THE "J" AMENDMENT

A NOVEL BY

GARTH H. HOLMES

Garth H Holmes

Copyright © 2007 by Garth H. Holmes

Cover design by Murphy Graphics Inc.

Printed in the United State of America.

Library of Congress Catalog Card Number: 2007904641

ISBN 978-0-9797223-0-1

DEDICATED TO:

My wife Dianne, an English teacher for thirty-two years.
She taught me the love of reading and writing.
Unfortunately, I lost her too soon.

PREFACE

Several years ago, it was suggested I write a novel as one of the things to do before I died. After my wife of forty-three years passed away, I did just that. This novel was a way of keeping myself busy, and fulfilling a life long dream to create something others may enjoy reading.

This story could possibly be true and conceivably happen. The Constitution of the United States, created in 1779, has been amended several times, but never could an amendment, such as the "J" amendment, create such turmoil in the conduct of the nation's business as depicted in the tale you are about to encounter

Many of the parts in the novel are taken from my life experiences, but are in no way related to any person living or dead.

I sincerely hope you enjoy the novel as much as I enjoyed writing it.

Garth H. Holmes
Olympia, Washington 2007

CHAPTER ONE

The stench and haze hung over the trash dump like a nuclear cloud. The broiling sun loomed high overhead like a large orange pumpkin, illuminating the heavy tractor, which was moving the garbage around from site to site. The mounds of stinking, decaying human leftovers were covered by swarms of dirty, small bodies seeking to discover something of value which could be sold to the tourists, redeemed for small amounts of money at a local trading post, or taken home to improve the lives of the impoverished families. Such was the existence of the unfortunate lost souls, without education, that were trapped in a perpetual cycle of eking out a livelihood, developing skin and lung cancer, and dying at an early age.

Even though he wore a bandana over his face, the smell and the heat were overpowering for young seventeen year old Juan Cardova, but he had no choice. His family, a mother, and five siblings, the youngest one just a baby, depended on him. The oldest of the brothers and sisters was Jesus Jr. who was ten years old. Then followed Carmen eight, Miranda six, Pedro three, and Pepe, the baby just one year old. Juan's father, Jesus had abandoned the family seven months ago, and left them with no means of support. The Cardova family was one of hundreds of poor Mexican families who tried to exist in the slum areas outside of Mexico City.

Juan was a tall boy for his age, a slight child with dark black hair, olive skin, and looks that could melt an iceberg. He was handsome beyond belief, with a charisma that charmed anyone who came into his presence. His nose was classic aquiline, inherited from the Spanish, and his high cheekbones a legacy of his Indian ancestors. He was nearing six feet, angular, and hard as a piece of beef sinew. He was not an introvert, but held his feelings close to his chest as if he were playing poker for a million dollar pot. He had a few close friends, Jose, Benji, and Alfredo who formed the nucleus of his social life, but no one else. They established a life long bond brought on by a common need to watch each other's back in the brutal and hostile environment in which they lived. All of their fathers worked as scavengers in the trash dump and land fill south of the city. That is when they weren't drinking, carousing, or abusing their wives. It was the lot in life handed to them for being illiterate and perpetuating the legacy they had inherited from generations past, which has come before.

Jesus Cardova really hadn't abandoned his family, he merely left them to find a better life, to break this cycle of poverty, to educate them, and to enjoy the short time he had to be with them. But his family would never know that. After many years of treading in the filth of the garbage pile, Jesus had contracted an aggressive form of lung disease. It had started as a small white spot on an x-ray taken at a secret examination he had arranged to keep his loved ones from discovering the truth.

Early one evening, Jesus slowly walked toward the local Cantina to mingle with the other caballeros and to drink a mixture of cervasos and tequila, a ritual he had done with his friends for many years. The cantina was constructed of the simple adobe brick manufactured in the region, and had been a watering hole for over one hundred years. The walls were lined with memorabilia from bullfights throughout Mexico, pictures of religious icons, and murals of past liberation battles expelling the French forces of Napoleon from their country. The interior was painted in rich, pastel colors slightly faded, taking on a dull gray look. The cantina smelled of stale cigarette smoke mixed with the acrid aroma of beer, liquor, vomit, and sweat. At first visit, the smell was repulsive, but after many visits, the smell was a welcome escape and the blending of brotherhood and purpose. Jesus was acknowledged by his friends as he entered. It was still early, but the place was filling up fast. It was a small building, so it didn't take long. Jesus glanced around the room and spotted Umberto in a far corner, signaling Jesus to come and join him. Jesus wound his way through the patrons, speaking to each one, shaking hands, and patting others on the back. Jokes were exchanged all in good fun. Jesus arrived at the table, drew the old wooden chair back, and sat down.

"Have you made the arrangements?" Jesus spoke to his friend Umberto.

"Everything has been taken care of. You are to meet the guide at midnight on the edge of town with the money we have promised him. You will recognize him easily. He will be driving a red pickup and will be wearing a white cowboy hat. Do not tell your family you are leaving for the United States, it will only complicate the situation. Carry only a small bundle of clothing and some food and water. The trip will be slow and dangerous, so be prepared."

Jesus was not sure he wanted to take this leap into the unknown, but he simply could not leave his family in this squalor any longer. For weeks, Jesus had been preparing. Each day when he went to the mound of hell, he wore an extra shirt or shorts, or stockings, which he hid, in a plastic bag inside a loose board of the trash dump's guardhouse. His wife never suspected anything. Finally, all of the things Jesus needed were gathered together. He was ready.

As his wife Carmela and the children were sleeping, Jesus arose from their bed as silently as a hawk diving for its prey. He stood in the darkness looking at his family, tears welling up in his eyes to temporarily blind him from the decision he had made. Gently, he leaned over and kissed each of them goodbye, knowing he was going to a better place. The children stirred gently, but did not awaken. Someday, he would return and bring riches for everyone. They would live in a suitable hacienda and would never starve or feel deprived again. He wanted to give his children what they needed, a lifestyle he had never known. Many other fathers had fled north, but few returned to their families. Many died in the big cities of America, or squandered their money, and were too ashamed to go back to their villages. Jesus vowed to avoid making those same kinds of mistakes.

Jesus was startled when Carmela arose in the bed. "What are you doing up this time of the night?" she asked.

"I couldn't sleep," he replied. "Go back to rest, it will be a long day tomorrow."

His heart was still racing as he watched her slowly drop her head on the hard pillow, close her eyes and drift off into the narcotic world of sleep. He did not want to awaken her again, so he sat in the broken, rattan chair he had found in the pile and waited. What seemed like hours, was only minutes, but he wanted to be sure Carmela was completely asleep before he made his exit from the shack.

The full moon's rays sifted through the broken window into the room. It would be a good night to travel. He wouldn't need any other light to get him to the pickup point he had been told about. As he sat there, he remembered the old days when he first met Camela. She was only 14, but in full bloom as a woman. He spotted her one day as she was walking from the fountain in the village square to her shanty. It was a torrid day, and she wore a short skirt and a low-slung halter-top. Her feet were bare and covered with grime, but he didn't care. He was struck with passion, the youthful surges of male hormones coursing through his body, tearing him apart. Later that evening, he waited for her outside her place. She appeared accepted his hand, and went with him into the blackness of the night.

She was fulfilled. Nine months later, Juan was born. Carmela knew she was pregnant from the moment they made love, telling her mother about it the next morning. Her mother knew Carmela loved Jesus, and began planning for a wedding as soon as Carmela had confessed her sins to the parish priest.

CHAPTER TWO

It was time to go. Jesus dressed quickly, waiting to put on his heavy boots until he was safely outside. In the distance, he would hear the cacophony of the city, the bright lights promising untold riches just over the horizon. The night was soundless, his heart beating so loudly he thought he was going to awaken the entire neighborhood. One by one, he took the first enterprising steps south of the village. The road was unpaved, so it was no traitor to him. As he walked along at a rapid pace, the smell of the putrefying mound became less and less. He stopped briefly to take in the fresh air his lungs so desperately needed. The experience was exhilarating and he thought for a moment he would swoon and pass out, but recovered and continued on. It seemed like he had gone a million miles. He was sure he was headed in the right direction, or had Umberto lied to him? He had no way of gauging the distance, but felt assured he knew what he was doing. Just after midnight, he spotted the red truck and the man with the cowboy hat. The man told Jesus to get in. He started the engine and drove for about two miles. There in the desert stood a semi truck, large, silver, outlined like an alien spacecraft in the moonlight. The cab was painted black and none of the rig had any markings.

As Jesus approached, he noticed three large men standing around the cab of the truck, smoking and talking. Jesus was large himself, but small by comparison with these giants. One of the drivers had a long, ugly scar that ran from his right eye to his left jaw. Probably sustained in a barroom fight thought Jesus. I wouldn't like to tangle with him or any of them for that matter he mused to himself. Best to just keep your feelings contained and do what they tell you.

Soon after Jesus arrived on the scene, others started to gather. At first just a few, then torrents of disheveled men in ragged clothes, carrying small suitcases or backpacks over their shoulders. In less than an hour, over 100 Mexicans had crowded into a small place no larger than a stockyard meant for fewer cattle. They milled around without a sound. Afraid to converse with each other, the men remained silent, lest the brutes running the transport would hear them and make an issue of it.

"Alright'" spoke one of the giants, "we don't have all night to mess around. Let's get this tribe on the truck and let's get this human cargo moving so we can collect our pay and get out of here."

The other two men moved quickly away and started to herd the men into the back of the semi. As each man was about to enter the truck, the drivers asked them for the money they were supposed to have brought with them. Each payment was counted to make sure the amount was right. It was a cool evening, but the inside of the truck was stifling. As the bodies began to compact inside, one could hardly breath. Jesus had been one of the first on board, and as he was shoved forward, he regretted having made this commitment and wanted to leave. It was too late, he was trapped and a victim of his own fate. The doors of the truck were slammed closed, and locked into place.

The truck engine coughed, then became a roar as the driver shifted it into gear and began to inch forward picking up speed rapidly. The men tried to sit down, but there was no room. It was hard to tell which direction the truck was moving, but Jesus sensed it was headed north toward the United States border. As the mass of human flesh pressed against him, Jesus prayed for the memory of his mother and father. He asked for their forgiveness, and for not being the religious person they had wanted him to be. His father had hoped that Jesus would become a priest like his brother, but that was not in the deck of cards life dealt him.

After what seemed like days, the truck came to an abrupt halt. The inside of the semi took on the smell of gasoline, meaning the rig had stopped to refuel before continuing its journey. Again, the semi moved, each man relieved that soon they would reach their destination and be free to work at a good job, to save some money, and to have their families join them in the land of opportunity. The second stop was an ominous one. A hush filled the deadened space with an eerie aura of foreboding. The shell of the trailer body was begining to heat up, the temperature inside rising rapidly. The men inside were becoming more and more agitated as time passed. Jesus reach for his water bottle to alleviate his thirst when another man withdrew a knife from his boot and pressed it against Jesus' throat.

"Give me your water, or you die." Growled the man.

Jesus felt a sharp pain just under his chin, followed by a warm ribbon of blood oozing down his neck and stained his flannel shirt. Jesus had but little choice, so he surrendered his bottle. The situation rapidly deteriorated, the men turning to desperate animals trying to escape the purgatory in which they found themselves. They were trapped, and they began to rail against the back and the sides of the truck. The doors did not yield even as the pressure increased. Jesus swooned and slipped under the feet of the strugglers and was crushed in the movement. He lost consciousness and everything went black. He would never reach his goal, nor see his family again.

The next day, agents of the Bureau of Immigrations and Naturalization Service (INS), found the truck with 135 dead bodies inside. The truck had been wiped clean of all traces of fingerprints and the occupants had no identification. No one cared about these human beings, so they were removed to a common grave and forgotten about, because the authorities had no way of knowing who to notify of their demise.

CHAPTER THREE

It had been over a week since Juan's father had gone from the area, and the burden of taking care of his loved ones had doubled. Juan arose extra early this morning, hoping to get a jumpstart on the day, and to find the more valuable items carried in by the garbage trucks from last night. It was a dream of all of the trash pickers to come across something of great value, so they could take some time off, buy a special present for their mothers or sweethearts, or stash something away for the future.

The sun had yet to come up in the horizon as Juan slipped on his clothes. He chose to wear his sandals and save his good leather boots for harder tasks. As he neared the dump, he looked around for his competition and found none. He began at the north end of the field, the place where the middle class discards were normally found. As he climbed the mound, his feet slipped on the decaying food and plastic bags, but he kept moving. At the top, he grabbed the first bag, tore off the tie, and began spilling the contents off to one side.

As he rummaged through the contents, he found the usual things, old magazines, letters, tin cans, plastic bottles, clothing, and glass bottles. His eyes scanned the goods and immediately found a hardly worn dress that would make a fine present for his mother. He would save it until Mother's Day and wrap it for her. He separated the cans and bottles into burlap sacks he would carry for recycling later. He labored for a couple of hours, musing about the value of the things he had found and resting before continuing his arduous task. As the sun shed light on his labor, out of the corner of his eye, he caught a glint of something shiny and bright. He thought it must be an illusion, because he could not find the source. He dug furiously, and there amongst the papers was a solid gold cigarette lighter casually thrown away. He could not believe his good fortune. A distant relative of the family owned a prosperous pawnshop, and Juan was certain the lighter would fetch a good price. He gingerly slipped the gold item into his back pocket and continued his quest.

After ten hours of shifting, sorting, and sacking, he ceased his labors, slung five burlap sacks over his shoulders and trudged down the mound. It had been a good day. First he would stop by the shack, deposit the dress under his bed, and move on to the recycling center hoping to get there before it closed. As he was approaching the center, the manager was hurriedly starting to close the wire gates and padlock the enclosure. Juan shouted at him, but the manager seemed more in a hurry to leave than to service a poor little Mexican kid even though the closing hour had not yet arrived. Juan turned his walk into a frenzied rush, running as fast as his youthful legs could take him. His lungs burned even hotter from the fumes and the exertion. He threw himself against the gate knocking the manager to the ground in the process. The manager, startled by the onslaught, rose angrily, but when he saw whom the intruder was, wrapped his arms around Juan and escorted him to the recycling building. For the past few years, Juan had brought more items to the center than anyone else, so the manager felt he owed Juan one last favor.

The manager explained to Juan that he and his wife were attending a wedding of a niece, and as the godfather of the bride, wanted to get to the wedding early to join into the festivities. But, there was still time to weigh Juan's sacks and pay him for the contents. The cans, plastic, and glass were put on the scales, the weight recorded for each, and paid for in cash. It had been a good day. For his efforts, Juan was given two hundred pesos, a kings' ransom for one day's work. His stellar efforts had paid off. He was so relieved and grateful, he assisted with the closing of the compound, stowed the money in his pocket, and strode off to the pawnshop.

CHAPTER FOUR

Carlos Gomez was the sole proprietor and operator of the local pawn-shop appropriately named "The Good Samaritan", to show his customers what a helpful person he was. The pawnshop was in the center of the village encased between a burrito shop, and a used clothing store. Like the other businesses in the village, the shop was reinforced with steel bars covering the windows, and a steel pull down gate, which was secured at the bottom by three heavy duty padlocks and a keyed dead bolt lock on the side. In the windows were displayed many items for sale or trade which had not been claimed by their owners within the allotted time. Fine classical guitars, watches, diamond rings, gold crosses, radio, Spanish hats, and knives beckoned the unwary, drawing them as a magnet.

Carlos was a large man with curly locks of hair, which hung down to his waist. His girth defied description, having grown to gigantic proportions after years of sitting behind his counter, drinking, and eating. Carlos had inherited the pawnshop from his father, a devious loan shark, who advanced money to the population of the little village when they needed it; demanding exorbitant rates of interest, which had to be paid, or he would send his Mexican strong arms to recoup the money owed.

Carlos, soft spoken, appeared to be meek in his demeanor, but inside was a ruthless, hardheaded individual who had learned well, having been brought up in the business. His primary tactic was to keep his customers waiting, making them anxious to leave. When he felt their nervousness peak, he would call them to the back counter and ask to see what they had brought him. Passively, he would inspect the merchandise much the same as a cat would toy with a mouse. He would mumble to himself, shushing anyone who volunteered to speak. By the time Carlos was finished appraising the goods, the customer just wanted to leave and didn't really care the amount Carlos was wiling to give.

Gingerly, Juan handed the gold lighter to Carlos. In typical fashion, Carlos took his own sweet time gently rolling the lighter over and over in his paw like hands. The lighter indeed was twenty-four carat, long and slender without any identifying marks or engravings. It was a cigarette lighter which could be purchased at any high scale jewelry store in the city, and not traceable to anyone. Juan knew about Carlo's tactics, and interrupted him often, demanding a quoted reimbursement amount. Carlos snapped at Juan to shut his filthy mouth and give him more time.

"What is your hurry El Nino? Is there a fire in your pants you want to quench? You must give me time to accurately determine what the value of such a fine item is."

"I am only bothering you because I have so little time. I must get back to work. My father has disappeared and my family will starve if I do not get to the market to get some food."

Juan did not want to tell Carlos that he just wanted to be finished with this business so he could take the rest of the afternoon off and play soccer with his friends.

Again he implored Carlos. "Please be kind and help me and my family. You know I am a hard working person, and a relative of yours. If you finish soon, I will tell everyone what a fine merchant you are, and they should consider you for all of their business in the future."

The flattery seemed to work on Carlos. He glanced at this handsome, strong willed boy, and reflected that Juan reminded him of himself when he was that age.

"Alright, I have made up my mind. Since you have come to me and will recommend me to your friends, I will give you one thousand peso, and not a peso more."

"But Carlos, the lighter is almost new, and gold. Surely such a fine piece is worth at least two thousand pesos."

"Humph, snorted Carlos. What are you a pirate, a Spanish invader who wants to rob me of my just reward? Maybe, because you are a good bargainer, I will give you eleven hundred pesos."

"Sixteen hundred pesos."

"Fifteen hundred pesos."

"Done."

Juan stood in awe as Carlos counted out fifteen crisp, new one hundred peso bills. Juan's hands were sweaty, but he didn't want Carlos to see the nervousness he felt, so he bit the inside of his cheek painfully, and the distraction held his fingers steady. When the final bill was dropped, Juan turned, without a word, and strode out the front door. He did not glance back, fearful that the money would be snatched away. As he left the shop, he paused to look both ways. There had been many instances of hoodlums waiting in the shadows of the alleys to jump Carlo's customers and free them of their money, goods, or possessions. Two vulgar looking, older youths were standing on the next corner, wasting away their talents by hitting on a newly rolled marijuana cigarette. Juan waited until they were well on their way to getting high before he continued his trip back to the village.

Juan chose to exit down the alley instead of walking by the group. One could never tell what someone high on drugs would do unexpectedly. As he neared the end of the alley, he saw the alley was blocked by a couple of vile looking and foul smelling boys about his age. Juan knew he couldn't fight both of them and win, so he turned around and started to run as fast his legs would carry him. As he rounded the corner of the building, Juan so startled the smokers, they had little time to react and by seconds missed their opportunity. Juan was much faster than they were, and after a few hundred yards, the gang gave up and went back to their illegal activities.

CHAPTER FIVE

Soccer was an international sport revered by millions of fans throughout the globe. Heroes like Pele were immortalized as gods and had statues built for them. Rivalries went back hundreds of years for bragging rights and to uphold the honor of the cities and countries the teams represented. Stadiums were filled with thousands of screaming, jubilant fans. Mexico was no different. More people crowded into the soccer arena in Mexico City than attended the bullfights on a Sunday afternoon. But, soccer was not only played in arenas or stadiums, but in empty fields and in the streets of all of the villages in the country.

Almost every small suburb or village around the huge Mecca of Mexico City sported some sort of field. In Juan's village, the populace had gotten together, and with materials they had scrounged from the dump, had fabricated a reasonable sports facility. The women of the village had taken string collected and woven it into nets which were suspended from cast iron goal posts put together by the men from discarded plumbing thrown away when a large commercial building was renovated. Seats had been constructed on both sides of the field, which were nothing more than stones cemented together and crossed with scrap lumber. Grass had not been planted. The summer heat was so bad, the grass would never have survived, and the people of the village could ill afford to bring water in to keep the grass growing. A work party would rake the ground smooth before each match. This afternoon,

Juan walked hastily toward the field and his friends. They had agreed to meet and to spend some time together practicing for a skirmish with some of the other hopeful teams that weekend. It was a dream of many of the male youths, to one day play on a village, town, city, regional or national team. Soccer offered them a way out of the depths of despair, and hopefully onto the golden road of fame and fortune.

Even though baseball was also a popular sport in Mexico, the villagers didn't have the capital to procure the equipment necessary to field a baseball team. The only requirement for soccer was a ball, and two goal nets. Lucky teams had matching jerseys, but most didn't, having to rely on the knowledge of who their teammates were in order to separate them from the opponents.

Jose, Alfredo, and Benji looked up in surprise as Juan approached. They had not expected him to arrive so early in the day. Juan usually worked longer than the rest and joined the group just before suppertime.

"Hey amigo", Jose blurted out. "What happened? Did you strike it rich?"

"Well, you dumb Mexican, what do you think? Here let me show you."

With this, Juan unfolded the wad of pesos he had stashed in his pocket. Cries of astonishment erupted from all three of them. They could not believe someone had gotten so lucky, but they were glad it had happened to one of their own.

"What are you going to do with all of that money Juan?" "Well, I am going to get us a new soccer ball for starters, then buy my mother a wonderful present, toys for the kids, and put something away for a rainy day. That's what I am going to do. Now, let's stop horsing around" Juan said. "Let's play some soccer."

The soccer ball they were using was indeed so old, it was held together by duct tape and would flatten whenever it was kicked. Gleefully the boys chased each other over the field like gamboling young colts on a thoroughbred farm. Juan was the fastest and most talented. Gracefully he darted in and around his teammates, his footwork moving with the precision of a flamenco dancer. From side to side he went, until at the end of the field he lifted the ball straight as an arrow into the goal net. Juan was so wrapped up in his activity, he didn't notice the stranger sitting high up on the bleachers in the shade taking notes of what was happening. The game continued for over an hour more, but the man didn't move, it seemed like he was an illusion or simply dead.

Travis Bentley was a deeply tanned, slightly bald, middle aged man who fit into his environment because of the many years he had spent scouting players from Mexico for major league baseball. He was especially attuned to recognizing potential in up and coming talent which could be incorporated in the minor league farm system, and groomed for positions requiring speed, agility, and stamina. Travis was a graduate of San Diego State University where he had majored in physical education, played on the school's outstanding Aztec baseball team, and remained as an assistant coach for a few years. While he lived in San Diego, Travis attended all of the San Diego Padres games, following them to spring training in Peoria, Arizona and back for the grueling one hundred and sixty two game summer season. He ingratiated himself to the players, coaches, and management by volunteering to help anyway he could. He so impressed the baseball club, they offered him a job as assistant bench coach for the upcoming grind.

Travis became an avid student of the game, monitoring all of the decisions the manager made, trying to determine the reasons, and observing the outcome. He attended all of the film sessions, asking pertinent about the game, and offering suggestions which were sound in judgment, reflecting his insight into the lessons he had learned. After the first two years with the club, because he was so fluent in the Spanish language, he was offered a job as scout in the Mexican area. His travels took him the full breadth and length of the country. His success in recruiting new talent was exceptional and his influence grew. Many clubs wanted his services, but he stayed loyal to the Padres. The world was his oyster, and he knew he could give young men with potential, a passkey to a life beyond their wildest imagination.

The four youths played soccer until they were totally exhausted. As the last goal was scored by Juan, he grasped his friends by the hair, shoulders, arms, and bodies, swinging them around and flinging them to the ground. They didn't seem to mind because they loved Juan so much, and were so happy to see his good fortune. As Juan looked up, he saw the darkly tanned man approach. Juan knew the man was not from the region, his clothes were much too fine. The stranger was dressed in a thousand dollar, dark brown suit with a cream colored, buttoned down shirt, and a matching tie and handkerchief. His shoes were alligator leather with tassels on the front. Juan could sense an aura about the man, a little intimidating. The friends withdrew a few paces as the stranger neared and spoke. Then they vanished into the late afternoon.

"Hi, my name is Travis, what is yours?"

Not sure if he wanted to answer, Juan blurted out his name.

"If you have a minute, I would like to talk to you. Let's not stand in the sun, let's take in some shade in the bleachers."

With this, the man sauntered toward the bleachers, arriving before Juan, turned around and waited. Juan felt a cool rush of anticipation take over his body, but it was not an unpleasant experience. In a strange way, Juan felt a saintly like calm. He made the sign of the cross, ducked his head, and was about to begin a journey even he could never have anticipated. Juan climbed to a couple of rows above Travis, a position of dominance, looking down on Travis and forcing him to turn sideways to talk. This way, Juan could control the action.

Travis wanted to put Juan at ease, knowing a suspicious teenager would not be receptive until a certain level of reciprocation and trust took place. Travis also knew he must disarm the youth, and establish a true relationship.

"How old are you?" Travis began. A couple of minutes passed and Juan replied.

"I just turned seventeen"

"What do you do in the village besides play soccer:"

Juan was a little taken aback by the question, but also felt proud of what he was doing to support his family.

"I sift through the rubble in the city dump, Juan replied. "I collect as many things as I can to recycle, sell, and take home to make my family's life as best as I can. We don't have much, but enough to be fed, be healthy, and comfortable with our surroundings."

"Tell me about your family, I would love to hear about them."

"My father left home without telling us, and my mother is trying to raise us as best she can. I have brothers and sisters who are younger than I am. I also have some aunts and uncles who live nearby, and of course, my friends you saw here today."

Travis asked Juan what he liked to do in the village and what might be some hopes he had for the future. The two of them talked about Mexico, world cup soccer, other sports, food, girls, and fantasies. After awhile, Juan relaxed and offered himself to a more open interrogation. Talking to this man is so easy Juan thought to himself. Maybe he has something to say which will benefit me. Juan stopped talking about himself and asked Travis who he was, and what he was doing there. Travis felt that was a fair question, so gave Juan a brief biography of his life.

"But I don't play baseball. Why would you be talking to me?"

The man and the boy conversed for several minutes more before Travis asked the question, "how would you like to come to America and play soccer for the San Diego State Aztecs?"

The question stunned Juan, his mouth went dry, and his brain failed to comprehend what Travis was saying. As the euphoria subsided, Juan regained his composure and said, "I could not leave my family, they need me so desperately. Besides, what do I know of America and the rich gringos. America might just as well be on the moon for all I care. Neither can I leave my friends who also need me."

Juan had run out of excuses, but in the back of his mind, the possibility of going north of the border acted like a narcotic, lulling him into a dream like state of mind.

"Okay, you don't have to make a decision now, but I want you to think about it. I have friends at the university who could make arrangements to get you a visa, a dormitory to stay in, a scholarship to pay for you books and tuition, and some spending money. I would even get you a good looking American girl to tutor you English and help you with your studies."

Juan tried to picture in the back of his mind, a female English tutor. Travis had got to be kidding. The thought of a girl helping him had appeal, but he didn't need any English tutor. Juan was not without education. His mother had often dreamed of him getting some book learning, becoming a priest, and breaking this cycle of poverty. Along with his attendance in the catechism of the Catholic faith, the parish priest introduced Juan to English; how to speak as well as read it. Juan was not going to let Travis know he was fluent in English since the entire conversation had been held in Spanish. That piece of information he would release sometime in the future if need be.

Travis knew he and Juan had reached a crossroads. He didn't want to push the youngster too far too fast. Over the years, Travis had learned that coming on too strong turned away many talented athletes. He found that feeding on a person's ego, handing out small treats, and instilling thoughts of a brighter future for the person to think about, returned in far greater dividends.

The initial conversation was coming to an end. "Talk it over with your mother and family. You don't have to give them too many details, but listen to what your mother has to say. I have found that most mothers have an insight more valuable than any university professor. Say, let's meet again next Sunday afternoon, same time, same place.

21

In fact, I'll treat you and your friends to the soccer match and some food afterwards."

Juan was ecstatic. The game was a rematch of the two district teams that fought for a chance to compete in the national tournament where the winner would be selected to represent Mexico in the World Cup. With this, Travis shook Juan's hand, giving it a firm, but gentle squeeze promoting a feeling of confidence about the transaction. Sunday was five days away, plenty of time for Juan to come to a decision.

The stranger departed the field, stirring up some dust swirls as he shuffled his feet, taking his time to leave. Juan watched him leaving, not quite sure what had just happened, and still light headed from the experience. The man grew smaller and smaller as he disappeared into the halo of twilight. Travis seemed like a ghost to Juan, an unearthly messenger who had landed in an alien spacecraft, touched his soul and lifted away.

Juan remembered going to the cinema a long time ago to see Strange Encounters of the Third Kind. Now he felt as though he had been part of the movie cast. He gazed after Travis until the sun was gone and darkness had set in. He rushed home to see his mother. As he entered the hovel, his mother shouted at him.

"Where have you been? You know it is dangerous to be out after dark in this part of town. You know I worry about you."

Don't be mad at me mother, I just met a man on the soccer field who has offered me something of great value, and I need your advice before taking or rejecting it."

Juan's mother listened in silence, fingering her rosary, until Juan had completed his tale of the stranger and the offer he had made. Juan poured out his feelings including all of the reasons why he couldn't accept. He was emotionally exhausted when he finished.

Carmela rose, placed her large, beefy arms around him and wept. Finally releasing him, she wiped away the tears and spoke in an angelic voice.

"Juan, rarely in one's life does such a chance come along. You must take this man's present as a gift from God. Find out more about how and when this thing will happen, and we shall make plans for it. Do not worry about me and the family. Your bother and sister are getting older and can handle the responsibility. You have many aunts and uncles who will take care of me and the other children. We will not starve, and when you are finished with your schooling, you will find a wonderful woman and a job, and we will be united again as a whole. Now, come and eat your supper, tomorrow will be a new beginning, and time to prepare."

Juan ate the food his mother placed on the table for him. It was a spicy chili stew, one of his favorites. The vittles had never tasted so good. His worries evaporated and he spent most of the night thinking through the day's activities and what turn of events his life was about to take. For the next few nights, his sleep was filled with fits and starts. He was so anxious to meet with Travis again, and to tell him that he would accept the offer. During the coming days, his relatives had heard, and all of them stopped by to assure Juan that everything would be taken care of. Even the priest arranged for a special mass to bless Juan and to ask God's protection in Juan's journeys. Before the mass, Juan wanted Father Gomez to hear his confession, and advise him about the feasibility of such an offer.

As Juan entered the church, he noticed the confessional booth light on, meaning the priest was there to listen to the sins of the people and to absolve them of those sins. Juan seated himself on the booth, slid the partition barrier back and began.

"Father forgive me for I have sinned. It has been a month since my last confession. I have done nothing terribly wrong, but I have lusted in my heart. Not for women, but for my own self gratification. I have decided to go to America, leave my family and attend a university. This is selfish of me, but my mother has so encouraged me, I had no choice. I have decided to take up a stranger's offer, but I know nothing of such an arrangement and need your advice.

Father Domonic listened intently. The father was a young priest, just barely out of the seminary. He was athletic, wearing his dark brown hair in a crew cut style. He looked like a cross between a clipped poodle and a Marine Corps drill sergeant. He had been a radical student, expressing himself against the orthodox teaching of the Catholic Church, wanting to move his country forward, and to liberate the masses from the oppression they felt pressed upon them by the central government and the evil empire to the north of them.

The seminary could not find fault with his attendance at class, or his dedication to his faith or purpose in life. Because of his radicalism, they graduated him from the seminary, but assigned him to the far reaches of the diocese, to Shepard the lowest of the low. The assignment could only have been worse if it had been to a leper colony. He accepted the assignment with relish, knowing someday, he would make the difference between good and evil.

After Juan had finished, the priest said, "you have not sinned my son, you have merely chosen a path totally foreign to the things you know. Your family will be well taken care of, so go to the north and get the education you so richly deserve. When I was in the seminary, I knew a fellow student who had been offered an athletic scholarship to an American university. He accepted it, got a good education, returned to the priesthood and now serves with distinction. He told me of the things that had happened to him, the agent who offered and the process he went through. I believe this Travis means what he says. Someday you will return as well and make your village a better place to live. To make your dedication strong, say twelve Our Father and twelve Hail Mary's, and let's go mass to celebrate your good fortune."

CHAPTER SIX

The appointed meeting day finally came. Juan consumed little of his breakfast and lunch meals, his stomach turning into knots in anticipation. He knew he could not lose a day in the dump, the money and goods were too important, so he worked from sunrise until early afternoon. Finishing up his labors, he raced toward the soccer filed. When he arrived, Travis was not there. Juan looked around the field and up into the bleachers thinking the sun had blinded his eyesight, but Travis was nowhere to be seen. Had Juan forgotten the right date and time? He was confused and shook his head trying to remember. No, he was not wrong. Travis said he would meet him on this day, at this hour, and everything would fall into place.

Juan sat in the bleachers for an hour in disbelief. His anger mounted like the innards of a volcano, belching forth bile from inside his stomach, which felt like molten hot lava. Juan felt betrayed, but what could you expect from an American. He often been told never to trust them, and now he had good reason. His friends dropped by asking him to play some ball, but he explained the tragedy which had befallen him, and how angry he was. He was far too irate to waste his time on the stupid game of soccer. He drove his friends away, wanting to kill himself with anything he could find. He shoved his hands deep into his pockets and started home. His head hung low and tears welled up in his dark black eyes. As he was leaving the field, suddenly a large, black, heavily chromed BMW screeched to a halt at his feet, almost hitting him. As the dust settled, Travis turned off the engine, and emerged from the car. Travis looked as though he had not slept all night. His clothes were rumpled and dirty, he was unshaven and smelled of old sweat, but as he glided toward Juan, his face was lit up from ear to ear. His eyes glowed with iridescent lights and there was a bounce in his step.

Juan could sense the power of this man. Juan knew something dramatic was about to seal his fate in life, a fate which would render him into a personality he had never dreamed he would be. All of the fears Juan had about the decision he had made melted away as if a soft, warm breeze had dissolved the last of the snowfall on the peaks nearby.

"I am so sorry I am late. I was afraid you would think I had abandoned you and would not keep my promise. I am so thankful you are still here."

Travis was speaking a mile a minute, and it was hard for Juan to keep up with this raving man, so he strained harder to listen to what Travis was saying.

"The reason I am late is because I just got off the phone with the athletic director at San Diego State. After I left you, I called him to set up a meeting about you. I want to make a proposal which I was sure he wouldn't refuse. I knew he is not "The Godfather", but he is a powerful person in the administration, and without his help, I would have to renege on my promise. That I did not want to do. I did not tell him the reason for the meeting, I will do that when I see him. I need to fly to San Diego to meet with him personally. I must convince the university to grant you a stipulated scholarship, and will accept you on the condition you pass the physical and demonstrate the ability to help their soccer program. You will be assigned to live in a dormitory with other soccer players, both old timers and newcomers, and you will be working the dormitory dining hall of some other place to earn money for your living expenses. Your books, tuition, and soccer equipment, will be furnished by the school. Classes start during the first week in

September, which is after freshman orientation week. That will give you a few months to settle your affairs here in the village, get yourself some new clothes, and make sure your family is provided for. Are you going to take the offer if the university agrees?"

Juan was thunderstruck. Even though Travis had promised him a chance of a lifetime, Juan was not totally convinced that the promise would be made valid, but it had now come true. Juan's head was spinning, not comprehending the gravity of the decision he was about to make. The sense of euphoria slowly disappeared, and without hesitation Juan told Travis he would accept the conditions the university wanted. Juan knew he was physically fit and could pass the medical exam. Juan also knew his soccer skills were more than adequate. Soccer was a relatively new sport in America. But in Mexico, it was the national pastime. America had competed poorly on the road to the World Soccer Cup, while Mexico had been world champions several times. This gave Juan confidence that he would match up better than most of his counterparts.

When Travis had completed his spiel, Juan confessed about his command of the English language. Travis was impressed with the honestly, and knew he had found a true diamond in the rough. Travis told Juan he would contact him when he got back from San Diego.

Getting the scholarship for Juan would not been easy. Travis chastised himself for making the promise without any guarantees. He felt deep in his heart that Juan was a gifted child, made to order for the university, and he felt no remorse for going out on a limb. He would have to become the best salesman he could to swing the deal.

After the initial meeting with Juan, Travis had returned to his hotel and booked a flight to San Diego that same evening. As the plane lofted itself into the dark, ominous sky, rational and irrational thoughts began to stream though his mind like the blending of a margarita. The good and bad seemed to mix like the sweet and sour of his favorite libation. He tried to get some sleep, but his brain continued to compartmentalize the discussion points of his argument to the University for accepting Juan. By the time the plane had landed, he felt like he had polished his position as well as he could.

Leaving the airport, Travis hailed a taxi and directed the driver to take him to a hotel near the university. This way, Travis knew he could spend the maximum time with the athletic director, and not waste valuable minutes traveling long distances. The taxi deposited Travis at his destination. After checking in, Travis threw open the blinds of the room to gaze on the azure seas of the Pacific Ocean, and the pristine sands of the most beautiful beaches in the world. He could have gone to his expensive home, but it was an hour's drive away from the city and inconvenient for his purposes today.

Travis reflected on his days at San Diego State, the beer parties on the beach, the torrid groping and lovemaking with young coeds, and the reverie of strolling the vast expanse of sand as the sun dipped into a crimson fireball beyond the horizon. San Diego was a city as close to paradise as one could get. The days were temperate, with a soft breeze blowing from the cooler sea to the warmer land. San Diego was filled with highlights. San Diego bragged that it had the best zoo in the world. Balboa Park with all of its museums, the Navy base, World War II ships of all descriptions anchored in the harbor, professional sports, great schools, Old Town, and Mexico just across the border.

Travis had scheduled his meeting with Wally "Chipper" Biggs, the athletic director of the university for 10 o'clock the next morning. As Travis rode in a taxi toward the campus, he paid little heed to the cars zooming around him. Travis and Wally had been roommates in an all male dormitory mostly inhabited by athletes. It was commonly called "The Jock Dorm" with a live in professor named Wilkins and his wife. They were no nonsense people who enforced a strict curfew during the week, and kept the lid on rowdy parties during the week-end. The dorm occupants all loved the Wilkins'. Many times Dorothy would invite them down to the apartment for freshly baked cookies and other goodies. To many, she was their mother away from home, someone they could turn to with a problem or advice. Even though Dorothy was barely over five feet tall, gray haired, and slim, she was no pushover, and tolerated no misbehavior whatsoever.

Travis and Wally had more than their share of the invites, both of them being two of Dorothy's favorites. Travis as an outstanding baseball player, a gifted infielder with a rocket for an arm, and a range reserved for most players from Central America. Wally on the other hand, was a huge man, appearing to have no neck and tipping the scale at over two hundred and seventy pounds. Wally had obviously been pro-football material, playing inside linebacker for the most part, but sometimes playing defensive guard as wells. Travis was a local kid from Southern California, but Wally had grown up on a farm in Iowa raising pigs and cattle as well as harvesting an abundance of crops native to that part of the country.

Wally had been recruited to attend San Diego State along with many offers from other schools. His parents wanted him to stay close to home in case they needed him to help with the farm, but his wanderlust filled his brain, and after a visit to the west coast, he was consumed with the desire to attend San Diego State. Travis had no parents. They had been killed in an automobile accident when he was young, and he was raised by his aunt and uncle. Travis could have commuted to school from his home, but chose to live in a dorm so he could devote more of his time to his sports, his education, and his friends.

On holidays, Travis would take Wally to visit the aunt and uncle and to explore the city of Tijuana. One Thanksgiving, Wally reciprocated the favor by whisking Travis to the Iowa farm to be indulged with roast beef, mashed potatoes, gravy, corn on the cob, hot biscuits, and apple pie ala mode. These exchanges, along with rooming together, forged a bond of brotherhood stronger than a steel cable, and had lasted as solidly as a perfect marriage. They shared everything, and had no secrets from each other.

After college, Wally was drafted by the Green Bay Packers, and spent six years in the NFL. An unfortunate injury prematurely ended his illustrious career, and he chose to coach back at San Diego State. After many years as a coach, he gravitated to assistant athletic director, and then was promoted to the top job. Under his tutelage, Wally saw the school's athletic program grow into a national powerhouse, competing with schools like Southern Cal, Michigan, Utah, and Notre Dame in a variety of sports. San Diego State was truly outstanding in not only football and baseball, but soccer, golf, volleyball, and tennis as well.

Travis on the other hand, was drafted to play baseball for the New York Mets, but after one season, they cancelled his contract. He had no stomach for the east coast and the harsh sports press. He contacted the San Diego Padres, and the rest is history. Travis arrived a few minutes early, which gave him time to wander the hallowed halls of the sports complex, stopping to look at the Aztec Sports Hall of Fame where he recognized many of the men he had played with, including the one and only Wally "The Chipper".

Wally was nicknamed Chipper due to an accident on the football field. During a scrimmage, a running back, while trying to jump a pile of defenders at the goal line to score a touchdown, kicked Wally under the helmet, breaking the strap, and chipping two of Wally's teeth. Wally's scholarship didn't cover dental work, so the teeth remained chipped until after he graduated.

CHAPTER SEVEN

Travis could hear the bell tower on campus peal the ten o'clock hour. His anticipation rose like a Phoenix Bird from the ashes, as did his blood pressure when he was forced to come face to face with his old friend and ask Wally to give a scholarship to a poor Mexican kid, sight unseen, because Travis had made a promise. Suddenly panic set in like a car careening out of control. What if Wally turned him down. He could not go back to the village and face Juan. Travis knew he would have to use all of his many negotiating skills to make this a done deal.

He entered the athletic director's office reception area. The room was filled with more trophy cases, matching the ones in the hall, and filled with action figures in gold and silver, attesting to the prowess of the athletic program. Behind the reception desk sat Margie, middle aged, efficient, and a fixture in the building for over thirty years. Although her hair was graying, she kept it tinted to reflect the dashing brunette she was. Her makeup was perfect and her dress conservative. She was sitting behind a computer screen, completing the day's correspondence when Travis neared her desk. As she looked up, a broad grin crossed her face and she jumped around the desk to give him a hug, which could be classified as sensual. She had always been sweet on Travis, often times asking him to participate with her in an affair. Travis wasn't interested in women very much. He was no lover of men, he just liked being a bachelor without any strings. Oh he dated, but it never went beyond an occasional good night kiss.

"My God it is so good to see you", she said, and with that, gave him another squeeze. "What brings to the university, and why didn't you tell me you were coming?'

"Well, Travis stammered, it was sort of a last minute thing. An opportunity has come up to recruit one of the most outstanding soccer players I have ever seen, and I wanted to have Wally hear my story first hand. Besides, I always get a nicer hug when I surprise you."

With that remark, Margie grasped his hand a little tighter, and began leading the way into the inner office. Wally's office was neatly appointed, a testimony to his political savvy. The walls were made of a high quality, medium dark wood, with thick deep red carpet. The furniture created from maroon leather, comfortable and long lasting. Almost all the visible wall surface was covered with certificates of accomplishments, or pictures of Wally shaking hands, or standing with some local, state, or national dignitary.

As Travis strolled in, guided by the tenacious Margie, Wally was looking out the window unaware of the two people now entering his office. Margie softly coughed to let him know they had arrived. Wally turned, let out a whoop, rushed forward and caressed Travis like a bull moose at mating season.

"My God man it is so good to see you. What brings you to my neck of the woods? How long has it been, five, ten years or more? I don't hear from you often, and now you show up. I tried to get you to tell me about your visit when you called, but you wouldn't tell me a thing. It must be really important to keep it from your old roommate."

Wally looked Travis straight in the eye, and invited him to sit on one of the leather couches with him. As they plopped their tired old bodies on the soft pillows, Travis hesitated just a few seconds, not knowing if his prepared speech would work. He could only hope.

"Wally, you and I have known each other for decades. We lived in the same room for four years, dated some of the same girls, played sports together, and got to know each other intimately. I consider you not only my brother, but one of my very best friends. I know you feel the same way about me. We can trust each other without reservation. Now is the time I need your trust the most."

"What are you talking about? Of course you can trust me, and I can trust you."

"Okay then, I need a favor. As you know, I have been scouting for baseball prospects for many years in the Mexican league for the San Diego Padres. Over those years, I have seen some of the brightest talent available. I helped the Padres win the World Series with some of my finds. I know I have a gift for evaluating the potential, and I use that gift wisely."

Travis paused ever so slightly watching deep furrows appear in the massive brow of his friend. With this hesitation, Travis felt light headed, and worried that he had made a mistake he could not take back. Would it ruin his relationship with Wally forever. He had no choice, his die was cast and there was no turning back. He had made the promise to Juan on a spur of the moment decision, and he simply could not disappoint him. Travis continued.

"Last week, I was scouting in this impoverished area on the out-skirts of Mexico City, and stopped at a local village soccer field to watch four young men play soccer. I sat high in the bleachers, out of sight, to take in the action. One of the boys, a tall, good-looking sort absolutely took my breath away. He darted like a gazelle, had foot action you can only dream about, and never seemed to tire. After the boys were finished, I talked to this future star and found out his name was Juan Cardova. He is seventeen, fluent in English, and highly intelligent."

Travis hesitated again, then almost croaked, "I told him San Diego State University would give him a scholarship in soccer. I told him the university would work with the INS to allow him into the country, and that his living quarters, books, and tuition would be paid for. I also guaranteed him a job to cover his personal needs in either the men's dining hall or at the gym. In short, I gave him assurances of a full ride here."

A look of bewilderment suddenly came over Wally's face. His face turned red, then crimson and his nostrils flared. He regained his composure, looked at Travis' shameful face, and seriously contemplated throwing him out the window onto the street below. The atmosphere in the room was electric. If someone had lit a match, the building would have gone up in the largest implosion known to mankind. His eyes rolled up into his sockets so only the whites were showing. Travis thought Wally was going to have a convulsion, a stroke, or would die, but the electricity subsided. Wally took a long and drawn out breath, then, in a loud voice, said, "You did WHAT!"

Travis really had no defense, so he reiterated what he had previously said. In addition, Travis again, emphatically stated that this child was one of a kind. That he would put the university on the world map in soccer, and the university would never regret it. "You will just have to trust me on this," Travis said.

"Trust you, you don't know a thing about soccer."

"Oh but I do. Remember I was on a championship soccer team for our fraternity when we competed in the intramural sports program, and I coached a local high school girl's soccer team as part of my physical education classes. Over the past many years in Mexico, I have attended dozens upon dozens of soccer matches. I was even fortunate enough to take in the World Cup matches one year. I also have a gut instinct second to none, and you know it."

Travis rested his case, watching his best friend's eyes go from blood red back to a normal blue, as if a soft wind had blown away the tempest. Travis waited for what seemed to be an eternity. The buzzing in his brain increased until he felt he was riding on the wing of a supersonic jet crossing the Pacific Ocean. I wasn't sure he was going to make it through the ordeal. Then he felt Wally's hands gently rest on his shoulders and a slight compression sent a chill down his spine, all the way to his toes.

"Travis, you make on hell of an argument, you have a deal. I don't know how I am going to convince the administration, but I will. You can take that much to the bank. The soccer program is a good one, but could be better. If we can pull this off, everyone in the university will benefit, and our alumni appeal will soar. Hell, I may even have something positive to say at the next alumni board of director's meeting."

And so the deal was done.

"I want to get the word to you as soon as possible, so when do you have to have the confirmation?"

"I have some time before I will be meeting with Juan, you can call me there when the decision has been made. I have to get back. Spring training will be coming up in a short while, and I need to finalize some of the paperwork on the prospects I have now."

"Okay, I will let you know by this Friday, that should give you plenty of time before you see Juan."

The two friends shook hands, and hugged again. Travis turned slowly to walk away, then reversed his stance, looked back at Wally and mouthed thanks. Wally merely nodded but said nothing. The die had been cast, an understanding consummated, and a promise confirmed.

CHAPTER EIGHT

The next step was to call in the coaches for the soccer team to let them know about his decision. He alerted Margie that he needed to see the soccer head coach and the two assistant coaches in his office as soon as possible. Margie picked up the phone immediately, and began placing the calls. In no time, she had conference called all three of the principals and told them to come to the office immediately. Margie's face reflected her concern, letting Wally know the coaches she had called all inquired as to the purpose of the meeting. She told them nothing, except the director would fill them in. Within ten minutes, into the office strolled Mark Goddard, the head coach, Tim Ryan and Bill Ferguson, the assistant coaches.

"Have a seat gentlemen," the athletic director intoned. They sat eagerly, rapt as to what was going to transpire. Wally spent little time filling them in on the details, and giving them instruction to find a dorm room, equipment, and locker space in the gym for the new arrival, and put it all on hold until the fall session started. It was his responsibility to complete the administrative responsibilities involved in the process. The next step, a session in the President's office only take twenty minutes. First Wally had to appraise the University President of the situation, obtain his permission, and then start the paperwork. Wally had a wonderful rapport with the President and the President seeing the value of such a transaction, would surely gave his approval.

The wheels could now be set in motion. Getting things started was a piece of cake for Margie who had done this task thousands of times. Wally also needed to contact the Dean of Housing, the Chief Financial Officer, the Scholarship Committee Chair, and the Public Relations Office. There was still plenty of time to get everything accomplished. It was only February. That would give him enough time to close all of the loop holes and have Juan on campus to start practice when Freshman orientation week was over.

Because of his exalted position, Wally wanted to meet with the President in person. The details could not be handled by phone, or by his other department aides. The meeting with the President didn't take long. Wally never had any problems once his ducks were in order. The potential for image enhancement always went well at the highest levels. Getting a visa for Juan might prove to be a little trickier, but Wally had contacts in both the INS and The State Department who were former alumni of the school.

In two days, all of the palms had been greased with flattery or promises of free tickets to some of the sought after sporting events, and the call was placed to Travis to get Juan ready, and bring him to San Diego by August 10th. Wally promised that all of the necessary forms and formalities would be sent priority mail to Mexico. All Travis had to do was get the signed consent and the completed forms from Juan and his mother and forward the consent back to the University. Wally. and Margie would handle all of the rest of the details.

As Travis got off the phone, he felt like a kid with a new toy. Tonight, he was going to treat himself to the largest steak in the city, garnished with sautéed mushrooms, a baked potato and steamed vegetables. He definitely was going to wash the meal down with several bottles of premium Mexican beer, and cheesecake with sweet cherries on top. It was only mid-afternoon, so Travis decided he had time for a long, hot shower and a short nap. He was exhausted from the exercise, having slept little last night, and had running for hours on an adrenaline high.

He would check out of the hotel in the morning, drive to his residence to ensure that it was being well maintained as he had instructed, and return to Mexico the next day. He could hardly wait to tell Juan the good news. He drove up to his house, a rambling ranch style set up in the hills, with a curved driveway, and beautiful landscaping. The gardener had definitely been doing what Travis had been paying him for. The grass had recently been mowed, the edges trimmed neatly, the hedges cut into the shape of figures. The swimming pool out back was free of leaves and debris. It looked so inviting, but he didn't have the time to spare. He opened the front door with his key, walked into the foyer and was overcome with the aroma of garlic, tacos, and salad. He had phoned ahead to his cook and housekeeper who had prepared him some lunch. She didn't want him flying all the way to Mexico after waiting in the airport clearing security without something to eat.

As he rounded the hall into the large, well equipped kitchen, Rosa was standing over the sink in final preparation of the repast he was about to enjoy. He sneaked up behind her, put his arms around her ample waist and whispered that he wanted to marry her. She broke free of his grasp, giggled, and declined the offer. It was a game they had played for years. Rosa had worked for the family seemingly forever. After Travis came into possession of the residence, she moved in to take care of him when he was in town, and the house when he wasn't.

She sat a place for him at the breakfast counter, and he ate with relish. The meal ended too quickly, and the time was fleeting. He had to leave soon, or he would miss his flight. He hurried upstairs, took off his clothes and jumped into a quick shower. As the hot water cascaded over his body, he remembered the many times he and his lady friends had taken showers together. How they had soaped each other's bodies, and made love in the steam room. He rarely thought about it in the past few years, but the remembrance was most pleasing.

He dressed in a pair of tan colored Dockers, a light blue knit shirt, and a dark Navy blue blazer. He completed the ensemble with a new woven straw fedora style hat. He packed a small suitcase, left the house and drove to the airport. The trip wasn't long, but the thought of having to go through all of the security again was upsetting. He was always prepared and had no problems, but inevitability, someone in front of him had forgotten to take their pen knife out of their pocket, or had stowed a pair of scissors in their purse, and the line would come to a screeching halt. He finally cleared customs, walked down the concourse to Gate 11B with about thirty minutes left until boarding time. Boarding was called and passengers began to exit through the door onto the ramp leading to the aircraft. The plane looked like it was going to be full. He found his seat in first class, settled in, and waited for the plane to taxi out to the runway and take off.

Normally he would have ordered a couple of drinks, tilted his seat back, and dozed off. This time he ordered only one. He had made this trip on so many occasions, he could almost tell you the exact position over the earth they were flying at any given moment. Sleeping would help pass the time since he had read the airlines magazine twice before on the flight home, and had forgotten to bring along a book. However, he could not sleep. He kept thinking about the possibility Juan might change his mind and not want to take Travis up on the offer. He sat bolt upright in the seat when the thought crossed through his cerebral cortex. Surely Juan would not do such a stupid thing, or would he? His reaction caused the hostess to come to his side and ask if there was anything wrong. Travis said no, and settled back in.

The flight seemed to go on forever. Travis again tried to sleep, but sleep still would not come. He slid the sleeve of his sport coat back to check the time, and found his watch had stopped. The battery must be dead, Travis surmised. He asked the hostess for another drink which she brought. He sat the drink on the tray, and turned to speak to the passenger next to him. In doing so, he caught the drink with his elbow, and it spilled all over him. The hostess assisted Travis in cleaning up the spill, offering to bring another, which Travis politely refused. At the rate things were going, these events were only increasing Travis' frustration. Were things going to hell in a hand-basket Travis internalized. He could feel an ulcer coming on. Relax, he told himself, things couldn't get any worse. Finally the plane landed and the shuttle took Travis to the parking area.

The shuttle arrived at the concrete island which separated his car from the street. He walked briskly to the shining black automobile, unlocked the door and put the key in the ignition and nothing happened. The batter was dead and things were getting worse. He dropped a coin into the payphone, dialed roadside assistance, and prayed the Mexican counterpart of AAA would be there. A pleasant sounding young Latino female took the call, asked for his specific location, color of car, license plate number, and informed him relief would arrive in approximately forty-five minutes. Travis paced back and forth like a caged animal. Why me? Why now? Is it possible that my luck has changed? Travis decided to stop deriding himself. This was only a minor glitch in an otherwise normal day.

As promised, the repair truck showed up, and headed itself to the front of the car. The mechanic leaped from the truck with a pair of jumper cables, lifted the hood and attached the red and black wires to the poles of the battery. He instructed Travis to turn on the key, and start the engine. The powerful motor roared to life. Travis let the engine idle while he signed the receipt for the service. When the truck had departed, Travis left the parking lot, and exited onto the expressway, which would take him to his apartment in the city. As Travis opened his apartment door, he could see the red light on the answering machine blinking. He was hungry and tired, but decided he needed to see who had called. He hit the replay button, and it was the director of player personnel for the Padres asking him where had he been. Travis was supposed to have given the director an update of the players Travis had scouted this week. The report was due two days ago, and Travis had forgotten. It was too late to call tonight. Travis promised himself he would do it first thing in the morning.

Travis stopped to realize how involved he had gotten with Juan, and how he had neglected his own job. He must be prepared to give a good explanation, but knew he couldn't think of anything rational at this time, so the morning would just have to be the time to bullshit the boss.

Travis was hungry, but when he opened the refrigerator, the only thing available was a TV dinner of bar-b-qued chicken. It had been a couple of weeks since Travis had been to the market, and had forgotten how low on food he was. He opened a bottle of beer, took the dinner out of the cardboard container, and slipped it into the microwave. The meal wasn't his favorite, but it met the need. He then undressed, showered, and went to bed. Travis spent a fretful night. He tossed and turned for hours, getting up often to pace about the house, trying to relax enough so he could sleep. Finally at two o'clock in the morning he dowsed off. He wasn't sure how long he had slept, but bright sunshine was streaming through a crack in his drapes. He turned the bedside clock around, and realized he had almost nocturnally devoured the whole morning.

He jumped out of bed, raced to the kitchen, and ate the remain cereal and milk he had left. He then dialed the telephone number of the player personnel office, and asked the secretary for the director. The conversation was short. Travis had no excuse, gave the director the report and hung up. Another shower made him feel better, as did the clean clothes. Travis exited his abode, entered his car, and headed toward the village soccer field and Juan.

CHAPTER NINE

The traffic through the city was horrendous, there had been a ghastly accident involving fatalities on the avenue he was traveling. He was stalled while emergency vehicles and ambulances darted by him with their sirens blaring for people to get out of the way. He sat in his car, grid-locked, for over an hour. He left the motor running to operate the air-conditioning, which he felt he could not turn off because of the heat and humidity of the day. The weatherman had predicted temperatures in excess of 100 degrees and humidity in the high 80 percentile. He also wanted to keep his windows closed to avoid the fumes of the cars and trucks which surrounded him. In a city of this size, the smell of gasoline and diesel fumes was overpowering. Mexico City was one of the most polluted cities in the world, with respiratory diseases occurring in a high number of its citizens. He glanced at the buildings in the city center seeing the corrosion eating away at their décor. Many of the buildings had been there for centuries, and it was such a shame to see the ruination.

He glanced at his gas gauge and noticed it registered less than half full. He would turn off the engine to conserve fuel only if he had too. Finally there was a break and the traffic began to move. He thought to himself, maybe my luck is changing after all. His car inched forward, then slowly picked up speed as he neared the edge of town. After locating the street he was after, Travis swung the car onto the graveled road leading to the soccer field. He parked the car, and went immediately to the field. When he got there, no one was in sight. Then he remembered he had not told Juan what day he was returning, but had only hoped the boys would be there engaged in their favorite sport.

No one arrived. He didn't know where Juan lived, so he set out for the dump to see if he could find Juan, or locate someone who knew where he lived. This late in the afternoon, there were only a handful of individuals left sifting though the trash. He hollered at one of the scavengers, but the noise of the dump tractors drowned him out. The only recourse he had was to trudge up the pile. The walk was like slogging through quicksand. With each step, his feet would sink in the muck and decay. His three hundred dollar a pair shoes, and his expensive pants would have to be thrown away Travis was certain, unless he could find a way to salvage them. About half way up the heap, Travis stopped a worker and asked if he knew Juan. The man said he did, and gave Travis directions to the boys home. Travis wasn't worried about showing up at the hovel in his condition because he would fit right in, smell and all.

After getting in his car, he knew he would ruin the carpeting, but hopefully he could find a car detailer who could remove the stains and smells. The worst part was the pungent odor coming from his clothes which permeated the inside, causing a wave of nausea to sweep over him. After a while, he got used to the smell, and it wasn't that far to reach Juan. Then Travis realized he couldn't possibly show up in this condition, so he stopped by a small laundry in the village, and bribed the owner into cleaning his pants while he waited in a small back room. While the pants were being taken care of, Travis took the liberty of cleaning his shoes off in a small sink. The laundry delivered the pants to Travis having done a reasonable job. Travis paid him handsomely, put the pants on and continued his journey.

He pulled up in front of a forlorn looking shed of a house constructed from boards, cardboard, and old bricks forming the walls, and sheets of tin metal functioning as the roof. The house looked reasonably solid, but run down as did the other houses in the village. He knocked on the door which was opened slightly by a middle aged woman of average height. She was a worn, bedraggled woman, but obviously had been handsome before a life of poverty had left its mark on her. Years of living with an abusive husband and bearing and raising a small brood of children had taken its toll. She was dressed in a colorful frock made of expensive material, most likely a rare find from the rich and affluent who had probably only worn the dress once or twice and then discarded it. Such was life, the haves and the have nots.

The old woman was leery of the slick looking man, a stranger and not to be trusted. In guttural Spanish, she asked him his name. When he told her who he was, she opened the door a little more to get a better look. She had remembered Juan telling her about the baseball scout, so she invited him into the house. Surprisingly, the house was neat and well kept. It was filled with furniture and some modern day appliances. Even a color TV. Very little of the furnishings matched, but Travis attributed that to the collection effort. She told him her name was Carmela and invited him to sit on the only sofa in the front room. The smaller children had gathered around her apron, and stared with deep brown eyes at the interloper. She shooed them into the bedrooms so she could have some privacy. She informed Travis that Juan was not home, but if Travis could wait, Juan should be arriving soon. Travis chose to remain, the message he brought was far too important to leave without seeing Juan.

Carmela served Travis a cold beer and they exchanged small talk as Travis mulled over his briefing to Juan on the progress Travis had made with the university. After a half hour or so, Juan appeared in the door. Travis arose and greeted Juan warmly. They sat down on the couch facing Juan's mother. Travis began his speech, hoping it didn't sound too rehearsed. Travis described his conversation with the Athletic Director, the dormitory where Juan would be staying, the class requirements, and the mentor that had been arranged to see Juan off to a good start.

After Travis finished, Juan asked if he could be alone with his mother to come to a final decision. Travis stood, excused himself, and walked outside for a much welcomed cigarette. Travis finished one cigarette and lit another with the glowing end of the first one. Six cigarettes later, Juan joined Travis outside. Travis thought to himself; what if Juan decides not to go to the university after all they had gone through. What would he tell the university if Juan does not accept the offer? Excuses came tumbling down his cerebral cortex like ice cubes being dispensed from the door of a refrigerator, with a resounding thud into a solid bottomed glass. He could tell them Juan had been killed by a gang, or had contracted some deadly virus from the dump, or simply that Juan was under such an obligation to support his family he could not leave them. No matter how many excuses surged through Travis' brain, none seemed feasible.

Juan appeared over Travis' shoulder. Juan smiled. "I have talked this over with my mother. My uncles and aunts have volunteered to help support the family, and it has been agreed on by everyone, I should take this opportunity to get an education in the United States. I know a chance like this only comes once in a lifetime, and I should not turn it down. Besides, maybe I can send some of the money I make working at the university back to my mother to help. I will go to San Diego, receive my teachings, and return to better the lives of those I will be leaving behind.

Relief made Travis light headed, and he feared for a moment he would pass out. His knees were shaking like Colorado Aspens, and he was devoid of speech. Juan's mother glanced at him in alarm, fearing he was having a stroke or heart attack. The concern was soon over when Travis broke into a grin wider than the Grand Canyon, grabbed Juan by the hand, and almost shook his arm off. From this point on, Travis filled in the details, showing Juan the papers that need to be completed to initiate the scholarship. In a couple of hours, the forms had been filled out and final preparations were planned. Juan would be leaving for San Diego in five months time. He would be on campus before the main body arrived which would give him time to become familiar with the surroundings, receive the freshman orientation, and begin soccer practices before the semester started.

Travis told Juan a first class flight would be arranged, and Travis would ferry Juan to the airport on the designated day, and away they would soar into this new and exciting adventure full of unknowns together. For the next few months, Juan spent most of his time raising as much capital as he could to hedge against any unforeseen problems with the funds necessary to maintain the household. He spent long hours in the landfill, striving to collect and resell as much as possible in the shortened time. On Sundays, he went to the city to buy clothes, shoes, and other essentials he would need. He also purchased a brand new piece of luggage to take with him on the plane.

On the day of destiny, Travis reappeared at the house to drive Juan to the airport. Travis had arranged some time off from his boss to make sure Juan received the very best in his services. The baseball pre-season was in full swing, and this was a time when the services Travis performed slipped into a brief lull. Juan kissed of his family goodbye, got aboard the car, and was off in a cloud of dust. Carmela waved goodbye until she could no longer see the dust cloud, then wept silently, and headed to the church to attend mass, and pray for her son's success and return.

CHAPTER TEN

The trip to the airport was reminiscent of two college boys headed to South Beach in anticipation of spring break. Travis and Juan chatted like two silly young girls about to go on their first date. Juan had a million questions, and Travis tried to answer each and every one the best he could. Travis told Juan about the city, the school, and the people who would be mentoring him. They talked about environment, the future, and the stresses Juan would experience. In no time, the airport loomed in front of them. Travis maneuvered around the traffic to find a space in the long term parking, as he always did, this time lucking out and finding a spot very near the shuttle gate.

They unloaded their baggage, and waited for the next van to pick them up and take them to the terminal. It wasn't long until the yellow vehicle pulled alongside the curb, and they hopped on. The van took them to the entry lounge and departed. The day was a scorcher, but as they breezed through the automatic doors, the coolness of the building inside refreshed them immediately. They proceeded to the counter to check in. They both showed the airline representative their tickets and passports, answering the standard questions all airlines asked about having anything dangerous in their luggage, and had their luggage been out of their sight since entering the terminal. Once the preliminary inquires were taken care of, the baggage tags were applied to the bags, and they received their boarding passes. They had almost an hour before the plane departed, so they found a seat in the boarding area and waited.

Juan was unnerved going through the security process. People ahead of him were showing their boarding passes and ID's and having their passes marked with a red pen. Then their fellow passengers had to go through an X-ray machine. The women were sent to a separate line to have their handbags inspected, and others were routed for a quick inspection of any carry on luggage. Travis had been through this routine so often, it didn't concern him at all. He never carried pocket knives or nail clippers as many did who had to surrender them to the security personnel. Juan jumped when a loud shriek sounded as one passenger walked through the archway which reminded Juan of a trellis in his mother's flower garden. Travis quieted Juan down and told him the person must have had something metal remaining on their body to make the machine sound off. Juan felt better when it was discovered the man was wearing an oversized belt buckle which triggered the mechanism. The man removed the belt, retraced his steps through the screening device to a deep sound of silence. It was Juan's turn, which went without incident.

There was still plenty of time to get something to drink and to visit the bathroom. Over the next few minutes, Juan was fascinated with the people. He had never seen so many different kinds. There people of every description. Men in business suits, girls in skimpy halter tops and levis trying to emulate American teenagers, mothers with children in strollers, older people who had been on vacation from California and other states, and people who looked like movie stars.

At fifteen minutes before the flight was to leave, the attendant at the gate announced that Flight 332 from Mexico City to San Diego was now available for boarding. Disabled passengers and parents with small children were boarded first. Next came the call for first class and VIP passengers. Travis nudged Juan to indicate their turn had come, and they should proceed to board the plane. They walked down the jet-way and on to the aircraft. They were seated in Row 2, seats D and E. Juan took the window seat, and settled into the soft, gray leather seat. Other passengers began boarding the plane, jousting to get down the aisles past idiots who were trying to stow their carry on luggage in the overhead compartments. In some ways, this reminded Juan of the overcrowded buses he would ride in when he traveled into the city, only with more manners from the travelers.

The flight would take three hours, the plane cruising at 33,000 feet above sea level. The captain came on the air to welcome everyone aboard and to tell them he expected a smooth flight and arrival in San Diego on time. When everyone was on board, the plane was pushed away from the gate, taxied to the strip and in seconds was airborne. Juan watched through the window in awe as he saw the ground disappear from sight and the plane become enveloped in dense white clouds. He had the sensation he had died and was being lifted to heaven. His ears popped like a tiny firecracker going off, a sensation he had never felt before. He opened his mouth to prevent it from happening again.

Shortly after takeoff, the first class cabin hostess, a young, trim Hispanic woman closed the curtain between their cabin and coach. She asked each of the first class passengers what they would like to drink and offered them a choice of food for the in flight meal. She spent a little extra time attending to the handsome young Mexican, a gesture not lost on Travis. Travis vowed he would make sure the staff at the university would keep Juan's head on straight and away from the women, although it would be a challenging task. After the meal, Juan watched as the sun set in the west. They were due to arrive in San Diego at eight PM not too much after all of the light had gone from the sky. Travis had a glass of wine and Juan a coke. They both chose the filet of sole with vegetables and a tossed green salad. The food was delicious and was devoured quickly. When the meal was finished and the dishes cleared away, Juan leaned his seat back, closed his yes, and immediately fell asleep, not dreaming and almost comatose. He was awakened when the captain announced for the passengers to fasten their seat belts in anticipation of the plane's landing. As the plane slowed and the wheels dropped into a locked position, Juan gazed out of his window at the thousands of lights which shimmered like tiny candles stretching for miles. He had never seen a city from the air, and it was beautiful beyond belief. The tires hit the runway with a screech and the pilot engaged the thrust engines to slow the craft. The hostess again announced the arrival to San Diego, thanked everyone for flying with them, and wished them a safe and pleasant stay in San Diego. The plane came to a rest at the gate and they deplaned into the brave new world.

CHAPTER ELEVEN

San Diego, a city of approximately one and one-half million people, lies 1400 miles north of Mexico City. San Diego, a city of charms, Juan was about to experience. Travis traveled so much between California and Mexico, he kept a car at both airports for convenience. They followed the same routine in getting to the repositioned car as they had done before. Because of the lateness, Travis decided to take Juan to his house for a few days until everything was settled at the university.

They drove in silence. Most of the questions Juan had were answered, so now was a time to reflect and tackle the new day. Travis drove up the curved driveway and parked in front of the house. Even though he had a three car garage, he didn't want to go through the rigmarole of having to engage the garage door opener, move inside, and unlock the back door. Instead, he parked the car at the curb, opened the massive wooden front door and helped Juan carry their luggage inside. Juan had never seen such luxury. He marveled at the cathedral ceilings with the dark wooden beams criss-crossing them. He felt the soft whir of the air conditioning and the muffled tones of cars on the interstate nearby.

Travis escorted Juan into the kitchen for a late night snack. As often happened, Rosa had left a plate of freshly baked cookies on the kitchen counter. She must have made them that afternoon. The aroma of melted chocolate still permeated the air. Travis took two glasses from the cupboard, filled them with fresh whole milk and handed one to Juan. In seconds, the cookies had disappeared. After the dishes had been rinsed and placed in the dishwasher, Travis led Juan upstairs to his bedroom, gave him a quick orientation of his room, bid him goodnight and said he would see him for breakfast in the morning. Even though Juan had slept on the airplane, he was so exhausted with all of the anticipation he slept the sleep of the dead. He could not remember being so tired, even when he had worked hard for twelve straight hours. He had not done any manual labor, but the stress of up-rooting his life, and the foreboding of the unexpected, had sapped his strength to the very core. Juan was not sure how long he had slept, but awakened refreshed and hungry as a mountain lion. He could smell the aroma of freshly brewed coffee, bacon frying, and other sounds emanating from below. Juan quickly took a shower and changed into fresh clothes exiting downstairs to marry up with Travis.

Travis was busy in the kitchen preparing the meal. He had given Rosa the day off, and relished the opportunity to practice his culinary talents. He asked Juan how he liked his eggs and poured the youngster a large glass of orange juice and filled a huge mug with the steaming hot brew. Four slices of toast went into the toaster. Travis preferred wheat, but put in two slices of white bread just to add a little variety. Soon the eggs were done, the toast buttered, and a second glass of juice devoured. Travis smiled as he watched Juan eat the meal as though he had not eaten in months. Ah the folly and appetite of youth, Travis thought to himself. Juan finished the initial helping, then asked for more, which Travis was certainly willing to oblige.

They wound up breakfast, put the dishes in the washer, and started their quest out the front door. The drive to the university would not take long, the first stop being at the housing office to sign in and get the key to the dorm room to which Juan had been assigned. The dorm housing for most of the student athletes was a two story, brick style building located near the southern end of the campus. It was one of the older buildings, but one that had been inhabited by sports scholarship recipients for decades. Each room was designed for two men, with two beds and nightstands, two desks, two closets, and a communal sink in the middle of the room. The toilets and showers were located at the end of the hall and were shared by all of the residents. Downstairs were the quarters of a professor and his wife who were managers of the dorm. The room was Spartan, but comfortable. Even as simple as it was, it was luxurious by comparison to what Juan had lived in at home for the past seventeen years. Travis helped Juan unpack his clothes, putting the shirts and pants in the closet and underwear, sock, and other items in the matching bureau. A roommate had been assigned to live with Juan but had not moved in yet. Juan could only imagine what the fellow might look like, but could not spend time thinking about it, he had too many things to accomplish that day. The next destination was the athletic department and a meeting with the athletic director and the soccer coaches.

Travis stopped his car in front of the building, bade Juan a fond farewell and drove off leaving Juan on the sidewalk alone and exposed. Juan was on his own now. Travis had to leave to get back to his duties, but knew the campus would become familiar soon enough and the exercise would do Juan good. They had furnished him a map of the campus, so as soon as his meeting with Wally was over, he would spend some time just walking around.

The day was sunny, with a slight wisps of clouds, high in the powder blue sky, normal for this temperate city. There weren't many students walking the sidewalks of the quadrangle formed by large classrooms, but a few. Some students were sitting on the benches provided under many of the trees, looking through the orientation materials or just relaxing. The athletic department was a large, mostly glass building with an imposing brick façade in front. The building not only held the offices of the coaches and their staffs, but also contained a weight room, conference rooms, a reception area, and an orthopedic consultation center. Juan vowed to keep himself out of that area.

Juan roamed the halls for a few minutes trying to locate the director's office. Suddenly he spotted the glass door with gold lettering indicating the right place. He pulled open the door, sidling up to the reception counter. Margie arose from her desk and said, "You must be Juan the new soccer player. Travis has told me so much about you, but he didn't tell me you were so good looking."

If it hadn't been for Juan's rich and dark brown skin, the redness he was feeling would have shown through like a beacon.

"Come on now Margie", the director spoke. "Pick on someone your own age."

"But there isn't anyone that handsome who is my age" was her retort said with a giggle.

Wally introduced himself and ushered Juan into his office asking Margie to join them for the initial visit. Once inside, Wally directed Juan to a chair in front of his desk, then sat down in his oversized leather chair, a gift from an admiring alumnus.

"Let me be the first to welcome you to San Diego State, Juan. We have a wonderful school here and an outstanding athletic program in over twenty different sports. I think you will like it here and I can guarantee that we will do everything in our power to make it so. Travis told me you were settled in you living quarters. We have decided to give you a roommate from the football program, a sophomore who has been with us for a year and knows our system pretty well. I think he can give you a hand in familiarizing yourself with the campus. Before you meet the soccer coaching staff, we need to get you enrolled, registered for your classes, your books purchased, and take you through your physical. I am going to have Margie type up some vouchers for you to use to pay for the tuition, the books, and the meal cards you will need to eat in the cafeteria once the results of the medical exam are in. These vouchers will be like checks in lieu of money. Please be careful with them. If they are lost, anyone can use them illegally. When you have finished today, take a break and we will see you back here at 9 o'clock in the morning. I have asked one of our women soccer players to take you under her wing and show you the ropes in getting everything accomplished. Let's go out back and meet her."

Wally had done all of the talking, which was fine with Juan, because he was so over-whelmed, he had nothing to say anyway. Together they walked out of the office down a long corridor, and through a set of double doors leading outside to a practice field. Gracefully manipulating a soccer ball with her feet was a slender, trim, gorgeous redhead, who stopped bouncing the ball when they neared.

"Juan, this is Shannon Stewart. She is now responsible for seeing that you are taken care of. Shannon, this is Juan Cardova from Mexico City, the newest member of the men's soccer team."

Shannon held out her long, slim hand. Juan had never seen a woman's hand with such long fingers. Her grip was firm and strong. She exuded confidence and there was an instantaneous chemistry between them. Not sexual in nature, more like a brother and sister.

"Shannon," the director spoke, "Margie has Juan's vouchers for you to pick up after we get the results of the physical. Would you take him to the student health center for the examination? The student clinic physician said he would expedite the exam which would allow Juan time tomorrow to get his books, pick up his meal passes, and complete his job application.

She nodded her head, grabbed Juan by the arm and off they went to the clinic. The student health center wasn't far away, but gave Shannon a little time to get acquainted with Juan. The center was a modern structure, having been added just recently to the campus. Inside the front doors was a modern facility which gleamed with shiny floors, new decorations, and the smell of cleanliness. Shannon and Juan checked in at the front counter. The medical records clerk had Juan fill out a medical history form, then led him down the hall to an examination room. Shannon sat on one of the chairs in the reception area and began reading a magazine. Soon, a nurse rapped on the door, introduced herself to Juan, took his blood pressure, his weight and height. She handed him some laboratory slips, one to get some blood drawn and a check of his urine. This was all so strange to Juan, but the nurse was assuring and guided him through the procedure. When the blood had been taken and the urine sample left at the lab desk, Juan returned to the examination room. In a short time, another rap sounded on the door, and entered a tall, young doctor in a stark white coat with a stethoscope hung around his neck.

For the next thirty minutes, the physician had Juan disrobe and probed every possible part of Juan's anatomy, making notes in Juan's chart as he went along. He told Juan he found nothing of concern, but would spend some time going over the laboratory results and then would send a report to the athletic director later that afternoon.

Most of the day had passed, so Shannon excused herself stating she had some other errands to run, but would meet Juan the next morning at the sports complex to see if he had passed the physical. Juan oriented his map and strolled back to his dorm room. He did some more arranging of his stuff and then went to the dining hall for supper. Juan found the food to be excellent. He sat with some of the other freshman athletes, conversing easily. That night Juan did not sleep well, he knew he was in great shape, but one never knew what possible problems might lie just under the surface.

The next morning Shannon was at the sports complex as she had promised. They walked together into see Margie, check on the results of the physical and if Juan had passed it, pick up the vouchers and get things moving. Margie was at her usual place and with a pleasant smile on her face, handed the vouchers to Shannon and informed Juan he passed the examination with flying colors. There was a noted bounce in Juan's step as they headed on the registrar's office to get Juan enrolled in the university. The office was located on the first floor of the administration building, an imposing four story structure made of natural limestone. It had been decided that Juan was to enroll in the communication curriculum with a minor in political science.

The first step was to obtain a class schedule for these subjects offered to incoming freshman. In addition to the pertinent subjects related to these two areas, Juan also had to select courses in English, mathematics, speech, a physical science, and a biological science. He would be carrying a load of 16 credit hours per semester for the first year. The administrative assistant in the office handed him a manila envelope containing all of the necessary forms, and class schedules. The assistant directed them to a large conference area where tables had been arranged for students to complete the forms. Shannon and Juan sat at one of the tables, opened the packet, and began to peruse the schedule.

Soccer practice was normally held early in the morning, so it was decided that Juan's first class should start around 9 o'clock. That would give him time to practice, get something to eat, shower, and get to class. After that, the day would be crammed attending class and studying. Efficiently they selected the classes from the course guide and slotted the classes into the schedule matrix the university had included. When they were finished, Juan was satisfied he could meet all of his obligations to the sports program and attend all of the necessary classes. They turned the forms in for review, but were told that his freshman English class was full and he would have to select another one at a different time. This threw the entire schedule out of kilter and process had to be repeated.

Juan sensed his growing frustration and almost tore up the papers. He didn't understand the workings of a bureaucracy. He swore in Spanish and started to get up. Shannon empathized with his frustrations, but encouraged him to continue to work through the problems. Shortly thereafter, the new schedule was completed and approved by the registrar's office.

The next stop was the bursar's office where Juan was to turn in one of the vouchers to pay for the first semester's tuition. The line winding up to the finance cage was long and slow. Juan and Shannon chatted to pass the time which seemed to be an eternity. It did however give them a chance to get to know each other.

Juan explained his background to the best of his ability, leaving out some of the sordid details of his meager existence. He thought she would like to hear a more glamorous story. She sensed he was lying, but was so skillful at it, she decided to accept it as the truth. She thought to herself, Juan would make a good politician.

Shannon told Juan she was a military brat. Her father had been in the Navy for over twenty years and had retired in the San Diego area and was now a consultant for an underwater demolition company which salvaged old war vessels under a Department of Defense contract. She talked about the family separation, the foreign countries they had lived in and her father's involvement in the landing at Inchon harbor and his service during the Korean conflict. She told Juan she was the youngest in the family. She had an older brother and sister. Her whole family had been involved in sports and she had chosen soccer to capitalize on her physical attributes and speed.

Their bonding and friendship blossomed and they spoke freely and easily with each other. By the time Juan reached the head of the line, he felt he had known Shannon all of his life. He turned in the voucher and waited for the clerk to enter the information into the computer. He was handed a receipt which told him they were finished with that step. Most of the morning had expired, so Shannon suggested they have lunch at the Student Union building cafeteria. It was her treat. When Juan protested, she would hear nothing of it. He could treat her some other time. The cafeteria was a bustling beehive of activity. The serving counter was like a silver snake contouring at different angles past steaming hot tables laden with a variety of food. He had never see so much food in one place in his entire life.

They exchanged personal background items freely during lunch.

Juan ate too much, knowing he would have to exercise that afternoon to work off the excess calories he had consumed. He vowed to control his appetite, and watch his weight. Being too heavy would certainly slow him down. The next stop was the Dean of Student's Office where Juan was to sign up for his job. Most of the scholarship athletes were given employment in college industries dealing with the Athletic Department. He was given a choice of tasks and he chose to be a custodian in the gym and to handle crowd control at sporting events such as basketball and football games when they didn't interfere with his soccer schedule.

Since Juan was now employed in the United States, he was issued a green working permit and expected to pay all of the taxes on his earnings. He filled out the W4 form listing five dependents. This would only extract the minimum amount of taxes. He decided to check in with the full time custodian at the gym later that afternoon.

The afternoon was warm and Juan was still feeling the effects of the jet trip, so they sat down on one of the benches strewn along the campus and rested. Not a word was exchanged. The two new friends just looked at the beautiful scenery and watched other new students as they trudged across the sidewalks getting settled in. The final stop was the university bookstore. The bookstore was located in the basement of the old student union building. It was filled with books needed for every class, but also university related clothing, decals, coffee mugs, glasses, magazine, pens, pencils, and a myriad of other objects to be purchased. Shannon gave one of the clerks working in the bookstore a copy of Juan's class list and followed as the clerk led them to the many aisles lined with publications.

The books were chosen and the voucher submitted to the cashier in payment. Again, a receipt was issued for Juan's records. Shannon walked with Juan back to his dormitory to stash his books away until classes began, then guided him to the gym for an orientation and meeting with his new boss. The gym was a massive building, constructed with the same style brick found on most of the other buildings at the institution. The basement floor housed the U.S. Army Reserved Officer's Training Corps (ROTC), administration, classrooms, and indoor rifle range. It also housed most of the heating and air conditioning systems, a laundry and storage areas. In the main part of the building were the ticket offices, the basketball court, a swimming pool of Olympic proportions, handball courts, weight rooms, gymnastic mats, and more classrooms.

They stopped by the chief custodian's office, but he wasn't there. Shannon knew he was on duty, so they traversed the building hoping to run him down. Sure enough, they located him coming out of the swimming pool area where he had just tested the water for the right mix of chlorine to keep the water safe.

Shannon shouted, "Hey Baron, here's your new slave."

Baron Nesbitt was the head custodian, a brute of a man. A former football player who had been tackled in the head and knees so many times, he had trouble remembering things and difficulty getting around. Shannon was certain he had gotten the job because of his disabilities. His nickname was "Baron of Beef" because of his size. A name whispered behind his back jokingly.

Juan introduced himself to Baron. They shook hands and Shannon left the gym telling Juan she would see him tomorrow. Baron spoke with Juan briefly, then they sat down in the custodian's office to explain his duties and develop a work schedule which would fit with his classes and practices.

CHAPTER TWELVE

Finally, the second day of Juan's new adventure was over. Leaving the gym, he felt like he had been dragged through a knothole backwards. Even as hard as he worked in the trash dump, he had never felt this tired. More mental than physical, but exhausted never the less. He decided he would lie down and take a short nap before the evening meal, then eat and explore the campus nightlife if there was such a thing. As he arrived at his floor in the dormitory, he noticed the door to his room was slightly ajar. He distinctly remembered locking the door and cautiously nudged the door aside, exposing the interior.

Bending over one of the bureaus was a student that made the "Baron of Beef" look small. The stranger turned around revealing a six foot six, three hundred and twenty pound monster. Juan thought there must be a mistake. No one he knew was that size. Juan cleared his throat. He did not wish to startle this gargantuan person.

The behemoth turned, spied Juan and in a deep voice said, "Hi, I'm Duane "Bubba" Wheeler. I'm your new roommate. What's your handle?"

Handle, what's a handle? Juan thought to himself. Then he remembered seeing the movie "Smokey and Bandit" and realized Duane was asking him his name.

"Hi Duane, my name is Juan Cardova. I'm here on a scholarship to play soccer."

"Glad to meet you Juan, I come from San Antonio, Texas home of the Alamo." Suddenly realizing the Alamo was the historical site of a battle between Mexican soldiers and famous patriots of American heritage, Bubba paused, a slow red coloring creeping up his shoulders and onto his face. You could not see the color on his neck, because he had no neck. Juan smiled and instantly the pressure was relieved. "I know what the Alamo is, I read it in a history book at the parish school. That is ancient history between my ancestors and some famous Americans. I don't hold any grudges. Someday, I would like to go to San Antonio and see the Alamo. They say San Antonio and its "River Walk" is one of the most beautiful cities in the United States."

Bubba grinned back, feeling the pressure abate. Bubba had a pleasant aura about him, including a bald head where once a blond mane existed. For the next thirty minutes, they explored each other's biography. Bubba had been recruited from The Lone Star State to play football. He, unlike Juan, was a sophomore on scholarship and still a little homesick even though this was his second year. He had been an all state offensive tackle on his championship high school team, leading the team to a state title which was no small task in a state where football was a religion, drawing 50,000 fans to high school games.

Bubba was an only child of a construction worker and a stay at home mother who doted on him. Bubba's father had also been a good football player, but never went to college, deciding instead to get married, settle down, and build tall buildings in downtown San Antonio. Bubba revered his father and emulated his work ethic into his sport. His father had wanted a college degree for his child, and had lobbied hard to encourage the high school football coach to find a school willing to utilize his son's talents.

The coach wrote letters to dozens of universities and when all of the replies seeking this outstanding prospect came, he read each one of them to Bubba and his father. Bubba agonized for days over which one to choose. He wanted to stay close to home, but also felt the allure of a far away place. One by one, Bubba eliminated schools until he was down to three, The University of Texas at Austin, San Diego State University, and The Ohio State University. Bubba decided to visit each campus before making up his mind. During the summer preceding Bubba's freshman year, his dad took some time off and accompanied Bubba to the schools.

The University of Texas was so big, Bubba felt like a minnow in a big pond. He didn't like the humidity and heat of Ohio and fell in love with the Pacific Ocean. Like a siren leading him on, the ocean closed the deal. The campus was to his liking, the university the right size, and the program geared to develop players to win and move on to the next higher level. Even though there was a dichotomy between the two men, the bonding was immediate. Juan knew Bubba would be a good and trusted friend.

CHAPTER THIRTEEN

Soccer practice began in late August. Twice a day the players met with their coaches, one in the early morning before breakfast and once in the late afternoon after each of them had a chance at the whirlpool to loosen up the aching muscles. Interspersed throughout the day was a chance to workout at the gym with the weights for toning, stretching, and running exercises. Many took advantage of the Olympic size swimming pool.

The head soccer coach, although an American was, a member of the Slavic team from Romania which had been a force in world cup soccer. Mark was tall for a soccer player, but very agile and brilliant in his strategy of the game. His hair was black, thinning in the back which made him look like a friar, and his face was wrinkled with laugh lines. He still spoke with a slight accent, but there was no misunderstanding him when he spoke.

The other coaches and assistants were a mixed bag. Some Americans and some outsiders of the country. Most of them had played either in college games or participated in match play or at some professional venue. A couple of them were young, but most of the staff were seasoned veterans. The players were divided up into offense or defense and at the beginning of practice, were played at the various positions on either side. This was to determine the best possible use of each player's talents.

Juan was in better shape than most, but for the first few days, his young body ached like the aged. Slowly, the pain subsided and finally went away. Catching his second wind became easier as he raced up and down the field. He got to know his teammates and a chemistry began to form between them. Coach Pernoski recognized the cohesiveness of the team and knew in his heart he had something very special, not only in the group, but in Juan himself.

The first semester began in early September, the campus bulging with arriving students to attend their undergraduate studies or complete their post graduate curriculums. The buildings echoed with muted sounds and erupted with cacophony when the bell sounded to end the instruction period and the students rushed to their next class or to the student union building to imbibe in a hasty cup of coffee or soft drink.

Juan's classes were interesting, but fast paced. The professors didn't have the time to devote to the needs of each individual as had the priests who taught in the Catholic parish. Juan knew he would have to expend extra resources to keep up. Between soccer practice and didactic instruction, his hours vanished like the wind. He found himself coming off the field exhausted, grabbing a quick meal at the local dining hall, then trudging back to the room to study.

Too often he would fall asleep at his desk, to be awakened by Bubba who was coming home from some social gathering down town. Bubba's motto was, "I won't let the books interfere with my education."

Juan recognized he needed help, so he sought out Shannon. She invited him to join her study group, students who were taking some of the same classes as Juan. The group met in a small room in the gymnasium in the early evening. It was a miniature setting, in space as well as number, which was good. Too many people tended to distract Juan from his assigned tasks.

Juan was readily welcomed into the group which consisted equally of male and females. They would take turns discussing the day's classes and underlining in yellow high-liter, the passages to reread in the textbooks which they thought might be on an examination. The process suited Juan well. He quickly fell into the routine and found he absorbed and retained more from hearing it verbally and then re-reading the main portions of the book.

He dreaded some of the first examinations he took, but was surprised on how well he had done. Midway through the first semester, he had amassed a grade point average (GPA) of 3.2 or just a little better than a grade B average.

He was so pleased, he invited his study group out for a few beers at a local tavern. Athletes weren't supposed to drink alcohol, but as long as they kept it to a minimum, didn't get drunk, or create a scene, it was generally overlooked. Juan met the group at Shannon's dorm and merrily they walked off campus and into the section of the city where students hung out. The clubs were buzzing with activities and noise. The group finally found a bar that was not quite so crowded, sat at a table and ordered a couple of pitchers of beer.

The bar catered to students, knowing they didn't have much money, so purchasing beer in pitchers was the most economical way to go. The pitchers came and the waitress sat them on the table along with glasses. They waited for the foam to settle a little, then Juan poured a glassful for everyone.

After awhile, Juan and Shannon sort of gravitated toward the dance floor where couples were gyrating to the music. Juan couldn't thank her enough for what she had done to help him, so while they were dancing, he leaned forward and planted a kiss softly on her lips. She didn't return the kiss, an indication that a repeat would not be welcomed. Juan was somewhat taken aback by this, sensing rejection for the first time. They continued dancing until the music ended, then returned to the group.

Juan thought Shannon was taken with him, but later as they walked back to the campus, found Shannon had a boyfriend in another town to whom she had committed to a relationship. They talked about it and agreed to stay best friends, but refrain from deepening any entanglement.

CHAPTER FOURTEEN

Of all of the classes Juan had, he seemed to enjoy the Reserved Officer's Training Corps (ROTC) program the best. As part of the federal government providing funds to the university, required the university to make ROTC mandatory for the first two years. In the third and fourth years, a cadet could elect to terminate his or her relationship with the program, or be enrolled in the Senior ROTC course leading to a commission in the U.S. Army. The head man in the ROTC program was a Lieutenant Colonel Rimmer. LTC Rimmer was short, wore his hair in a butch cut, stomped around like Napoleon and in general lorded it over the cadets. His one desire in life was to be promoted to bird Colonel before he retired. He was an artillery man and hard of hearing because of all of the cannons he had fired during his career had affected his ears. He said what? a lot, but denied he was afflicted by any malady. He was known as "The Professor of Military Science and Tactics", or PMS&T. Juan remembered seeing the movie "Patton" in the city some years ago, and Rimmer reminded him of the great general in many ways.

The ROTC cadre consisted of several Captains and Lieutenants who taught most of the classes, and non-commissioned officers (NCO's), sergeants who handled the administration and supply functions.

Before classes started, Juan reported to the ROTC area to be issued his uniforms to be worn each Thursday. The uniforms consisted of a dark green jacket, dark green pants, a light green shirt, black tie, black shoes, black socks, a black belt with a brass buckle, and a dark green cap with the ROTC insignia pinned on the left front side. They were also issued a utility uniform called fatigues, complete with black leather combat boots, and a soft cap.

One of the NCO's instructed the first year cadets on the proper wearing of the uniform and scolded them to ensure the uniform was clean and neat, and the shoes were shined to a high brilliance, and the belt buckle shone so you could see your face in it. Juan enjoyed putting the uniform on. It gave him a sense of purpose and belonging. He enjoyed the classes also. Wearing the uniform across campus brought jeers from some of the students who opposed war, but the jeers had no effect on Juan.

The classes Juan took in ROTC included map reading, small unit tactics, physical fitness, how to march, weapons firing and maintenance, military history, and chemical warfare. At each class, the cadets were formed into ten man squads and forty man platoons. Each squad had a squad leader, usually an enlisted position and each platoon had a platoon NCO with a platoon leader, a cadet lieutenant.

The squads lined up on command and were put through the proper manner to salute, facing movements, handling of the rifle and marching. At first, Juan's squad was a little uncoordinated, but after some excellent leadership, they began to coalesce into a group akin to a marching band. Juan enjoyed the discipline and the team spirit. Juan was a born leader and soon was promoted to Private and put in charge of the first squad of the fourth platoon in "A" Alpha Company. He studied the military subjects hard and did well in them. His dedication to duty would serve him well later.

The university campus was divided into an upper campus where the buildings were devoted to athletics, education, and the medical arts. The lower campus encompassed the liberal arts college, law, graduate studies, drams, engineering, chemistry, and the library. As Juan strolled from upper to lower campus, he took in the sights and sounds of students studying under the many trees found scattered about. It was estimated there were over four hundred species. He noticed a group of botany students ardently listening to the professor describe the flora and fauna which abounded. He also saw some coeds in the throes of making out, oblivious to anyone around them. Juan likened back to Shannon, but knew he had no chance to woe her, she was just too committed to her boyfriend.

The day had tired Juan out and he fell quickly to sleep even though Bubba was giving him a diatribe about his prowess on the football field. Juan tossed and turned, but didn't dream. He had a sense of ominous happenings about to occur.

Suddenly, a bright light flashed in his face. He awakened with a start and stared into a large flashlight, high beam, black in color which reminded him of a snake. He sat bolt upright in bed and demanded to know what was going on. One of his soccer teammates softly spoke, "we are going over to the girl's dormitory on a panty raid and we want you to go with us."

"I'm tired and I don't have time for this foolishness", Juan blew back.

"Oh come on, don't be such a party pooper. It is just some little harmless fun. We will only be gone a few minutes and then you can get your beauty sleep."

Begrudgingly, Juan cleared the fog from his head, put on his shirt, jeans, and Keds. He ran his fingers through his hair and donned an old baseball cap. The commotion woke Bubba up demanding to know what was going on. When the situation was explained to him, Bubba thought a panty raid sounded like a great idea and decided to join in. There were only two soccer buddies who had crept into his room, but when he arrived outside, the throng had swollen to over one hundred rowdy, college stallions. Down the campus they raced, arriving at the backside of the girl's dorm which had been securely locked for the evening.

They had no idea how to enter the building until one of the mob discovered the kitchen window on the first floor had been left ajar. He deftly climbed the shoulders of a friend, removed his pocketknife from his pants and cut a small opening in the protective screen. He slipped his hand through the incision, pushed the window up, removed the screen from the sash, and tumbled into the kitchen. He was now in the inter sanctum. His skin crawled with anticipation. He located the back door which he gently opened allowing the horde to rush through.

Up until now, the adventure had been reasonably quiet, but when the door crashed open, the noise reached a staggering crescendo. Down the halls they tore, opening doors which weren't locked and darting into rooms when some of the ladies opened them to see what was causing the commotion. Lights came on, screams were heard, bureau drawers were opened, and out of the rooms raced the terrorists with handfuls of lacey undergarments.

Outside the dorm, campus and city police cars were arriving, having been heralded by the dorm proctor Dean Ottness. Some of the men made it out of the building to escape capture, while others, trapped on the second and third floors, attempted escape through windows, dropping themselves onto some shrubbery which scarred their arms and legs as they plummeted to earth.

Search lights from the police cars played across the bricks of the building, highlighting the escapees. Some were captured, handcuffed, and taken into custody, but most made it away free.

The next morning, the panty raid announcement was blazoned across the front pages of the local papers. Nothing had ever happened like this at San Diego State and the administration was determined it would never happen again. For those who were caught, a disciplinary hearing was held at the insistence of the Dean of Students and those in attendance were put on probation for the remainder of the school year. One more foul-up and they would be kicked out of school. Luckily, Juan was not one of the students identified as being part of the raid.

As Juan finished one of his morning classes, he exited the building and rounded the corner of the History Building, one of the oldest on campus. He marveled at the frescos and sculpture work on the façade. This building was one of the original and reflected the Spanish architecture of the early years. He noticed a crack in some of the stones, needing repairs, but money was hard to come by from the state legislature to get things repaired the way they needed to be.

He mused to himself, "if I were in charge, there would be money to fix things up." He had only taken a couple of steps when he felt a sharp pain to his shoulder. Someone had struck him there in a hurtful manner. He was shocked to see Shannon standing there. Her face was as red as her flaming hair, and a look of total anger filled her youthful countenance.

Juan had never seen Shannon mad before and astonishment drove him back against the side of the building. As if a volcano was about to erupt, she said, "you dumb cluck. What do you think you were doing going on the panty raid? You were just lucky you weren't caught and sent before the disciplinary board. You could have been expelled and lost your scholarship!"

Juan had no response, he just stood there agape as she walked away. Over her shoulder, she shouted, "don't ever try anything like that again," and stormed off past several students who had witnessed the confrontation.

That night, he sought Bubba's counsel. "The best thing you can do is call her and apologize. Invite her out for coffee after she has had some time to cool down and assure her you won't pull a stupid stunt like that again." The giant suggested. "Enough said, now get to bed, you will need all of the sleep you can get. Tomorrow is the first scrimmage game and you need a clear head." Juan had a hard time going to sleep, but he knew Bubba was right. He would await his opportunity and then rendezvous with his friend and mend a few fences. After waiting a couple of days, Juan invited Shannon for coffee. She accepted and as they sat in the cafeteria staring down at the brown tempting brew, Juan apologized. Shannon accepted his apology and they moved on.

Soccer practices had now turned into inter-squad games and finally into league play. Juan demonstrated he had the makings of a superstar on the field. The coach was pleased they had made the right decision bringing him into the program. For the first time in many years, the Aztecs were leading their league, compiling the first winning record in decades. Time just seemed to melt away for Juan. No sooner had he begun his academic safari, than it was the end of the semester. He had studied hard and had exceeded his own expectations, which greatly pleased the athletic director's office.

Juan was featured prominently in the local sports pages of the newspapers and the stands were now filled to capacity. The soccer program was paying for itself. Some of the alumni were so pleased, they offered to fly Juan back to his village for the break. This would have constituted a violation of the NCAA rules, so Juan declined. He ached to go back and see his family, but knew it would have to wait until the school year was finished.

Travis had promised him a free plane ride at that time, giving Juan some extra free air miles he had accumulated. Although there was no money involved, and there was no connection to the university, Juan declined. Juan had come close once before in embarrassing his university, he was not going to chance it now. He was sure the thoughtful alumnus could have disguised the payment for the airfare, but de didn't want to be politically incorrect. His mother had taught him to be truthful and he didn't want to ever disappoint her. Even though Juan wasn't able to see him family, he did correspond with her often, slipping a few dollars in the envelope to help with the family's expenses.

The semester break gave Juan a chance to do some traveling in and around San Diego and its environs. Some of his classmates lived nearby and invited him home to meet their families. This also gave Juan a chance to sample the food of the American's and to expand his socialization skills. He did all of the things the tourists did. A couple of days at the zoo, a day at Sea World, visiting the museums, and absorbing the naval history of the area. He had read about the Spanish Armada, but marveled at the size and greatness of the modern naval fleet station nearby.

As he roamed the streets, he would stop to watch a chess match in progress and to chat with the participants. He had a cool drink outside of a quaint street café and mingled with the patrons. He had spoken so much English, there was hardly a traceable accent to his speech. He made friends easily and was soon assimilated into the fabric of the community.

CHAPTER FIFTEEN

The second semester began much the same as the first had. More classes, more wearing of the Army green uniform, and more soccer games. The festive life of the school increased with dances every Friday night, mixed in with concerts, musicals, and plays. One of the biggest dances to take place was the "Sadie Hawkins Day Dance", where everyone dressed up like the citizens of Dog Patch, Arkansas. The girls all wore tattered skirts, tight blouses and their hair in pigtails. The boys all wore bib overalls, boots, flannel shirts, straw hats and fake beards.

Part of this gala blast was the choosing of the Lil Abner and Daisy Mae roles. All of the sororities in the Greek system selected candidates from the male population and the fraternities from the female side. Advertisements were run in the campus newspaper and jars were placed in various locations to collect one penny for each vote for a particular selectee. Not only did this system determine the winners, but raised money for the organizations to use in their welfare and charitable projects. The male winner was declared the "Ugliest Man On Campus". The female winner was given a much better title. The candidates really weren't really ugly, the contest was more of a popularity recognition. All of the ugliest to be were expected to campaign for their sponsors. Juan was nominated by the Gamma Phi Beta House. This experience gave Juan his first shot at selling the public on his worthiness.

The Gamma Phi House and Juan organized the campaign, placed posters on telephone poles and trees, gave speeches, and traversed the grounds shaking hands and extolling the attributes of their man. Juan was immensely popular and won handily. This was to give him his first taste of the political process. He savored the rush and the adulation. Somehow, Juan's DNA told him this was his destiny.

The dance was a tremendous success. At intermission, Lil Abner and Daisy Mae were crowned and awarded gifts which has been solicited from downtown merchants. Juan was so exhausted, he barely remembered going home a falling asleep. Juan wasn't certain he was going to finish his first year at this pace. The next morning he awakened still fully clothed. After showering and shaving, Juan set off for breakfast at the dining hall.

A sudden emptiness overcame him. The elation that filled him the night before was replaced by a sense he was any empty shell needing to be filled again. In the back of his mind, the idea to run for a student office consumed him.

The second semester ended with Juan achieving even higher academic levels and leading the soccer team to a highly successful season. He had the summer free, but knew he had to return home to Mexico to determine how his family was coping. After all his first allegiance was to them.

Travis, true to his word, dropped by Juan's dormitory a couple of days before the term ended to make arrangements for Juan to meet him in three days hence out in front for a ride to the airport and home. Juan had checked with the athletic department and since the ride did not involve any money or influence, the trip was condoned. During the ride, Juan was silent for most of the way, but erupted in a flurry of statements, overwhelming Travis with the adventures he had undertaken and the plans he had contemplated for the future.

"Hey, slow down", Travis said. "It will be a long flight and you will have plenty of time to give me all of the gory details."

Juan took a deep breath, looked out of the car window at the passing scenery and continued his dialog at a much slower pace. He recounted meeting Shannon, getting settled in his dorm, his new roommate Bubba, the soccer games, the studies and the dances.

Travis listened unabashedly, noticing the glow Juan seemed to emanate like the halo of a saint. Travis never interrupted or offered a comment, but just listened. The time went quickly and they were at the long term parking lot of the airport once again. Travis found his favorite spot near the shuttle and they unloaded their bags.

The crowds entering the airport were small, most of the heavier laden flights having gone out a couple of hours ago, mostly with tourists who wanted to get into Mexico City and settled in their hotels before it became too late to enjoy the ambience of that mystical city so steeped in Spanish history and culture.

The air-omatic doors slid effortlessly open as they approached. They stopped for a few seconds to look at the departure console to determine from which concourse and gate they would be leaving.

Travis entered the ticket's electronic code into the in-processing station at the bottom of the escalator which would take them to the gate. The computer did its usual thing. Verified the passengers, asked them if they carried any dangerous things in their luggage, and other inane inquires. Juan could never figure out why the machine did this. There wasn't a lie detector in the machine, so how did it know you weren't lying. Not to worry, you could lie straight faced to a ticket agent with enough practice. They were leaving out of Gate C-29, the last gate in the concourse. Travis hated to walk so far, but Juan didn't mind, youth versus age. They passed a stream of customers just de-planing from a packed aircraft coming in from Seattle. They could tell the passengers were from the north, lacking in sun tans and wearing clothes not really suited for the warmer climates they were about to encounter in Southern California.

Juan loved to people watch. The young girls with the hip huger levis, short tops, pierced navel jewelry, and tattoos just above the crack in their backsides. What a mix of humanity. America was truly the melting pot of the world. Juan leaned forward to a group just ahead of them to determine what language they were speaking. He couldn't tell. Juan enjoyed being immersed in this atmosphere. People smiled at him easily and he returned the smiles.

They soon arrived at the designated departure lounge. They found a couple of seats by the window where they could watch the departing planes lift effortlessly into the fading dusk. Juan sat mesmerized, but was brought back to reality when the gate attendant announced the first boarding call for their flight.

The first-class section was comprised of the first six rows of this aircraft. Juan and Travis were seated in row six, not the most desirable, since the last row was placed against the bulkhead and the seats could only tilt back a few inches. Travis hated this row, but had no choice because it had the only seats left available when the tickets were purchased.

They settled into the soft, gray leather seats and loosely buckled their seat belts. The first-class cabin attendant served each passenger an ice cold bottle of water and a hot steaming cloth to wash their hands and face. The cloth had a slight odor of lemon, which Juan found refreshing and relaxing. Ah, the comforts of first-class.

The attendant was a young twenty-ish latino girl with a broad smile, deep dimples, black eyes, and black hair done up into a twisted knot. The hairdo did much to accentuate her high cheek bones and olive skin. She smiled at Juan, not in a sensual way, but friendly and alluring. Juan could tell she had been on this run before and had practiced her smile on quite a few young studs, or other wealthy looking travelers.

Juan thumbed through the airlines magazine, noting the routes the company flew and high lighting the golf courses to be played at the final destinations. The magazine was filled with advertisements for hotels, restaurants, real estate, and business opportunities. In the back was a section devoted to items one could buy on the internet. The items were very expensive, but so appealing. Juan wondered if some day he would ever have enough money to buy some of these items for himself and his family.

Once the aircraft had reached its cruising altitude of 35,000 feet and leveled off, the sweet thing knelt by each of the rows and asked each person what would be their preference for dinner. The choices were a small tenderloin steak or a pasta dish. Juan chose the steak. He knew what red meat did to your circulatory system but he didn't care. Travis chose the steak as well, he didn't care either.

The steak reminded him of a story he once heard. The saying goes: "The Chinese eat lots of rice and have fewer heart attacks than do Americans. The Spanish eat lots of red meat and have fewer heart attacks than do Americans. The Germans drink lots of beer and have fewer heart attacks than do Americans. The French drink lots of red wine and have fewer heart attacks than do Americans. The moral of that story is eat and drink what you want, just don't speak English."

After the dinner debris was taken away, Travis settled for an after-dinner glass of brandy. Juan could smell the rich pungent odor of the caramel colored liquid, but chose not to join him. As Travis slowly savored his liquor, Juan continued telling him about his life so far. Travis nodded as Juan related his love for the military, the sense of satisfaction he got from playing on a winning soccer team and his thirst to be part of a crowd, leading them on any crusade. Finally Juan ran out of verbiage which didn't matter anyway. Travis's head was on his chest his soft snoring just barely audible. Juan gazed at his mentor's countenance and silently thanked him for all he had done.

CHAPTER SIXTEEN

They taxied up to the gate, gathered their carry-on luggage and deplaned. As soon as they hit the gateway, the smell of pollution and years of poverty consumed them like a thick coat of paint. Juan had a hard time breathing. He had forgotten what living in an atmosphere like Mexico City had been like. He wondered how he had survived in this city of millions under these conditions. How little the government had done to correct the situation. Most of the air smog was coming from older model automobiles purchased in the United States and still driven using leaded gas which was no longer legal north of the border. The American and the Mexican governments didn't care. It was a source of revenue which made a small percentage of the population rich and corrupted the politicians.

Juan vowed some day he would change all of this. Things must be changed so that his brothers and sisters and their offspring could avoid lung cancer and other maladies. He felt light headed and had to pause for a few minutes to catch his bearings. He stopped by a water fountain for a drink and was repulsed by the taste. He knew then and there he could not return to Mexico. California would have to be his salvation. He would make the most of it in the land of temperate climes, where the anti-pollution laws were becoming some of the strictest.

Although the drive to his village wasn't long, it seemed like an eternity. His body assumed the position of time traveler in an old space mobile. He felt the years recede backwards into time. He felt his youth slowly seeping away and he was becoming wrinkled and old. He shuddered and brought himself back to reality. Travis stopped the car in front of Juan's house, bade him farewell until the return trip in the fall and drove off. Juan had asked if Travis would like to come inside and say hello to his mother, but Travis declined. Juan watched as his friend left in a burst of smoke suddenly feeling melancholy and out of touch.

The sensation didn't last long. He had written his mother, telling her the approximate time he would be arriving and she had heard the car approach with her son. As she looked out the front window and spotted Juan, she gather the siblings in the house and raced for the front yard. She looked at her son in amazement. He had grown so tall, was so dark, and so muscular. He was handsome enough to be El Cid, the legendary knight of Spain who saved the nation from the Moors. He leaned forward and held her tightly in his arms. He did not remember her being so frail and small, but he didn't mind the passing thought. He picked her from the ground, swung her around and deposited her amidst the screaming horde of siblings vying for his attention.

It took Juan a few minutes to separate and quiet his siblings, but he relished the procedure. He unlocked his luggage and extracted gifts for everyone. To his mother he gave an expensive tatted lace shawl to wear to church. Her eyes glistened at the sight and a tear encroached the corners of her eyes. That evening his mother fixed the meal of a lifetime. Homemade frijoles, tortillas, beans, jalapeno peppers, and rice. His mother told him to keep eating even though he was stuffed to the gills. He could not remember such a fine meal. As the repast was winding down, everyone started to speak at once.

They all wanted to hear about the land to the north and the riches it held. Juan tried to tell them as much as he could. Their dark orbs expanded with each word. They shook their heads in disbelief. Nothing could be that grand, but they knew Juan would not lie to them. When their curiosity had been sated, they helped clear the table and finish up washing the dishes and other cleaning chores. The evening had transpired so quickly, their bedtimes were approaching, but they didn't want the story to end. With much cajoling, the mother escorted them to their sleeping chambers, kissed them goodnight and rejoined her son. The older children wanted to stay up, but realized they must get their rest so they would be fresh to start a new workday. From the far reaches of the back rooms, each of the brothers and sisters called out to Juan, thanking him for the gifts and wishing him a good night.

Juan sat on the couch, glancing about the familiar room. Not much had changed. The religious paintings and pictures dominated the walls still and air still hung heavily with the burning of incense. The furniture exhibited a few more scars where the younger ones had bumped into it or abused it in some other way. Juan made a note to see if could replace some of it with sturdier things.

Quietly, Carmela sat next to her oldest. Her aged, liver spotted, wrinkled hands grasped Juan's. She gently squeezed his hands and looked into his eyes. She spoke softly.

"It is so good to have you home my son. We have missed you."

"How has it been for you mother?" Juan replied.

"Everything is okay. Your uncles and aunts have been providing for us well and some of the children have worked hard to provide money and goods to keep us living well. You have also helped so much with the money you have sent."

Juan started to speak, but then hesitated. Carmela sensed a foreboding in his demeanor.

"What troubles you Juan?"

"I don't know how to say this, but I have decided to become an American citizen and to live in Southern California. I want to finish my studies, get a job, and have you and the children join me in a few years. In the meantime, I will come home each summer until I have completed my goals."

Carmela sat silently, her face a mask of bewilderment slowly changing to understanding as Juan spoke of his dreams and aspirations.

"Mother, I want to go into politics, to make us a better place to live, to get married, raise a family, own a nice house, drive a big car, and be respected. I can't do that here, only in California. It won't be long and we will be together again in a utopia and away from this awful smell and horrible existence."

Carmela knitted her brow. Searching for the words to answer him, she reflected back over the past many years. She couldn't remember anything but poverty and deprivation. It was the only way of life she had ever known. She was overcome with a strange euphoria. Could it be possible to break this cycle and enjoin in a better life? Or, would they be jerked out of the only existence she had known and thrust into an alien environment of which they knew nothing.

Carmela could speak a little English, but the children were still young or only just beginning to attend school to accumulate the knowledge they would need to survive. What would they do without their relatives who had expended so much energy to aid them? This paradigm shift made her head swirl. She felt nauseous and wanted to throw up her dinner. The ramifications were overwhelming. She couldn't think.

"Let's take a walk away from the house and the stink and let our heads clear", she said.

Gracefully she rose like a conqueror going out to accost her foes, knowing there would be resolution somehow. Juan joined her as they exited the humble abode. They swept southward toward the green belt which lay just beyond the confines of the village. In this place, the children played in a small stream which trickled by, and climbed the stunted trees which had not been cut down yet for firewood.

They walked for what seemed like hours, but was really only minutes. They came to rest on a fallen stump devoid of its bark and rubbed smooth by the many little ones who had slithered across it in playful jostling. The night was warm, but Carmela held her scarf tightly against her drooping shoulders, deep in thought. She nodded her head up and down as if in a trance. She seemed to have slipped into state of possession, unable to be reached. Gently, Juan shook his mother's shoulders to see she was alright. She stirred, then opened her dark eyes and reached out to hold Juan close to her bosom.

"Forgive me Juan, for leaving you in my thoughts. I was praying deeply to our patron Saint for his guidance. While I was praying, a bright light shown through the shadows of my mind and the darkness parted to give me the answer. I want you to return to the United States, to finish your studies, to become an American citizen and to achieve your dreams and ambitions. We will be fine here. You can visit us in the summers and when you are through with college, we can make a better decision then."

Juan felt like a large weight had been lifted from his back. "Thank you my dear mother. I will not disappoint you, ever."

They sat like two carved figures on the stump for a while longer enjoying what little evening light was left, then trudged back to the house.

CHAPTER SEVENTEEN

Juan's stay with his family was far too short. Way too soon it was fall and he must join up with Travis and return to San Diego. The last few days tugged at his heart and he really didn't want to leave, but knew he must. An urge, stronger than family, was now taking over his being. He had never thought so clearly in his life. As he heard the familiar sound of Travis' car, he gathered his loved ones about him, gave them each a hug and a kiss in turn and without fanfare, entered the sedan and was gone.

The flight back to San Diego was a silent one. Travis instinctively knew what course Juan had chosen, so he didn't pressure him for any details. Juan slept most of the way, only taking time out to enjoy the dinner served in the first class compartment.

The second year at the university went pretty much the same as the first. He enjoyed his new classes, especially one in public speaking. In this class, each student was expected to present a series of speeches to his classmates and to be critiqued on each speech. The first speech was one without notes, impromptu was the word they called it. The instructor asked each student, in turn, to come to the front of the class and tell the group, in five minutes, who they were and a little background into their lives.

When it was Juan's turn, butterflies suddenly enveloped his stomach. He wanted to hightail it out of there. It was worse than preparing for a soccer game. He sensed a state of panic and almost didn't make it to the front of the room. He stood there speechless. The words would not come. He felt as though he had a large balloon in his throat and his mouth was dry as cotton. He felt his knees buckle, but stood his ground. The professor approached him, laid a hand on his shoulder, and said "take your time Juan, you are experiencing what they call stage fright. Please be assured you feel far more nervous inside than you are showing us."

Juan stood there with his hands crossed over his crotch like a fig leaf on Adam in the Garden of Eden. He coughed lightly, then began his tale of self and family. The five minutes seemed like hours, but he made it through. From that point on, speeches were given on different subjects of interest to the student. One was to be humorous, one filled with facts, one about history, one to demonstrate a product, and other topics. Each student was required to prepare an outline of their speech, not to exceed ten minutes for each one. Since not all of the students could give their speeches on the same day, they traded turns, rotating the starting student when the entire group had been heard from on each round.

With each speech, Juan became more comfortable. The professor filled in the days with helpful hints on how to gesture with their hands, how to maintain eye contact, how to start the speech with an attention getting phrase and how to make emphatic points.

By mid-term, Juan was feeling like an old pro. The nervousness was gone and the critiques were filled with more praise than scorn. Juan had a gift. He could mesmerize the audience by the time the term had ended. He received an "A" for the class. This experience would aid him greatly in the years to come.

The second year of ROTC was even more exciting and fun than the first. He was promoted to squad leader and had his first chevrons sewn on the sleeves of his uniform jacket. He was now in charge of people and given a chance to hone his leadership skills. The time eventually came, when the PMS&T requested that all sophomore cadets declare their intentions as to whether they would continue on to the last year, Senior ROTC courses leading to a commission in the U.S. Army.

Juan received a letter to this effect, asking him to meet with his counselor to discuss his choice and options. Juan met with Captain Jackman, a tall western Kentuckian with a slight drawl and raw bony features. Jackman was a member of the regular Army, Infantry Branch. He was a graduate of West Point, the epitome of military schooling for the Army. Even though Captain Jackman was a West Point graduate, he explained that many of the officers of the armed forces came from the ranks of the ROTC program and went on to illustrious careers, many making the General Officer status rank.

He used Colin Powell as an example. Powell was commissioned through a program in New York City, served in Vietnam and now was a fellow in the Department of Defense at the Pentagon. Everyone knew this man was destined for four stars and a position as the Army Chief of Staff some day.

The discussion didn't take long before Juan was convinced this was the path he wanted to take. He told Captain Jackman he wanted to join the Senior Program. He was also glad to hear that cadets in the senior ROTC program were given a $90 per month stipend to help with their scholastic needs. But, Captain Jackman reminded Juan, "You need to become an American citizen before I can sign all of the necessary documents. Since you speak, read and write such good English, this should not be a problem. Your next stop has to be the Immigration Service in the Federal Building downtown."

As Juan rose to leave, Captain Jackman grasped his hand, shook it rapidly up and down. "Congratulations Juan, I think you have made a wise choice. If there is anything I can do to help you, please do not hesitate to ask."

That afternoon, Juan contacted Shannon and invited her for dinner at one of the local restaurants catering to the college crowd. He wanted to relay the day's events to her and ask for her advice on getting his citizenship. They agreed on a time Juan would pick her up, with Juan arriving right on time at her dorm. They only had a short way to walk and the evening was cool, with a soft breeze blowing off the Pacific Ocean.

Shannon could see Juan was about to burst with his news, but he waited until they were seated in the eatery. The restaurant was called "The Bomb Cellar". It was owned by an overweight, white haired, ex World War II pilot from the Army Air Corps. The owner's name was Sandy Sanford and he played the piano for his guests as well. The restaurant was in the basement of an office building near the campus and was decorated with memorabilia from the big war. There was a one hundred pound bomb suspended from the ceiling and pictures of aircraft and troops festooning the walls. The tables were grouped tightly together, so close, one could almost feel claustrophobic. The place was jammed on a Friday night. The quaff of the day was beer drawn on tap, served ice cold in large pitchers, with glasses for everyone at the table.

The waitress appeared with a pitcher of beer, two glasses and menus for them to choose their dinner. The specialty of the house was a Southwestern hamburger. Two large patties of ground beef, covered with salsa, Monterey Jack cheese, bacon, lettuce, tomatoes and onions. Of course, there was a choice of French fries or onion rings that would melt in your mouth.

Shannon had to cut her burger into four sections. Her small mouth could not engulf the sandwich as it was served. They got right to the task at hand, devouring the meal, wiping their mouths with the cloth napkins and leaning back with a satisfied sigh.

Shannon sipped gently from her glass and said, "okay Juan, what is it you have to tell me?'

Juan gazed into her radiant face and related his conversation with Captain Jackman and his need to begin the process of becoming an

American citizen. Shannon tingled as he spoke. When he was done, Shannon agreed to go with him to the Federal Building at noon on Monday to see what need to be done. On the way back to campus, they giggled, laughed and just enjoyed each other's company. The commitment had begun.

CHAPTER EIGHTEEN

Juan's class load was light on Mondays. He had an early 8:00 AM communications session, but then didn't resume his other instruction until 2:00 PM. This would give him plenty of time to go to the Federal Building downtown and determine the procedures he would have to go through to apply for his citizenship.

To improve his mobility, Juan had purchased a small economy car from the wages he earned working at the gym. It wasn't much to look at, sporting several shades of paint from previous botched attempts to repair dents and scratches, but the motor was sound and the door fit. It didn't take Juan and Shannon long to arrive at the Federal Building. The structure was a high rise office building made entirely of tinted glass and steel. The building did not fit the atmosphere of the city, but the intent was to show San Diego it still belonged to the Federal Government.

Juan was fortunate, he found a parking place just three blocks away, parked his car, and they walked up to the formidable tall glass doors emblazoned with gold letters marking it as "The Federal Building". Inside the spacious marbled lobby, Juan found a building directory fastened on the wall next to a bank of elevators. The directory was so typical of the federal bureaucracy, black pegboard with white letters, encased in a chromed frame. Juan scanned down the directory and found Naturalization Services Room 1204. Juan pressed the button of the elevator and watched as the red light indicator marked the movement of the car from the upper parts of the building to the lobby floor. The doors silently slid open and a crowd of people emerged, many dressed in suits, headed to the café for their coffee break, or just to get outdoors for some fresh air and sunshine. A small crowd had joined Juan and Shannon as they entered the cavernous elevator and the doors closed on them.

The ride to the twelfth floor was quiet and effortless. It seemed as though only a few seconds has passed when the ding of the bell announcing the twelfth floor sounded. The car disgorged its passengers into a corridor with a highly polished floor, accommodating rows of offices enclosed in frosted glass, again with gold lettering to indicate each office's function. Juan located Room 1204, opened the door and entered the room.

The interior was separated into seemingly miles of cubicles and protected by a wooden counter with protective glass which spanned the front of the area. In the center of the counter was an opening in the glass, behind which sat an attractive Latino female about Juan's age. She smiled demurely and inquired as to what business he had with the office. Juan explained his purpose and the young lady handed him a packet containing, she said, all of the essential information and forms he would need to apply for citizenship. Coyly, she told Juan if he needed any extra help, he could arrange to take her to dinner for the service, but Juan demurred. She was attractive, but he had other things on his mind. Shannon kidded him all the way back to campus.

The morning had almost expired, so Juan left the packet of information in his car, which he would retrieve later and examine. After dropping Shannon off, he made for the student union building to have a quick lunch, then headed for the shade trees on the main campus to peruse the material pertaining to his next class.

CHAPTER NINETEEN

The second year of his education was nearing the midway point and Juan knew if he wanted to continue in the Senior ROTC Program, he must become a citizen. He opened the packet he had taken out of his car and read the requirements. There was a lengthy application form containing all of the demographic information about himself and his family. There was a requirement to provide legal documents establish his date of birth, parents, visa data and other necessities. The U.S. Bureau of Citizenship and Immigration (formerly known at the INS) suggested the applicant be careful in filling out the application. The process could take from a few months to a couple of years if things were not documented properly. Knowing he would eventually need proof of birth, Juan had arranged that summer to obtain the birth certificate from the local health office. He made an extra copy of the proof just in case the original copy would get lost.

In addition to the application and documents, Juan would need two recent photographs of himself. Juan knew Shannon had a Polaroid camera, so he asked her to take the pictures. When he received an appointment letter, he would have to go to a specified location to be fingerprinted. The USC&I had a website with helpful hints and an on-line service of which Juan took full advantage. He began filling out his application forms and gathering his paperwork. Because of his attention to detail, Juan received notification his application had been approved and the only remaining requirement, was an interview with an immigration official and the successful completion of the written test on American History and Law. Earlier Juan had practiced on sample questions the service had provided along with the book he had to read.

In only two months from start to finish, Juan completed his application, took the test with flying colors, and was scheduled for his interview. Because of his school schedule, the federal interviewer made an allowance to have Juan come to the office in the Federal Building on a Saturday morning. The night before the interview, Juan hardly slept, tossing and turning for most of the night. It kept running through his head what questions the interviewer might ask and would he give the right answers if there were such a thing. He sensed he had been doing more of this in the past few years than he had the rest of his life combined. Somehow, he would have to learn to calm himself and to divorce the stress from his mind. Sleep deprivation was not something Juan needed right now.

The interview was scheduled for nine o'clock, but Juan was up and dressed hours before. He was so uptight, he didn't even feel like eating anything. Bubba insisted that your brain could not function without fuel, so Juan accompanied him to the dining hall picking at his food like a love sick puppy, but finally managed to get something down.

Juan arrived at the Federal Building fifteen minutes early, giving him plenty of time to find a parking space and zoom up to the interviewer's office. The letter of instructions indication Juan was to be interviewed by a Mr. Wesley Short in room 615. Juan again took the ornate elevator to the sixth floor and located room 615. Like all of the other offices, Juan had seen in the building, room 615 had the same frosted glass door with gold lettering as well, stating, "Wesley Short, Immigration Services".

Juan rapped lightly and a soft voice from inside asking him to come in. Juan gingerly opened the door into a non-descript room, filled with government issue furniture, the steel gray variety of desk with gray armed chairs and dark green vinyl padding.

A short, middle aged man rose from behind the desk and invited Juan to take a seat. Wesley drew up another identical chair and sat down beside him. Wesley was the typical government employee. He wore a white shirt with a bow tie, suspenders, dark pants, and brown shoes. Wesley could be described as slightly overweight, with thinning hair and a ruddy complexion belying his apparent English linage.

He had a pencil thin mustache under a large red nose, which looked as if it was either painted on or tattooed. He extended his hand, shook Juan's and introduced himself. With the formalities over, Wesley commenced the interview. The questions Wesley asked ranged from Juan's background, to the reasons Juan wanted to become an American citizen. Juan talked about his desires to serve the U.S. in the military and to get involved in American politics to help improve the relationships between the two countries. The interview lasted approximately an hour and seemed to go smoothly. Wesley informed Juan that the interview was over and Juan had done extremely well on the examination. There were no faults on the application form and the process had been satisfactorily completed. Wesley told Juan a letter of determination would be sent out within a week's time, giving the government's statement of acceptance or rejection of Juan's application. The two men again shook hand and Juan left. He didn't even remember getting back to the dorm or what was said in the interview. Had he blown it? His palms were sweaty and cold, but he couldn't worry about it now, he had done the best he could.

Juan used his classes, conversations with Bubba and Shannon, and his soccer to keep his mind occupied. At night he again didn't sleep well. He normally dreamed in Technicolor, but for some reason, his dreams were in stark black and white, the subjects totally unfamiliar to him. Juan hoped someday his life would mellow out and he would see nothing but restful sleep filled with pleasant memories.

As promised, the official letter arrived at his student mailbox. His name had been typed on the front with a signature blue return address so like the other federal items he had seen. He took the envelope outside into the sunshine, afraid to open it. He sat in his favorite spot on the quadrangle and just stared at the white, business style object. Finally summoning up enough courage, Juan opened his penknife and slit the spine of the envelope, withdrawing the tri-folded piece of paper.

"This letter is to inform you that you have been accepted as a candidate to become a citizen of the United States pending your signing the enclosed acceptance form and returning it in the postage paid return envelope." The letter went on to give a date, location, and procedure for the swearing in ceremony. November eleventh, Veteran's Day, was the date selected to entrust the aliens to their new country. The ceremony was set to be held in the auditorium of the Federal Building at one o'clock on that day. When Juan arrived, the auditorium was filled with over three hundred people of all descriptions. Folding chairs had been arranged in rows for those being sworn in. Members of the various families ringed the outside of the chairs. Juan felt remarkably as if he had just walked into the bowels of the United Nation's Building in New York City. He found a seat next to a man with a dark complexion, Juan was not sure of his native origin. The man was wearing the native sarong of the Country of India.

All of the men in the group either wore a suit, sports coat, native dress, or a white shirt with a tie. Juan had picked out his best suit for the occasion. He wanted to portray his very best image to his new countrymen. The room was abuzz with chatter which ceased immediately as a regally robed judge entered at the far end of the room. The judge spoke into the microphone at the elevated dais. As Juan glanced around the room, he spotted Bubba, Shannon, Wally, and several players on the soccer team. He had told them about the ceremony, but didn't realize they were going to attend. He was thrilled his friends thought that much of him to want to share in this momentous occasion.

The judge asked all those present to stand, raise their right hand and to repeat after him the oath of allegiance to the United States and to affirm they would abide by the laws of this land and protect America from all dangers both foreign and domestic. The assemblage, each with a miniature American flag grasped tightly in their other hand, rose as one body. In unison, Juan repeated the words, ending the last sentence with, "I do". The judge then told the new initiates they were now officially citizens, and they were to approach the podium as their names were called. One by one, the newly sworn in citizens stood in front of the judge to receive a Certificate of Citizenship and the congratulations of the presiding figure. With the colorful piece of parchment in his hands, Juan moved toward his friends, who surrounded him with congratulations and an invitation to go to dinner with them to celebrate. The dinner on them of course. His dreams of a meaningful career and a better life for his family were now becoming a reality.

CHAPTER TWENTY

Juan completed his sophomore year, returned home to his village that summer, went back to school that fall, and endured. The third year was much the same as the rest, only now Juan was completely familiar with the routine. The soccer team did well again. Juan enjoyed his classes and participation in campus politics became a segment of his life. He railed for change in student government, fostered worldly causes, and organized voter registration to improve the percentage of students who had never cast their ballots, although they had been eligible to vote since age eighteen. Juan could not understand why such a small percentage of this age group did not take the right to vote more seriously. What a privilege it was to be able to exercise one of the basic freedoms guaranteed under the Bill of Rights.

Because of his newly acquired status as an American citizen, his academic achievements and aptitude for the military, Juan was accepted into the Senior ROTC Program. He was now in a higher leadership position. His demonstrated abilities soon earned him a promotion to platoon leader, a position normally held by a cadet Second Lieutenant. He stood proudly when the PMS&T pinned on his first "pip", a circular silver ornament denoting his new rank.

As his experience grew, he was again promoted to the ranks of First Lieutenant and then to Captain in charge of a company of soldiers, approximately 150 men and women in total. He enjoyed the interaction of drilling the younger cadets on the marching field, of disciplining those that needed it, and participating in the planning of each Thursday's drill period.

It is a normal progression, following a cadet's Junior year, to attend a military summer camp at an Army base in the region accessible to the university. The summer camp would last eight weeks, starting in June. The military base chosen to host the San Diego State University ROTC cadets was Fort Lewis in Washington state. Juan would visit his family at the conclusion of the camp for an abbreviated time. He wrote his mother to let her know.

Fort Lewis was located midway between the capitol city of Olympia and Tacoma, just thirty miles south of Seattle, on old highway 99, now called Interstate 5 which ran from the Canadian border to the Mexican border south of San Diego. Fort Lewis was nestled in the grandeur of Mount Rainier, one of the six sister mountains aligned in a chain stretching from Northern Washington to the Northern part of the State of California. It was one of the largest training areas in the Army service, fulfilling the duty of training soldiers for deployment to all corners of the globe as it had done since World War I and World War II, as well as training ROTC cadets. It had recently been designated as the training ground for Special Forces Operations and boasted of having the toughest Ranger Battalion in the service. Many of these two elite groups, distinguished by their distinctive berets, were to become many of the instructors and cadre running the exercises the cadets would encounter.

Juan and some of his fellow cadets decided to drive from San Diego to Fort Lewis, expecting to arrive on a Friday, one day prior to the required starting date which was to occur on the first Saturday in June. They loaded themselves into a convertible one of the comrades owned and off they went. They enjoyed watching the scenery change as they drove up the wide highway through the sprawling metropolis of Los Angeles, the country side of the Napa Valley wine country, the

San Francisco Bay area, and into the forested reaches of the Mount Shasta region. As they passed through Oregon, Juan was overwhelmed with the amount of pine trees covering the landscape. He had never seen so many trees in all of his life. The forests were a rich dark green, sometimes taking on a blackened hue. He could only imagine how the settlers must have felt as they colonized this part of the world.

They arrived at Fort Lewis early on the expected Friday and followed the directional signs to the ROTC in-processing center located at North Fort. North Fort was located west of the main post, separated by the interstate. It was inhabited with hundreds of old two story, wooden, World War II constructed buildings which were designed to house the troops to be trained and smaller single story buildings which were used for administrative purposes.

The cadets were assigned to platoons and companies by alphabetic order, so the San Diego State cadets were destined to be separated for the duration. They located the in-processing center, checked in with the administrative sergeant in charge, and were given the building number of the platoon each of them had been assigned to. A platoon consisted of forty-four men, half located on the first floor and half on the second floor of each building. Each cadet was given a metal cot with a mattress to sleep on, an olive green wall locker to store his clothes in, and an olive green footlocker to store his personal items. The Army had taken away the identity of the individual. From now on, Juan was a number in the larger scheme of things. Everyone was the same. Civilian clothes were limited and all the lockers had to be arranged in a pre-designated fashion. Each Saturday, there would be an inspection to ensure the lockers contained the essential ingredients and the ingredients were arranged in the prescribed manner. To have a can of shoe polish out of order meant an immediate demerit and too many demerits meant no weekend passes to visit the surrounding community.

In the front of each barracks building there was a room where the platoon First Sergeant lived. This non-commissioned officer was assigned to the ROTC program at either a college, university, or high school setting and performed their duties for the summer as part of their lives as active duty personnel. The door to the platoon sergeant's quarters was identified with a simple white sign upon which was stenciled Sergeant First Class (SFC) Hamilton, Los Angeles High School.

After every cadet had been in-processed and issued his or her uniforms, meals cards, identification cards, and bedding, Juan settled in his barracks apprehensive of what the following days would bring. Over the course of the afternoon, cadets began to filter in, introducing themselves to the earlier arrivals. The cadet bunked next to Juan was a Chinese American from Idaho State College by the name of Chang. During the course of the summer camp, Juan and Chang would become fast friends.

CHAPTER TWENTY-ONE

When everyone had signed in, there was a mass formation of the company and the active duty company commander was introduced. He outlined the summer and the expectations he had for his company. He let it be known, his company would be the best at camp and if the cadets under his tutorship performed to his expectations, they would reap untold rewards, namely time off over the weekend after each Saturday morning parade.

Sunday was a period of relaxation and getting acquainted with the platoon members. Over fourteen colleges and universities were represented, involving over two thousand cadets and support staff. On Monday morning early, all hell broke loose. At 4 o'clock, SFC Hamilton turned on the lights and shouted for everyone to get out of bed, get shaved, showered, their beds made up, get into uniform, and report to the mess hall for chow at 0500 hours, military time an hour from wake up. All of this accomplished, the cadets lined up outside the mess hall door waiting to get fed. Before they could enter the building, each of them had to do twenty pull-ups on a cross bar which had been erected just outside the door. If this was not done, the cadet went to the back of the line until it was his turn again. Anyone failing the second time was scheduled for additional physical training.

After the cadets had eaten, they were to report back to the barracks for cleaning the latrines and making sure their barracks areas were squared away for the day. They were then directed to form into their platoons outside the barracks and were spirited away in gray Army buses for destinations in the training areas. The first day broke hot and dusty. Juan had been led to believe it always rained in the Pacific Northwest, but this summer, that was not the case. The summer would prove to be the driest and hottest on record.

The days started early and ended late. The cadets were driven by bus to various locations to practice map reading, chemical warfare, rifle firing, small unit tactics and all of the other military subjects they had been taught back at campus. The cadets were driven to exhaustion, not realizing how much the human body could endure. They cried when they had to remove their protective masks and be exposed to tear gas, and choked on the dust when they marched behind tanks down the field of simulated battle.

Surprisingly, the week went fast and the first Saturday's inspection was due. The cadets in Juan's platoon got up early, finished their morning tasks and proceeded to spit polish their living quarters. After chow, they prepared for the ritual that would make them officers. The inspector was going to be the battalion commander, a Lieutenant Colonel from Washington State University. At the pre-arranged hour, the cadets assembled at the foot of their bunks and waited. Juan mentally went through all of the instructions he and the others had received. Had he arranged everything correctly, had they cleaned and shined the chrome in the bathrooms to specification? He didn't have a chance to reconsider changing things. The cadets were called to attention by SFC Hamilton and the Colonel marched onto the first floor.

Lieutenant Colonel Miller was a craggy faced, tall, Armored officer, having seen service during the Korean War. He reflected the bearing of a dedicated officer, standing ramrod straight with a uniform devoid of mistakes. You could see your reflection on his brass buckle surrounding his pants. In turn, he stopped by each cadet, asking them questions, inspected their lockers and noted to the platoon sergeant any deficiencies in the established protocols.

He lithely moved from cadet to cadet and from floor to floor. As he left the first floor area, the cadets were given the command "at ease" and remained in place until the inspection was finished. It took about thirty minutes for the tour to be completed. The inspecting party departed the barracks with a flourish. When the smoke had cleared, SFC Hamilton announced the platoon had mustered the inspection with flying colors. The next step was to participate in the weekly Saturday parade at the massive parade field on main post. Normally a roosting ground for seagulls, this day it was covered with hundreds of cadets in their battle gear, arranged in companies as far as the eye could see. The marching band to accompany the cadets was furnished by the 9th Infantry Division Band.

After the cadets had been formed, the Adjutant's Call was sounded by a bugler, and the mass of troops was called to attention. The commander for the day sounded, "pass in review" at which time each company commander gave the order, "right face, left turn march". In unison, the companies made two left turns and were headed west, parallel to the group of dignitaries in the reviewing stand. As each company came in front of the stand, the company commander ordered, "eyes right" and saluted. This was repeated until the last of the companies had passed.

As Juan heard the first command and then heard the band start up with the Sousa march, "Washington Post", the hair on the back of his head stood on end, his spine straightened and pride overwhelmed him. Never in his life had he experienced such an emotion of patriotism as then. He hardly remembered beginning to march and it was over. His company had marched well, so they were given the afternoon and the next day off on pass and were to report back to the barracks on Sunday evening. Back in the barracks, the cadets were all a buzz. "Where should we go", said one of them. "Let's go into Olympia and take a tour of the Olympia Brewery", said another. The platoon agreed this was a good plan and off they drove to the south, to the capitol city just twenty minutes away.

They had a map and found the brewery easily. As they entered the front doors, they were greeted by a brewery staff member, who guided them through the plant. They were shown the brewing vats, settling tanks, the aging process and the storage facility. The last of the tour was to arrive at the "Tap Room" where each guest was given a glass with the brewery seal on it and filled up with freshly brewed beer. The beer was ice cold and delicious. Juan had never tasted anything so good on a hot, dry, and dusty Saturday afternoon. The glass was drained before he had a chance to really savor the malt like taste. As luck would have it, the bar tender offered each of them another round. This too was consumed in a hare's breath and the third and last round was drawn from the tap. After each tour, members of the platoon vowed to expend extra energy to outperform the others, to get another Saturday pass, and revisit the brewery. Next time, though, they would skip the tour and go straight to the Tap Room.

CHAPTER TWENTY-TWO

The remaining weeks of summer camp were grueling. The future officers got up early and were trained late. They mastered the weapons assigned to them on the ranges and wiped away the tears as they again experienced removing their protective masks in the gas chamber. They spent hours on a day and night compass course, trying to find predetermined locations on the ground and return to their starting place using only a compass, and land navigation. At night, most of the cadets got lost and had to be found, by the active duty cadre.

Juan and his partner Chang, maxed the course and qualified expert in all of the weapons. Still more came in the form of physical training, leadership courses, and extensive drilling in a variety of military subjects. When the last day of summer camp was over, Juan eagerly went to the bulletin board to see how he had fared in the ranking of best to worst of the cadets. The results weren't posted until the next morning and by the time he arrived there was a crowd gathered, shouting and groaning. Throughout the course of the summer camp, fifteen percent had failed at some point and the rankings that had been posted were for those who had completed the camp and were in line for bragging rights.

Finally, Juan made it to the listings. He scanned down the sheets of paper stapled on the bulletin board and squelched a short shout as he noticed his teammate and cot mate next to him, Chang had achieved distinction of being the number one cadet. Juan went further down the list and found his name in the number four position. He had qualified for the outstanding cadet awarded to the top ten finishers. At the final parade, the ten outstanding cadets joined the reviewing stand to be honored. They proudly saluted when the companies passed by. An adventure was over and Juan had gained a new dimension in his personality.

Juan finished his last year of college and graduated in early June. As the President of the University called each graduate's name, the individual rose and strode to the podium to receive his sheep skin. Each of the senior ROTC graduating cadets were also to receive their Army commission and second lieutenant bars at the same time. Juan felt about ten feet tall when the diploma was handed to him and the President and the PMS&T pinned the golden bars onto his uniform.

Juan was commissioned a second lieutenant in the Infantry Branch as a Distinguished Military Graduate. He now awaited his call to active duty for assignment. Juan received his orders from the Department of the Army to report to the Infantry Officer's Basic Course at Fort Benning, Georgia. His reporting date had been established as early August, which gave him ample time to go back to Mexico, check on his family and return to the American south.

Juan did return to his village to ensure everything was okay and returned to Fort Benning. Benning was one of the largest military posts operated by the U.S. Army. It was a beautiful post, well groomed and bustling. He had been assigned to one of several Bachelor Officer's Quarters (BOQs) where he would be housed for the next eight weeks.

Not unlike ROTC, many of the courses were taught in the classroom and many taught in the large training areas. Some courses were repeats of what Juan had in school, but many new ones were introduced. Subjects like personnel management, leadership, terrain analysis, task forcing, logistics and communications were hurled at him. Classes commenced at precisely 0800 hours in a three story building devoted to didactic instruction. Each class lasted fifty minutes with a ten minute recess between each class. Many basic course attend-ees used these ten minutes to go outside for a cigarette. Juan didn't smoke, so he used the precious time to read up on the next class assignment.

Field training included small unit tactics, more map reading, on the ground reconnaissance, weapons utilization, hand to hand com-bat and day and night land navigation. During the noon hour after a short lunch, each class of officers would assemble in the parade field to practice marching and giving marching commands. Each officer had a chance to lead the group through the precision drills mandated by the manual on drill and ceremony. Each officer was graded by a cadre member on their ability to master the proper techniques, their command voice, and their leadership skills.

Juan enjoyed this training and he especially enjoyed being an of-ficer with the privileges it afforded. His evening and weekends were free and he had access to the Fort Benning Officer's Club where they served fine food, offered entertainment almost every night and lots of camaraderie.

It was usual practice, after the last class of the day, for the officers to retire to the club for a drink and a leisurely dinner. As they strolled from the classroom area to the club, they were saluted by the enlisted men on the post that walked by and they saluted the higher ranking officers as they passed. Saluting was a mandatory part of the military stemming from many years of tradition, recognition, and respect and for the esprit inherent in the Army.

Juan studied hard and did well. He was in the upper echelons of the course and received an outstanding efficiency report, his first one. It was with sadness the officers in his class met for the last time at the club. They had each received further orders as to their assign-ments. Some would be going on to airborne training at Fort Bragg or remaining there at Fort Benning to train troops. Some would go to Special Forces Training in Florida and some to Ranger School. The majority of the class would be assigned to infantry divisions scattered around the world.

Juan stopped by the personnel office on the day he graduated from the basic course to see what the fates had in store for him. A young female personnel enlisted person had him wait at the counter as she extracted his file from a drawer of a cabinet situated behind her desk. She withdrew several pieces of paper, went to the copy machine, and returned to Juan with his orders. Juan sat down on a lounge sofa in the office to confirm what was in store for his future. Even though the day had been cool, he broke out into a feverish sweat as he read his order, "Vietnam".

CHAPTER TWENTY-THREE

The year was 1966 and the U.S. Army was in the throes of the massive buildup characteristic of the Vietnam Conflict. Thousands of soldiers, marines, airmen and civilian personnel were arriving in country by any means available. Juan was directed to report to Fort Ord, California where he was assigned to an infantry battalion being formed there for shipment by sea to southeast Asia. His assignment was as platoon leader, first platoon, Alpha Company of the 23rd Infantry Battalion, 25th Infantry Division (Tropical Lightening). He flew from Fort Benning to San Francisco and was then taken by Greyhound bus to Fort Ord. Again, he was assigned to a BOQ and settled in to meet his new unit.

The day after he arrived, he found the orderly room of Alpha Company, handed the company clerk a copy of his orders and signed in. His adventure, for good or bad, had begun in earnest. The executive officer and second in command, a first lieutenant, came forward to greet and welcome Juan to the company. They entered the execs office for a quick briefing and then went to the company commander's office. The company commander, a Captain, was an older, seasoned veteran. Captain Benson, a product of the Citadel Military Academy was tall, blond, tanned and exemplified the very meaning of an infantry officer. He talked in brief but to the point statements. The briefing didn't take long and Juan knew he would follow this man into battle without hesitation.

During the next four weeks, Juan spent most of his time getting to know the forty-four men who made up his platoon. They were a mixed breed, an experienced platoon sergeant with one tour of Vietnam already under his belt, some experienced squad leaders and the rest recent graduates from basic training.

The battalion was also a mix of active duty soldiers and reservists called to active duty to complete the need for manpower to serve. Most of the company's activities were to in-process the personnel, complete the immunizations necessary for travel to a disease ridden area, load the unit's gear in hundreds of steel conex containers and get to know each other.

At the end of the month, the battalion arose at the crack of dawn and formed, in full combat gear, in front of the battalion headquarters. Once a head count had been taken and all men accounted for, the troops were loaded on buses for transport to the Oakland Army Terminal where they were to board a U.S. Navy troop ship which would be their home for the next three week as they sailed the Pacific Ocean to Vietnam.

The officers were assigned to the upper decks of the vessel and the enlisted men to the bowels of the vessel. They say rank has its privileges and that was for sure. The officers had their separate dining room and were served by contract Filipino waiters. The food was fresh and delicious. The enlisted men, however, ate in one large mess area, eating in shifts and going through a long cafeteria style line to receive their vittles. The officers also had separate compartments housing two to four officers per space. The enlisted men were housed in canvas cots attached to the bulkhead of the ship, stacked four high.

The ship, a gray World War II troop carrier had been pressed into service because there wasn't adequate aircraft available to transport the masses of soldiers headed for the combat zone. The sailing across the placid blue waters of the Pacific was smooth, but boring. The troops held physical training on the main deck three times a day, but there was little else to do. The ship had an air-conditioned chapel, which doubled as a movie theater, showing old classical movies during the afternoon and evenings. There was also a library containing volumes of the classical works of the older authors. Card tables were strewn about a large room where energetic youngsters played pinochle, spades, gin rummy and cribbage. Juan took advantage of the library and read many of the books he had heard about and wanted to read. Juan also was required to inspect the enlisted areas when his turn came up, an experience, which made him glad he was one of the privileged few, and not one of the masses. Seasickness was rampant and the stench almost made him throw up as well.

Although there was no liquor allowed on the journey, the officers had smuggled aboard a sufficient supply to ease the tension of the trip. Each afternoon, happy hour would take place in a pre-designated cabin for those who wanted to participate. At these occurrences, Juan got to know his fellow officers and enjoined in the revelry to the maximum extent possible.

About two weeks into the journey, the ship crossed the 180th parallel which created the need for the induction of all first timers into the "Order of the Golden Dragon", a society to symbolize such a crossing. At a specified time, all new inductees were gather on the top deck, wearing only their shorts and tennis shoes. As the individuals assembled, they were washed down with salt water to indicate their new baptism. They were ordered to crawl on their hands and knees down a canvas tunnel, which contained cottage cheese, eggshells, coffee grounds, and other fowl smelling ingredients.

As they emerged from the tunnel, they were greeted by King Neptune and his Queen Neptune, who sat regally on their thrones. King Neptune was covered by a sable cape and a stomach smeared with cold cream. In turn, each inductee had to kneel down and kiss King Neptune's stomach. After bearing allegiance to the society, each soldier then crawled the rest of the length of the deck and were swatted with wooden paddles on their posteriors.

Although the process could be classified as harassment, Juan felt a sense of comradeship and belonging. It was an experience he would never forget. The next day, the ship pulled into Subic Bay, to dock at the main port of Manila in the Philippines, to replenish the stores required for the completion of the trip. All on board were given liberty for the day to visit the city, with orders to return to the ship by midnight or be counted as AWOL.

Some of the officers went into the capitol, but most stayed to drink and talk in the officer's club at the naval base. At the club was Juan's first introduction to slot machines. These gaming devices, programmed to make money for the club, soon sucked up what few coins Juan had. He decided gambling was not his style, but he enjoyed watching other win or lose as the chance may be.

The day passed quickly and the hour was fast approaching for everyone to be on board as the tide was becoming ready for departure. Soldiers and sailors began arriving in all types of conveyances. Mostly drunk and rowdy, they piled aboard, were taken below and put to bed. As the lines were about to be cast off, a speeding taxi roared up to the ship sounding its horn as loud and long as it could. Four drunken soldiers departed the cab, paid the driver, and barely made it to the gangplank and on to the ship. Fortunately, there was no one left behind.

CHAPTER TWENTY-FOUR

The ship completed its odyssey and slipped into its berth at the port city of Vung Tau on the lower southeastern portion of the Republic of Vietnam. The troops soon began the process of disembarking from the ship and forming up into their battalion units. Once another head count had been completed and the battalion commanders were satisfied everyone was accounted for, the troops were quickly loaded onto awaiting deuce and one-half ton trucks for transport to the Ben Hoa Air force base for lift to their final destination, Chu Chi, the base camp of the 25th Infantry Division.

The feeling of foreboding engulfed everyone. They were in a super heated, damp and dark green environment, a place in which they felt strange and unwanted. As the trucks moved along the dusty country roads, they passed small villages where the houses were made of brick or mud and covered with tin or other metal for their roofs. For some strange reason, the scene reminded Juan of his village minus the foliage.

They passed religious icons built in fields to ward off the evil spirits and shops doing a brisk business with the military. Many building were demolished, with the remaining walls inscribed with political slogans, warning the Viet Cong to stay away for fear of death. Street vendors selling flavored soft drinks, or skewered meats lined the sidewalks. The population all seemed to wear black pajamas with a conical straw hat, typical of the culture of the nation and its farmers.

The region was well known for its rubber plantations and rice fields, which was one of the primary resources the French sought when they occupied the country for decades. Vietnam, formerly known as French Indochina, had gained its independence in 1954, but the French influence could still be seen in the buildings and landscaping.

As the trucks traversed the countryside, small children with bare feet ran alongside asking for goodies. Many of the soldiers had candy they had saved from their trip into Manila and they tossed what they had to the waifs, who delighted the troops with their squeals of pleasure. Bicycles were forced out of the way, with angry glances thrown at the men in the trucks by the riders. The truck drivers didn't care; they hated the slopes and would just as soon have run over them.

As Juan looked over the side of the truck, he saw in the distance a large, black butte standing amidst the rice fields. This black monolith was the landmark of the Ta Ninh province, the district within which the town of Chu Chi was subordinate. He could smell the fumes of the diesel emanating from the exhaust, but he also smelled the human and animal waste that was used to fertilize the fields.

The journey took about an hour and at last they were stopped at the gates of the compound housing the air force base. An American Military Policeman checked with the head driver, opened the gates and allowed the trucks to enter. The base was very modern, with a mixture of concrete and metal buildings. The grounds were neat and orderly, resembling anything a person would find at any air force base in the U.S.

The day was beginning to get very hot and the reflection from the concrete reinforced the temperature. There was no wind to alleviate the inferno. The palm trees stood like lonely sentinels whose branches hung like lifeless arms point to the ground. The trucks convoyed around several buildings and ground to a halt on the tarmac. Across a short field were lined up three C-130 aircraft, which would be used to ferry the troops to their final scene of existence for the time being.

The soldiers were ordered to dismount and form into their respective companies. Each company commander then ordered them to march in single file to get aboard the aircraft. As Juan entered the rear of the plane, the heat inside was almost overpowering. He felt a sense of being suffocated and wanted to pass out, but resisted because he didn't want to set a bad example for his platoon.

As soon as each soldier marched on board, he found a canvas sling seat to sit in. Most of the men immediately took off their steel helmets, which brought some relief, but not much. As soon as the plane was full, the engines started with puffs of billowing black smoke and roared into action. The planes, in turn, taxied down the runway to line up for departure. When the go ahead was given from the control tower, the planes gathered speed and accelerated until they reached sufficient speed to become airborne. As soon as the crafts left the ground and started to gain altitude, the interior of the plane began to cool off. The commander of the craft had left the tailgate slightly ajar to help with the circulation of cooler air, something greatly appreciated by the men.

Looking out the window, Juan was amazed at the beauty below. For miles, he could see the expansive fields of rice and other crops. Soon the Mekong River, the lifeline of the country came into view and beyond that the Capitol City of Saigon. As they neared Saigon, the city seemed to meander in all directions, the streets filled with all forms of transportation, a beehive of hustle and bustle.

Approximately 50 miles northwest of Saigon was the base camp of the 25th Infantry Division. The camp had been carved out of an old growth rubber tree plantation and was located about three miles south of the town of Cu Chi. Cu Chi was a town of approximately 2,500 and was situated at a cross roads of Vietnam Highway 1 which went northwest to Cambodia and northeast to Da Nang. The country of Vietnam was divided into districts, which were subdivided in sub-districts, which were divided into towns, then into villages, and then into hamlets.

The road from the paved Highway 1 through Cu Chi was dirt. From the major intersection, turning south, a traveler would pass by a fortification at the center of town where a policeman stood directing traffic. From there they would progress down the road toward the camp. Along the route were sprinkled business adventures, which had not been there ten years ago. The businesses had colorful names like, "The Peppermint Lounge", "The Jiffy Jeep Wash", and the "Do Drop In Bar". The buildings were ramshackle, made of temporary materials and covered with tin roofs. The temporary structures smacked of frivolous enterprise. Any fool could tell that the owners were there to make as many a quick buck as could be made and then forget the Americans had ever arrived.

The entire division compound was surrounded by several sections of concertina wire, piled three rows high and contained within three separate barbed wire fences. One road entered the compound, vehicles having to pass through an elaborate network of baffles and wired gates. At all intervals of the compound and at the front gate, sat M-60 tanks to ensure the safety of the area. Ringing the compound were listening posts, placed to detect any unauthorized movement from the outside. Searchlights bathed the main gate and the perimeter.

The planes landed at the airstrip in the central part of the compound, taxied to a halt and disgorged their passengers. The troops were met by several trucks and were quickly loaded and driven to their barracks where the men would live for the next twelve months, or would be evacuated if they were wounded, or if they would die as a result of enemy fire.

CHAPTER TWENTY-FIVE

The compound was a small city, containing a population of almost 40,000. Several main roads intersected, leading to the major components of the base camp. In the center was the division headquarters surrounded by matching buildings used for administrative purposes. At the north end was a battery of 175mm howitzers, to the east, the headquarters of the signal battalion and communications center. To the west was the petroleum dump and airstrip. To the south were the quarters for the infantry units. Sandwiched amongst the buildings was a 400-bed evacuation hospital, which treated the injured, returned them to duty, or removed them to other medical facilities within or out of country.

Almost all of the buildings were made out of wood and were single story, or were constructed out of tin Quonset hut kits. The metal huts were used mainly for administrative purposes. The wood building sides were louvered halfway up, then screened in. The roofs were made of metal and shone brightly with the afternoon sun. They were sandbagged up to six feet or had bunkers within a short distance to be used in case of small arms fire, mortar attacks, or rockets launched at them.

Each barracks building housed twelve men, the officer's quarter being separated from the enlisted men. Inside the barracks, each man was given a metal cot with springs, a metal wall locker, a wooden footlocker and a wooden field table. Juan was struck with the similarity between his new home and the summer camp he had attended at

Fort Lewis, only this time, there wouldn't be any inspections, parades, or weekend passes.

As part of their in processing, everyone was required to go through the jungle warfare school to orient them to the environment in which they would be fighting. The school was set up just outside the compound in a secure area enclosed in thick jungle vegetation. The school started with an introductory speech by a Special Forces NCO who was now serving his third tour in country. Displayed on the platform where SFC Wilson stood was displayed an array of weapons and other explosive devices used by the Viet Cong.

After the initial briefing, the platoon was led single file into the canopy of the darkest green Juan had ever seen. The sunlight became muted and the path dim until the eyes grew accustomed to it. After a few turns, the unit was stopped and the guide pointed out a booby-trapped grenade hanging from a nearby tree. Everyone spent a few minutes tracing the guy wire from the explosive killer to the ground where a soldier's foot would trip the wire and ignite the grenade, blowing off a head, or arms, or otherwise killing the individual.

Other turns led them past holes in the ground cleverly concealed by a trap door and covered with indigenous leaves. As the NCO lifted the trap door, below were sharpened steel spikes, capable of piercing someone's foot or leg. The spikes were normally covered in human feces to increase the likelihood of a serious infection, which would incapacitate the soldier for days or months.

Other steps along the trail revealed concrete slabs suspended above, also with steel spikes, which when released, would drop down on the unwary victim. The more the men traveled, the more the tension grew. What had they gotten themselves into. All of the tactics Juan had learned came from the classic warfare manuals, which pitted one enemy in front of another to do battle. In Vietnam, the enemy was everywhere and nowhere.

After the tour, the platoon spent some time handling the weapons and explosive devices to become familiar with their size and shape. There wasn't much conversation. A somber mood enveloped the men emphasizing the importance of the lessons they were being exposed to. Each of them knew this training might someday save his life or the lives of their buddies.

During a lull in the training, Juan struck up a conversation with SFC Wilson. Wilson, a large black NCO, was a former Newark, New Jersey policeman who had gotten tired of his job and was looking for something more adventuresome. He had enlisted in the Army, gone through basic training, airborne training, and Special Forces training. He had acquired all of the necessary skills to operate with a small team of like members who could engage the enemy at close range and operate independently. He was an expert in hand-to-hand combat, communications, explosives and medical care.

That evening Juan invited SFC Wilson to have a beer with him and his men to follow up on the day's instruction. After evening mess, the platoon met in a small park used by the troops to play volleyball, touch football and watch movies on occasion. A cooler full of iced beer was brought out and cans passed around to everyone. The war stories began. Wilson related exploits of his first two tours where he and his Special Forces team had ambushed a Viet Cong unit, killed most of their members and brought a few prisoners back to base to be interrogated for military intelligence purposes. He talked about visiting Vietnamese villages to ferret out the Viet Cong, which couldn't be discerned from the farmers working in the fields. To SFC Wilson, everyone wore the black pajamas and spoke the same language whether they were friend or foe.

He talked about surprise raids on smaller hamlets, discovering weapons caches hidden in the ground under the living quarters, or cleverly hidden in the jungle. He had become an expert in flushing out the enemy, and for his expertise he was given the position of running the school during his third tour. After leaving Vietnam, Wilson was scheduled to attend school at the Criminal Investigation Detachment (CID) for the Military Police. Using his police background, he wanted to move into this field hoping to use it at some later point in his life. Juan was impressed with the demeanor of Wilson, but little did he know that this huge Special Forces sergeant would play a significant role in Juan's future life.

CHAPTER TWENTY-SIX

For the first two weeks in Vietnam, the platoon saw no action. They were kept on base to become acclimated to the oppressive humidity and hot sun. They received extensive briefings in ambush tactics and guerilla warfare from other battalion members who had been around longer. They also received information about an unusual aspect of their mission, the disruption of the tunnel system used by the Viet Cong.

For twenty years prior to the entrance of American troops, the Viet Cong had constructed an elaborate network of inter-connecting tunnels covering hundreds of miles. Military intelligence had discovered this system and had placed the 25th Infantry Division directly atop one of the largest complexes. Contained in these tunnel systems were hospital sites, ammunition dumps, eating facilities, living quarters and command centers. These tunnels could be entered and exited by a series of openings in the ground, which had been camouflaged to look like the surrounding terrain.

The division whose mission it was to enter these tunnels, find the enemy and kill them was recruiting men of small stature. The "Tunnel Rats" were a strange breed of individuals. They would spend days looking for the tunnel entrances, then entering the claustrophobic spaces, would seek out their foes. They were armed with only a small weapon, a flashlight and their wits. Some of Juan's platoon volunteered for this duty. Juan hated to lose good men to this function, but he was proud of them and he found replacements elsewhere.

Soon it was time for Juan's platoon to join the company and do what they were sent to Vietnam to do, find and annihilate the enemy. The majority of the tactics used; were search and destroy maneuvers. From reliable sources, the Viet Cong would be located and armed troops would be sent out to engage them either by armored convoy or by the famous and versatile Huey (Dragon Fly) helicopter. The main mode of relocating the soldiers was the helicopter because the tanks and armored personnel carriers had so much difficulty crossing the rice paddies and would get mired down, becoming easy targets.

For the next ten months, the company moved about the zone. All of the training and indoctrination the men had received started to come true. The Viet Cong would wait in ambush, strike and then fade into the jungle as if they were ghosts. Sometimes the Cong would cross into Cambodia, a region forbidden to the American soldier. From there the Cong would regroup and rearm for coordinated attacks back in Vietnam. Juan soon began to doubt the validity of the decision made to support the South Vietnamese government. The casualties began to mount with no apparent gain on the part of the war effort.

For years prior to Juan's arrival there, American military advisors had been training the Vietnamese Army, apparently to no avail. On one occasion, Juan's company was conducting a joint operation with a like Vietnamese company when they came under fire. The Vietnamese soldiers ran and left the flank of the Americans exposed to deadly crossfires. Eight percent of the company was either wounded or killed. Juan lost half of his platoon. When the fighting was over, Juan knelt down and cried over such waste. He thought to himself, the only persons to win a war are the survivors, and what have they won.

It was common knowledge around the base camp that most of the people who were killed, were killed in the first or the last month of their tour. No one knew for sure if this was true, but the rumor persisted.

Once back at base camp, the men needed to relax. Most of them did this by having a few drinks and telling tales to their comrades at one of the many clubs interspersed throughout the camp. Juan's favorite hangout was the officer's club at the hospital. In fact it was one of the most popular because of the female nurses who took care of the patients. There were approximately sixty females, or round eyes as the GIs called them, including nurses and women who worked for the American Red Cross.

Juan wasn't much of a drinker, but did like to socialize. Late in the afternoon, he walked the short distance from his barracks to the hospital club, which was located in one half of a long Quonset hut, the other half being used to sort, or triage the wounded as they arrived to be treated. The bar was decorated in a jungle motif and music blared in the background. Tables and chairs made of rattan were placed about the room which was filled to capacity.

Juan squeezed himself up to the bar and ordered a glass of orange juice and glanced about the crowd. His eyes rested on a miniature female, with dark hair, and flashing ebony eyes. She had thrown her head back and was laughing at a joke someone at her table was telling. Even in the baggy, green Army fatigues, it was obvious she had a nice body. Juan couldn't keep his eyes off her and asked the bartender who she was.

"Her name is Mary. She is one of the nurses in the intensive care unit who just got here recently" he said.

"Is she connected with anyone?" Juan asked

"Not as far as I know, but then you never know. Some of the nurses are married and some aren't. Some are connected and some are not. They don't flash that knowledge around, so you will just have to find out for yourself."

In about thirty minutes, Mary arose from her table, said goodnight to the group and started toward the door. Juan had to find out more about her, so he started to pursue her, but lost track as the crowd seem to seal off her path. He finally made it outside, to see her walking toward the nurse's quarters some distance east of the hospital. He didn't want to frighten her, so decided to wait until another day.

Juan's chance to meet Mary came at an unexpected turn. One morning he needed to get some shaving cream from the small Post Exchange and was standing outside the door waiting for the sergeant in charge to open. As he turned around, there stood Mary. Juan was sure he sounded like an idiot when he asked, "Are you Mary?"

"Who wants to know", came the reply.

"Oh, I'm sorry, let me introduce myself. I am Juan Cardova, a platoon leader of one of the infantry units."

"How did you know my name?' came back the challenge.

"I must confess, I saw you at the hospital officer's club the other day and I asked the bartender who you were. I am sorry if I seem to be too forward, but I have never seen someone so beautiful and I had to chance getting to know you."

Juan thought he detected a slight blush, but couldn't be sure.

"Well, if you want to get to know me, let's go for a walk after we shop. I don't have to be on the ward until after 1500 hours, that should give us plenty of time to get acquainted."

Juan could not believe his good fortune. His head began to swim and he thought he was going to throw up. He had dated some women, but none had struck him so forcefully. They walked around the exchange, making small talk and looking over the limited merchandise. Mary selected a chrome Seiko watch and told Juan it was a birthday present for her father who had always wanted a Seiko watch, but couldn't afford one in the states. Juan looked at the price tag, thirty dollars for a watch that could easily have been sold for over one hundred dollars in an American jewelry store.

Mary also bought some snacks to eat later on in the ward, some postcards and stationary, and some sunscreen. Juan bought some shave cream and a fresh supply of disposable razors. He didn't need much else, but was enjoying Mary's company every second. After they paid for their purchases, they began their outdoor stroll, finally arriving at the small park near division headquarters. They found a small bench beneath a tree and sat down.

Juan discovered that Mary, like himself was from Mexican ancestry. Her mother was Mexican and her father Irish. Her parents had met in Southern California, fell in love, married, and raised five children with Mary being the only girl. Mary confessed she was sent to a convent as a young woman to become a num. While there, she discovered her aptitude for nursing and was sent to school by the Catholic Church. After three years, she had completed her training and was about to be ordained a sister in one of the Catholic orders and assigned to a hospital near San Diego.

Somewhere along the line, Mary had a change of heart, dropped out of the order, married, and then lost her husband of just two years to cancer. She was so devastated, she had to get away and do something extraordinary, so she joined the Army Nurse Corps and asked for immediate assignment to Vietnam.

Juan listened with compassion and understanding, nodding at the right times and offering simple words of sympathy. When Mary was finished, Juan related his background. They never took their eyes off each other. A chemistry was born and grew as the time passed. Suddenly Mary jumped up and exclaimed she had to get back to her hooch, get changed and get to work. They agree to meet at the club after her shift ended at 2300 hours.

At precisely five minutes after 2300 hours, Mary walked through the door of the club. She glanced around the room, which was filled to capacity, not spotting Juan immediately. One of the other nurses she knew, nudged her on the shoulder and told her handsome himself was sitting against the far wall. As her eyes adjusted to the dimness, she saw Juan. She hurried to him, put a slight kiss on his cheek and sat down.

"What would you like to drink?" Juan asked.

"Oh, just a beer, I am so tired. I am afraid anything else would put me to sleep here at the table."

Juan got up and went to the bar to order her request. She waited, listening to the noise from the jukebox, nervous without knowing shy. Had she made a mistake taking a liking to this person she barely knew. It was too late to change her mind and leave. Juan sat down beside her and deposited two beers in front of them.

The next hour was spent trying to hear each other. They bantered about with small talk and finally Mary told Juan she had to leave. She needed to wash her hair and get some sleep. It would be a busy day tomorrow. The division had several missions planned and the casualties might be coming in at any time. In this war, the work was never planned. In hours, wounded and dead GI's could overwhelm the hospital, straining its resources to the maximum.

Sure enough, four hours later, a Chinook helicopter landed on the hospital landing pad and like a large dragon, disgorged thirty-six casualties. Every available person was pressed into action, carrying the wounded and dead into the triage area where a tall, six foot four inch male nurse directed traffic. It was his job to determine which person was to go immediately to the operating room, which person could wait for a while, which person was expected to die and which person only needed minimal attention. Mary was press back into action.

CHAPTER TWENTY-SEVEN

Juan's platoon was called out for an insertion into enemy territory the next day. A battle that would last four days and again see the majority of the company either killed or wounded. So far Juan had been lucky. Once a bullet from a sniper had grazed his helmet, but it did nothing more than give him a headache for a few hours. After the perimeter of their area had been secured and the shooting had stopped, Juan took a few seconds to assess the situation. He called together what was left of his platoon and realized he didn't recognize many of the dirty faces staring back at him.

He told his men to take time out to get something to eat, rest in place if they could and they would be moving out in an hour. The majority of the last day of the drive was devoted to seeking out the Cong that had ambushed them. They met with little success. Again, the black pajamas had vanished into the dark green jungle without a trace.

After the company returned, the commander kept them busy regrouping, filling in with new replacements, cleaning their weapons and getting some sleep. Juan had not seen Mary for a week and he ached all over. That evening, he went to the hospital club but when he arrived Mary wasn't there. One of the nurses he had been introduced to let him know Mary had been called in to work on one of the wards where the surgical patients were sent after they had been operated on.

Juan walked the length of the hospital complex, striding along newly poured concrete sidewalks with newly constructed covers to keep the monsoon rains off the patients when they were being transported from hut to hut. Each Quonset hut had a wooden sign signifying the function of the hut. He walked past the Emergency Room, past the X-ray, past the operating rooms and finally stopped at the sign, which read, "Post Op".

Cautiously, he opened the door and entered. The room was air-conditioned and brought a welcome relief from the overbearing oppressive humidity of the outside. The room was dimly lit, smelling of human flesh and disinfectant. Several doctors and nurses were attending to the wounded. IV solutions were hanging from metal tripods, the long vinyl tubes like spider webs, were attached to arms barely visible under the clean white sheets. Low moans could be heard all around.

Juan stopped at the front of the ward, not wanting to interfere and stood by quietly as possible. He was amazed at the efficiency of the staff as they moved about taking care of the maimed and disfigured. Someone had once told him, if he were ever wounded in the field, because of the helicopter and the medical personnel, arriving at this hospital would guarantee his life would be saved nine times out of ten. He knew, if he were ever wounded, he would want to come here to be saved.

He hadn't noticed, but Mary had come up behind him and gently put her arms around his waist. He felt her warmth, turned to face her and kissed her passionately.

"Not here", she said. " I know a place where we can be alone." Before they left, Mary found another nurse. She whispered into her ear and the nurse nodded. Mary told Juan she had informed the other nurse they would be leaving for a few minutes and to cover for her.

Mary guided Juan out of the post op ward and across the center of the quadrangle formed by the wards and into one of the last buildings on the opposite side of the hospital. This building had been designated for use in treating Vietnam civilians who were cared for by the hospital in emergency conditions. It had last been used when a bus had run over an explosive device embedded in the road. Several women and children had been hurt, taken care of in the emergency room, put on this ward to rehabilitate and had been released. The ward was now empty, waiting until the next travesty came to yet another innocent civilian life.

The only light was a night-light that barely illuminated the room. The contours of the building reflected what little light there was giving the ward an eerie look and feel. A chill ran down Juan's spine. Mary took his hand and led him to the far end to a bed still made up, surrounded by a curtain connected to an overhead track, which could be shielded off to offer some dimension of privacy. They stood in the near darkness groping for each other. Kisses were feverish, hands found private parts, and then Juan slowed and gently began to undress Mary. When she was without clothes, she returned the favor and they became one.

The rest of his tour in Vietnam for Juan was much of the same. When he received his commission from ROTC, he incurred a two-year obligation with the Army. He was now nearing that period of over a year and was also nearing the end of the twelve months in Vietnam. During one mission, Juan's company came under attack and during the ensuing firefight, Juan led his soldiers to the flank of the Cong, lobbing grenades onto their position and providing covering fire as the wounded were evacuated. He was slightly wounded in the fight, treated at the hospital and was awarded the Purple Heart for wounds received as a result of hostile fire. For his bravery and leadership, he was also awarded the Bronze Star for valor. One of the highest decorations a combat leader could obtain.

Before his tour was over, he arranged to take a rest and relaxation (R&R) trip out of country to rest from the purgatory he was going through. He invited Mary to go with him. She accepted. Each of them requested and was granted a five-day visit to the British Colony of Hong Kong.

A friend at the aviation battalion flew the lovebirds to Ton San Hut airbase in a helicopter where they were processed and boarded a jet for a three-hour flight to the island paradise. For the first time since they had arrived in country, they were in the khaki uniform, the one required for entry into another country. It seemed strange not to be in the familiar fatigues they were accustomed to wearing. It would seem even more strange to put on civilian clothing which they rarely did at base.

They sat together on the plane, talked almost non stop and fell more deeply in love. The flight ended with a thrilling approach over the bay of Hong Kong. The landing strip was built out of coral rock dumped into the bay and it seemed as though they were going to land in the ocean. As they approached, Chinese boats, called "Junks", were floating all over the harbor plying their trade and transporting goods throughout the orient.

After they disembarked from the jet, they went through an in-processing station, were given a briefing on the customs of Hong Kong, converted their military script into British currency and assigned to a hotel. They caught a taxi for the Hong Kong Hilton, a newly constructed, beautiful structure overlooking the bay.

When they arrived, they were shown to their room by a uniformed bellman. After they tipped the bellman, they glanced around the well-appointed room, which contained two queen-sized beds, fresh fruit on the desk, flowers on the pillows and soft music playing. Only one bed would be used during their stay.

For the next five days, they slept, made love, enjoyed the cuisine and toured the island. Across from Hong Kong was the Chinese mainland of Kawloon where shopping was supposed to be the finest in the world. One morning, after a delightful breakfast, they took the ferry for the short ride from Hong Kong to Kawloon. They spent the day dropping in from store to store. Mary bought a blue sapphire ring and Juan bought a camera. That evening, they took the elevator to the top floor of the President Hotel where they drank wild concoctions, ate wonderful food again, and watched the sun set over the city. The trip could not have been more perfect, but the reality soon set in when they were on their way back to the battle zone.

Juan received word his reassignment order had come through and a port call for shipment out of country was being requested. He stopped by the company clerk's office, received a copy of his orders and returned to his quarters. He slowly read the orders. He had been assigned to the training cadre at Fort Polk, Louisiana as an instructor for basic trainees. He was to leave Vietnam in a few days.

Mary managed to get her chief nurse to grant her a couple of days leave so she and Juan could be together. They took a jeep ride into Saigon for those two days to enjoy the city's French cuisine and wine along with increasing the bond between them. After the leave was over, they returned to the base camp and the inevitable that neither one of them was anxious for.

At the appointed hours, Mary held Juan closely, then with tears streaming down her face, watched as he entered the side door of the helicopter, which would transport him to the 8th aero-port to connect with the jet bound for the U.S. Juan looked back from the chopper, watching the small figure of his loved one diminish in size and eventually fading out of sight. He was lost, a ball of pain forming in his gut, but he knew someday they would be together forever. They had agreed to write as often as they could and to see each other when Mary returned to the states. Maybe they could even be stationed together and make the Army a career. Anything was possible.

The chopper landed at the 8th aero-port in mid-morning. Juan waited until the rotor blades had come to a complete stop and then departed the craft. He was directed to a section of the Saigon International Airport designated for processing incoming and outgoing troops. The day was typically hot and the processing station teemed with bodies fuming to get airborne and return to their loved ones in their native land.

Juan handed the clerk a copy of his orders and port call. The clerk gave him a precursory glance and directed him to sit in an area reserved for those who were departing. The uniform to board the outbound plane was again the Army khaki uniform, this being only the second time he had worn in since he arrival some twelve months ago. Juan carried a small suitcase, which contained only some underwear, toiletries, a few gifts and a change of civilian clothes. Most of the presents were for his family and personal effects he had were shipped in a wooden footlocker to Fort Polk.

Just before noon, a Boeing 747, "Flying Tigers" airliner landed and taxied to the tarmac adjacent to the area in which Juan was waiting. The plane came to a halt, shut down its jet engines and opened the passenger door. A portable ramp had been wheeled to the entry way and the new replacements began to descend from the opening in the fuselage. To the cheers from the assembled gathering, taunts of "FNG", "Fuckin New Guys", sounded from the masses of those who had served their time. The FNG's weren't sure what all of the banter meant, but twelve months from now, would fully understand the significance. They seemed in awe as they passed their counterparts, noticing a chest full of decorations and awards. Looking down at their chest, was a solitary ribbon, the American Defense Medal, one some would die for.

It took a couple of hours for the crew to service the plane. The waiting began to wear on Juan. He had served his stint and wanted to exit this God forsaken country. As he looked around him, enlisted men had broken out some playing cards and were merrily engaged in games of different sorts. Most of the officers were deep in retrospect, seemingly oblivious to their surroundings. The fighting and the stress had taken it's toll. Deep lines and streaks of gray could be seen on every head.

Juan brought with him a paper back book, but had a hard time concentrating on the story. He must have started over a dozen times with the same paragraph. All he could think about was Mary, his family, and his new assignment. A loud, whisky soaked voice ruptured over the public address system. It was time for members of Flight 881 to board the aircraft. From the protection of the shade, the flight members entered the scorching sun and onto the already hot interior. The doors were shut, the air-conditioning turned up to full blast and away flew the freedom bird.

CHAPTER TWENTY-EIGHT

The flight from Vietnam to San Francisco was just slightly over eighteen hours with one stop at the airbase in Guam where the plane was again serviced and a new crew came on board. The Military Police would not let anyone off the base, but they did allow the passengers access to the terminal building where they could smoke, get something to drink, or just walk around.

In a short time they were ordered back on the plane and the journey home had began. Juan left Vietnam on July 7th and arrived in San Francisco on July 7th. The day he had lost on the ship crossing the 180th parallel was given back to him. What a strange planet we live on Juan deduced.

The landing at the airport in San Francisco was routine and soon everyone was disembarking. As they passed close to the civilians cursing through the passageways, Juan ducked into the men's bathroom, removed his uniform and donned his civilian clothes. They had all heard about other soldiers who had criss-crossed the country to be spat upon by individuals who were against the war. Juan didn't want to take that chance. Even though he was now dressed like everyone else in the airport, many gave him a disgusted leer, knowing he was a member of the military because of his short haircut. Intolerance was as thick as butter and hung in the air with an acrid odor. The Army had given Juan a thirty-day furlough before reporting to Fort Polk.

In about an hour, he made the connecting flight to Mexico City and his family. He would have liked to stay in San Francisco for a couple of days. The "City by the Bay" was one of his favorites, but he wanted to maximize his time with his loved ones.

Juan finally made it to Mexico, deplaned and caught a taxi to his village. He didn't have many presents for his mother and siblings, but the presents would come later in his baggage. He did, however bring each of the boys a watch and each of the girls a golden topaz necklace he had purchased on his R&R with Mary. For his mother, he brought a solid Jade set of prayer beads to use when she attended Mass.

His month on leave dissipated in what seemed like seconds rather than days. Much of his stay consisted of visits by the relatives, massive food orgies, music, games and catching up. His mother was worried that he had lost so much weight, but she would take care of that. The food, all of Juan's favorites, filled several tables with Juan and the guest gorging themselves like pigs at every gathering. On one occasion they had even made a special Piñata for Juan filled with candies and other treats. Juan was blindfolded and given a stick. He was then spun around and aimed at the Piñata. In two strong and swift strokes, the Piñata broke into a dozen pieces and the treasures were spewed on the ground to the delight of the children.

Juan was not particularly a religious man, but he did attend Mass with his mother a couple of times. He thanked God for his safe return and asked for divine protection over his family for the upcoming years. Juan was not sure what fates were in store for him, but knew he would be spending more and more time away from Mexico.

As his free time was about to expire, Travis appeared on the scene, hugged Juan until Juan thought he was not going to be able to breath. The reunion of old friends put the icing on the cake of devotion. Juan took the time to squirrel Travis off to a local bar, to be alone with him and to tell Travis about his experiences, most of which he could not tell his family. It was difficult recounting the horror, death and destruction Juan had witnessed. He told Travis about Mary and his hopes for the future.

When the bar closed, they staggered back to the village to sleep off the jubilation.

CHAPTER TWENTY-NINE

Juan's leave was over and he started his overture to his new assignment. Fort Polk is the Joint Readiness Training Center for the Army. It is located southeast of Shreveport, Louisiana and north of Lake Charles. Fort Polk was stabled in 1941 and named in honor of the Right Reverend Leonidas Polk, the first Episcopalian Bishop of the Diocese of Louisiana and a Confederate General.

Thousands of soldiers learned the basics of combat here during the World War II Louisiana maneuvers. Afterwards, the post was opened for the Korean War and then closed. It wasn't until the 1961 Berlin Crisis that Fort Polk was reactivated on a more permanent basis and became an infantry-training center in 1962. Subsequently, it was selected to conduct Vietnam oriented basic and advanced training.

It was during his assignment to Fort Polk that Juan was promoted to the rank of First Lieutenant. His golden bars, symbols of initiation into the armed forces, were exchanged for silver bars denoting the higher rank. The center commander, a Brigadier General, and Juan's immediate supervisor a Captain, pinned the shiny new metal bars on his shoulders.

Juan was given the task of assisting the staff at the center's operations center. His job was to coordinate the incoming new recruits, assigning them to the various units for basic training and eventual shipment to Vietnam. His immediate supervisor was also a Vietnam

War veteran. It was while Juan was in this capacity that he became introduced to the internal workings of the Code Of Military Justice, the military law used to discipline wayward soldiers. Although Juan had received some instruction in The Code, he never had to exercise it's contents and knew very little of it's application. No matter how hard the cadre tried, there were always problem children in basic training. Soldiers who would write bad checks, go absent without leave (AWOL), get into fights at the local pubs and other crimes of more or lesser degrees.

Being a fairly junior officer, Juan was given the responsibility of formulating the charges against a wrong doer, determining the level to which the charges would be referred and scheduling the various courts martial to try, acquit or convict and dole out the appropriate punishment. The simplest punishment, reserved for very minor offenses was an Article 15, which could be administered by a Captain or below who were the commanding officers of the soldiers in question. It was up to a single individual to review the charges and make an objective determination as to guilt or innocence. If the determination was guilty, the punishment was generally confinement to the barracks for a short period, loss of pass privileges, or extra duty around the post. The next level was the Summary Court, one officer, in the rank of Major or above who performed the same process at the Article 15, but could levy fines, place in the stockade, or give increased amounts of extra duties.

As the offenses grew in stature, the soldier would be referred to a Special Courts Martial. This Courts Martial was usually a committee of three individuals, usually one officer and two NCOs. Their judgments could extract money, confine in jail, or order the individual be discharged from the service for unsuitability with a general discharge or a bad conduct discharge. The latter could prevent the soldier from ever having the opportunity be in any branch of the armed forces again, but retaining all of his civil rights.

The final authority constituted by the Commanding General, was the General Courts Martial. This court heard only the most heinous crimes, like murder, assault with intent to kill, treason and flagrant insubordination to leaders to which the accused was entrusted. This court could recommend the offender, if found guilty, be placed in the Federal Prison at Fort Leavenworth, Kansas, be discharged with a dishonorable discharge, reduced in rank, fined, or a combination of all three.

If a soldier received a dishonorable discharge or was placed in prison, the results were the same as committing a civil felony, taking away the individual's rights to certain civil liberties guaranteed by the U.S. Constitution.

Juan spent an extraordinary amount of time memorizing The Code, reviewing the charges and the outcomes and forwarding the recommendation on to the approving authority who had the responsibility to uphold the decisions made by the courts, modify the judgments, or dismiss the charges outright. It was at this juncture that Juan felt this tingling sensation creep up his neck and recognized a deepening desire to become involved in the legal system.

Juan had only incurred a two-year obligation to remain in the Army as payback for the support he received in the Senior ROTC Program, but he was under no obligation to stay after that period. As his two years were coming to a conclusion, Juan was called into his cadre commander's office for an end of tour counseling session.

This commander, a Lieutenant Colonel Watson, opened the door to his office as Juan knocked on the hardwood frame. The office walls were covered with symbols of duty to which Colonel Watson had been exposed in his career to this point. Juan noticed a glass case, which entombed the medals, and decorations Watson had earned. Like himself, Colonel Watson had received a Bronze Star for Valor and a Purple Heart for wounds received by enemy fire. Colonel Watson also had a Silver Star for Valor and a Combat Infantry Badge with two stars as testimony to his expertise as an Infantry leader and his bravery under fire. The Colonel invited Juan to sit down in the soft, red leather chair alongside his desk.

"Juan", the Colonel commenced. "You are coming to a crossroads in your life and you must make a decision soon. Your performance of duty in the operations center has been outstanding. You are well liked and respected by your subordinates and superiors and you have a bright future in the Army. I would like to recommend you for a position in the Regular Army and see you put in thirty years of service. You have the leadership potential to go all the way to General. Your country needs men like you, officers who command respect and get things done. Your resources are still untapped. What have you thought you might like to do?"

"Colonel Watson, you are most generous in your praise, but I have made the decision to leave the Army and to attend Law School. Some far away voice is telling me I should render myself to the betterment of society and justice. I have this ache in the pit of my stomach to maybe some day return to Mexico and to better the relationship between my native country and the United States. I will leave the Army with great sadness, but I know it is the right decision."

Colonel Watson slowly rose from his desk, walked around to Juan as Juan was standing and grasped Juan's hand in a firm grip.

"If that is your decision, so be it. The Army has lost a fine officer and gentleman, but I wish you the very best of luck in your chosen direction and if there is anything I can do to help, please do not hesitate to ask it of me."

With that, Juan exited the office and within the next few months, would clear post and receive his discharge papers making him a civilian again. His journey had now taken a new twist. Had he made the right decision? Did he really have the potential to become a lawyer and to make the world a better place in which to live? How would he get into law school? What did he have to do next? Where would he start?

One of the nights before his departure, Juan struck up a conversation with Captain Hurley who was a lawyer assigned to the Staff Judge Advocate Corps. Hurley's chief responsibilities were to sit on the courts martial boards as an advisor to the court. He was a graduate of the University of Virginia Law School and like Juan had an obligation to serve in the Army for repayment of his support while in the Senior ROTC program as compensation for the Army putting him through law school.

"I want to be an attorney Captain Hurley, but I don't know where to start. Can you help me?'

"Well, the first thing you should do is drop by my office in the morning. I have a publication, which encompasses the subject of application to law schools and the things you will need to do to get in. There is an appendix in the back, which lists all of the law schools in the United States and the addresses you can write to for application forms. The publication is full of helpful hints and I am sure it will give you the right steps to take. Then again, there is always the Army path that I took. That choice, of course, will be up to you."

Juan felt like the weight of the world was beginning to left from his shoulders. A small light was beginning to emerge from the tunnel of doubt and uncertainty. Juan made sure Captain Hurley was well supplied with imbibing liquids for the rest of the evening.

The next morning Juan crossed the quadrangle from his BOQ to the JAG office of Captain Hurley. The day was humid as was typical of Fort Polk, but cool. As he crossed, squads of basic trainees marching to class under the guidance of their drill instructors, wearing the "Smokey The Bear" hats, intercepted him. He waited on the sidewalk as they passed in the street, the NCO rendering him a salute as was befitting an officer.

The JAG office was on the second floor of an old World War II wooden building, typical of the many which were built during that era and just like the ones at Fort Lewis. The building was scheduled for demolition in the upcoming months, but in the meantime still sprouted window air-conditioners sticking out of the sides of the building like overripe zits. Juan walked up the creaky staircase, arriving at the reception area manned by a female specialist. She asked the nature of his business and nodded that Captain Hurley had indeed informed her to show Lieutenant Cardova in when he arrived.

Captain Hurley was engrossed in the paperwork at this government issued desk not noticing Juan at first, but then smiling when he looked up. Hurley arose without comment and moved to the wall where a bookcase, stuffed with texts, was located. He extracted a paperbound volume about the size of a telephone directory and handed it to Juan.

"Everything you need to know is in here. When you are finished, just bring it back and if I am not here, give it to the specialist at the reception desk."

Juan thanked Captain Hurley, shook his hand and left.

That night, Juan opened the book to the table of contents, got a birds' eye view of what the book was about and began scanning the text. When he had finished most of the introductory words, he turned to the appendix, which listed all of the law schools by geographical location. Juan wanted to return to the west coast, so he thumbed to the pages listing the schools in California, Oregon and Washington states.

The reference outlined the process of applying to the school, so Juan began typing letters as instructed and addressed them to all of the institutions. The next day, he purchased stamps and mailed the letters off, not knowing what fish would be caught as he trolled for acceptance.

CHAPTER THIRTY

Since leaving Vietnam, Juan and Mary had written to each other at least once a week. Mary numbered her letters in sequence because the mail out of country was sometimes unpredictable and arrived at Juan's mailbox out of order. When letter four arrived before letter one, two and three, he held the letter until the others came.

Holding onto the letter, Juan could smell the faint hint of Mary's perfume. It aroused in him all of the primeval feelings he had experience with his love. He felt a momentary depression, but he soon regained his composure, put the thoughts to the back of his mind and focused his contemplations to the future.

Soon the initial letters arrived and Juan hastily opened them wanting to devour the contents in a hurry, but took his time savoring each and every word. Of course Mary missed him and wanted to be with him. She told him of the lonely nights, the casualties who had increased in number and the losing battle America was waging. In letter three, Mary told Juan she had received her reassignment orders. She was to report to The Walter Reed Army Medical Center near Washington D.C.

Juan was stunned. That meant she would be a continent away. That was unacceptable Juan wrote back. Wasn't there a hospital closer where she could be assigned? She replied the Army Nurse Corps was firm, she would be going to Walter Reed.

Juan suggested as an alternative, a monthly flight linking the two lovers until Mary left the Army and was permanently settled near Juan. This seemed to be a less than desirable solution, but they didn't have much choice. They agreed to this arrangement knowing it would only last until Juan was nearing the completion of is second year of schooling.

Along with Mary's letters, application forms with instructions began to trickle in from the law schools. All of the schools had a myriad of forms to complete and required at least five letters of recommendation. Juan was hard pressed to consider to whom he would turn for these recommendations, deciding he would ask Travis, the athletic director at San Diego State, his commanding officer from Vietnam, and his supervisor at Fort Polk. Juan was now hard pressed to think of a fifth person to help him out.

After contacting each of these individuals, Juan was informed by Travis that a California state senator, named Kyle Smith and an old friend of Travis, offered to help Juan get into a California law school. Senator Smith, like Juan, was an alumnus of San Diego State and was more than willing to assist. That very night, Juan wrote to Senator Smith asking for a letter of recommendation and thanking him for the kind generosity shown.

As promised, the letters of recommendation started to arrive. When the last one was in, Juan made copies of the letters and the applications forms just in case they might get lost in the mail. The letter from Senator Smith was neatly typed on his government letterhead and like the others addressed "To Whom it May Concern". Attached to the official letter was a hand written note from the Senator. The writing was bold, with large sweeping letters, a mark of a person in authority according to a graphologist.

In the text, the Senator wrote, if Juan needed anything to just let him know. The Senator listed his phone number for his office in Sacramento and his residence phone, which diabolically was in Santa Barbara, a beautiful city where Juan had always wanted to live.

Juan hoped he had allowed plenty of time for the applications to get to the schools, to be reviewed and an answer given back to him. With only a month left before he was to leave Fort Polk and three weeks before the term of school commenced, letters came from all of the institutions Juan had applied to.

He hurriedly opened each one. The first one, from the University of Washington began, "Dear Mr. Cardova, we were pleased with you application, but must inform you, the class starting this fall is filled. Please feel free to apply again."

Two more letters bore basically the same message. They didn't want Juan or he was not ranked high enough. Juan suddenly felt nauseous. His stomach felt as if an M-80 firecracker had exploded in it. What if he failed to get accepted to any of the schools? What would he do, he couldn't let his dream evaporate like a puff of smoke. He had turned the Army down and he was sure they wouldn't want him back.

Calming his fears, Juan opened yet another letter. This one from The University of California at Santa Barbara, which opened, "Mr. Cardova, we are pleased to inform you of your acceptance to our law school, the first term to begin....." Juan immediately began jumping around the room like a crazy child. Bouncing off walls, cavorting over the furniture, kissing the letter and yelling at the top of his lungs. He rushed to his desk and composed a short letter to Mary, telling her of his good news and asking her to begin making plans to come to Santa Barbara as soon as she arrived back in the states.

Financing his education would pose no problem for Juan. He had the G.I. Bill paying for the first two years and he had saved enough, he felt, to cover the last one. If worse came to worse, he could seek a student loan to be paid back later after he had a job. Then again, he could always look for a position as a paralegal, but only if he had to. Juan wanted to devote all of his time to his studies and not be distracted in any way.

Juan hadn't needed a car while he was stationed at Fort Polk. He lived on post and could walk to work, and many of the officers had offered to take him places when the need arose. Now he was on his own and needed transportation. He had to make a decision to buy a car in Louisiana or fly to California and purchase one there. As he was clearing post, he stopped by a bulletin board and noticed an announcement posted by one of the officers at the training center who were shipping out for Vietnam and was selling his Pontiac GTO convertible.

Juan had always wanted a convertible and the GTO was one of his favorites. This was a true muscle car, and Juan had fancied it when he watched television. He jotted down the telephone number, found a pay phone and dialed. The seller answered and agreed to meet Juan that afternoon. In no time, the deal was consummated and the title was signed over to Juan when the cash transaction took place. The GTO was black with a white interior, the only way a GTO should be. The license tabs had not expired, so Juan decided not to license the car locally, but would do that when he arrived on the west coast.

Early in the morning he loaded the trunk with his suitcases, put the top down and drove to the interstate highway, which would carry him across the countryside. Since he couldn't carry everything in the car he owned, the Army shipped his goods to a warehouse in Santa Barbara where it would be stored until he claimed it. The morning was beginning to turn into an inferno, but Juan didn't care. He was on his way into another galaxy of stars, bolstered by his sense of elated joy. The wind mussed his hair as he drove along. He didn't care.

He traversed the States of Texas, New Mexico and Arizona before entering the familiar grounds he knew as southern California. Along the way, he marveled at the landscape as it changed. He didn't realize how big Texas was. He thought to himself, no wonder the Texans think they are better than everyone else, they own most of the land.

On the way he stopped to get gas, feed his famished stomach and check into motels which showed vacancy signs and looked clean. He now understood why New Mexico was called "The Land of Enchantment". The mountains glowed like pink candles in the sunset, finally arriving at that color after changing from hues of yellow to red to orange to pink. In Arizona, the mountains stood like sentinels out in the desert. The cactus pointed their arms to the heavens, welcoming him to their domain. He wondered how anything could exist in this wilderness, but marveled at the flowers that bloomed along the way.

He had taken Interstate 20 out of Shreveport, angling from there through Fort Worth and into El Paso. For some strange reason, the Marty Robbin's song about this city kept running through his mind and he hummed along trying to remember the words. Eventually Interstate 20 connected with Interstate 10 through Phoenix and on to Las Angeles, his final destination.

CHAPTER THIRTY-ONE

Juan knew the cost of living in Santa Barbara was one of the highest in the state, so he decided to look for a cheap motel room in the interim where he could live on a week to week timeframe until he found an apartment meeting his needs. Near the center of the city, he found a Spanish style motel, aged, but with grounds which were well groomed and taken care of. In the courtyard in front of the office was a fountain with a statue of a Saint holding a water ewer, spilling the precious fluid into a granite pond.

As Juan opened the office door, he was greeted by the aroma of freshly baked bread and scents of other spices used in making Mexican delicacies. A small bell jingled as the door broke its plain and a dark skinned man appeared, wiping his hands on a soiled towel. Juan explained his situation, asking if it were possible to lease a room on a weekly tenure for the short term. The office manager stroked the stubble on his five-day-old chin whiskers and looked skyward as if in deep meditation. The manager said he had a room with a kitchenette for cooking an individual's own meals, but would only agree if Juan was willing to put up a security deposit of fifty dollars and pay the first two weeks rent in advance. After that point, the rent would be negotiated on a weekly basis and when Juan left, the deposit would be returned to him if the room remained as Juan had found it.

Juan agreed to the terms, signed the register and was handed the key to Rom 103. Room 103 was located to the rear of the motel, away from the noise of the street traffic for the most part. Juan parked his GTO in front of his room, inserted the key and opened the door.

The space he had paid for was small. The bed, desk, chair, lamp and bureau being in the same room as the kitchen. The kitchen really wasn't a kitchen, but a segment of the room where there was a cupboard and counter on one wall, a two burner electric hot plate and two chrome and vinyl chairs parked beneath a chrome and hard plastic topped table. There was a drape covering a standard sized window in the front, and a smaller window off the kitchen adorned with simply made curtains.

The room was clean and functional. Juan sat on the bed and the mattress was firm and responsive to his weight. The walls were painted a light yellow and the carpet an ugly green shag, so typical of the décor of that period. It wasn't much to crow about, but it was his first home away from home other than the BOQ and the tent the Army had provided him.

The evening was wearing on and Juan was exhausted. He didn't feel like fixing himself dinner, so he walked across the motel's parking lot to the street in hopes of finding an inexpensive eatery. As he glanced up the street, he spied an old railroad car, which had been converted into a diner. A large red, neon sign was affixed to the top, which read "EATS". The neon on the "S" had burned out, so "EAT" was good enough for him.

Inside the diner against one wall was a galley with a window through which the cook passed the cooked meals. An older, matronly woman was extracting the food and placing it on a counter running the length of the diner under which six bar stools were attached. On the opposite wall, skirting the four outside window, were four double booths, which could accommodate four people if no one was obese.

The waitress noticed as Juan sat down at the counter and without a word poured him a cup of coffee and handed him a menu. The food smelled good and the prices seemed reasonable. He chose a hamburger and fries for now and a piece of apple pie ala mode for later. The hour was still early, so few patrons were eating. As Juan's food arrived, the small place started to fill to capacity. Most of the diners coming in looked like blue-collar workers on their way home.

Juan finished his meal, his appetite sated for the time being. He tipped the waitress, picked up his check and went to the cash register to pay. A younger girl was seated behind the register, probably the owner's daughter, Juan thought. She took the money and gave Juan his change. After Juan returned to his motel, he undressed, wrote a letter to Mary, took a shower and fell into a deep and restful sleep.

The next morning, Juan was awakened by a bright light streaming through a small crack in the front window drapes. He glanced at the digital clock on the nightstand and was amazed to observe it was after nine in the morning. This was the latest he had slept in ages. He surmised his body clock was getting adjusted to the west coast and soon his getting up early would become routine.

Juan spent most of the first week looking through the classified ads of the newspaper, circling those apartments which seemed to be within his budget. Juan had purchased a city map at a local gas station and indicated the locations on the map for the addresses he was interested in. The week left Juan totally frustrated. Either the listed apartment had just been taken, or was being renovated, or was so filthy, Juan would not want to live there.

He stopped by some of the more expensive layouts, which were unfurnished. They would assuredly exceed the limited budget Juan had. He felt somewhat like he was being squeezed between a pair of pinchers and was afraid he wasn't going to find a place to live by the time he was to begin classes.

Out of desperation Juan called the home of Senator Smith. On the second ring, a female voice answered, "Smith residence, how may I help you." Juan volunteered his name and asked to speak to the Senator. "I'm sorry, I don't know anyone by that name and the Senator is busy in his office at the moment".

As the woman was about to hang up, Juan beseeched her to listen to his story. He described the letter he had received from the Senator and pleaded with her to allow him to speak to the master of the house. Apparently Juan was convincing. The person on the phone said, "wait a minute, I will see if Senator Smith is available."

A few minutes elapsed and a deep resonating voice came on the line. "Juan, it that you?"

"Yes it is Senator. I have finally arrived in Santa Barbara, but I am having some difficulties finding a place to live. I was wondering if I can impose on you further for some assistance."

"Why certainly Juan. Why don't you drop over to my place this afternoon and we'll if we can work something out." Juan agreed and stated he would see the Senator shortly after noontime.

Juan found the location of the Smith residence on his city map, estimating it would take him about thirty minutes to get there. He skipped lunch and entered the stream of cars going in his direction. Juan found the mansion without difficulty. It was on the side of a hill overlooking the ocean and nestled in amongst homes that were equally as beautiful. He parked his GTO in the front driveway and rang the doorbell. A middle aged Mexican woman answered, told Juan to wait in the foyer and she would fetch the Senator.

A few minutes elapsed and striding down a long hallway came a man of means. Kyle was tall, a little over six feet, around the age of fifty plus, dark black hair and dressed in the style worn by most of the rich people who lived in this part of the universe. He wore a Hawaiian print shirt, pulled loose from his white canvas pants and hanging about mid thigh. He wore sandals without socks. He was deeply tanned.

From his looks, Kyle could have easily been a corporate CEO, an athlete, or a used car salesman. He carried the mystique of someone in charge, knowing how to make decisions and commanding respect.

He grasped Juan's hand, pumping it like a farmer pumped a siphon to get water from a well. He smiled easily, showing perfectly matched and whitened teeth.

"Juan, it is certainly a pleasure to meet you. Travis has spoken so highly of you and your potential."

Not wanting to appear ungrateful, Juan replied, "and what would that potential be?"

"Oh, I know a lot about you Juan. I make it my business to know lots about people who interest me. I made my fortune in the fuel business, starting out as an accountant for an oil company and eventually acquiring small businesses in like enterprises. I now own a conglomerate of nuclear, oil and natural gas companies, which supply most of the state. Over the years, I have come in contact with a multitude of young men and women and I must say I pride myself in determining those who have potential and those who do not. Don't be offended, but I spent hours grilling Travis about you and studying your military record."

The next few minutes were spent with Kyle recounting Juan's athletic scholarship to the university, Juan's outstanding career on the soccer field, being a distinguished ROTC cadet and his valor in Vietnam. He knew more about Juan than Juan's mother.

Kyle paused, "Why don't we take a walk to the pool and have a glass of refreshment. It is a little early for a drink so how about some iced tea or lemonade?"

Juan really didn't have a choice, so like a new lamb, followed the ram to the pool. The pool area was breathtaking. The Olympic sized pool was filled with crystal clear water and emblazoned with tile made in Mexico which Juan remembered festooning some of the cultural buildings in Mexico City. The plants surrounding the pool were green and lush. Flowers brightened every corner of the yard, which was immaculately kept.

The two men settled into a pair of overstuffed lounge chairs set around glass table with a large matching umbrella set in the center. Kyle motioned to a young maid, who approached.

"Maria, would you please bring Mr. Cardova and me some ice tea with some lemon and sugar on the side. And also, would you ask Mrs. Smith if she would join us."

"Certainly Senator" she replied, "I will get right to it."

Juan watched as Maria walked away. She was probably in her late teens, with a curvaceous figure and a suggestive walk, which must have turned the heads of many a young man. She glanced back over her shoulder and gave Juan a flirting look, inviting him to stare at her a little longer. Smith could not help but notice the exchange. He grinned a knowing grin and continued the conversation.

"I know you will be starting your law courses soon, but in the meantime where are you staying?"

"Oh, I rented a kitchenette in a motel near the center of the city. It is clean and cheap, but isn't anything I want on a permanent basis. I've been apartment hunting and so far everything that would fit my needs is just a little too expensive for my budget. All I have is the G.I. Bill and what little money I have been able to save from the Army. If I don't find something soon, I fear I won't know what to do."

Kyle mused for a few minutes, his dark eyes becoming darker. Juan thought he could almost see lightening flash through them as the Senator contemplated Juan's remarks. When he had gone through his thought process Kyle said, "I think I might have a solution to your problem."

Juan had barely met this man, yet there was an aura of trust that seemed to radiate from his person.

"Juan, I own a small, two bedroom condo near the university where you will be going to school. I use it mostly for out of town guests who come to visit, but haven't used it much lately. I know you would not accept it on a gratuitous foundation, but I would be willing to rent it to you for a figure which you feel you can reasonably handle."

Juan was overwhelmed. Had he heard the Senator right or was he dreaming? "You are much too generous Senator, I could not accept such a favor."

"Not so fast Juan. I am not giving you a favor, the offer comes with a catch."

"And what might that be."

"Well, I have been a Senator in the California State Legislature for the past six years and I have my mind set on a bigger prize, a seat in the U.S. Senate in Washington D.C. I am looking for bright, talented young people to help me achieve that goal. I need staff that can bring in the votes necessary to get me elected, especially the Hispanic vote. I think you could fill that bill nicely."

"But Senator, I can't work on a political campaign and go to school at the same time."

"I know Juan, but I won't be seeking the position for the next two years. That should give you time to almost complete you education before you go to work for me."

"But Senator, I will need at least three years to finish."

"Not necessarily. In the State of California, you can take the bar exam without ever going to law school. If you pass, you are a lawyer by default. I feel certain that after just two years of study, you will be more than qualified to take the bar exam. I also feel you have the brains to take on an extra workload during the term and then consume the third year's classes during the two intervening summers."

Juan had never heard of such a thing, but the Senator explained that California was the only state in the union which had this provision in it's legal system.

A whiff of an exotic perfume preceded her into the room as Mrs. Smith joined the men. She, like her husband, was tall, athletic and commanding. She wore a flowered sarong, which moved in sync with her lithe body. She was also tan and smiled that brilliant smile as she approached. Kyle rose as she neared like a Greek God paying homage to his lover Kyle led her to the table and held her chair as she sat. Kyle took her hand and kissed it before introducing her to Juan. Maria brought a glass of iced tea for Tara.

"Juan, this is my lovely wife Tara."

"My husband has told me so much about you, Juan. I feel I have known you forever and you are a member of the family. I hope you can join us for dinner."

"That would be my pleasure", Juan cooed softly.

"By the way, what is for dinner, Maria?", Kyle asked.

The menu the maid outlined sounded like a feast for Kings. Juan suddenly realized he hadn't eaten anything since early morning and was famished.

The three principles bantered about for a while, then departed for the dining room and the meal, which awaited them. They started with a shrimp and crab cocktail, followed by a cold raspberry soup. Assorted cheeses were passed around to whet the palate before the main course, which was poached halibut. The halibut was served with a vintage Chardonnay wine, the finest California wineries could provide. The fish was complemented with au gratin potatoes and fresh peas. The desert was a fruit medley followed by more wine.

The meal was interspersed with a little chatter, Tara wanting to know about Juan's family and his hopes for the future. She asked if he had a girlfriend. Juan suspected she already knew all of the answers to her questions, but he played along never the less. Juan gave her a quick biographical sketch and an overview of Mary and their relationship.

The dinner ended far too quickly for Juan. He could have remained and savored the delicious taste for hours, but the time was getting late. Kyle walked Juan to the door with instructions to stop by his office at ten in the morning so they could consummate the lease agreement and get Juan settled in his new abode. Tara gave him a maternal hug and a light kiss on the cheek and bade him a good evening.

On his way home, Juan drove through the Smith's neighborhood, lined with palatial estates, hidden behind black wrought iron barriers, the residents afraid someone would enter their inter sanctum and do them harm. Or perhaps they just wanted to keep the world of ordinary people at bay and preserve their privacy.

The night was cool with a soft breeze blowing, so Juan pulled to the side of the road and lowered the canvas top. The movement of the car started to clear his head of the quantities of wine he had consumed and by the time he reached his motel, he was relatively sober.

CHAPTER THIRTY-TWO

The next morning Juan arose early and went for a run around a small park located within a short distance of the motel. He had not really exercised for some time and his muscles reacted to the stress they had not been made to endure for some time. After a few minutes, Juan caught his second wind and sprinted around the perimeter of a lake in the center of the park and back to his room to take a shower.

He dressed casually, stopped back at the diner for a simple breakfast and drove downtown to meet Kyle. Kyle's office was located on the top floor of one of the many downtown office buildings. The building was not tall, the city having banned any building over six stories, and was encased in a dark reflective glass shell. Juan found a parking space a few blocks away and walked to the building with ten minutes to spare.

This gave him a chance to enjoy the exquisite interior of the lobby, adorned with marble and gold. The floors were highly polished, giving the impression that one was walking on water. A simple fountain stood in one corner, the figure of a Greek goddess placed in the center. Juan moved across the spacious lobby to the express elevator, which would take him to the top floor. Inside the elevator, classical music was playing a soft relaxing melody. The car arrived at the sixth floor and the doors opened into a well-appointed reception area manned by an attractive secretary behind a large dark wooden desk. He introduced himself to the young woman, marveling at the beauty before him. Kyle certainly surrounded himself with good-looking specimens.

She spoke into the inter-office console on the surface of the desk, letting Kyle know Juan had arrived for his appointment. A few seconds passed, then Kyle's office door opened. Kyle waved Juan in and closed the door behind them.

Kyle asked Juan if he wanted something to drink. Juan accepted a soft drink. Kyle poured the soda into a crystal tumbler filled with ice cubes, and handed it to him. Kyle poured himself a small amount of Scotch into a similar glass without ice. The two men sat on a comfortable sofa next to an enormous coffee table constructed of inlayed Teak. On the table was a document bearing the letterhead of Kyle's business. Kyle extracted the document from the table and passed it on to Juan.

"This is the lease for the condo I want you to use while you are attending law school", Kyle said. "Please read it carefully. I have left out the amount of the monthly rent. I would like you to fill in the amount, like I said, for a figure you would feel comfortable with on your budget."

The lease was a straightforward, boilerplated lease agreement outlining the location of the condo, the rent to be paid, the due dates for the rent payment and assurance the renter would maintain the quality of the place.

Juan spent some time looking the agreement over and finally entered an amount he felt he could afford. Kyle agreed and both of them signed the lease. Kyle's secretary witnessed the agreement and made a copy for Juan with the original to be deposited in the office files.

That done, Kyle replenished his glass and rejoined Juan on the sofa. For the next thirty minutes, Kyle outlined his plans to run for the U.S. Senate in two years time. The California Senator now serving in the Congress was about to retire and the Republican seat would be vacant. Kyle felt he had an excellent chance to win with the Senate now controlled by Republicans, but didn't know who the Democrats would find to challenge him.

Kyle had already created a war chest to fund his campaign, had procured a headquarters in Los Angeles and was making overtures to hire staff. He expressed his desires for Juan to aid in his bid for this high office when the time came. Kyle guaranteed a hefty salary for his time, and encouraged Juan to join up right away. Juan expressed his desire to help, but hedged a little about coming on board with a full class schedule facing him for the next two years.

"Let's take that trip one step at a time", Kyle countered. "How would you like to start working on the campaign here in Santa Barbara on a part time basis until you get your feet wet. I will be starting up offices all over the state and need a good man to work with the crew here. As you progress through your studies, you can determine how much time you would like to commit and if things get too much for you, you can take some time off to regroup."

"Senator, I can only tell you how generous you are being to me and that I will give it some serious thought. I can't make any promises now, but I will definitely give you an answer soon. Who knows, maybe someday I might like to run for office myself."

Kyle laughed and patted Juan on the shoulder, affirming a true friendship in it's infancy. Kyle then gave Juan the keys to the condo and instructions on how to get there. The place was fully furnished, so the logistics of outfitting a new pad would not be a burden.

It didn't take much to find his new digs. The drive from downtown swung toward the ocean and bay upon which the university was located. As he neared the street address, the homes took on an elegant posh look. The street was lined with antique lampposts made of bronze with curls near the globe holding baskets of flowers in a profusion of colors. Juan felt as though he were driving through a kaleidoscope. Juan never used drugs, but had an inkling of what a trip on LSD might have been like. He had somewhat of a feeling for the experience, having known several free love students at San Diego State.

The yards were beautifully landscaped, sidewalks swept clean, windows washed and all cars stowed neatly inside two and three car garages. Juan had the top down on his car and could smell the blending of bouquets of ordors mixing sweet and tart smells with the gentle scent of the ocean salt. He admired this neighborhood, noting the contrast of the two other places in which he had lived. Surely this must be the nirvana his ancestors dreamt about when they reached heaven.

The houses gave way to town houses and condominiums reaching to the water's edge. Juan located the one he had leased. It was a three story, split level affair abutted next to the sidewalk. The one car garage was on the street level. Outside the garage there was a staircase made of concrete, which led to the ornate front door. The staircase was trimmed in the same materials as the lampposts, acting as holders for zonal geraniums flowing out of containers affixed to the railing.

The condo was white stucco with a red Spanish tile roof pointing like a wounded finger to the azure blue sky. The windows were done in colored crystal and lead reminding Juan of the windows in the church he attended in Mexico. He was impressed and made the sign of the cross to acknowledge his good fortune and to thank the Redeemer for providing him with this great opportunity.

Juan pressed the garage door opener, watching the vinyl covered aluminum door glide effortlessly up into the ceiling. After the car entered, Juan turned off the engine, closed the garage door and sat to let his head clear from the day's heady experiences. He still couldn't bring himself to believe all of this was happening.

After a few minutes Juan exited the condo through a side door of the garage and walked up the short flight of stairs onto a landing with a door which entered into the front room. On the first floor of the condo was an efficiency kitchen incorporated with a breakfast nook and a great room. The architecture made the room flow from wall to wall, giving the impression you were standing in one room, but as you moved, the room became separate rooms. From the great room, through an archway was the living room, foyer, the front door to the street and a clothes closet. The second floor consisted of a bedroom, a bath and a den easily adaptable for Juan to use as an office. Third floor contained a master bedroom and a walk-in, tiled shower and Jacuzzi. Off the main bedroom were French style doors opening out onto a veranda and which offered a spectacular view of the Pacific to the west. Juan stood there mesmerized as the sun began to turn into a fiery ball and sink into the placid water.

The condo was furnished in an art deco motif. Most of the furniture was white leather with chrome tables, lamps and other fixtures. A large television sat in one corner of the front room and a like stereo system sat in the other corner. Area rugs in colors to match the paintings adorned the white carpet. A professional must have decorated the house, it was so well done.

The kitchen was stainless steel with marble counter tops. A large mobile hung from the ceiling supporting a variety of cooking utensils in Teflon black. The cabinets were white with chrome handles. Juan noticed a fairly large wine cooler wedged between the refrigerator and the stove. It was filled to capacity with different kinds of wine, of which Juan had never heard of or what they tasted like. He made a mental note to buy a book at the local bookstore on wines. He didn't want to appear to be stupid to his benefactor.

The second floor was toned down just a little with colored walls sporting more traditional artwork. The master bedroom likewise was more conventional with an oversize king bed, nightstands made of oak and a very large walk-in closet. The kitchen was well stocked, but Juan decided to eat out for the evening until he had a chance to move his belongings in and go to the grocery store for supplies that he liked, but didn't see in the pantry. He would also check out of the motel the next day.

A few blocks away, Juan found a small, cozy Italian restaurant tucked in the back of some shops. The sign read "Petero's Fine Italian

Cuisine". The restaurant looked clean from the outside, but it was the aroma of the food that drew him in. The inside was typical Italian. The tables were covered with the traditional red and white, checkered tablecloths. Each table had a Chianti bottle, wrapped in straw with a candle placed in the center. The tables were crowded together. The headwaiter, dressed in a long sleeved white shirt with a black bow tie, black pants and a white apron motioned him to a small table for two by the window.

Juan ordered a glass of red wine and some veal scaloppini, which turned out to be delicious and very filling. He ordered another glass of wine and stared out the window at the people passing by on their way home or to do some shopping. His mind drifted away to Mary. He had not gotten a letter for almost a week and was worried about something might be wrong. If only he could reach her by some means.

Juan finished his meal, paid the bill and retired to his new living place. It was still early, but he was exhausted. A hot shower and bed was the order of the day. Tomorrow he had to visit the Law School campus to get oriented. It didn't take him long to fall asleep, slumbering to a dreamless state when his telephone rang startling him awake.

"Juan, its Mary, I love you and wanted to get in touch with you just as soon as possible. I know it is late in California, but I couldn't sleep."

"Are you okay and how did you find me?"

"Oh, I'm fine and I got your number from Kyle Smith. Remember you told me if I ever needed to reach you, I could find out where you were through him. I had his number copied from one of your letters. I just wanted to let you know I will be leaving Vietnam at the end of the month for my new duty station at Walter Reed Army Medical Center. I have taken a month's delay in route and will be flying into L.A.X. I was hoping you could meet me and we could spend some time together."

"Meet you? Wild horses couldn't keep me away. Give me your flight number and arrival date and time when you get them, and I'll be there to greet you."

"I don't have all of that information yet, but when I do, I will call you and let you know. I won't be interfering with your schooling will I?"

"Of course not. The timing couldn't have been better. I start classes about the end of your leave time, so it shouldn't be a problem."

"Thanks darling, I can't wait to show you what you have been missing all these months. Take lots of vitamins or eat lots of oysters, you are going to need them."

"I'm headed for the kitchen as we speak, I'll be ready."

"I have to go now, the operator at the MARS station is signaling me my time is up. Someone else has to have their turn. Sleep tight my love and I'll be in touch when I have things a little firmer."

With that, the line went silent. The MARS system had always intrigued Juan. It was a station set up by the signal battalion at the base camp allowing a soldier to call home for free. It was a radio to telephone link, so when a person was through talking into the mike, they would release a button the side and say "over", that would let the other party know when it was their turn to speak. Juan had used it several times and always appreciated the Army providing such a wonderful service to its members. Juan gazed at the phone as if it were a Genie's bottle emitting forth golden phrases of intimate feelings. Go back to sleep. You have got to be kidding Juan said to himself.

CHAPTER THIRTY-THREE

The next day, Juan arrived at the Law School at UCSB to receive his orientation. The new incoming students were to gather at 10 o'clock in the lecture hall. Juan came a few minutes early and found a seat on the aisle near the center of the room. Slowly the room filled to about half full. The class would number almost two hundred. After everyone was seated, a distinguished looking professor moved to the dais on the podium at the stage in front of the hall. He waited for the students to stop talking. He then began his welcome.

For the next hour, the professor went over the rules on attendance, class scheduling, administrative paperwork, grading system and study hints. Forms were filled out to obtain parking permits for the cars, a student identification card and personal information to be put into each student's file. After the orientation, the students were then escorted on a grand tour of the school. They visited the classrooms, the law library, administrative offices, cafeteria and bookstore. Juan knew he was in the right place. As they journeyed through the law library, Juan felt as if a warm cloak had been thrown around his body and had enveloped him with a feeling of comfort. It was like being tucked in bed by his mother. He knew things would be okay from here on out. Juan stood in awe at the expanse of the library. Thousands of bound leather volumes sat on wooden shelves like sardines packed into cans. The room was almost mystical. He felt vibrations of great justices and lawyers past. Supreme Court Federalist John Marshall, Oliver Wendell Holmes, Clarence Darrow, Melvin Belli, Abe Lincoln and other personages whom he had studied to pass his citizenship examination.

The new law students had been given a course outline and the required book list they would use to buy the texts from the bookstore. After getting his parking permit and student ID card, Juan found a shopping cart and went from area to area in the bookstore until he found everything he needed. After waiting in a long line, Juan made his purchases, tossed the books in his car and went back to the condo. He unloaded the books and placed then on the shelves of his new office where they would be in easy access.

As suggested by the professor, Juan returned to the administrative center to put his name on a sign-up sheet for a study group. The school found students could be more efficient if they formed small groups. This way, the assignments could be divided equally and shared at group meetings without each student having to read everything. Once everyone had signed up, the administrative staff would decide the composition of each study group, giving the assemblage a flavor of gender, ethnicity, age and geography. The pairing would be posted the following Monday.

Juan spent the weekend perusing the books he had purchased, running his fingers over the slick outer covers and admiring the thickness of each one of them. As he scanned each volume, he wondered how he was ever going to learn all of the material. Putting the books aside, he then looked over the course syllabuses, which gave the student directions for which chapters to read to coincide with the times of the classes. The courses were sequenced around the various aspects of the legal system. General information about probates, contracts, corporate dealings, financial information, tax law and a myriad of other subjects were hidden within the hardness of the writings.

Juan tried to relax, but found his nerves tingling in anticipation of meeting his new study group. They would have almost a month to get to know each other before classes started. Sunday night, he fell asleep at his desk and was awakened with a start by the ringing of his phone. Sleepily he answered.

"Juan, its Mary, you know the one you love. I just got my port call and will be leaving Ton Son Hut on Pan American Airlines next Wednesday. I am scheduled to arrive in LAX the same day at noon aboard flight 272. Strange, but I am leaving and arriving the same day. How weird is that? Anyway, I will only have two weeks to spend with you, then I must get to the D.C. area, find a place and get checked into the hospital. I wanted a month, but the chief nurse said two weeks was all she could spare. She said they were receiving so many soldiers from Vietnam, the staff is completely exhausted and overworked and they need some relief. I wasn't very happy about it, but I guess I have no choice. You don't mind if I stay two week with you do you?"

"Mind; if you don't come, I think I would commit some sort of self mutilation and hire a contract assassin to polish you off. But then again, I might just look for another gorgeous female named Mary and start all over again."

Mary laughed. For the next few minutes, they shared an intimate conversation and then Mary hung up. Juan jumped up from his desk and charged around the room liken to the Tasmanian devil in heat. This calls for a celebration he thought as he opened the refrigerator and extract a cold bottle of pinot noir, his favorite. He hadn't intended to drink but one glassful, but soon had polished off the entire bottle. He felt the glow of the alcohol filter through his brain and body and a calm come over him. His world was good and going to get better.

That night, he slept the sleep of the dead, not arising until late morning. The weekend zoomed by and now it was Monday, the day of infamy. Like the Japanese attack on Pearl Harbor, this was a day to be remembered for the rest of his life. He was going to become a member of a legal team.

Juan raced to the administrative building to look at the team postings. Beside his name were four others. The first was Candice Wright, the second William Peterson, the third Henry Solomon and the fourth Daniel Chan. Beside his team's listing was a meeting date and location which would give the team a chance to introduce themselves and work out the necessary logistics over the span of the term.

The first team meeting took place in a small conference room adjacent to the main lecture hall. Juan was not the first to arrive. Two others were there, the final members following along shortly. They each introduced themselves, shook hands and began to relate something about themselves.

Candice was a thin, almost bulimic, light skinned Afro-American. Tall, her skin so translucent she could have easily passed for a Latino or a Caucasian if it had not been for her black, penetrating eyes. When she smiled, her mouth was filled with perfectly straight teeth which reflected the light like a highly polished marble statue. She was dressed in a simple white blouse with a plaid skirt and low-heeled pumps. She wore her hair pulled back into a bun held in place by a brightly accented scarf. A small strand of miniature pearls adorned her neck and she wore a gold ankle bracelet.

Candice told the team she had grown up in the Deep South, daughter of a schoolteacher and a local business man who had done well. She had attended public schools through the 8th grade, then her parents enrolled her in an all girl's academy. She graduated summa cum laude from Emory College in Atlanta, majoring in English and political science. Her minor had been in foreign languages. She, like the others, had applied to several law schools and had been selected to attend UCSB because of her high academic ranking. She was an only child, privileged, but not arrogant.

William was a large, white farm boy looking specimen. He was the middle son of a family of five boys, raised in the rural Midwest. His father was a successful farmer, raising a variety of crops and animals.

Most of the boys stayed to help run the acreage, but William wanted to get away from the small town atmosphere, where everyone knew your business and marked the birth of a child nine months after they saw a girl kiss a boy.

William was a religious individual, having been born again. His convictions were to the conservative right. He was against big government, for education and a dyed in the wool conservationist. He felt global warming was the ruination of our planet and he wanted to finish law school and practice environmental law. He felt there was room for both business and land use and he wanted to dedicate himself to that end.

Harry was a diminutive Jewish man from New York City. His parents operated a small delicatessen in the city, but lived in the suburbs. His father was moderately well to do by New York standards, but not rich. Harry had an older sister who studied music at New York City College and was now working as an assistant director of musicals on Broadway. Harry had a prominent nose upon which rested a pair of gold rimmed spectacles. He wore a Tommy Hilfiger shirt, open at the neck and short sleeved. His pants were neatly creased, covering a pair of highly polished shoes and white socks.

Daniel Chan was from the San Jose area. His parents ran a Chinese restaurant, an establishment handed down over the generations from father to son. Dan, as he preferred to be called, had two sisters who helped their parents operate the eatery, but Dan wanted nothing to do with it. Dan was tall, well groomed and soft spoken.

For a couple of hours, the team conversed about the upcoming session and established a work-plan to address their relationships. The chemistry, which would bond them together later, was apparent from the onset.

After their initial study group meeting, they decided to go out for a drink to celebrate their new friendship. One of the more popular places nearby was a tavern catering to the college students and staff.

None of the group had much money, so they decided to go at Happy Hour and save a few dollars.

The afternoon was still early, so when they arrived the place was only partially full. The outside windows were covered with advertising, so the amount of light in the place was at a minimum. They found a table in the back which would fit their needs and sat down. A young waitress asked for their order and soon returned with their drinks.

The discussions had left them thirsty and dry. The drinks were consumed much too quickly and another round was ordered. Somewhere Juan found a few extra dollars in a secret pocket of his wallet. The gesture endeared him to the group. They joked easily with each other, stopping on occasion to play a game of darts. The competition was fierce with William winning the first game and Candice the second. Juan knew he was in for the time of his life with this aggressive bunch.

CHAPTER THIRTY-FOUR

The date of Mary's arrival came at last. The drive from Juan's condo to L.A.X. would take about an hour, so Juan left early enough to make sure he was at the arrival gate when she walked through the portal. It had been some time since they had been together and Juan wondered if the love they had come to know was still there. Juan's anxiety level seemed to spiral upward as the minutes ticked off the clock. Why hadn't he taken those Yoga classes he had read about.

As he was about to explode, Mary walked into view. She was the most ravishing thing he had ever seen. She was still in her khaki uniform, with three rows of colorful ribbons emblazoned on her left chest. Decorations for the service she had provided to her country. On the right side were two meritorious unit citations for the work the hospital had done supporting the infantry division and the Vietnamese Army.

In a couple of long strides he reached out, whisked her up into his arms and kissed her savagely. She returned the favor with great intensity. For a few moments after they separated their lips, they just gazed into each other's eyes. The love was there, they both could feel it.

They soon claimed Mary's luggage, found the car in the parking lot and started back to San Barbara. Juan wanted to know all about the recent past and what plans Mary had for the future. She slowed him down a little and answered.

"I will be able to stay with you for just two weeks as I told you before. Then I have to move on to the hospital for the required introductory tour of the facility and assignment to one of the wards. That will give us a chance to have some fun together before your schooling starts. I want to finish up some time on this tour of duty, so don't be mad at me if I suggest we wait a while before we decide to get married."

Juan knew she was right. They had talked at length about getting married when they were in Vietnam, but had not made any definite plans. Juan knew they didn't have the money to support two people but the only the feasible choice of waiting gnawed at his stomach.

"Besides", Mary continued, " I can always catch a military hop from Andrews Air Force Base to the base outside of Santa Barbara several times a year. This will save our precious few resources and we can still see each other as our fate moves along. I have also decided to complete my obligation to the Army and then find a job in a civilian hospital here in southern California. By then you will be finished with your schooling and with both of us working, we can get married."

"You are a marvel, so logical and so beautiful. I will hate to be away from you again, but hopefully the time will pass quickly and we can consummate our relationship for all time."

Mary asked about Juan's progress so far. He told her about Kyle Smith and his help. He also delved into the makeup of his new group and how much he liked them. He confessed he wasn't sure how well he would do in law school, but felt, with the support of the team, he would do just fine.

Before they knew it, the condo was in sight just up the street. Juan slowed the car to let Mary savor the surroundings. She was enthralled with the lovely homes, the manicured lawns and the wonderful weather. Unlike Vietnam, the temperatures stayed moderate most of the year. Each morning a light fog would rise from the ocean, but soon the day would become sunny. A soft current of air would waif onshore, giving the atmosphere a hint of salt spray. Mary knew she would fall in love with a city like this.

Mary stepped out of the car and waited until Juan unlocked the trunk and retrieved her luggage. He then led her up the steps, setting the bags down long enough to unlock the front door. As Mary entered the main portal, she said, "What a beautiful place. Who did you say rented this to you?"

"Let me tell you about that later. For now, why don't you take a shower and change into something a little more comfortable."

Juan wanted to make love to immediately, but sensed she was tired and didn't want to spoil her homecoming. He placed her things in the guest bedroom and showed her where to find the towels. He turned to leave her alone, letting her know he would fix dinner for them to eat on the patio.

Juan was not a gourmet cook, but did know enough to make a passable meal. He knew Mary's favorite was salmon with a lemon dill sauce and small red potatoes served with a light Chardonnay wine. He had purchased a couple of filets and decided to put them on the small Hibachi grill he had outside. The lemon sauce he had purchased from a deli, which specialized in take out creams and sauces. The small red potatoes he put in a steamer and turned it on. He sat two place mats on the glass table, along with matching cloth napkins and silverware. He had also managed to procure a vase full of fresh flowers and a candle to add atmosphere to the setting.

He commenced at once to fashion a tossed green salad and put the filets on the grill to cook. As the ingredients were beginning to be done, he opened the wine to let it air just a little. The timing couldn't have been better. Just as the food was finished cooking, Mary stepped into the kitchen in a pair of Bermuda shorts, sandals and a halter-top. Her hair was still wet from the shower and hung limply from her head. She looked like a nymph just emerging from the mist of the forest. Juan handed her a glass of wine and took her outside to see the view of the city and the ocean.

As she gently sipped on the delicious liquid, Juan finished up the meal, placing the salads on the table along with some Blue Cheese dressing, then dished up the potatoes, with fresh asparagus and went to retrieve the salmon. They sat, pouring the lemon sauce from a small pitcher over the fish. They didn't say much, they just enjoyed looking at each other and savoring each wonderful bite.

When they had finished the meal, Juan cleared the plates, telling Mary to sit still and then Juan refilled their glasses with the remainder of the bottle. Juan embellished his story about Kyle Smith and his graciousness. He also elaborated about his study group and the beginning courses he was about to tackle. He asked her about her trip and her next steps. They didn't approach the subject of getting married, which had already been decided. The wine was taking effect and Mary shuddered with exhaustion. Juan escorted her to the bedroom, helped her get undressed and placed her in bed. She immediately fell asleep. Juan stood over her like a guardian angel and watched the peaceful demeanor pass over her tanned face.

For the next two weeks they made love often, toured the city, met the study group, walked on the beach and in general just enjoyed each other's company. One day, they dropped by Kyle's office so Juan could show Mary off. Kyle then took them to lunch at a very expensive restaurant.

"Well Mary, you certainly are a sight for these tired old eyes. Juan said you were beautiful, but he missed the description by a mile. You are far more than beautiful. I can hardly wait for the two of you to get married. And if you decide to join me in politics, I will make sure everyone gets a chance to benefit from you charm."

Mary blushed slightly. "Kyle, you don't know how much I appreciate that. I do hope everything will work out for Juan and you. In case Juan hadn't told you, we plan to unite in holy matrimony as soon as Juan passes the bar. I have had enough of Army life and am looking forward to settling down and being catered to by the most handsome man on earth."

The next hour was filled with small talk and a delicious desert. Kyle excused himself, telling them he had to get back to the office for an appointment, but they could stay as long as they liked. He motioned to the matre'd, letting him know the lunch was on the business account and the couple at his table were to be well taken care of. Kyle slipped the headwaiter a hundred dollar bill to ensure his attention to Juan and Mary.

CHAPTER THIRTY-FIVE

The vacation ended much too soon, but both Mary and Juan knew they must move on to getting the necessities done in their lives. Juan took her to the airport, sat with her in the terminal until her flight was announced and then walked her to the gate. He kissed her gently and watched as the tunnel swallowed her up like Jonah and the whale. He remained in the boarding area watching her plane taxi and then lift off on it's way to Washington D.C.

That Sunday, Juan attended Mass. Juan wanted God to know he needed His help as much as possible. He received communion and lit a candle for his lover.

Monday, all hell broke lose. Juan attended his first lecture in the grand hall. The room was overflowing with students. The atmosphere sounded alive with a hum reminiscent of a beehive. The students were a mixed bag, like a crowd in mid city Los Angeles. Males and females of every description and hue. Some knew each other and were nose to nose in heated discussions like angry bulls. Others were looking about the hall seeking out a possible lay for the evening, or someone to follow up on later. Some sat silently in their seats, their eyes diverted to the ceiling or the floor. Juan sat with Candice, William, Henry and Daniel about halfway up the row of seats.

The day outside was sunny, clouds drifting along like wisps of cotton candy. Even though the temperature was in the high 70s, the heat generated from the assemblage seemed almost overpowering. How could anyone think in this situation Juan thought to himself. Suddenly, like a suspense filled moment at the end of a horror movie, a hush came of the crowd. Everyone's eyes turned to a small, ornate door to the rear of the stage.

A short, grossly obese, balding professor entered carrying his briefcase in his right hand. He approached the podium, opened the case and deposited a sheaf of papers on the dais table placed next to the podium. He extracted a few pages off the top and placed them before him. He was dressed in a woolen, plaid sports coat with a pair of non-matching slacks. His shirt was a black button down variety with an orange bow tie, which seemed to give his lower jaw the glow of a Halloween pumpkin. His shoes were brown and he was not wearing any socks. Professor Tillman began his lecture.

Professor Tillman was a local phenomenon. His stature was legendary in the legal education business. He had written over twenty texts used in almost all of the universities in the nation and in several foreign countries. He was the Dean of the Law School and a force to be reckoned with. By word of mouth, everyone was told to keep their mouths shut and listen. A person would be ill advised to cross swords with this man. It was rumored if you garnered his favor, he could help you get into any position in any law firm you desired. None other excelled his placement of students, in lucrative corporate firms and in government positions.

Professor Tillman gazed at the class and the words began. Even though the warmth of the room made everyone drowsy, no one dared to bring down his wrath by catching you falling asleep. At one point, Juan wished he had brought along some tape to affix from his eyelids to his brow to keep his eyes open. Somehow, as if a miracle had occurred, the forty-five minute stint was over and Juan was still awake. As the professor exited the hall, Juan shook his head to clear away the cobwebs, rose with his friends and shuffled off to the next class. The ordeal had begun.

When the first day was over, Juan couldn't remember when he had been so tired, but as promised to the study group, he caught a quick bite to eat and joined them in one of the student study closets. The group looked like a row of washed out socks hanging on an outdoor clothesline, but after a cup of coffee and some donuts gave them a sugar high, they settled into the task at hand.

The session went well and the bonding strengthened like adding reinforcing rods to cement. The assignments handed out at the lecture were divided up with each member researching his or her share in the library the next morning. Time management became an absolute necessity for them. Even though they didn't have classes all day long, there was so much to read and discuss, the morning, midday and evening hours were critical.

And so their learning evolved. For the next four months, they crammed their heads as full as a stuffed turkey at Thanksgiving. There were times when Juan felt as though his cranium was going to burst open like an overripe watermelon. They made up cue cards to test each other and devised other tricks to help them remember the salient points of each subject. As the end of the term examinations loomed, the stress level grew to that of expectant parents about to deliver their first child. They felt like rookies on the verge of their first major league baseball game facing a Cy Young winner on the mound.

Drinking coffee didn't always do the job keeping them awake to study, but an answer to the need to be alert came in an unusual package. One of the pre-med students the group had met at the local watering hole also worked in a local pharmacy which had two doctor's offices in the back of the building. One of the tasks the pharmacy employee performed each evening was to open the drug samples the nurses next door brought over and put the samples in the stock bottles on the pharmacy shelves. The nurses didn't mind helping out the pharmacy owner, because the pharmaceutical companies plied the offices with far more than the physicians could hand out.

One of the prized samples were capsules filled with dextro-amphetamine, uppers used to treat obesity, but was also prescribed, on the sly, to truck drivers to keep them awake on long hauls. Back in those days, the amphetamines were not put under control as were the narcotics, so slipping a few into the pocket and disbursing them to friends didn't seem like a criminal act.

One capsule would last for twenty-four hours. The night before the final exams, Juan doled out one precious capsule to each of his friends and the marathon began. Juan couldn't believe how powerful these drugs were. The tiredness disappeared and his mind became razor sharp. His thoughts raced like a hundred yard sprinter and everything came into clear focus as if he were adjusting the lens of a pair of binoculars.

Into the night they studied, not stopping to eat since the drug suppressed the appetite and none of them were hungry in the slightest. They didn't even realize the sun had come up until Juan looked at his watch and it was only an hour before the reckoning. They all decided to take a shower, change their clothes and get to the examination area. They bid each other the best of luck and went their separate ways to clean up.

At the stroke of the hour, each student was seated in their assigned chair type desks and handed two small notebooks with light blue covers and two sharpened pencils. They were instructed to enter their names in the upper right hand corner of the first blank page, the date of the exam and the exam title. Juan carefully folded back the blue cover and did what he was asked. When everyone had completed this simple instruction, the mentor handed out the exam. The race was on.

As the end of the two-hour period came to a close, a warning was given that the students only had ten minutes left to finish. At the end of the ten minutes, a horn was to be sounded and the students were to cease their writing whether they had completed the exam or not. Upon ceasing their writing, they were to close the covers on the notebooks and wait for the notebooks to be picked up. The mentor, a teaching assistant of Professor Tillman's, a dour, chestnut haired witchlike looking individual sounded the horn and circulated herself through the group collecting the books and pencils. The class was then excused.

When Juan got back to his condo, the effects of the capsule had begun to wear off. He had been escorted to the highest levels of awareness, but now was being dropped into the vast depth of darkness. For hours, every neuron in his brain had been firing. Now, like a stalemate on the battlefield, every fiber in his body relaxed and he barely made it to his bed before he fell into a comatose state.

When he woke up, the sun was going down in the west. He glanced at his bedside clock and it registered early evening. Good, he thought until he realized he had slept for over twenty-four hours. You dummy, he chided himself, it is a blessing that it is a Saturday and he had nowhere to go. He didn't feel like sleeping anymore, so he moved on to the kitchen to fix himself some food. He set the coffee maker in motion, opened the refrigerator door and withdrew a carton of orange juice and a tray of eggs. He broke three eggs into a bowl, added some milk and sloshed the mixture into a greased skillet. He popped some toast into the toaster and set the table. He stirred the eggs into a scrambled state and removed the skillet from the burners as he buttered his toast. He liked a little salsa on his eggs; luckily he had some in the cupboard. Juan was famished and wolfed down the eggs he had prepared. Juan spent the rest of the evening watching the late shows on TV and went back to bed after midnight.

The next morning, Juan showered, shaved and put on a clean tee shirt, his jeans and a short jacket. He left the condo and walked down the street to an all night convenience store for the Sunday newspaper. The morning was filled with a light mist, giving the street the feeling of being covered in cobwebs. He should have worn a baseball cap he thought to himself, but didn't mind the weather soaking his hair.

He spent the rest of the day reading the paper, catching up on the local and national happenings. The next election year was over eighteen months off, but the paper was filled with the initial gamblings of those who were thinking about running for some sort of office either at the state or national level. The trade deficit was increasing, as was the national debt. How stupid can the President and Congress be Juan internalized, to let this be happening? "This wouldn't happen if I were President" Juan said out loud. Crime was also on the rise, especially in the aftermath of the Watts riots. This alarmed Juan, knowing something had to be done to reverse this trend, but what could he do except wait until he was in a position to do something about it.

The next morning since classes had been suspended because of the exams, Juan had Monday off. The sun was rising in the east like an orange colored balloon, chasing away the mist like a chambermaid sweeping the floor. Juan had changed into his jogging outfit and took off toward the beach to burn off the food he had consumed. To his surprise, the beach was filled with early morning sojourners, some with playful dogs and some with significant others. As he ran, Juan shook the last vestiges of school from his head and picked up the pace. By the time he reached the pier at the center of town, he was exhausted and leisurely strolled back home. He took another shower and called Mary.

"Hope I didn't wake you", Juan said into the telephone.

"No darling, I have the day off, but have been up for a couple of hours. I thought I would sleep in, but I couldn't. To what do I owed the privilege of this call?"

"Nothing in particular, I just wanted to tell you I love you and to let you know I took the final term exams on Friday. We'll know the results in a few days, I hope I did well."

"A man with your looks and brains, no sweat."

"I wish you were here with me when I find out, but that is only wishful thinking."

"Don't worry, I am flying out in a couple of weeks to see you and I can assure you, we will celebrate a very successful outcome."

Juan and Mary chatted blithely about trivia mostly, and then rang off. Life was good and continuing to get better.

CHAPTER THIRTY-SIX

Juan had done extremely well in all of the examinations he had taken. The rest of the school year raced by reaching super sonic proportions. Before Juan knew it, spring had come and gone and summer was raising its beautiful head. Juan had availed himself of every moment to indulge in the mastery of the law. When he wasn't studying with the group or attending classes, he found himself in the law library cross-referencing the cases, which had set the precedence for the way society conducted itself. His brain was soaking up information at a rapid rate, filling his gray matter like a gigantic sponge until it was saturated. Juan wasn't sure where he was going to put another atom of information, but his brain seemed to expand with each session.

The quest didn't cease with the summer. Juan enrolled in the summer sessions to keep the momentum going. The sessions from May to September were of even more value to Juan. The classes were smaller and the teaching assistants to student ratios were very low. This gave Juan a chance to exchange debates with the mentors, while at the same time sharpening his argumentative skills.

When fall exploded onto the scene, the hard work Juan's hard work had come to the attention of Professor Tillman. Word had filtered to the dean about Juan's dedication, his charisma and his expanding knowledge of the law. Although it was usually given to a third year student, Professor Tillman awarded Juan the editorship of the monthly law review for the college. The UCSB review, like the Harvard Review, was the most prestigious position around. It gave Juan the opportunity to write and present his arguments for how the law might be altered or applied depending on the cases before the various courts across the country. The review was not only read by the students, but was widely circulated throughout the State of California and exchanged with other law colleges.

After performing as the top man, Juan was jubilant when the UCSB review was given the American Bar Association's award for best publication among the nation's law colleges. The presentation was to be made in Washington D.C. at the ABA's annual meeting. Juan, and professor Tillman were granted release by the college to attend. Together they flew back east, which gave each of them time to get to know each other personally. During the flight they conversed amiably, sharing insights into their respective philosophies and life styles. Juan did more listening than speaking, a quality that would serve him well in the future. Professor Tillman gave Juan many pointers on how to circulate within the arenas of legal application and what pitfall to watch out for.

"Don't trust anyone is the best advice I can give you. As the old adage goes, keep your friends close, but keep your enemies closer. Learn to trust your instincts. If your gut tells you something is amiss, then it is amiss. Develop an attitude of scrutiny, while never letting on you are trying to discover the hidden agendas of people in the profession. Over time, you will know who your allies are and who you need to cultivate to help you out."

Juan and the professor were met at the airport by a representative of the association and whisked away in a long black limousine to the hotel. They had been pre-registered and were taken immediately to their rooms. The presentation was slated to take place at the awards banquet the next night, so it gave Juan the entire day to look around D.C., and to inhale all of the history the center of the world's greatest superpower had amassed. He had already called Mary and told her he was coming, so they made arrangements to meet and to do the town.

Juan was staying in a room at the Hyatt Regency, a massive hotel near Georgetown and the site of the Bar Association's meeting and banquet. Juan and Mary spent the day doing what most tourists do, visiting the Lincoln Memorial, the Washington Monument, strolling past the reflecting pool, marveling at the displays in the Smithsonian Museum and viewing the White House. After a fun filled day, they took a shower, made love and took a short nap. Then it was time to get ready for the awards ceremony.

Juan had never worn a tuxedo before, so Mary assisted him in placing the black onyx studs in the front of the stiff shirt, placing the similar links in the cuffs and tying the black bowtie around his neck. Juan marveled at himself in the full-length mirror. He stared back at an image which reminded him of the undertakers in Mexico City who carted away the dead to be buried. He shook his head repulsed at the idea, then felt a sense of gratification at how fortunate he was.

Mary was dressed in an evening gown made of a thousand sequins and reaching to the floor. Her shoes matched the dress and she wore long diamond earrings. Her hair was piled high on her head and secured in place with a faux diamond tiara. When she made her grand entrance from the bedroom, Juan swooned. He had never seen anything so beautiful in his life.

Juan had ordered a small bottle of champagne for the occasion. He withdrew the bottle from the ice bucket left by room service and popped the cork. He filled both glasses to the brim and proposed a toast. They looked into each other's eyes and slowly sipped the potent potable.

Professor Tillman had made prior arrangements to meet them in the lobby at six o'clock. That was the time the schedule of events indicated was the hour to start the festivities. The banquet was preceded by a social period where guests were to mingle and renew old friendships or create new ones. The social hour would be followed by the food and the awards.

The hotel had set aside two very large ballrooms, one for the gathering and one for the banquet. A sliding door separated the two rooms until 7 o'clock, then the doors would be withdrawn into the walls and the guests would wander to the numbered round tables. As the three of them made their way into the first ballroom, Juan could not believe his eyes. The room was filled with over a thousand people all dressed in their finery. The room reminded Juan of a documentary he had seen once on the National Geographic Channel about penguins. Everywhere he looked, he spied men walking around in stark black and white.

There were lawyers everywhere as well as invited dignitaries. The women had taken out all stops in their apparel. There were attorneys from across the nation, lobbyists from the D.C. area, Senators and Congressmen and foreign wannabees there for the connections. Professor Tillman suddenly spotted a familiar face, raised his hand and beckoned toward the individual and his spouse. A tall, distinguished man nodded in recognition, grasped his wife's elbow and steered her toward them.

The two men clasped their hands and pumped their limbs feverishly. Tillman gave the woman a perfunctory kiss and a greeting. He then turned to Juan and Mary.

"Mr. Vice President, let me present my two friends Juan and Mary. Juan and Mary, this is the second most powerful man in the nation and a former student of mine."

The Vice President, Mark Chandler, shook both their hands, smiled a well practice smile and spoke.

"So this is the latest in a long line of protégés? Juan, I have heard so much about you. The professor says you have the intelligence and drive to someday take my job. I certainly hope you give me some time before you do." He finished with a genuine laugh. He then introduced his wife Paula who likewise shook their hands.

Mark was a mountain of a man and soulful looking. His face was lined with deep furrows, which had occurred either through many periods of laughter, or many hours of deep thought and concern. His eyes were gray and searching. He was aging as was evident by the liver spots on the backs of his hands, but he carried his age well.

Paula was a matronly woman, shorter than her husband and broader due to the availability of the exquisite cuisine found at the many parties she and her husband had to attend. She wore a black gown to hide some of the weight. The gown was low cut and the generous cleavage looked deep enough to hide a business length envelope without any trouble. She was younger than Mark, probably a trophy wife at one time. She moved in on Mary, took her under her wing and whisked her off to meet some of the other guests.

The Vice President took it upon himself to maneuver Juan and the professor about the facility, stopping to chat and introduce them to some of the powerful luminaries of the Washington scene. Juan was overwhelmed by the names. Corporate CEO's, majority leaders, key strategists, power brokers and an array of judges whose names tripped lightly off Mark's tongue. Juan floated about the room as if he were in a stupor or a fantasy akin to a Walt Disney movie. But before he knew it, the social hour had ended, a bell chimed and the walls slid silently aside exposing the luxuriously furnished banquet hall.

Since Juan was one of the recipients of an award, the Vice President directed them to an aide who escorted them to the head table. Mary had rejoined Juan and they located their place cards and stood behind their chairs until all of the head table participants were assembled. The salads were already on the table and the President of the Bar Association started the meal by lifting his fork and stabbing a piece of lettuce. Soft music began in the background played by an orchestra chamber ensemble.

Juan was seated next to the Vice President who was chosen to deliver the keynote address. Mary was placed next to the Veep's wife. During the meal they exchanged small talk, and Juan enjoying the exchange immensely. When the dinner was finished and the keynote speech rendered, the awards ceremony began. The emcee was a young attorney with a great gift of gab and a robust sense of humor. In no time, he had the crowd in a jovial mood. As each award recipient was called forward, they gave a short acceptance acknowledgement and receive a rousing round of applause. When Juan's name was called, he arose and moved forward to the presenter. When he was handed a beautifully engraved plague, the emcee shook his hand and they posed for the obligatory photo. Juan faced the crowd, thanked everyone and announced that someday he would be head of his country. Everyone chuckled, thinking he meant Mexico, not realizing he meant the United States.

The meeting was fun, but tiring. The next morning Juan said good-bye to Mary and saw her off in a taxi. When she was gone, Juan and Professor Tillman checked out of the hotel and returned to Santa Barbara.

CHAPTER THIRTY-SEVEN

At the end of the second year of law school, Juan felt he had met all of the requirements to take the bar exam. He had focused so hard on the material he needed to know and had so deprived himself of all worldly pleasures, except for of Mary, he felt he had earned the right to do this. He met with Professor Tillman, receiving the old man's blessing and encouragement. The next day he applied for and was granted the right to take the bar exam. The exam was a grueling exercise in cerebral evacuation. Juan felt like every cell in his gray matter had been squeezed dry of information implanted there over the past twenty-four months. He had never done anything this exhausting. He felt as if he had run two marathons, back to back and winning both at great expense. He could now only wait for the results. They finally came. Juan had passed the bar on the first try.

Juan couldn't wait to relate the good news to Professor Tillman. He knew the professor had class at this time, but the class would be over in less than half an hour, so Juan strolled leisurely across the campus to his office. Juan had become friendly with the teaching assistants and the secretary for the dean, so he had no difficulty being allowed to enter Tillman's office, find a comfortable seat on one of the overstuffed chairs and lean his head back on the cushion.

His mind became a marquee of colors. Millions of possibilities began to surface into his thought process. What would be his next move, where would he go, what job should he apply for? Like a rapid firing machine gun, more questions surged out into the open. He was sure the professor would give him some sage advice.

Juan heard the familiar shuffle of Tillman's feet coming down the hall. Juan arose as the professor came through the door. "My secretary said you had something important, something that you couldn't wait to tell me. Well, what is it."

"I passed the bar", Juan blurted out and began to mutter almost incoherently, his request for assistance.

"Hold on just a second, slow down and let's get to the bottom of this."

Juan paused, gathered himself and began again. "Professor, there isn't anyone else in the world I respect more than you. I value your judgment above all others and I desperately need your assistance. Having passed the bar, I won't be attending classes anymore, so I need some strategic plan for my future. I immediately thought of you and all of the guidance you have given me in the past. I hate to intrude on our relationship, but I don't know where else to turn."

"Well, let's take a few moments to savor your achievement and then we will discuss the possibilities." The dean then moved toward one of the paneled walls, stuck a key into one of the boards and opened a secret hiding place where he kept his personal stash of libation for special occasions. He withdrew two crystal, solid bottomed glasses and filled them with two fingers of twelve year old Scotch. He swirled the caramel colored liquid around and handed one of the glasses to Juan.

They each took a long sip, relishing the smoothness of the fine whiskey. Juan wasn't much of a hard liquor drinker, so the fluid burned his throat slightly, giving him the urge to cough. He took in a breath of air and felt the alcohol begin to bring a flush to his cheeks and a warming sensation to his body. They both sat on a couch nestled against one wall and the counseling session began.

"First, we need to find you a position where you can learn the intricacies of the field of law and a position where you can launch yourself into the political arena. I do know Kyle Smith also wants you to help him run for the U.S. Senate and I think I have the solution that will accomplish both ends. I know you have been working part time for Kyle, but that hasn't given you much of a head start. You just haven't had the time to devote to that effort. The best way to proceed, in my opinion, is to work for the county district attorney's office. This will give you trial experience and exposure to a great many issues passing through the state and federal courts. It will also expose you to the media, the public defenders office and the city government. The job as an assistant DA doesn't pay that much, but will provide you with sufficient income to meet your needs. It will also give you enough flexibility to help Kyle with his campaign. Let me make a few phone calls and I will contact you later in the week with what I am able to do for you."

With that, they finished their drinks and Professor Tillman excused Juan from his office. As Juan left the building, there was a lilt in his step and a contented smile complimented with a background of brilliant white teeth. Life is good and about to get better.

Juan couldn't wait to get home and call Mary with the good news. The time was right for the two of them to stop the transcontinental flights and get down to some serious togetherness. He couldn't imagine a life without her. As he drove home, it seemed every car that passed held someone who was smiling at him. People sharing his good fortune and happiness. Juan waved at each and every one of them, exuding joy from every pore of his body.

He unlocked the door; kicked his way through the living room, vowing this weekend he would clean the place up. He quickly dialed Mary's number from memory. The phone rang the obligatory four times and then diverted the call to an answering service.

"Whomever you are, I am sorry I am not here to speak to you directly. Please leave me a good reason to return your call and I will try. No promises."

Juan spoke his message into the phone and gently reseated the phone onto its cradle. Juan smiled, went to the refrigerator and opened a fresh bottle of his favorite wine to celebrate. He hadn't really planned it that way, but before he knew it, the bottle was gone, as had a second one. Juan didn't care. On top of the Scotch he drank in Professor Tillman's office, he was the happiest man on earth at this very moment. He danced around the kitchen like a lovesick ninny, wrapping his arms around himself in mock affection. He crashed into the cupboards several times before he realized how drunk he was and collapsed onto one of the kitchen chairs. He buried his head in his hands, laughed and then cried with joy.

Sobering up a little, Juan went to the bathroom vowing to stop this type of behavior in the coming years. He turned on the hot water into the tub, removed his clothes and submerged himself into the steamy relief. He soaked until his skin took on a reptilian luster and the water had turned cool. He emerged, toweled himself off and fell into bed naked. At three o'clock in the morning, the telephone rang sounding like a fire engine inside Juan's head. His head couldn't have hurt any worse even if he had pounded it with a sledgehammer. He managed to whisper hello.

"Juan, this is Mary, are you all right?"

With his head clearing, Juan replied, "I am now. Just hearing your wonderful voice has made things all better." He went on to explain his celebration and to tell her about his good fortunes. They chatted for over an hour agreeing to be married when Mary's tour of duty at Walter Reed was over, which was due to happen in a few months. They agreed to live in the condo if it was okay with Kyle and then look for a place of their own later on. They ended with kisses into the voice box of the phone. Juan crept out of bed, found two aspirin tablets in the bathroom cabinet and swallowed them dry. He was repulsed when the acid flavor of the medicine descended down his throat. He turned on the cold-water faucet and diluted the sting. Feeling somewhat the worse for wear, he returned to the bed and didn't wake up until well into the morning.

CHAPTER THIRTY-EIGHT

When Juan was fully awake and functioning, he fixed himself some breakfast. As the eggs and bacon were simmering in the frying pan, he popped a couple of slices of wheat bread into the toaster, turned the bacon over and poured himself a cup of the dark molten brew he called coffee. Slowly, but surely, the gauze covering his eyes was starting to dissolve from the confines of his brain. He finished his morning repast, washed up the dishes and utensils and began the task of straightening up his condo. Partly through his labors, the phone rang again. This time, the pain was gone and he answered in a slightly more coherent way.

This time, the call came from an unfamiliar feminine voice. "Mr. Cardova, this is Sarah Blume, the Santa Barbara District Attorney, are you free to talk."

"Certainly Ms. Blume, or is it Mrs. Blume, I want to be politically correct."

"Oh, it's Mrs. Blume, but please call me Sarah. I don't stand much on political correctness when I am hiring a new employee."

Juan was flabbergasted. Here was a high profile individual offering him a job without having ever seen him. Juan tried to picture Sarah, he had never seen her either. Her voice was low, almost contralto in range, with a slightly sexy tone intermingled. He imagined her to be tall, brunette, white skinned with a California tan, and her hair pulled back into a severe bun.

"Did you say, hiring a new employee?"

"That I did."

"But you don't even know me."

"I don't have to. The word of Professor Tillman and State Senator Smith are good enough for me. I've had a chance to read your resume and I am convinced you are the round peg I need to complete my staff. I would like to meet you however, just to make things appear to be on the up and up. The interview shouldn't take too long and then I can have my chief assistant district attorney escort you through the office and get you settled in. Can you come by my building, say 3 o'clock tomorrow afternoon?"

"That would be great. Thank you so much for extending me this great privilege. I know you won't be disappointed."

With that, Sarah rang off. Juan didn't move. He held the phone in his hand as if it were a sacred icon spouting favors to the unworthy. The next day he wanted to present his best side, so he chose a dark blue, single-breasted suit with a white buttoned down collar and an Ivy League style diagonally striped tie. He put on black socks and wore his lace up black shoes. When he was finished, he admired himself in the mirror. Internally he remarked to himself, what a hunk!

The drive to the District Attorney's office was leisurely. The day had arrived sunny after the usual morning happenings and the temperature remained in the moderate range as it always did in this part of the state. Juan found a visitor's parking stall in front of the building. The regulatory sign said "One Hour Parking", which he felt would be more than adequate for his needs. He applied his parking brakes, turned off the engine and remained in his seat for a few minutes to gather his thoughts and clear any clouds remaining from his celebration. When he felt everything was in place, he exited his car, straightened his suit and tie, glanced up at the multifaceted plate glass building and entered through the rotating glass door.

Security was always tight in buildings housing law enforcement agencies; the District Attorney's building was no exception. Just inside the front door was a reception area restricting access to the elevators and the inner bowels of the structure. Behind the reception desk sat a security guard who could have Bubba's twin. A huge, thirty year old type with no neck and a uniform of light blue with contrasting dark blue pocket flaps. His brown hair was cut in a military style "Butch" haircut and he was clean-shaven. His eyes were deep and gave a no nonsense look.

Juan approached the desk, remaining still until the guard noticed him.

"Could I help you sir," the guard said in a clipped way.

"Yes", Juan replied, "My name is Juan Cardova, and I am here to see District Attorney Sarah Blume."

The guard withdrew a clipboard from a corner of his desk, running his fingers down the columns until a stubby digit rested on Juan's name.

"Yes, Mr. Cardova, your name is on the register. Do you have some sort of photo identification to verify who you are?"

Juan took his wallet from his back pocket, extracted his driver's license from one of the plastic slots and handed it to the guard. The security person glanced at the card, then looked into Juan's face and returned the card.

"Wait here a few minutes. I will call upstairs for an escort for you."

With that, the guard, his nametag stating he was Jeff, picked up the phone and in an efficient and well-rehearsed manner, dialed a three number sequence. Covering the phone with his hand, Jeff spoke softly and returned the hand piece. "An assistant District Attorney will be with you presently, please have a seat."

It wasn't long until a young, slightly plump blonde appeared from one of the elevators. She walked with confidence across the expanse between the elevator and the security desk until she had reached Juan's location. She extended her slender, well-manicured hand to Juan as a token of introduction. She didn't smile, but held her face in strict reserve. She told Juan her name was Terry, one of the many assistant district attorneys in the building. They exchanged pleasantries as Terry led the way to the sixth floor, the seat of power.

No conversation was exchanged as the elevator slowly glided up its path. They came to a stop at the appointed floor, the doors opened and they disembarked. The main foyer of the District Attorney's headquarters was nice, but not overwhelming. It did not reek of the opulence found in the federal courthouses, but bespoke a certain sense of efficiency and status. The hallways were filled with photographs of previous District Attorneys and historical pictures of past Santa Barbara scenery. In the center of the hallway leading to Sarah's office was an aquarium filled with a mixture of tropical fish, gliding along in their mesmerizing fashion.

Juan and Terry entered Sarah's office as the District Attorney rose from her high backed chair to greet them. Sarah was exactly as Juan had imagined. She is a woman who commanded attention. She had a presence that one cannot mistake. Her handshake was firm and dry. She excused Terry and invited Juan to sit on a nearby settee.

For the next fifteen minutes or so, they chatted about Juan's background, his law school experiences, his military prowess and his goals for the future. When they had finished, Sarah wanted Juan to know that she felt all of her assistants must master the entire workings of the office, and rotating Juan through the various departments she supervised would accomplish this. She was well aware of the need State Senator Smith had for Juan's services and let Juan know there would be ample time for him to work on Smith's campaign and also do his own job. Juan got the sense Sarah was a political animal as well and certainly having a token minority around would do much to enhance her potential.

Juan would start in the fraud division and then rotate through vice, homicide, and do some research with the city DAs. Sarah concluded the interview and left her door open to Juan if he ever needed her advice. Terry led Juan out of the office; back to the elevator and down to the second floor, the hub of operations for the assistant DAs. It was a large open area divided into separate working spaces partitioned off by six-foot high, padded moveable walls. In the center of the room was the stenographer's pool where all of the filing, typing and other administrative functions took place. Terry found Juan a space and left him temporarily to look around. The cubicle was approximately twelve feet by ten feet. Not a lot of room, but sufficient for Juan's needs. There was a corner desk, which took up two walls and held an efficiency desk with shelves. In the corner were a computer and printer. On the other panel were bookcases filled with law books Juan would need for instant research. The main law library was on the third floor and this would save Juan from having to leave his so-called office very often. There were a couple of upholstered chairs, an end table with a lamp and a small sofa. The panels were devoid of any decorations, the office leaving that to the personal taste of the occupant.

The space was clean and well lighted. Juan felt he would like this place.

CHAPTER THIRTY-NINE

Before Juan assumed his duties as assistant DA, Sarah graciously gave him some time off to get married. Mary had completed her tour with the Army Medical Department and would be moving her belongings to California. Mary lost both of her parents in an automobile accident when was just a little girl, so she had no one to help her plan the wedding on. Her prayers were answered when Kyle Smith and his lovely wife Tara agreed to assume that responsibility. Kyle insisted the wedding take place at their manor overlooking the ocean. Juan could not imagine a setting anymore wonderful.

As promised, Mary arrived at the condo, her car stuffed to the gills with personal items. She explained the Army would be sending the remainder of her things in a short time. Part of separating from the service is the benefit of having your things sent to a final destination. As Mary exited the vehicle, she was more radiant than Juan remembered. He rushed down the agate-surfaced staircase, sweeping her into his arms. He gently kissed her on the lips, then kissed her much deeper and with greater feeling. Mary threw her arms around his neck and returned the favor.

They separated, then looking lovingly into each other's eyes, oblivious of the neighbors staring at them. Hand in hand, they walked up the stairs and made a beeline for the bedroom. When they were finished, they lay there exhausted, but realized someone might find the open car tempting goods. Quickly they got dressed and retrieved everything from the street.

The next week was a flurry of activity. Mrs. Smith took Mary to the area's finest clothing outlets to procure a wedding dress and arrange for the bridal party. In the meantime, Juan had asked Kyle to be his best man and Kyle had readily agreed. Mrs. Smith had arranged for her eight year old twin niece and nephew to be the ring bearers. Tara placed an immediate call to their church's pastor begging him to perform the ceremony. Fortunately, he was free for the set date. Photographers, caterers, parking valets and bar tenders were all secured. The Smith's backyard was miraculously transformed into a lover's Eden. A guest list was prepared and the invitations sent out. The guest list included not only Wally, Bubba, Travis, Shannon, Professor Tillman, and many other friends that had been in Juan's life, but also included some of the most influential personages in the state and federal governments. No expense was spared.

As the sacred time neared, Juan insisted there was no way he could accept Kyle's generosity and vowed he would repay every penny spent. Without hesitation, Kyle clasped Juan tightly in a bear hug, and assured him he would be handsomely repaid in the very near future.

Knowing the ladies had the proceedings well in hand, Kyle invited Juan into his inner chamber for a Scotch and a cigar. Kyle's den was a masterpiece of affluence. The walls were solid mahogany polished to a high sheen. The room was filled with soft beige colored suede chairs and sofas. There were expensive oil paintings hanging about, each with it's own portrait light shining from above to accentuate the delicate stokes. Juan didn't know much about art, but did recognize a Monet and a Picasso from some magazines he once read. Against one wall was a massive desk with a matching high backed chair. Off to the side were matching bookcases and computer console. Kyle stepped to one side, hit a switch and one wall was immediately transformed into a full size bar complete with glasses resting on glass shelves, a refrigerator and an assortment of alcohols.

Kyle reached in and withdrew a pinch bottle of Scotch. He set up two thick glasses on the bar counter, added a couple of ice cubes and filled each glass to the brim with the golden liquid. He handed one glass to Juan, proposed a toast to the soon to be newlyweds and clinked Juan's glass for good luck. For the next several minutes, they chatted about the upcoming nuptials and life in general. Juan thought to himself, I could get used to this Scotch stuff, I only hope someday I can afford it. As the powerful drink hit Juan, he hesitated for a moment and asks Kyle a question he normally wouldn't have asked.

"By the by Kyle, I haven't seen your maid Maria around your house lately. Where is she?"

"Oh, she is no longer with us. Her parents were having some problems with their health and she returned to Mexico to care for them. I certainly do miss her, she was an excellent worker and as yet, we haven't found anyone who can replace her even though we have used several maids since."

Juan let the statement sink into his foggy brain. He was feeling the effects of the liquor and the explanation just didn't register. Didn't Maria tell him at one time her parents were dead? He couldn't be sure, but he thought he remembered her telling him this. Oh well, he must have been mistaken. Kyle poured Juan another drink then opened a humidor and took two hand rolled Cuban cigars out of the box. He took a gold clip from his pocket and snipped off the ends of the two elongated tubes and gave one to Juan. Kyle licked the exquisite tobacco from tip to tip, reached for a gold lighter on the coffee table and lit each cigar. The pungent aroma filled the room. Juan had never smoked and at first the smoke he inhaled caused him to cough and his head to become euphoric. He felt as though he was about to vomit, but repulsed the idea. Another sip of his drink and the feeling faded. After a few puffs, he savored the experience. The two men sat in facing chairs and enjoyed the exchange.

"Son, and I hope you don't mind me calling you that, because I do consider you as if you were one of my own. Now is the time to outline how you can repay me for what I have been doing for you. I guess you know that Professor Tillman and I were responsible for getting you the job with Sarah. We did it because we knew you were one of the most promising young attorneys available for the job. We also knew that Sarah owed us a favor for helping her get elected to her high position. That's what life is all about, doing favors for each other. Sarah has agreed to allow you sufficient time to help me on my campaign for U.S. Senator. I plan to activate all of the campaign offices I started in each of the six geographical areas of the state and will be picking a permanent manager for each site. Asking you to be a manager would be too heavy a load for you to carry along with your job, but your assisting the manager to corral the Hispanic voters in the Santa Barbara and Los Angeles areas would be a windfall for me. I do hope you will say yes, but I don't expect your answer this instant. Think it over and let me know after your honeymoon."

CHAPTER FORTY

The wedding day dawned sunny and warm. The sky was free of fog, an artist's canvas dotted with puffs of cottony clouds floating by in random formations. Juan remembered back to his youth when he had lain on his back and pretended to see animal shapes in the white fluffiness. The day was even more special because arrangements had been made to bring his mother to Santa Barbara to see the nuptials. His mother was still asleep in one of the guest rooms, fatigued from the long and tiring flight. Juan and his mother hadn't spoken much to each other, there was always time for that she said, but she was a little disappointed they were not going to have a church wedding. She hoped that would happen some time in the near future. The wedding wasn't scheduled until 5 o'clock in the afternoon, so there was plenty of time to hear about the brothers and sisters still in Mexico and the relatives who were taking care of them.

The day streaked away and the hour of bliss was upon them. Juan had retired to a dressing room to don his formal attire. He was joined by Kyle and Professor Tillman, as well as an attendant from the tuxedo shop. Juan found the tuxedo confining, but when everything was in place, he admired his image again.

A sharp rap on the bedroom door announced the time for Juan and his male friends to come to the improvised altar to begin the ceremony. All of a sudden, Juan felt more nervous than he had felt at anytime in his life. Why was he so nervous? He was marrying the most wonderful woman in the world. A woman who had shared his bed and a woman he had explored every inch of her body. They had told each other everything; so why did Mary emerge as a stranger in his mind. He shook off the doubt and gracefully walked down the rose strewn aisle to the altar, positioning himself to the left side of the pastor. Professor Tillman joined him. No sooner had Juan and Kyle arrived than the music from the organist echoed the bridal march, "Here comes the Bride". Juan turned his eyes to the rear of the crowd and saw Kyle bring Mary along the same path Juan had just traversed. The halo around Mary was iridescent. She looked like an angel descending from outer space. Her soft white hands held a bouquet of white roses trimmed with satin and lace. Her head was held regally high and she seemed to float with the soft breeze.

Kyle, acting as Mary's father, kissed her gently on the cheek and relinquished her to Juan and the pastor. The words were spoken, the rings exchanged and the ritual was complete. Mary was no longer a stranger, but Juan's beloved wife. It was now on to the reception and the honeymoon.

Kyle had offered the honeymoon as his wedding present to the couple. Mary and Juan chose Cancun. Even though Juan was a native Mexican, he had never been to that side of the country. He had heard it was a wondrous place to get away with your beloved. The showering of the rice at the end of the ceremony, the trip to the airport and the two weeks at the beach resort went by in a wink.

CHAPTER FORTY-ONE

The honeymoon was over. It was now time to get back to work. Juan and Mary arose early, took a quick shower together, remembering the fantastic time they had had on their vacation. The memories were still fresh in their minds as they dried each other off and got dressed. Their visit to Cancun was far too short, but the memories would last forever. Juan put on his best suit, white button down collared shirt, regimental striped tie, and his wing tip loafers, which were highly polished, a trait the military had taught him. Mary wore a form hugging sheath, sandals, and a single string of beads at her throat. She gathered her hair in the back and secured it with a matching clip. They stood for a moment admiring each other, so much in love, and then went to the kitchen for some breakfast.

This was a special day. Juan made his specialty, a southwestern omelet with bell peppers, onions, crushed bacon, and topped with salsa. He popped in some whole-wheat toast, and poured each of them a glass of freshly made orange juice. They sat across the kitchen nook table and feed each other with their forks, gently wiping small dribbles from each other's chin.

When the meal was finished, they cleaned up the dishes, tidied up the kitchen, went through the front door, kissed each other good-bye, and got into their retrospective cars. Juan was off to the district attorney's office for his initiation into the field of civil crime and Mary off to the hospital for new staff orientation. To each of them, it seemed like starting college. Each was a little apprehensive, not knowing fully what to expect, but confident that everything would okay, and their expectations would be met to the fullest.

On the way to the office, Juan glanced out of his car window to marvel at the beautiful day and surroundings. He was so glad he had chosen Santa Barbara as a place in which to live and work. There wasn't a better place to inhabit. Soon he was at the district attorney's office, noticing a special parking place had been designated for him. At the end of the building was an open lane with a newly painted white sign attached to the curb. It read, "Juan Cardova, Assistant DA". Juan's ego took a gigantic leap upward when he saw the sign. His only concern now was whether or not he could perform to the high standards he had envisioned for himself. His self-doubt returned, but soon faded away as he entered the building.

Inside, Juan met his counterparts, a nice mix of genders and ethnic groups. He felt a comradeship with this group on his first day, and knew that he would like working here. He found his cubicle that Terry had shown him before, settled in, looked around to orient himself, and made mental notes on how to decorate an otherwise drab place. He turned on his computer to see the icon configurations and the programs he was going to be working with. The system was an up-scale system linked to the other computers and printers in the office through a very complex LAN system. What he saw so far pleased him. This was going to be a very nice place.

He clicked on his email icon and immediately noticed many messages, most of them from friends who were wishing him good luck in his chosen profession. One email, however, was from Sarah, assigning him his first case. The case dealt with fraud by a city employee. Juan downloaded a brief of the charges and the references, which were being held in the chief clerk's office. Apparently, one of the bureaucrats in the disbursement office of the Mayor had been embezzling money from the mayor's account, and moving the money into a private bank offshore in the Cayman Islands. Over a period of three years, this individual had managed to move over five million dollars, unaccounted for until now. The scam probably would not have been detected if it has not been for an eagle-eyed accountant in the audit division. When the accountant reviewed the expense reports, a red flag immediately jumped up at him and he reported it to the DA's office. Juan made arrangements to convene a Grand Jury to see if the charges were sufficient to bring this case to trial. His first order of business was to interview the embezzler to get his version of the story. The accused was presently housed in the city jail to which Juan had easy access. Juan called the jail administrator, explained his purpose and set up a meeting for the following week.

On Monday, the first day of the new week, Juan met with the accused to determine the circumstances behind the crime. Present with the accused was his attorney, a young man directed by the court to be his defense counsel. Juan began to question the suspect, who told him little upon the advice of counsel. Armed with this rebuttal, Juan convened the grand jury.

The grand jury met in the county courthouse on the third floor, a room usually reserved for the Superior Court, but which was available on this day. The grand jury, a group of twelve citizens of various backgrounds sat in the jury box, the accused sat in the witness chair. As is the legal process of a grand jury, the defense attorney was present, but could not participate. The DA's office can ask the defendant any question they want, and the individual being questioned must answer.

Less than thirty minutes into the Grand Jury session it became apparent there was sufficient evidence to render an indictment and take the case to trial. After the Grand Jury was dismissed with Juan's thanks, the suspect and his defense attorney neared Juan and asked for a private session with him at that very moment. With no one in the room, the client and defense attorney asked if there was a possibility of a plea bargain. Juan hesitated at first, then agreed after realizing the advantages of saving the county money and getting a conviction on his first case would put him in good stead with his boss.

For the next five hours, Juan asked the individual accused of the crime questions about the embezzlement and who was involved. As fate will sometimes enter the picture, the crime was committed to help fund the re-election campaign of a U.S. Senator from California, the very same Senator that Juan's friend Kyle Smith was thinking of running against. Juan stored this piece of information away for future reference.

The next day, Juan and the defendant appeared before the judge to announce the plea bargain agreement. The sentence was rendered, and the accused taken away to serve his sentence in a state prison facility. Juan was jubilant with his victory, but dismayed with the thought of the information he had obtained about the California Senator. Thoughts surged through his mind as to whether or not he should inform Kyle Smith of this revelation or to keep it to himself. He knew it was unethical to reveal confidential information, but also realized what value it had, especially in the enhancement of Juan's career in both law and politics.

When he returned to his office, he was greeted by the DA and the rest of the staff with a celebration party. Champagne flowed and slaps on the back and handshakes abounded. Juan was off to a good start in the office. The feeling was warm inside Juan, but a cold sweat sprouted from his brow when he thought of the information leak. After the party, Juan went home still trying to decide what to do. Mary sensed the turmoil Juan was experiencing, but Juan brushed her off with an excuse that the first trial was hard, but he would get over it. After they went to bed, Juan tossed and turned. His dreams were more like nightmares. Around four o'clock in the morning, Juan sat bold upright, covered in cold sweat. Mary rose with him, put her arms around his shoulders and comforted him.

"What's the matter Juan", she asked. He replied, "Oh nothing, just a bad dream". Mary knew this wasn't true, she could feel the tension in his muscles, but knew that she must trust Juan. She knew he would tell her in his own good time. Juan lay back down, closed his eyes and drifted off into a troubled slumber.

The next morning Juan drove to the office, having gotten over the nightmare. He felt better, pushing the thoughts he had dreamed to the back of his mind. He didn't have time to worry about things like that, he would make a decision to tell Kyle later when he could think more clearly.

He parked his car in his assigned space and got out. Juan noticed a black limo parked next to the curb across the street. Instantly, the skin on his head tightened and his knees went weak. The limo belonged to Kyle Smith. What was he doing here, Juan muttered to himself.

As Juan entered the building, everything seemed normal, but his intuition told him things weren't as they seemed. He couldn't place his finger on the feeling, but knew something was going to happen. He rode up the elevator to his office, walked down the hall and through his office door. Kyle was standing by the window staring at the beautiful landscape and ocean.

As Juan came through the door, Kyle turned to greet him. Kyle was dressed to the nines with a dark blue pinstriped suit, blue silk shirt, and a flashy tie. His hair had just been cut to perfection, and his complexion glowed.

"And to what do I owe this visit", Juan asked.

"Well Juan", Kyle replied, "I just wanted to let you know that I have finalized my run for the Senate of the United States. In the meantime, I am putting together my campaign team, and as I told you before, I want you on it. I know that you have just started a new career with the District Attorney's Office, but as I told you, Sarah has agreed your caseload will be reduced so you can spend more time on my campaign. This way, you will have the best of both worlds. You can practice law and learn the political ropes at the same time. I can guarantee you that you will be well rewarded for your efforts. I just wanted to set a salary and a time schedule with you."

Juan paused for a few minutes. He knew that Kyle Smith had his sights set on the Senate seat in the U.S. Congress, and nothing would stop him nor would any expense be spared. Juan had only just begun his new career and there was so much to learn, but an opportunity like this only comes once in a lifetime. Juan knew if he were to attain his goals, getting involved in politics himself, now was the time to seize the brass ring and run with it. He knew it would be the ride of his life. Kyle outlined the schedule and the salary. Juan was impressed, and readily agreed to both subject to Sarah's blessing.

"Kyle, I have to discuss this with my boss. Can you give me twenty-four hours to do this?"

"Certainly Juan, take as much time as you like. The path you have chosen is a big one, and I want you to feel comfortable with it. Give me a call when you are ready. If you agree to the terms, I will make arrangements to hold a staff meeting to plan our strategy."

The two friends shook hands and Kyle left. Juan reached for the phone. He had to talk to Sarah about this stage of the development and to get her guidance. His hands shook as he dialed the interoffice number. His fingers were so sweaty, they almost slipped off the buttons. Twice he dialed the wrong number. He chastised himself as he tried to get a grip on the situation. Juan took in a big breath, held it for a few seconds, and then dialed the number correctly.

He got Sarah's voice mail, telling the caller she was unavailable and would return their call as soon as possible. Juan toyed with the idea of going to her office, but decided to stay where he was and wait. He had plenty of work to do, but found himself just sitting there like a statue, unable to concentrate on anything. After what seemed like an eternity, the phone rang. Juan wasn't expecting it, and it startled him. He reached for the handset, held it to his ear and asked Sarah if he could have a few minutes of her time to discuss a very important item.

"Can't you just tell me over the phone?" Sarah asked.

"I wish I could, but this will take some special explaining, and I don't want anyone else in the office to overhear our conversation."

"Okay, come by my office in twenty minutes. I have a few things to finish up, then I will be able to spend whatever time we need."

For the next twenty minutes, Juan paced back and forth in his office. He looked out of the window unable to focus on anything really. He tried to work on a case that he had been assigned, but it didn't make any sense to him. He simply could not stay focused. The sun was starting to settle in the west, its color changing from yellow to a brilliant orange as it sank into the azure sea called The Pacific Ocean. He stood mesmerized as the scene unfolded before him. A soothing calm suddenly overtook him, and he felt as though everything was going to turn out fine.

The twenty minutes seemed like molasses oozing through a cold sieve. No matter how hard Juan tried, he could not make the time go any faster. He paced back and forth like an expectant father, the tendons in his neck reaching a high-strung pitch giving him a migraine like headache. He clutched and unclenched his fists, twisting his head from side to side to relieve the tension. He moved to his desk, took out a couple of Ibuprofen tablets and washed them down with a cup of water. In a few minutes, the medicine seemed to work. His tension was somewhat gone and the headache had disappeared.

Finally the time had passed and he left his office to walk down the hall to Sarah's. He approached her office door, which was locked, and rapped gently a couple of times. He heard Sarah's muted voice inviting him to come in. She had her back turned and was just finishing up some typing on her word processor. She shut the computer off and turned to face Juan. Her brow became furrowed when she saw the tension in Juan's body language. She invited him to sit on the couch next to her desk. She asked if he would like a drink, something he accepted readily. It was nearing the close of the office hours, so neither of them felt ashamed to have a little toast to go along with their conversation. Sarah poured each of them a bourbon and water. She added two ice cubes to each, and passed one of the glasses to Juan. They each took a sip, let the golden fluid trickle down their throats, savoring the instant, warm glow. They both relaxed. Juan opened the dialogue. He told Sarah about the arrangements he had made with Kyle and wanted her to approve, but it would be her decision.

Sarah stood, sighed a deep sigh and leaned against her desk. "Juan, I have a story to tell you. It delves into some of my darkest secrets, and when I finish, I do not want you to repeat any of it to anyone. If you do, I will deny I ever said it, and will do everything in my power to destroy you. Do you understand this?"

Juan assured her that he would hold her secrets inviolate, and would never reveal them to anyone.

Sarah nodded, cleared her throat and began.

"I will do anything that Kyle asks. When I was a first year law student, I hung out with a sort of wild group. It wasn't unusual for them to study together, and then go to a deserted part of the park, drink beer and smoke a joint of Mary Jane. One night they invited me to go with them. They offered me this marijuana cigarette after I had a couple of beers. I refused, never having had tried dope, but they were insistent and I gave in. The feeling was wonderful. My head was light, and I just seemed to float on some sort of heavenly cloud. I don't remember much of what happened that night, but the next morning I woke up in bed naked. As I became aware of my surroundings, it dawned on me that I had been raped by one of the men in our group. I never did find out who it was, but that is of no consequence. I was so ashamed, I didn't even want to report it. I went on as if nothing ever happened. A month later, I missed my period and had a strange awakening in my stomach. I knew I was pregnant. A month later, I stopped by a local drugstore, purchase a pregnancy test, and it came up positive. I was in total shock. I didn't know where to go, or what to do. I could see my law career going down the tubes, and my life ruined. I had no means to take care of a baby, nor did I have any family to assist me. Hell, I could hardly take care of myself. I just wanted to kill myself and be done with it. One day, Professor Tillman stopped by the study hall and saw the forlorn look on my face and asked me if there was something the matter. I told him I just wasn't feeling well, but he intuitively surmised that something was in fact wrong. He walked me outside the library building and we sat on a bench in a quiet and secluded part of the campus. He grilled me until I told him. I tried to hold back, but my feeling just spewed forth like a volcano erupting. I told him of my predicament, and that I wanted to end my life. He listened with great intensity, nodding from time to time until I was finished.

After I was through, he took my hand and said he would take care of it. A couple of days later, he called me into his office and told me that a benefactor had come forward, and would pay for me to have an abortion in Mexico. He guaranteed me the abortion would take place in a highly respected clinic used by many celebrities who wanted to keep things like this quiet. A lull was coming up in the term, and the arrangements were made. I received a telephone call that a car would pick me up at a certain date and time, and would escort me south. The car came and I went to the clinic. The procedure was profession- ally handled and I stayed in their area for two days to make sure the procedure had gone well, and there was no infection. I was given a clean bill of health, and driven back to campus.

I didn't have a roommate, so I didn't have to explain my absence to anyone. I finished law school, found a job, and immediately decided I wanted to get into politics. I didn't have much experience, but I knew I wanted the challenge of running for the office of District Attorney of Santa Barbara. Most influential insiders told me I wouldn't have a chance, but out of the clear blue sky, a man came to visit me, explaining he had been hired as my campaign manger. We spent several days planning my run for the office of District Attorney for Santa Barbara County. Suddenly I had a staff which materialized from out of nowhere. A bank account was established to support my candidacy, and the money began pouring in. In no time, I had a war chest twice as rich as any of the other candidates.

The next few months were like a whirlwind. I had television ads on all of the major networks, ads in the newspapers, posters on front lawns, speaking engagements, visits to senior centers, and a myriad of other activities. I had people who wrote speeches for me, and coached me on how to deliver them. The campaign began, and wonder upon wonder, I won. Soon after I was installed in the office, I had a visit from Kyle Smith. He told me that he knew who had raped me and would use the information about the rape and the abortion unless I agreed help him later. He also told me he was the funding source for my election. I found out that one of the things he wanted was for me to hire you as an assistant district attorney, and to allow you to work on his campaign for the U.S. Senate. I felt I was being blackmailed in part, but I was go grateful, I agreed. The rest is history. I have never gone back on my word, so I hired you and I will make sure your case load is such that you can work for Kyle to get him elected."

Juan knew Sarah trusted him unconditionally, or she wouldn't have told him such an intimate secret. He also knew this was an opportunity to enrich his own life, and fulfill a desire to enter into the political arena himself. He stared at Sarah for a short time, looking deeply into her soft eyes, seeing a chemistry emerge of true allies. As long as Sarah stayed in the job, and Juan had every reason to assume she would, he was on his way to his Valhalla, paradise in the sky, power of the influential, a dream come true.

"Okay Sarah," Juan said, "I think it will be a pleasure working together. Now let's sit down and work out the details of my employment from here on out." Sarah moved to her highly stylish desk, and withdrew a five-year calendar, a note pad, a pen, and a calculator. She moved to the polished small conference table she had in her office and put the items on one side. She pulled out two chairs, side by side, and sat down with Juan. She ordered coffee for the two of them. It was going to be a hectic hour or so.

CHAPTER FORTY-TWO

Over the course of the next few months, Juan's caseload diminished and his courtroom appearances were less and less. Juan had reached a juncture that would influence his life from now on. He and Mary had often talked about what was happening, and they both agreed that it was the way to go and the best thing to do.

While Juan was working at his desk one balmy afternoon, the phone rang and Kyle Smith was calling. Kyle wanted Juan to come to his downtown headquarters to be briefed on the duties Juan would be performing over the next year or so. Juan told Kyle that he was ready to assume those duties and would see him in the morning.

Juan glanced out of his window at the panoramic view, marveling at the scenery surrounding his area. His thoughts went back to his childhood, to his family, to his experiences in Vietnam, his marriage to Mary, law school, and politics. He knew he was destined for great things. He felt confident in himself and his friends. He knew he was going to acquire more acumen in this arena, and would prosper to heights he could not yet imagine. The day was ending and the sun was setting over the ocean, it was a good day. Juan reached for the phone and called Mary. He wanted to take her out to dinner to celebrate his good fortune and thank her for all of her wonderful support and love.

They dined that night at one of the more fashionable restaurants in Santa Barbara, one of Mary's favorites. Juan decided to make the night a very memorable occasion, so he ordered Mary's choice of a classic Chardonnay. The waiter presented the wine to Juan and poured a small sampling in his glass. Juana expertly swirled the wine around the crystal glass, gazed at its clarity, smelled the sharp aroma, rested a sip of the gold liquid on his tongue and declared the wine to his liking. The waiter filled up both of their glasses and took their order.

They started with escargot, followed by a small crab and lettuce salad. Juan ordered the "fish of the day", which was Mahi Mahi, and Mary settled for the small prime rib done medium rare. The food was delicious and the evening passed by too quickly. They spent the rest of the evening relaxing, watching a DVD of their favorite movie. They went to bed knowing that the morning would spring a new beginning.

Kyle Smith's campaign headquarters occupied a small space which once had been a boutique in the middle of downtown Santa Barbara. The space had been empty for some time, and the owner was willing to lease it to Kyle for a reasonable fee. There was a small sign in the front window announcing Kyle's candidacy for the U.S. Senate, but other than that, the front of the headquarters took on little change from other surrounding buildings. Kyle didn't want to ruin the ambience of the downtown area, or take away from the quaint nature of the downtown area. Juan parked his car in an area behind the building and sat for a few moments pondering the impact this adventure would have on his life, and also wondering if he had made the right decision. The day was picture perfect, and Juan almost decided to go for a drive to the beach, to walk alone and clear his head, but he knew he had made a commitment, one he had to honor.

Juan left his car, locked the doors with his remote and strolled through the alley. The city took pride in itself, and the alley was free of trash, the dumpsters freshly painted and stacked neatly in rows. Once past the dumpsters, Juan rounded the corner of the building and strode up to the front door of the headquarters.

As he entered, Juan encountered a cacophony of activity. Staffers were busy putting together signs, and stapling the signs to wooden slats to be pushed into the lawns around the city. Others were working on the computers, sending emails to as many people in the region as they had addresses for. Phones were actively engaged, people speaking into them, asking for contributions and extolling the virtues of Kyle Smith, the next U. S. Senator from the state of California.

All of the interior walls had been removed, leaving just one very large room to house all of this activity. Desks were strewn around the room denying it of any privacy. There were TV sets in various locations displaying the various advertising clips that would be used on local network stations around the area. Individuals were busy watching the ads, taking notes, and making plans for revising the ads, or contemplating where and how the ads would be aired in the coming months. TV advertising was a very expensive proposition, so tons of care were being expended to ensure Kyle got the biggest bang for his dollar.

Kyle was a charismatic person, a very adept fundraiser, and had cajoled hundreds of men, women, and businesses into providing as many funds as the law would allow. Kyle through his fund raising efforts was now qualified to also receive federal matching funds for his campaign. Juan marveled at what money could buy. The ads were very slick and extolled the greatest virtues of Kyle and his caring for the citizens of California and the nation. Kyle didn't want to launch a smear campaign against any of his opponents, Kyle felt that the smear tactic would come back to bite him in the rear end and would be counter productive.

Juan spotted Kyle at the far corner of the room, conversing with a handsome young woman, giving her directions of what he wanted done as the launch of his involvement in the race had begun. Kyle noticed Juan, finished his business with the lovely thing, and motioned Juan to join him in the only office enclosed with glass. Kyle shook Juan's hand, put his beefy arms around his shoulders and gave

Juan a Smith bear style hug. Juan harkened back to his college days and the embraces that he has received from Bubba and others at San Diego State.

Kyle pointed to a soft chair for Juan to sit. He walked to a sideboard cabinet made of bright cherry and opened the doors. Inside was an array of whiskeys and chasers. He asked Juan what he would like and Juan opted for a scotch on the rocks. Kyle poured each of them a drink. He was very generous with the amount. Juan was beginning to notice his tolerance for alcohol was increasing. He wondered how much more it would take to get the same effect as the first drink he had. He chastised himself and agreed internally to put a lid on the excessive use of this potent potable.

Kyle handed the drink to Juan and took a sip himself. Juan swirled the bright yellow liquid around in his glass, savoring the aroma of the distillate brew. He sipped gently and felt the warm glow as the amber fire traveled down his throat and into his stomach.

After a few more sips, Kyle began.

"Juan, this conversation never happened. I am going to tell you how I want this campaign run, and if any of it leaks out of this room, I will deny every word. I want you to focus your time on wooing the Hispanic vote in this area. Spare no expense. I have millions in the bank from favors I have called in from big companies I can help when I get elected. I want you to go to their churches, their businesses, their shopping malls and into their home if need be. I want you to kiss babies and hug the wives and shake hands with the husbands. I want you to take Mary along with you when she has the time away from the hospital. I will furnish you with a car and driver, just tell him where you want to go once your have developed your battle plan."

Juan felt as though he were back in Vietnam at an operations briefing. He had been given his objective and his marching orders, now it was his turn to develop the strategy for getting the job done. Accomplishing the mission so to speak. Juan knew the drill well.

"To continue," Kyle said, "You know that I have decided not to run a smear campaign. But I also want you to know that I have decided to squeeze each of my opponents until they either drop out of the race or are exposed. I need you to start digging into the backgrounds of each of them. I want you to find skeletons in their closets, things that we can leak to the press, or can confront them with. I need leverage, I won't call it blackmail, just leverage. Can you do this?"

Juan was awestruck. This was his first exposure into the true nature of politics. He had heard such things were possible, but never in his wildest dreams did he think he would be involved. Juan was caught on the horns of an ethical dilemma. He could picture the proverbial red devil sitting on one shoulder who says go for it, and the white angel sitting on the other shoulder, telling him to refuse. Between the alcohol and the conflict, Juan's head began to swim in a torrent of crashing waves. In all of his years, with all of the decisions he had to make, this was to be one of the most difficult.

Juan asked Kyle if he could have a couple of minutes to get some fresh air. Kyle agreed and Juan opened the back door of the office and slipped out onto the back patio. A cool breeze had come up and Juan held his face to its healing effects. His head cleared and he went back into the office.

"Kyle", Juan said, "I want you to know this decision is very difficult for me. On one hand, I want you to win this race as all costs. The country needs you and your skills in Washington D.C. But at the same time, I am not sure I am the man for this job."

At this point, Juan revealed the information he had gathered from the embezzler.

"Thanks for that information. I can see the frustration in your face Juan, and I don't want to press you on this until you have had some time to filter out the pros and cons and developed an action plan. Take the rest of the day off. Be with Mary, go walk on the beach, take a cold shower, or do anything you need to, but I must have a decision by tomorrow."

Juan thanked Kyle and left the office almost in a trance. He didn't even remember driving home. After he walked through the front door, he began to pace. He wanted another drink, but knew that that would only gum up the process. He needed a clear head in the worst possible way. Kyle had made a wise suggestion. Perhaps a walk on the beach would be good for him.

He extracted his car keys off the foyer table, ran down the front steps, and jumped into his car. The beach was only minutes away, and at this time of day, it would probably be as deserted as it was going to get. He parked, took off his shoes and felt the warm sand squeeze between his toes. The sand was like a sponge, draining away the mystery and giving Juan confidence in his ability to come up with the right solution. After walking the beach for an hour and watching the sea gulls turn and dip softly in the afternoon up currents, he arrived at his answer. He didn't want to wait until tomorrow to speak to Kyle, so he stopped by a pay phone, called the office and hoped that Kyle was still there. The phone rang three times before Kyle answered it. Juan asked him to wait there until he could get back to the office. Kyle said he understood, and said he would wait.

Juan drove slowly back to the campaign office. On the way, he noticed things he had not noticed before. The city was lined with green foliage on the margins between the sidewalks and street. Flowers had been planted around the trees, and the grass in the margins had been neatly trimmed. It was a mark of a compulsive city. Juan wondered if living in the city had in some way changed him, and made him more compulsive.

The buildings were clean and orderly, a symbol of wealth and power ensconced by the people who live here. There was an aura of priority abounding. People walked and drove with purpose, not to be deterred. Juan surmised that this was the compelling force driving Kyle. Juan made up his mind to hear Kyle out and unless there was out and out illegality, Juan would bend as much as possible to compromise with Kyle.

Juan parked his car in a space designated for the campaign hierarchy, shut off the motor, and stepped out. Again, he took a deep breath and opened the door.

Back inside Kyle's office, Kyle was having another drink. The day was getting late and Kyle had nothing planned for that evening, so he felt he could indulge himself.

Juan spoke. "Kyle I have decided to listen to what you have to say and if there isn't anything illegal in what you propose, I am willing to meet you half way."

Kyle slipped like a snake over to Juan, put his arm around Juan's shoulder and led him to the leather couch on the side of the room.

" Let me reiterate Juan. I think we should use the strategy of finding inappropriate backgrounds to give us the edge. I don't propose to do anything illegal, just find out the information we can that would help us meet our objectives. Most of what I need can be found in the public records, or by interviewing people who know the other candidates. It is a simple matter of private investigation. What we need is a top notch PI to help us out. I would be willing to conjure up a salary, which should entice the very best. Do you know anyone that would fill the bill?"

Juan thought for a minute. "When I was in Vietnam, I was acquainted with a Special Forces sergeant who was the best criminal investigator I have ever seen. I don't know where he is, but he is our man."

CHAPTER FORTY-THREE

Juan's old friend from Vietnam, SFC Wilson immediately jumped into his mind. No one was more capable of doing what need to be done than Wilson. Over the months they had know each other in country, Wilson never ceased to amaze Juan with his innate ability to find facts, apply those facts, and come up with a conclusion that fit the situation perfectly. Wilson could move behind the scenes like a clandestine CIA operative, searching through records, piles of trivia, and data bases without ever being heard or seen. Juan remembered one case where Wilson had uncovered the girlfriend of a high ranking officer. The girlfriend had often gotten the officer drunk, plied him with her sexual favors and extracted valuable secret information about his unit, which she then turned over to the enemy. Before they could bring the girl to trial, she had committed suicide. The officer was reassigned to the United States and was retired. Wilson's involvement in the case was never discovered.

The question now was, how could Juan find him? Juan assumed the best place to start was with the Department of Defense. There were two locations where information about former military personnel was located, the finance center in St. Louis, Missouri and the military personnel center in the Pentagon in Washington D.C. Juan knew accessing either of those two places would be difficult. Juan sat down at his desk, and called operator assistance to get the phone numbers of the finance and personnel centers. The operator gave him the central telephone numbers for each, but could not assist him in reaching the specific office he needed for the information.

Juan called the finance center first. On the third ring, a young female voice answered. "Department of the Army Finance Center, specialist Young speaking, how may I help you?" Juan explained what he was looking for and was informed that information of this nature was classified and could only be given out by written consent of the commanding general of the center. She suggested that Juan write a letter to the center, stating the reasons for the requested information and asking for permission to receive it. The specialist hung up and the phone went dead.

Juan couldn't afford the time to write and wait while some bureaucracy stalled and may or may not get back to him. Juan then tried the personnel center with the same results. Frustrated, Juan didn't know where to turn, then he remembered Wilson had given him the address of his parents just in case anything ever happened to him. If Wilson were to get killed in combat in that god forsaken Asian land, he wanted Juan to take his effects back to his parents. He didn't want some Army officer and a Chaplain doing it. Juan made the promise to him and demanded Wilson do the same for him. Fortunately, neither of them met an untimely demise.

Juan rushed back to his house trying to ascertain where he had kept the address of others he had garnered in the jungle they called home for a year. Juan searched the storage area in the attic, the place where he would have stored things from Vietnam. Behind a pillar was a footlocker that Juan hadn't opened since moving in the new abode. The footlocker was covered with cobwebs and dust and reeked of mildew. Juan wasn't sure if anything inside was still worth extracting. He had put a combination lock on the footlocker, and now, looking down at the lock, he tried to remember the combination. Suddenly, the combination came to him. It was the numbers in his Army serial number backwards. The centerpiece of the lock was slightly rusted, but with a little urging, started to turn. It didn't turn freely, so Juan sprayed a few drops of WD40 lubricating oil on the face. Working the dial back and forth, it soon operated as if it were new. Juan twisted the dial, right 18, left 34, right 56, left 13 and right to 04. The lock snapped open with a little pull.

Gingerly, Juan lifted up the lid and memories of jungle humidity, death, diesel fuel, helicopter noises, and sleepless nights came flooding back to him. He reeled for a moment, his head swimming with the recall, but after taking a couple of deep breaths, his head cleared.

Juan pawed through the contents of the footlocker. Inside were a set of fatigues he had worn, the camouflaged patches still in place with his rank and name sewn over the pockets. There as also a cigarette lighter given to him by the unit with the unit crest soldered to the front. A good-bye plaque made out of brass and crafted by a local village artist. The brass coming from artillery rounds the Vietnamese had policed up from around the area. There were pictures of his platoon and buddies. What youthful faces they were at the time. There were other things, but Juan found the leather folder he was looking for. he closed the footlocker and retreated to the kitchen.

Juan mixed himself a stiff drink, opened the folder and took out the scraps of paper inside with the addresses of the men he had known best. Wilson's parent's address and telephone number had been dulled with age, but Juan could still read them.

Juan slowly removed the phone from the wall bracket and punched in the number. The phone began to ring, once, twice, a third time. Juan was afraid Wilson's parents might have moved, or had their phone disconnected, or had died; but on the fourth ring, a quiet, almost hushed voice said, "Hello."

Juan found he was talking to Wilson's mother, a woman who was now in her 80's and apparently dulled with age. Juan told her who he was and the relationship he had shared with her son. She recognized the name and said her son had mentioned him many times in the correspondence he had sent from Vietnam and during the discussions they had when Wilson was visiting. She asked Juan to hold for a minute and she would see if she could find the address and telephone number to reach her son. Juan heard the phone clink as it was placed on the counter. A long pause ensued.

What was only a few minutes seemed like days. Juan's anxiety level was beginning to climb when the mother came back on the line. She asked if Juan had a paper and pencil. When Juan replied in the affirmative, she recited the information, which Juan repeated to her to make sure he had it correctly. She told Juan they hadn't heard from their son for some time and hoped the address was still valid. Juan thanked her profusely and told her he would give her regards to her son if and when he made contact.

The address Wilson's mother had given Juan was an upscale area in which the small town of Bristow, Virginia was situated. Bristow, a nondescript little berg, was located just a few miles for the town of Manassas, the first Battle of Bull Run. Juan recalled his Vietnam buddy was an ardent student of the Civil War. He talked about it at great length, recounting the prelude leading up to the conflict and every battle which had taken place. He described in great detail the commanders and the staff of the two opposing sides. He also described the tactics, be they good or bad that were used in the encounters. Juan had been mesmerized by the knowledge Wilson possessed and vowed some day to visit all of the battlefields with Wilson if and when they ever ran across each other.

CHAPTER FORTY-FOUR

Juan didn't want to call Wilson, he would much rather surprise him. Juan worried he wouldn't recognize his old friend, but quickly theorized everyone changes, but the true self will always shine through, and the recognition would occur spontaneously. Juan had one of the office staff book his flight from Santa Barbara to Dulles airport, the closest facility near Bristow. The United flight would take Juan from his airport to a connecting hub in Chicago where Juan would change planes and journey on to Dulles. The flight was just over six hours with the change of planes, so Juan opted for First Class. This way, he could stretch out on a comfortable leather seat, get some food, and have a few drinks to calm his nerves and make the time go faster.

As the plane was filling up, Juan noticed the window seat next to him was still vacant. The flight attendants were getting everything in order in preparation for departure from the gate. Juan had gone through this drill, he could almost predict the exact moment when the hatch door would be closed and the plane, tethered to a small motor car, would be extracted from the jet way.

One of the flight attendants in first class was a well proportioned black woman in a Navy blue blazer with matching skirt. The blazer covered a white blouse with a striped red, white, and blue scarf. The outline of a shapely body was not hidden by the apparel. Juan motioned to her and jokingly asked if she could search the plane for a good-looking female to fill the window seat and keep him company. The attendant, flirting with Juan, said she would see what she could do.

In spite of Juan's best intentions, a young businessman excused himself, and asked if he would occupy the window seat. Juan stood up, moved to the aisle and allowed the gentleman to pass him into the seat. When they were buckled in, the shapely flight person came back the aisle. Juan stopped her and enquired if the guy was the best she could do. The two of them laughed, the man not understanding the private joke. After the dinner and drink requests were taken, Juan introduced himself to his traveling companion and explained the laughter. The ice was broken, and they each shared personal information to begin the flight.

The traveler was a sales representative for a major software company located in Silicon Valley on his way to Philadelphia to attend a convention for business owners who were likely targets for his company's products. His connecting flight left from Dulles, so the two of them would have ample time to talk.

The time sped by and soon the plane was making it's final approach. Juan heard the distinctive clunk as the landing gear slipped into place and then the screech of the tires on the hard concrete surface. Juan deplaned, and found his luggage at carousel number two. He exited the terminal, crossed the median and waited for the rental car shuttle to arrive. After procuring his car, he started for Wilson's home.

Bristow, Virginia is a bedroom community about an hours drive from Washington, D.C. Deep in the heart of the Civil War country, Bristow is embedded in the middle of Prince William County, an upscale, mostly white, upper middle class neighborhoods. Bristow, a city of approximately 30,000 has excellent schools and entertainment possibilities. People tend to get along with each other, offering to chauffer each other's children to soccer games, little league, and music practice. The parents are active in the PTA and often hold outdoor parties for the people who live in their areas. They leave behind the drudges of governmental America and opt for the genteel way of life, away from the maddening crowd.

As Juan drove from the airport, he headed west by southwest along Interstate 66 until he crossed state route 28 which took him through Manassas. The evening was getting on and the sun was slowly sinking on the horizon. Juan wanted to find the house before it got too dark. Finding residences in unfamiliar territory is always more difficult at night.

Soon after leaving the outskirts of Manassas, Juan approached the entrance of the city of Bristow. The town welcomed the traveler with the usual sign, made of a pile of stacked stone, announcing the various civic and social clubs which added civic pride to this typical rural community. The Rotary meets here every Tuesday, the Lion's Club meets every Thursday, etc. Juan had seen these entrances a million times, but it still gave him a thrill to know that people still cared for people. He never recalled seeing these signs as he went into the slums of the big cities. Why haven't these organizations moved into the area of down trodden people Juan mused to himself. He guessed it was because there just wasn't the organization or the money there to support arrogance of those at the top.

Rather than try to guess how to get to Wilson's house, Juan stopped at a local convenience store to ask for directions. Behind the counter was a lovely young lady wearing the standard garb of the company she worked for. There was no one in the establishment, so she gave Juan her full attention. It never seemed to amaze Juan how young ladies were always welcoming of good looking strangers, late at night, on a boring shift. Juan lingered a little longer than he should have, but the conversation was pleasant. He even had a chance to kid with her for a little while. She gave him the general layout of the city and directions to the street Juan was looking forward. To thank her for her help, Juan purchased some breath mints, which he really didn't need, but felt obligated some how to buy. She invited him to stop in anytime, and maybe she would show him the town. Returning to see her was the furtherest thing from Juan's mind.

Bristow was divided into blocks like so many other communities scattered across America. The streets running north and south were named for trees and the streets running east and west were designated by of numbers. Wilson lived at 1603 Elm Street. As Juan turned out of the convenience store, the first street to draw his attention was Ash Street, followed by Burch, then Cedar, then Dogwood. Juan was not surprised the next street was Elm, which followed in alphabetical sequence. He was on 4th Street and he turned left, crossing 3rd street. Realizing his mistake, Juan performed a perfect U turn and headed in the opposite direction. He then crossed 4th Street again, then 5th, eventually coming to 16th. Wilson's house was situated on the corner. A large lot, beautifully landscaped with a large oak tree in the center of the corner and bushes nestled up against the front windows.

Parked in the driveway was an older model Ford Mustang, a classic 1964, something Wilson would acquire and take meticulous care of. The house was dark. Even though there was a porch light, it was not turned on. The house gave off an eerie burst of energy, like the sense of looking at a crypt in a cemetery. Juan stopped his car in front, turned off the ignition and opened the car door. He hesitated for an instant not knowing whether or not he would approach the door and knock. What the hell, he said to himself, I didn't come all this way to be frightened of seeing an old buddy.

Juan had a small flashlight attached to his key ring. He switched in on and located the doorbell. He pushed the smooth white object and heard the melodious strains of the Marine Corps anthem. Juan remembered Wilson has once been a buck private in the Marines before quitting and joined up with the Army Special Forces. Wilson never explained why he had made that choice, and Juan had never asked. It did seem strange though. Rarely would a Marine ever give up the Corps for some other branch of service.

No one answered, so Juan pushed the bell again and waited. He peered through the glass in the front door. The front room was dark, but there was a soft flickering light emanating from some back room. Glimmers of light strobed across one wall, the intensity of the light constantly changing. Juan assumed it was a television set someone was watching, or had left on.

Juan decided that perhaps someone was in the house and had failed to hear the doorbell. The sound from the television seemed awfully loud. Juan made a choice to go around to the back of house and try the back door. The backyard was fenced, with a wooden gate at the end of a short sidewalk. Again, Juan turned on his flashlight, and found the latch to open the gate. He closed the gate gently behind himself, not wishing to wake up the neighbors who might call the police to investigate the possibility of a burglary occurring next door.

Juan flashed his light across the back door, but was unable to spot another doorbell. As he was about to rap his knuckles on the hard-wood casing, Juan felt the sting of cold metal pressed against the side of his head. Juan had not heard even a single footstep. The stealth of the weapon holder was amazing. Juan remembered hearing about individuals like that in Nam, but had never encountered one.

In a soft, almost inaudible whisper, a deep baritone voice said, "If you twitch, you are dead!" Juan felt his knees almost buckle and the blood rush from his head. He was confused and startled. The adrenalin started to flow, and Juan was torn between dropping or running or remaining calm. Juan slowly raised his hands into the air and pleaded, "Please don't shoot, I am only looking for an old friend."

"And who might that friend be," came the response.

"A no account, cheating, Vietnam card shark by the name of Wilson."

The atmosphere shattered like bullet piercing a plate glass window. A hearty roar came from the person sporting the gun.

"Turn around you wimp. Didn't I teach you anything when we

were in country?" "How could you let anyone sneak up on you so easily. What has happened to your senses and training, have you gone soft on me?"

Juan spun around and in the dim light, came face to face with someone he thought he recognized, but wasn't sure. Gone was the short, dark hair, replaced with a silver sheen. The tanned Adonis body, replaced by a beer gut and foul breath. But the demeanor was unmistakable. It was Wilson, many years later.

Wilson grasped the brass doorknob, opened the kitchen door, and turned on the light. The kitchen was small, but neatly kept. There were no dishes in the sink, and the floors had been swept of any debris. Some military certificates were hung on the walls along with pictures of family members. The room would have reminded one of the 1960s when Harvest Gold and dark green shag rugs were all the rage. The counter tops were Formica and a side by side refrigerator, with and a controlled temperature storage area on the bottom of the fridge, sat next to the counter.

Wilson told Juan to sit at the kitchen table, then went to the cupboard and took down a bottle of Scotch and two glasses. Wilson returned to the freezer, withdrew a tray of ice cubes, smacked the tray against the side of the counter to loosen the ice. He then dropped a couple of cubes into each glass. He poured not two, but four fingers of Scotch into each glass. The amber gold liquid clung to the sides of the glasses, attesting to the expensive nature of the Scotch.

Wilson then took a couple of coasters from a stack on top of the counter, placed one in front of Juan and put the drink down. He repeated the procedure next to Juan and sat down himself.

"Now, my old friend, what brings you to my house?"

Before answering, Juan looked around Wilson's kitchen. It was spotless and well organized, not the type of kitchen you would expect from a man with Wilson's background. He had color coordinated everything in matching yellows, rusts, browns, and whites. The other structure in Wilson's kitchen was an office alcove, which housed a desk, a computer, and a telephone. Nestled in the alcove were certificates of the medals and decorations he had been awarded and pictures of his military buddies, mostly from Vietnam.

"Excuse me," Juan said. "I think I see a picture of the two of us, do you mind if I take a peek." Wilson nodded his assent allowing Juan to get up from the counter and approach the picture. Juan immediately had a flashback to that era conflict. He remembered the incident in vivid color and sound. Even though the two of them looked serene, Juan could still hear in his mind the clamor of helicopters buzzing overhead on their way outbound to deliver troops, evacuate the wounded, or fire on enemy positions.

Wilson joined Juan at the framed countenance, bringing Juan back to reality. Without comment, the two buddies returned to the counter to resume their drinks and conversation.

Wilson coughed out, "Now again, what's up?"

For the next hour, Juan went into a diatribe about his involvement with Kyle Smith's campaign, and the expectations Smith had laid on Juan. Juan explained the strategy that was being employed to gather background information on the opponents with the purpose of using any derogatory information as leverage in a well orchestrated smear process, without seeming to be derogatory.

Wilson listened intently, nodding in places, but not offering a word or question as Juan traversed through the reasoning behind the strategy and the work they would like Wilson to perform. Juan went into extensive detail about the timetable and the information release points during the campaign. Finally, Juan recognized that he had covered all of the pertinent information, and asked Wilson if there were any questions.

"Wow" offered Wilson, "that is a basketful of bees you have just handed me. I am not sure I want to get involved in those kinds of shenanigans in the first place, but since I owe you so much, please let me think about it."

"Alright," replied Juan. "I will be staying at a local motel for a couple of days and you can reach me at this number." Juan handed Wilson a piece of paper containing the name of the motel and its telephone number.

Wilson asked why Juan couldn't stay with him, to which Juan countered, "I want you to have the time to think by yourself, without distractions. My being here might influence your decision, and I don't want that. I know you will have some demons to deal with, and I know you will want to be alone to meditate and come to your own conclusion."

"Fair enough. Give me forty-eight hours, and I will telephone you at the motel with my decision."

Juan rose, reached out with his hand, but gave way to a crushing hug from his old friend. Juan could see the depth of concern in Wilson's eyes, but was sure Wilson would make the right choice and help the campaign along. After Juan was released from the grip, he turned, without looking back, and strode out of the house. It was getting late, and Juan had not eaten, so he stopped by a twenty-four hour café. He wanted another drink badly, but knew the café didn't sell hard liquor, so he settled for a cheeseburger and French fries along with a diet Coke.

The next two days were tough on Juan. He couldn't contact Kyle, because he didn't have Wilson's answer yet. He watched some television, but soon became bored with the drivel on the boob tube. He walked to a nearby convenience store to get a newspaper and a couple of magazines, which he devoured in no time flat. He tried napping on the bed, but only stared at the ceiling of the room, unable to focus on his thoughts, failing to make sense of what he was feeling.

He arose, took off his clothes, took a shower and donned fresh duds. He decided to take a drive around the city and the countryside to pass the time away. It was a lovely city, steeped in the Civil War tradition with statues of Confederate officers in the town square and in front of the courthouse. It was an orderly and clean city, lots of flowers festooning the park, and weeping willow trees adding a sense of mystery to the setting. It was the kind of city Juan knew fitted Wilson. Throughout their days together, Wilson was almost obsessive compulsive about his person, seeking neatness in everything and beauty everywhere. Juan knew that Wilson was from a small town originally and was a Civil War buff.

Juan drove around for most of the morning, stopping at a local drive in to get a cup of coffee in a Styrofoam cup to go. He parked at the city community area and walked a short distance to a park bench where he sat, took the lid of the cup, and smelled the pungent aroma of the brew. He watched young mothers tending to their charges on the grass, and senior citizens walking their dogs to get in a little exercise to keep the arthritic bones from giving way. The day was calm, crisp, and smelled of fall. What a place to live, thought Juan, but his destiny was not in this place, but back in California.

As noon approached, Juan headed for a local café for lunch. He chose a Cobb salad, a measure to keep his waistline down. Since he had been on the road and had not exercised much, he was concerned about a growing midriff. He had always been in excellent shape, and didn't want things to change now. He finished his meal, continued to drive around the lovely area, and returned to his motel room.

Juan tried to watch television, read the newspaper, finish a crossword puzzle and nap, but his mind was so wrapped up with concern about what Wilson's answer might mean, he couldn't really concentrate on anything. Late afternoon turned to dusk, so Juan decided to take in a light supper at a local restaurant and then go to see a movie. The meal was adequate and filling and the movie a class B non-descript thriller filled with car chases and violence. The movie theater was only half full, so Juan had his choice of seats. He chose to sit on the aisle about half way down. He had purchased a small bucket of popcorn and a small Coke, you simply couldn't go to the movies without popcorn and a soda. The movie began, and about half way through, Juan had seen enough. The plot was shallow and the acting abysmal. What a waste of time Juan thought to himself.

After departing the theater, Juan walked a few blocks down the street to a local watering hole before going back to his room. A red Budweiser beer neon sign announced the establishment as "Joe's Place". The bar was in the middle of the block, an apparent holdover from many years past. The bar was made of a highly polished Teak wood with vinyl topped swiveling bar stools made of chrome. Scattered around the room were green felt top tables, a jukebox, a dartboard, and a pool table. The room was dark and smoky and only partially filled. Being that it was a week night, most of the patrons were working class people who had stopped in for a beer before going home, and a few hang on drunks who had no where else to go.

As Juan approached the bar, all of the eyes in the room moved toward him. He was a stranger in town, and wasn't going to go unnoticed. The bar tender asked him what he wanted, and Juan settled for a draft beer. The bar tender pushed a bowl of salty nuts toward him and then drew the glass of beer. Juan swallowed half the beer in the first gulp. It was cold and refreshing, and it had been a long time since Juan had had a beer. Maybe he should switch back to the malted beverage and stop the hard stuff.

Juan didn't stay long before returning to his room. He again tried to watch some television, but couldn't concentrate. He finally gave up, took a hot shower, and hopped into bed reading a pocket book he had picked up in his travels.

Sleep soon overcame Juan. He awakened at the crack of dawn. He jumped out of bed, put on his jogging clothes, and headed out towards the park. He found a well manicured path leading through the park. It surprised him that so many people were out this early either walking their canines or jogging themselves. Many of the runners looked like white collar workers probably employed in the local offices, or they were part of the grey panther set, just out for a little exercise to keep the weight and cholesterol down.

Juan finished his run back at the motel, took another hot shower and decided to take in some of the Civil War battle sites nearby. He stopped in at the visitor's bureau staffed by town volunteers and obtained an information sheet with maps indicating where the battles were fought and how to get there. He took off, spending most of the day reading markers placed in historical areas, or actually walking the fields where the skirmishes took place. He stopped frequently and looked out over the slightly rolling hills, trying to imagine what a war between brothers must have been like. He didn't mind killing the Viet Cong, because they represented a threat to the free Vietnamese and the American way of life. They were also different than the race he came from or the white race he had been assimilated into, but he had a hard time comprehending the slaughter like personages.

Juan again spent the evening having a few beers at "Joe's Place". This time when he entered the establishment, the eyes didn't turn to focus on him, they had seen him before, and the premise was that he wasn't really a stranger any longer.

He hadn't been at the bar long, when a buxom blonde cocktail waitress sidled up beside him, and occupied a stool to his left. She introduced herself as Sharon, a high school drop out who couldn't leave town because she was married to a worthless husband and had three children and no education. Juan really wasn't interested in her story, but he listened just to be polite.

Luckily, the bar tender told Sharon some of the customers at one of the tables needed some drinks. Before Sharon could get the men served and return to the seat, Juan finished his last beer and left. This night was not unlike the night before, De Ja Vu all over again. He finally made it through the sleepless ordeal, nodding off in the wee hours of the morning, just to hear the phone ring as he was about to be enveloped into a hazy, unconscious state.

The ringing startled Juan. He sat up in bed not quite knowing where he was, but then realized the phone was next to where he had been trying to sleep. He spoke a hello into the receiver, waited, and then heard Wilson come on the line.

"Good morning Sunshine, thought you would have been up by now. It must be nice to be pampered and get to sleep in."

It was five o'clock in the morning, so Juan knew Wilson was only giving him a bad time.

"Before you say anything, hear me out" Wilson said. "I have been weighing the pros and cons of your proposal. I sat up most of the last two nights with a pad and pencil, making two columns. The pros in a column on the left, and the cons on the right side. When I was finished, I had more cons than pros. I didn't sleep much. I paced the floor mostly, had too much to drink and I have a monstrous headache. With that said, I have made my decision."

As Juan was listening intently, his heart sank. He felt like he was sinking in quicksand and he was about to go under and die a slow and painful death.

Again Wilson spoke. "Meet me for dinner tonight at The Starlight Café downtown, it is on Main Street, you can't miss it. Meet me at 7:00 o'clock sharp."

Juan knew better than to question Wilson, and he knew the hours remaining until their rendezvous would be torturous at best. The rest of the day moved like slow flowing lava, the stress and tension becoming unbearable. Finally Juan said to himself, if Wilson turns me down, I will just have to find someone else. I don't know who I can turn to on such short notice, but that is the ills of war.

It was less than a ten minute walk to the café, but Juan left ten minutes early just to make sure. As Juan walked along the tree lined street, he breathed deeply to reduce the tension and commanded himself to think positively. He had had worse disappointments, so he would survive this ordeal as well.

When Juan entered the café, it was sparsely inhabited so Juan had any choice of seating location he wanted. He was met by a young, attractive hostess who asked were he would like to sit. Juan chose a booth toward the rear of the room where more privacy would be ensured. After he was seated, he let the hostess know he was expecting someone and ordered a Martini on the rocks very dry. Even though Juan always felt Martinis tasted like kerosene, he needed the stiffest drink he could think of.

At precisely 7:00 o'clock Wilson came through the front door. He looked as though he had been dragged through a knothole backwards. His clothes were disheveled, he had a two day growth of beard, and his hair had been hastily combed. Juan thought to himself, if I owned this café, I would kick this bum out. However, the hostess knew Wilson and as Wilson nodded towards Juan, the hostess retreated into the kitchen.

Wilson sat across from Juan, looked him squarely in the eye and said, "I will do whatever you ask. Just don't make me tell you what the two pros were for me making this decision, and don't come back here until this is all over. Send me instructions on what you want done by overnight express and I will see to it. Now, lets have a steak and get wasted."

CHAPTER FORTY-FIVE

Truly, Juan and Wilson did get blown away. After far too many drinks, the proprietor of the establishment had to call a halt to the drinking. The owner ushered the two drunks into taxi cabs, paid the drivers, and gave the drivers instructions on how to dispose of the former military men.

Juan woke up the next morning in his motel room bed, completely naked, wondering how he had arrived at that state. He swallowed a couple of pain pills, washing them down with a beer, sat on the bed and flopped backward to sleep for another hour. When he again awakened, he felt much better. Juan remembered he had left his car at the bar, so he called a taxi and went to retrieve it. He had promised Wilson he would leave without any further association, so he showered, packed and left Virginia for home.

It was late when Juan arrived back in Santa Barbara, but he was rejuvenated when he unlocked the front door and opened it to see Mary standing there in a see through nightie and two glasses of sparkling wine in her hands. It didn't take much seduction for Juan to figure out what was going on. He thought about checking with the office and unpacking his bags, but both of those could wait.

After an enjoyable night of love making, Juan slept the sleep of the dead. He was so tired from all of the stress that the caresses from Mary acted like a tranquilizer. When he awakened, the sun was up, but it was still early. Mary was already showered and dressed, and was in the kitchen fixing their breakfast. Juan got out from under the blankets, took a shower, shaved, and went downstairs.

Mary didn't have to be at the hospital until later that afternoon, so the two of them sat out on the patio with their food and enjoyed the early morning. The day was cool, and promising to be sunny and mild all day. They chatted about Juan's trip to Virginia. When Juan told her about the offer he had made to Wilson and the particulars that were involved, Mary grew very silent. Juan asked her what was wrong. Mary didn't answer immediately, but then responded.

"Juan, I have never been one for dirty tricks, and I strongly disapprove of the strategy Kyle has cooked up for his run for election. It is a messy business and may come back to haunt you some day in the future. Kyle has lots of money, a good appearance, a strong platform, why does he need to go into this kind of dirty business?"

Juan understood her concern, and agreed that dirty politics were awful things, but it was the way the game was played. As their breakfast grew cold, he spent almost twenty minutes explaining the reasoning he and Kyle had gone over. Finally, Juan won Mary over to his side, but with great reservations. She said she would support him, but if the strategy failed, he was on his own to explain. She would not stand by him if disaster ensued.

Their jubilant mood had been tainted with the discussion, so they picked up their dishes, scraped the food into the garbage disposal and prepared themselves for the rest of the day.

Juan drove to the downtown campaign office with a heavy heart and many intrepidations. As he entered the busy office, the din suddenly stopped and a tremendous roar erupted. Everyone came forward to give Juan an embrace and welcome him back. Juan acknowledged the acclaim, sent the forces back to their jobs with friendly jibs, and retreated to his office. His secretary had sorted his mail. In one pile were letters demanding some sort of immediate attention, and those which could wait a few days, or those that probably could be discarded.

Juan's first priority was to contact Kyle and set up a meeting to discuss Wilson's involvement in the next few weeks. Through the intercom, Juan asked his assistant to call Kyle. In just a matter of moments, the phone rang directing Juan to line two. Kyle also welcomed Juan back and set up a meeting for the following morning, early at 7:00 A.M. before the start of the business day.

The day zoomed by for Juan. It was filled with his giving directions, approving the design of signs to be place in windows and on yards, dictating answers to the immediate letters of concern, and handling the drafting of speeches Kyle was to give during the next few days. Before Juan was aware of it, the clock struck 8:00 P.M., and he realized he hadn't eaten anything but a container of yogurt and consumed countless cups of dark coffee. He was famished, but he knew that Mary was still on shift and had probably eaten at the hospital cafeteria. He decided to step next door to a local café where most of the staff ate supper.

Juan liked the café. It was decorated like an old country inn with relics of farming implements displayed on the walls, and cotton print curtains on the windows. It had a counter, circa the 1950s, and tables scattered around the room. One could see the cooks slaving over hot stoves from anywhere in the room and the aroma of the cooking was truly American. Juan selected a table by the window and drew the menu from its holder. He ordered a T-bone steak with mashed potatoes, gravy, vegetables, and a glass of the local micro beer. The beer came first, and Juan was amazed the deep, rich taste. He must remember to order that brand again.

The meal came, cooked to perfection and steaming hot. Juan used a little steak sauce on the side, but didn't want to ruin the flavor, just enhance it. He ate slowly, savoring every bite. When he was finished, he wiped the corner of his mouth with the napkin, asked for the check, and added a generous tip to the total. He departed the café, went to his car, and drove home.

The next few weeks vanished like a time warp. There was so much going on, Juan hardly knew reality from fantasy. Meeting followed upon meeting, speech followed speech, and the days blended together like a montage. Kyle had filed for the primary elections just to make everything official. Two other candidates had also filed to compete against him within the Democratic Party. The first opponent was Phil Miller, a local businessman and millionaire. Phil had never been involved in the political scene except to provide money to other campaigns, but for some unknown reason, he decided to parlay his fortune into what he perceived as a position of power. Juan knew Phil was a political novice, but he also knew Phil was smart and a formidable foe. He looked like a center for a basketball team, average, good looking in a rugged sort of way, prematurely gray for his age, but with the physical looks of a movie idol. Phil had made his money by being an astute individual, using every dirty trick in the book to have things go his way. Juan also knew Phil would stop at nothing to win the primary and enter the run off with the Republican choice who was on the GOP side of the primary without opposition.

Phil would be a hard nut to crack, so Juan gathered as much information on him as possible, and sent it to Wilson for investigation. The other Democratic opponent was Dale Shawley, a local attorney who at one time had been a prosecuting attorney in another part of the state. Dale was not a political novice, but had been around the scene as a city councilman, a district party chairman, and a campaign manager for several successful state legislators. Dale would be another worthy combatant, but in Juan's estimation, not the measure of Phil. Dale was a dowdy man, prone to wearing rumpled suits and letting his unsightly beard go untrimmed. Juan wasn't sure how the man ever got involved in government in the first place. There must be something about the man that was an unknown quantity, but Juan never underestimated anyone. Again, Juan gathered the information he needed on Dale and sent it off to Wilson.

A couple of weeks went by and Juan still hadn't heard from his Vietnam buddy. Juan wasn't unduly worried, because he knew Wilson had all of the facilities to get the job done. Juan's days were filled with daily activities which seem to run on like the river of no return. He had met so many people, he couldn't possibly remember all of their names, but he shook their hands at receptions, remarked on how nicely dressed the women were, and urged those attending the parties to vote for Kyle.

Shortly after the primary campaign began, the first polls came out. Phil was leading Kyle by 30 points capturing 58 percent of the take with Kyle holding his own at 28 percent. Dale was a distant third at 10 percent with 4 percent undecided. Kyle called Juan into his office obviously disturbed by the numbers. It was time to call for a gathering of the key strategy people to see what was needed to reverse this trend.

The group met and proposed Kyle invite Phil and Dale to an open forum debate on the issues affecting the state of California and the nation. The debate would be held at local colleges around the region, open to the public, and designed along the same lines as the Kennedy versus Nixon debates. It was also agreed to ramp up the television spots during prime time for greater exposure of the philosophies Kyle stood behind. The money had been pouring in at a steady rate, and the budget could certainly handle the increased expense of the new media blitz.

Juan contacted the offices of Dale and Phil, and was soundly rejected. They wanted nothing to do with any debates. Let the people decide as they hear each of us individually they said. Juan advised Kyle on this development, and new plans were made to hammer home in the new ads this lack of backbone by Kyle's anti-debate opponents. Juan located another ad manager who had developed just such ads for other people who had successfully achieved seats in the U.S. Senate and House of

Representatives. A contract was consummated with the new ad manager, and script writing and taping of the new ads began.

The new approach seemed to be working. In a week, the margin between Phil and Kyle had narrowed to 15 points, the lead cut in half. There was every indication their new strategy was paying dividends, and that the margin would continue to close. Over the next few weeks, the margin truly did narrow, then widened, then narrowed, and suddenly took a turn for the worse. All of the gain Kyle had made seemed to be dissipating into thin air. Panic in the office seemed everywhere. The gloom was so thick, one could cut it with a knife. It was almost palpable. No matter what turns Juan could put in place, Phil was able to side step them and come off as the best choice.

Juan still hadn't heard from Wilson, and only three weeks remained before the primary balloting began. Juan was not sleeping nights. He shunned Mary's advances to make love, and he hardly ate. Large, dark blue circles began to form under his eyes and his clothes hung on him frame like a robe on a skeleton. He knew it would take a miracle to stem the flow, and then the miracle happened.

A FedEx truck pulled up to the front of the headquarters, double parked in the street and a uniformed delivery specialist entered the office. A staffer asked to assist the driver, but the FedEx employee told him that his instructions were to give the package directly to Juan and no one else. The staffer escorted the driver to Juan's office where Juan signed for the package on the appropriate line and dropped it onto his desk as the driver left. Juan stared transfixed at the package. The return address on the upper left hand corner told Juan that Wilson had sent it. Juan was full of uneasiness, not knowing whether the contents would spell success or doom. It was late in the afternoon, and Juan was exhausted. Should he open the package and be done with it, or should he delay the inevitable until the following morning when he was fresher, and more able to take the consequences.

Oh what the hell, Juan grumbled to himself, let's get this over with.

Juan kept a bayonet in his desk drawer, a reminder of his days in Vietnam, to open boxes and large packages. The weapon, sharpened to a fine edge, sliced easily through the paper tape which sealed the insides. The file in the envelope was approximately two inches thick, containing typed pages and photos arranged to coincide with the text. Slowly Juan began to read through the file.

Phil came from a privileged background. His father was a prominent attorney, and his mother a college professor. He attended only private schools where the rich were not to mingle with the common folk of the city. After elementary school, he attended a prestigious military prep academy. Juan looked at the picture of this handsome lad in his cadet uniform. Charisma was written all over his face, and one could surmise from the photo this young man was going to succeed in life. As Juan continued to read, the fact that although Phil had attended a military high school, he had never spent on day on active duty or in the reserve components. Juan made a note of this on his long, yellow legal pad.

After the prep school, Phil applied for and was admitted to Stanford University in Palo Alto. He majored in political science and economics, and according to his college transcript was an above average student. He joined a Greek fraternity, the largest on campus. The fraternity jokingly called itself, not by it's real name, but the name touted in jest was, "I felt a thigh". Another note was made. When Juan turned the next page, rockets exploded and Juan's hair stood on end. The information on the page jumped off the page and shouted, "We hit the mother lode."

The pages which followed were a copy of court transcripts dated during Phil's freshman year when he was seventeen years old, soon to be eighteen. Apparently the humorous Greek name the fraternity adopted had meaning. Phil was accused of participating in a gang rape of a freshman coed in the fraternity house. Six members of the fraternity were involved, all older than Phil. The parents had tried to buy off the accusers, but had failed and the case had gone to a hearing. The older members where hauled into superior court, but Phil had his hearing in juvenile court since he had not reach the age of majority.

Phil was found guilty by the judge and sentenced to a hefty fine and three years of probation for his crime, a mere slap on the wrist. Juan was astounded that this court record was in the file. Normally, juvenile records are sealed by the courts and never opened to the public. How Wilson got a hold of these records amazed Juan, but he didn't ask any questions. The majority of the file chronicled Phil's life. He graduated from Stanford, went on the law school, and joined his father's firm. The final section of the file was almost as damning as the rape record. Documents indicated that Phil had been involved in influence peddling. Juan was sure that, without the knowledge of Phil' father, Phil had used the firm to put pressure on Congressional members to pass legislation favorable to the interest Phil had in a corrupt development firm. This firm was set up to rake in money by scamming unsuspecting investors.

Juan took the notes he had made and the file to Kyle. It was decided a private meeting with Phil was in order. Kyle asked his secretary to make the arrangements. In just minutes, the intercom buzzed. Kyle's secretary told Kyle she had contacted the opponents' office and he was on the line, wanting to know what in the hell was going on. Kyle picked up the phone, chatted briefly with him and returned the phone to its receiver.

"The meeting is set for three o'clock this afternoon. I think Phil will see it our way. Have everything ready, Phil is coming to our turf with his personal lawyer."

In less than half an hour, Phil and his sidekick stormed into Kyle's office, barging past the secretary as though she was invisible. She tried to stop the two of them, but they were like raging bulls in a China shop. She jumped to one side, barely escaping a shoulder, which would have thrown her against the wall and possibly done her bodily harm.

Phil threw open Kyle's office door and stood in the doorframe. His face was so red, it was hard to distinguish the color from the red, white, and blue striped tie he wore. He was so frustrated, the words would not erupt from his lips.

His personal attorney wedged himself between Phil and the door forcing both of them to spill into the room. Phil placed his hands on his hips and grunted, "I repeat, what the hell does this meeting mean?"

"Before this conversation goes any further," Kyle shot back, "I think we ought to close the door so the whole world in not privy to this conversation. Would either of you like a drink to take the edge off?"

"I won't drink your damned whiskey," Phil snorted. "Let's get to the bottom of this shit pile now!"

Kyle didn't delay in breaking the news they had acquired about Phil and his past life. The effect was one of pure deflation. The steam went out of Phil as if the pressure gauge had broken and let off a fountain of hot mist. Phil slumped to the leather couch sitting next to the wall and hung his head in his hands. His attorney knelt down beside Phil and asked if the information was true. Phil nodded dejectedly to the affirmative.

The sidekick stood slowly, looked at Kyle and asked how they had obtained this information from sealed court records. Kyle wasn't about to reveal his sources, so he remained silent. The air was so thick, a surface to surface missile would not have penetrated it.

Phil rose. "You are going to use this against me aren't you?"

"And why not, I am merely using the same tactics you have used all of your life against others. How does it feel to finally have the shoe on the other foot?"

"There is no way I can dissuade you?"

"None, that I can think of."

"How much would it cost me?"

"I wouldn't stop now for all the money you salted away in some off shore bank for your future retirement, and I am sure that is a considerable amount."

In the next split second, Phil reached inside his coat pocket and withdrew a small 38 caliber chrome pistol. He aimed it squarely at Kyle and demanded that the file be handed over immediately. Kyle felt the adrenaline rush to his head, making him feel faint, but quickly recovered stared Phil down.

"Go ahead and shoot, you Lilly-livered coward. Don't you know if you kill me you will go to the gallows and be hung for the true criminal you are. You will lose everything including your life. But, I will make you a deal, withdraw from the race and I will turn everything I have over to you and no one will be the wiser."

"Let me think it over, and I'll let you know."

Phil and his attorney left much slower than they arrived. In minutes they had exited the building, entered their car and drove off. Kyle and Juan let out a sigh of relief, broke out two glasses and downed three fingers of Scotch. The next morning, they read in the newspaper that Phil had committed suicide. No apparent reason was given, there was no suicide note.

CHAPTER FORTY-SIX

Now that Miller was out of the picture, the California polls showed over 80 percent of his votes had shifted to Kyle. Simply stated, Kyle would walk away with the primary by a landslide. Even knowing this, the campaign stayed in high gear. Juan and Kyle were not leaving anything to chance. They knew once the primary was over, and Kyle declared the Democratic nominee, the race for the Senate seat would be much easier. It was a well known fact that congressional leaders from the state were generally Democratic even though the governorship had been Republican from time to time.

The primary arrived without fanfare. Kyle and Juan went to their respective precincts to cast their ballots. Kyle took every photo op that he could as he inserted his ballot into the ballot box. Juan waltzed in and out without notice. Kyle, Juan, their wives, and party workers gathered at a hotel in Santa Barbara to wait for the election returns. The ballroom with festooned with red, white, and blue balloons with matching bunting on the guest of honor's table, and similar trapping hanging from the walls and ceiling. Round tables seating a dozen people per table were scattered around the room. Waiters were standing by with chilled bottles of champagne awaiting the decisive moment. In the meantime, a hosted bar was open serving the favorite beverages to those attending.

There were television sets scattered around the room so that everyone could see the countdown. The sets were tuned to all three major networks although the information was the same. Kyle thought it only fair that the three be represented so as not to show favoritism, and besides people did have their preference to broadcasters.

The evening started with the final results as the polls closed across the nation. Some of the primary elections went the way the pundits had predicted, but others were just too close to call. As everyone but Kyle and Juan were getting politely stewed, the initial count from California was announced. With four percent of the votes counted, Kyle Smith is leading his opponent Dale Shawley. Kyle didn't like the closeness of the race, but only four percent of the votes had been counted, and the Smith strongholds of Los Angeles, San Diego, and Sacramento were still to come in.

The evening dragged on. Kyle was starting to wear down. The adrenaline rush had passed, and the letdown phase was kicking in. The temperature in the room was like a sauna bath. Kyle just wanted to get the damn thing over with and move on to the next phase, the head to head race with the Republican challenger, Dan Daniels. As the clock was ticking near midnight, the announcer returned to California and stated that fifty percent of the votes had been counted, and their network was predicting Kyle Smith the winner by a landslide. Corks exploded like a twenty-one gun salute. Wine glasses were filled to overflowing and everyone broke into a chorus of "He's A Jolly Good Fellow". Staffers and invited guests alike all took their turns expressing their congratulations and best wishes to Kyle. Finally it was over, the televisions were turned off, and the crowd dispersed for home. Kyle and Juan had rented rooms in the hotel for their families, so up the elevator they went, hopefully to sleep.

The next few months were used to prepare for the November presidential and congressional elections. Again, Juan and his staff followed a meticulous path they had been planning for some time. In the interim, Wilson had compiled and sent to Juan another large file on Dan Daniels. Juan wasn't sure they would need it, so he placed the file in his safe just in case he would have to use it. Juan didn't even bother to open it, knowing the expertise of Wilson, assured that all the information they would need was there.

As expected, Kyle also won the general election by a wide margin. The fight had been fought and had been won. Another celebration party was somewhat of a let down for Juan, there wasn't the ferocity in this segment as there was in the primary. Juan was always looking for a good fight and the close ones where cherished so much more. Over the ensuing weeks, Kyle and his wife packed up and moved to Washington D.C. and his new job as a freshman Senator.

Juan received correspondence from Kyle describing the new office, the orientation and the challenges to be faced. Kyle even offered a job to Juan as one of his in house aides, which Juan turned down with appreciation. Juan wouldn't have minded going to the seat of power in the United States, however, the timing was not yet correct. In Juan's gut, he felt something like this would happen. But only time would tell. Juan closed up the campaign headquarter, paid the staff for their services, and returned to his primary job as assistant District Attorney. He said goodbye to as many of the helpers as he could, knowing some of them had gone with Kyle to the Congress in a supporting role.

Getting back to work posed no problem for Juan. Sarah had seen to it his caseload was small upon his return, giving him time to readjust to the local court business. When he walked into his office on the first day back, there was a large bouquet of flowers on his desk, along with a fifth of Juan's favorite whiskey and a note from Sarah applauding his return. Juan appreciated the gesture. He had been drinking so much of that type of whiskey, he was getting rather used to it.

The cases were prepared and taken to trial. Juan, as usual, won a majority of them and was establishing himself as a young Trojan in the legal trenches. Sarah was more than pleased with his performance and often told him so joking from time to time that she had better watch out or Juan would soon be having her job. She never realized how prophetic that thought would prove to be.

It didn't take long for Juan's job to become mundane and boring. The cases he tried were the same thing over and over. He was afraid of losing his political edge doing this kind of work. He didn't sleep well at night and longed for the challenge of the political arena. Again, he knew he was destined for bigger and better things in the future. He began laying his plans to run for the Office of District Attorney of Santa Barbara County. He revered Sarah, but she was getting along in years and was now following a predictable approach to business as usual. She was not attacking the kinds of crime which Juan knew the populace was worried about. She was taking on the slam dunk cases she knew they could win and ignoring the corporate fraud and ineptness of the police department. There were rumors on the streets and in the editorials in the newspapers hinting the District Attorney's Office was not serving the county well.

Juan knew Sarah's term of office would be up in one year. He didn't want to stab her in the back, but knew now was the time for him to make his move. The District Attorney's weekly staff meeting was just ending late Friday night. Juan waited around until everyone left, so he could approach Sarah alone. He sat in his chair at the conference table while Sarah bid her goodbyes to each assistant, wishing them a good weekend of fun and frivolity.

As the last member of the staff exited the room, Sarah turned to Juan. "I expect you wanted to talk to me alone. What's on your mind?"

"Sarah, your term of office will be up in a year, and I don't know what your plans are, but I wanted to let you know about mine. You have been a wonderful boss, and I hope you have found my loyalty to be of the highest standard. Because of that, I am telling you that I propose to seek your position in the next election. I didn't want you to find out about it in the newspapers, or on television, or from a friend. I know this must come as a shock to you. I have thought it over and over, and have found I desire the political arena more and more. I want to start here, and work my way up the ladder to the highest possible position however long that takes."

Juan let his statement ferment in Sarah's physche for a short while. Then Sarah spoke.

"Well Juan, thank you for your candor and loyalty. I kind of had the expectation you might like to see me retire and leave the job to you. That might not be a bad idea at all. I have served the citizens of Santa Barbara County for many years, and I am at the age when I would like to spend more time with my family, especially the grand-children. I don't need the job for the money. I just wanted to stay active as long as my health remained good. I do have some outside interests that I have been wanting to pursue for many years, and this might be the best timing I could have hoped for. Yes, I think I will retire and help you get what you want."

Juan was overwhelmed with Sarah's remarks and he sat there in stunned silence.

She continued. "What we need is a planning session with the local Democratic chairperson, Fritz Brimmer. Why don't I give him a call and arrange a meeting between the three of us as to exactly how to proceed."

"Sarah, I don't know what to say. I was hoping you would be ame-nable to the proposition, but this is too good to be true. You will never know how much this means to me. Please let me know when we can meet." Juan was so appreciative that he didn't have to use the services of Wilson.

As Juan arose from his chair and started his exodus to the door, Sarah stopped him with a maternal hug, the kind a mother would give a son. Their eyes met directly, and a partnership crossed between them. Juan was on cloud nine and all aglow. He couldn't wait to tell Mary.

When Juan arrived at their residence, Mary had gotten there ahead of him. That was strange thought Juan, Mary's shift at the hospital wasn't due to be over for a couple of more hours. Juan found Mary in the kitchen, stirring her cup of coffee randomly without purpose. Her face had taken on a demeanor Juan had not noticed before.

Juan sat down at the table across from her and said he had something to tell her. She held her fingers to his lips and said she had something to tell him first. She almost shouted out, "I'm pregnant!"

"Darling, that is just so wonderful. I wondered why you were home when I got here. When did you find out?"

"This afternoon. Doctor Whittaker confirmed the test and told me. He says I'm about six weeks into the term and everything looks good. He says I am healthy and should be able to continue to work unless something comes up which he doesn't expect. He wants to see me every two weeks for the next six months, then weekly as I go into the third trimester."

"Does he know whether it will be a boy or girl?"

"No, silly, he won't know that for some time when he does the ultra-sound. Then again, do you really want to know, or do you want a surprise?"

"I guess you're right. I don't care as long as the baby is healthy and looks like you."

They prepared their light dinner, Mary having a half a glass of wine, knowing that soon she would have to give up alcohol all together. They washed up the dishes and went to bed. Before they nodded off, Juan asked Mary, "can we start another one so the first one will have a little brother or sister?"

"No, but we can try."

Juan could hardly contain the joy he felt in his life. He could not imagine another soul living in their house, giving them such joy. He had always wanted children, tons of them. He missed his own family in Mexico greatly. Since he had left, he had revisited his mother and siblings as often as he could. He returned home a couple of times each year when he was in college, but wasn't able to see them until his tour of duty in Vietnam was completed.

During law school, working, and getting involved in the political games, he had only been able to travel to Mexico once a year. Each time his mother seemed to grow older and grayer. He wasn't sure if she would be on the planet for too many more years. He contained the remorse he felt, but knew he was doing the very best that he could under the circumstances.

With this exciting news, he had to share this unbelievable phenomenon with those most precious to him. He asked Sarah for a few days off, and with Mary's consent, winged his way back to the garbage dump and home. He had been able to provide some money to his family and had moved them into a nicer house, but he could not convince some of his brothers there was a better life than picking through the throwaways of other people. One of his sisters had graduated from high school and had gone on to a trade school, learning to cook, but the others remained mired in the way of life only they could understand. The fear of the unknown was just to overpowering for them to break its grip.

Visiting his mother was becoming more and more of an improbable task. Juan suspected she was developing a severe case of Alzheimer's disease, but in Mexico they didn't recognize the condition and just called it old age.

His mother seemed to be doing well. She had hired a niece to take care of her daily personal needs and to clean the house. Everything seemed to be in order. As Juan talked to his mother, she would stare off into space and methodically finger her Rosary beads. Juan wasn't sure she really heard what he had to say, but she mumbled and nodded as if she did.

Juan spent some time visiting his brothers and sisters and visiting the old haunts. Carlos Gomez, the pawnshop owner had died, and a new, younger man had taken over the business. The new owner impressed Juan as being from the new breed of gang members who would just as quickly shoot you as do business with you.

Juan wasn't sure how much longer his mother would remain on this earth, but he couldn't stay any longer. He kissed her gently on the cheeks and detected a small tear cascading from her left eye. She held him tightly and wished him God speed and good luck in his new job. His new job was several years old, so Juan just dismissed the comment at part of getting old.

CHAPTER FORTY-SEVEN

After Juan returned from Mexico, he finished up his cases, and set about formulating his plans for obtaining the District Attorney's Office. True to her promise, Sarah had arranged a meet with Fritz Brimmer at an out of the way café in downtown Santa Barbara.

The three of them agreed to meet after the lunch hour. That would give them the chance to get to know each other, and explore the possibilities which lay ahead. The Café was called "The Lark", a small but very chic place, catering to the well to do and up and coming middle class of the city. It was nestled between a florist and tall men's shop on a street which intersected with other streets taking people to their offices. The décor was superb. It smacked of richness. In one corner was a sports type bar outlined in expensive teak wood, and filled with memorabilia from Santa Barbara's past. The tables were spread around the floor, spaced adequately so that private conversations could not be heard from table to table. The walls were lined with expensive art, probably the private collection of a good patron who had loaned them to the owner. There were Monet's, Piccasco's, Renoir's, and other famous artists. The paintings must have cost a fortune. Juan wondered if the owner had sufficient insurance in case of theft from a break in.

Juan was just walking up to the door when Sarah's car, a platinum colored Jaguar pulled to the curb. Luckily, Sarah had located a parking place almost in front of the eatery. Sarah emerged from the driver's side and a man from the passenger's side. Juan assumed the fellow must be Fritz Brimmer. Fritz was a tall man, well over six foot and large, but not fat. Fritz had been a farmer in a valley just north of Sacramento, growing a variety of things, but mostly Blue Diamond almonds, which individuals in that part of the country called "amonds".

Juan was struck by the informality of Fritz's dress. He was wearing a pair of jeans with a long sleeved flannel shirt, cowboy boots, and a baseball cap with The Blue Diamond logo emblazed on the front. Under the cap Fritz's hair was a mix of gray and black, and he wore standard bifocal lens glasses. He was adorned as Juan could only imagine farmers from Northern California must appear to be. Fritz looked like a country hick, but Sarah had warned Juan, Fritz had more political savvy than just about two thirds of the members of the state legislature.

As they met on the street, Sarah introduced Juan to Fritz. As the two men shook hands, Fritz's grip was strong, but not overpowering. His hands were calloused, reflective of the many years spent laboring with them. Sarah then ushered them into the café with the caveat she was hungry and they should be getting something to eat before she starved to death. Discussions could come later.

The hostess led them to a table in the back of the room to ensure absolute privacy, seated them, took their drink orders, and left them with menus to peruse. Fritz let everyone know that he normally didn't drink at lunch, but this auspicious occasion a bottle of the best wine in the house was in order. Fritz ordered a dry Merlot from the Napa Valley, and the waitress disappeared.

As the three of them began to talk, the waitress reappeared with the bottle, opened it with a corkscrew and poured a small sample into Fritz's glass. Fritz, like all good wine connoisseurs in California, swirled the wine around in the glass, held it up to the light to check the clarity, rendered a sniff with his nose, then swished a small amount in his mouth to finalize the procedure. Fritz announced his pleasure and the waitress filled each glass half full and placed the remainder of the bottle into the ice bucket.

She then took their orders. Sarah wanted the Cobb salad with vinaigrette dressing on the side. Juan ordered the fish and chips, which Sarah had told him was the specialty of the house, and Fritz rounded out the order with a club sandwich on toast.

After savoring the wine, Fritz opened the conversation.

"Juan, Sarah tells me that you want to be the next District Attorney of Santa Barbara County, is that right?"

"It is indeed, and Sarah told me you are the one who can help me attain it."

"Sarah is much too generous, but I think I can certainly help. I have worked for the Democratic Party in this state for many years, and have had considerable success doing that. We have established a broad base of support, and we have a treasure chest of local contributors whom we can count on. It certainly is a plus that you are Hispanic. We have been trying for years to get the legal Hispanic population registered to vote, and have amassed potential numbers that are mind boggling. Unlike the general American population who have become so lethargic over the past century, the new citizens are frothing at the mouth for the opportunity to exercise their new found right to vote."

"It sounds great, Juan said, where do we begin?"

"First we need to get you known to the community. Outside of the courtroom, you are an unknown quantity. To begin with, Sarah will hold a press conference and announce her retirement. You will attend the conference and have your picture taken with Sarah. I'll help prepare some short remarks for you to render to the assembled group. Then we will file your application to run for the office at the appropriate time. In the interim, I will go with you when we attend meetings of the various associations who are most interested in the job you will do. We start with the Chief of Police's office and work with him when his group meets next. We want to do the same thing with the Chief of the Fire Department, the Public Defenders Office, and the judges of the Superior Court. Then I want to have you speak at the Rotary Club, the Kiwanis, and the Lions Clubs of Santa Barbara. We should culminate with the Latino organizations, the places which will have the greatest impact on your voter base."

Before Fritz could continue, the food had arrived and was placed before them. Juan's head was in a whirlpool. He felt like he had developed a severe case of vertigo and wasn't sure he would be able to hold his food down. He paused for a moment, took a large gasp of air, and cleared his head.

They ate the delicious food at a leisurely pace, savoring each morsel, and washing it all down with some more wine. When the trio was through, they each wiped their mouths with relish, and placed their napkins on their now bare plates almost as if they had been rehearsing the ritual. They looked at each other and almost laughed in unison as each recognized what had just happened. As with Sarah, Juan felt at ease immediately with Fritz, sensing a camaraderie between them.

Fritz leaned back in his chair and rubbed his ample potbelly with his hand. He wanted to belch, but avoided the notion.

"Juan, I have several things to do this afternoon, and in as much as tomorrow is Saturday, why don't we take a couple of days to formalize how we think this thing should take place, get together Monday and compare notes."

"Sounds good to me Fritz. Where and when would you like to meet?"

"Let's say at 1:00 P.M. in Sarah's office. Bring your notes."

"Sounds good, see you then."

With this they arose from the table, said their good byes and left. Juan had his first taste of the political process as it was to affect him directly. Up until this time, he had been doing things at the wishes of Kyle, and now the shoe was on the other foot. It seemed like unfamiliar territory, but as Juan walked back to his office, ideas began to form in his mind, a coalescence of options to be considered. Juan knew the tack they were going to take would be different than that of a senatorial race, but the underlying principles were the same. Juan must come across as a positive and viable candidate. He must polish his speaking abilities, even though his courtroom manners had always been exemplary. He must conjure up a list of potential staff members to assist him, and think about individuals he could invite to some social functions, a necessary part in raising the capital he would need.

Juan attempted to slug through his work that afternoon, but his head really wasn't tuned into it. He somehow managed to get done what needed to get done, and still leave the office by a reasonable hour. He called Mary and told her he was picking up Chinese, so she wouldn't have to fix anything for dinner.

The next several months became a blur in Juan's memory. The meetings, socials, and speeches seemed to blend together. Juan had taken Fritz's advice, hired a speech writer, and had become a very polished orator. Juan's platform was simple. It contained two major planks. One was reduction in crime, and the other the prosecution of corporate fraud and abuse.

Since the time Juan first came to Santa Barbara, there had been a steady increase in violent crimes, especially armed robbery, gang related murders, and assault. The citizens of the city and county were alarmed as to the direction this trend was going, and wanted something done about it. The letters coming into Juan's office indicated the general population felt the streets were not safe any more, and Juan had vowed to take them back. No one would have imagined a city as affluent at Santa Barbara would have as much crime as was being witnessed, but times had changed. Like John Dillinger, they sought out Santa Barbara cause that's where the money was.

Likewise, because of the affluence, corporations were scamming millions of dollars for their businesses. Presidents of corporations were using their employee retirement and trust funds as their own personal bank accounts, living lavish life styles at employee expense. This too must be stopped.

Juan felt ashamed he was spending so much time away from Mary, but she didn't mind. By the time Juan was elected to the District Attorney's job, the baby would have arrived and would require her full time attention. Mary spent most of her off duty hours preparing the guest bedroom as a nursery. She reveled in shopping for items to fill the room. Juan and Mary decorated the room in neutral colors, not knowing which gender the baby would be. There were pictures of animals put into frames and hung on the walls. Matching wallpaper strips were glued next to the ceiling. They found an antique crib at a local antique store, painted white with gold trim that matched the décor perfectly. They also purchased a matching reclining couch where Mary would nurse the baby. Mary was a firm believer in nursing, the statistics had proven that nursing babies were better adjusted and less prone to disease than bottle fed ones.

The nursing staff at the hospital had given Mary a baby shower, filling in the gaps of supplies an infant would require as he or she grew. One of the nicest gifts was a two year contract for a diaper service so Mary wouldn't have to mess with the untouchables. There were also the blankets, booties, sweaters, pajamas, and sheets.

Mary had decided to work up until the delivery date. Then when the baby was born, she would take a two year leave of absence to be with the child. After that, she opted to find a nanny to care for the child so she could return. Juan wanted her to stop working and be a stay at home mom, but Mary felt she needed to resume her work to be mentally challenged. She finally convinced Juan her way was the best, and as usual, he caved in. He never could win an argument with her.

Since the Democratic Party was so dominant in Santa Barbara County, Juan's opponent for the District Attorney's position was merely a token put up by the Republicans to save face. Juan won by a huge margin, the voter turn-out being a record for the county. Nothing was more in evidence than the percentage of Hispanic votes in comparison to the others. Fritz knew where the power base was to get Juan elected, and he used it wisely.

Juan experienced the winner's celebration party, only this time, he was on the receiving end. His ego had never been stroked so much before, and he felt a power surge which almost overcame him. He was so energized and pumped after the party, he could hardly sleep. Unlike Kyle, he and Mary went home after the victory party. Mary took a shower and went to bed, nodding off almost immediately. Juan could not sleep. He thought he would watch television for a while, and then retire. Nothing on the boob tube took his fancy, so he turned it off. He had read a person should not drink alcohol before going to bed because it disrupts the sleep pattern, but Juan had already had a shipload of sparkling wine, and felt like a stiff drink was needed to help bring him back to earth.

He fixed a double shot of single malt scotch with two ice cubes and strolled out onto the patio. Finding a patio chair, Juan gazed at the pitch black sky and listened to the traffic as it roared up the interstate, people seemingly going nowhere with lots of noise. Juan sipped his drink and contemplated his next move. There would be a transition period before he officially would take office, which would give him some time to wind up his old job, take a short vacation and then assume the awesome new duties.

As he watched the stars glimmer above, the thought crossed his mind, why not take a cruise? Mary had never been on a cruise and what a golden opportunity it was to get away, have someone make up your bed every day, lie by the pool, see great entertainment, and gamble the night away. Juan made a note to stop by a travel agent's office tomorrow and pick up some literature. Many of their friends had talked about taking a cruise, extolling the virtues of such an adventure. Juan nodded his head as if in agreement with some unknown genie, finished his drink and staggered off to slumber land.

Mary thought a cruise was a brilliant idea and agreed immediately. It was decided to embark on a seven day adventure from San Diego to the Mexican Riviera with stops in Puerto Vallarta, Mazatlan, and Cabo San Lucas. Holland American was touted as the best company to book with, but the choices were difficult to make with so many cruise companies vying for the travel dollar. Juan worked out the details with the travel agent and made arrangements for a limo to take them to the port in San Diego to board the ship.

Juan and Mary attended an orientation hosted by the travel agency telling the customers what to wear, how to pack, and what to expect. Mary spent most of the next week shopping for clothes and packing for the trip.

The day of the cruise arrived with every indication the weather would be perfect for the next week. The instructions found in the dark blue leather folder furnished by the travel company instructed Juan and Mary to be at the pier in San Diego at one P.M. This would give them plenty of time to arrive, be processed by the cruise line employees and be shown to their cabin before the ship sailed at the appointed time of five P.M. The folder also included colorful luggage tags, a nameplate to be worn on their clothing, a diagram of the ship indicating the location of their space, a list of the ship's services, and an itinerary of the trip.

Juan had made arrangements for a Lincoln Town car to pick them up at their residence and transport then to the ship. The limo arrived approximately ten minutes before the scheduled time, which pleased Juan. The driver was a young man, possibly in his mid thirties, dressed in a dark black suit, white shirt and black tie. He was hatless and his shoes highly polished. He asked Juan for their luggage which he deftly handled and placed the pieces in the trunk. He held the door for the couple, backed out of the driveway, and was soon on the interstate to the rendezvous site.

The driver carried on a stream of light banter, guessing this was the first trip the fare had ever taken on a cruise liner by the questions they asked. He told them it would be a wonderful trip. He and his wife had cruised a couple of times, and he felt cruising was truly addicting. In what seemed like no time at all, the limo pulled next to the curb adjoining the pier. As Juan and Mary exited the car, they looked skyward for what seemed an eternity at the gigantic behemoth. The white luster of the outside shell of the vessel glistened in the bright sunshine like a thousand watt searchlight. The bottom half of the ship was painted a Navy blue adding a stark contrast to the scene. Juan counted twelve decks starting from the portholes, which the information Boucher indicated was the first level. To the rear or aft of the ship was a monstrous black smoke stack with the cruise line's company logo painted also in white, belching a slow, curling cloud of light gray smoke.

Juan had heard about the consumption of large amounts of fuel and the potential these big ships had for contaminating the harbor. It didn't take a genius to knew why. It was another concern for Juan to put into his memory bank for later consideration.

The driver assisted them with the baggage, depositing the cases in a luggage holding area just inside the terminal building. Juan lavishly tipped the young man, and off the holiday couple went to be in-processed.

The holding area was starting to fill up, and they were asked by a cruise line staff person, dressed in a dark blue skirt and white blouse to join one of five lines through which they would eventually come to the ticket in-processing station. The staff person asked to see their passports, their tickets, and some form of identification. Once that formality was over, the line started to move at a moderately steady pace. Juan told Mary to take a seat provided by the company for those who weren't necessary to sign in. Finally Juan approached the service counter and was warmly greeted by an attractive young woman wearing the same garb as the other female staff members. After taking a swipe of Juan's credit card to be used for on board purchases, checking his documents, and verifying Juan's signature, Juan was directed to another area where cocktails, juice, and finger foods were being offered. It was explained that Juan and Mary would now have a chance to mingle with the other guests while their luggage was being stowed in their cabin.

The refreshment center was a mob scene. The ship held almost three thousand sojourners all seeming to be talking at once. Juan and Mary were standing apart from the crowd, not sure what to do, when an elderly couple tapped them on the shoulders and asked them if this was their first cruise. Juan replied in the affirmative, and the couple immediately took Juan and Mary under their wings explaining they had grandchildren just about Juan's age who had cruised with them just this past year.

This couple professed to having taken many cruises to all parts of the world. To Juan's surprise, the gentleman was also a California attorney, recently retired from the Los Angles area. He introduced himself as Carl Evans, and his wife Nedra.

About an hour before the ship was to sail, an announcement came over the public address system directing the passengers to begin embarking onto the vessel. The acoustics in the building were so awful, Juan strained to hear the announcement and had to ask a cruise employee what was being said. Everything was clarified. They were announcing the boarding by groups. They had just called groups one through four. Juan looked at his plastic card which read group twelve. They would have a bit of a wait.

There were three gangplanks set up at a slight elevation into the fifth deck, where the purser's office and main reception areas were located. The lines moved fairly quickly, the crowd seemed to be in a festive mood, of course enhanced by the drinks that were served in the processing area.

As Juan and Mary entered the ship, they came face to face with one of the most beautiful sights they had ever witnessed. The center of the deck was an open atrium that soared to the ninth deck. Against one side was a cascading waterfall, and against the other was a glass enclosed elevator to the upper lofts. The space was completed with gift shops, salons, and a bar. Everything was gleaming like a starlit night. The glass, brass adornments, and marble floors sparkled like polished diamonds. Juan was almost afraid to step on the tiles, they were so beautiful. As if mesmerized, they just stood and gaped at the surroundings. What a wonderful start to a glorious vacation.

Juan located another elevator closer to the side of the ship where their cabin was situated. Their cabin was on the ninth deck, about mid-ship and near the elevator. This allowed Mary the convenience of not having to walk too far to access the other parts of the ship. The locks on the cabin door had slots where the plastic key cards with their names embossed on them were inserted. Juan tried his key, heard a snap, and after pushing down the handle opened the door to their home for the next seven days.

The cabin was one at the upper level of comfort. Juan didn't want a cheap inside cabin without a view of the ocean, nor did he want to spend the money for a suite. A quick glance told him they would be very comfortable indeed. Just inside the door to the left was the bathroom, with a double basin, a toilet, and a glass encased shower. The bathroom was small, but adequate. To the right of the door were a pair of matching closets with built in drawers where they could stow their clothes for the trip.

The room widened out with a king size bed snuggled up against the wall on the left, and a dresser, television, storage bureau on the right. A beautiful, heavy velvet drape hung across a room in a wide arch behind which were a two cushion sofa, a coffee table, and an upholstered chair. Beyond the sitting room were two sliding glass doors, which emptied out onto a balcony containing two plastic chairs and a plastic table. Sitting next to the table was a stand with an ice bucket crammed to the brim with their favorite white wine, compliments of the travel agency through which they bought their tickets.

The five o'clock sailing hour had arrived, announced by a sharp blast of the ship's horn, which could be heard for miles. Gently, the assigned tugboat nudged the massive ship away from the pier, rotating the tons of steel and passengers toward the open sea. Juan opened the wine, poured each of them a glass and they reclined in the chairs to watch the skyline of the city slowly pass in front of them. Juan felt as if he had been swept up on Aladdin's magic carpet and was riding a fairy tale into a far off land.

Juan had signed up for the early seating in the main dining room. In addition to the main dining room there was a smaller dining room and four restaurants, which required reservations if a passenger decided they didn't want to eat in the assigned area. They thought eating in the main dining room would be a good way to go until they had time to explore the contents of the ship and determine what amenities were there. They were greeted at the entrance by the Matre'd, dressed regally in a black tuxedo with a black bow tie and highly polished shoes. Passengers were assigned to tables of six. Part of the fun of the trip was to meet new people who one might meet at every meal, get to know personally, and perhaps become friends.

Soon after Juan and Mary were seated, two other couples joined them, rounding out the table. Introductions were made all around. The four strangers introduced themselves as being from the Baltimore area in Maryland. They explained they were touring the west coast and had decided to include the cruise from San Diego in their itinerary. The couple was a few years older than Juan and Mary, but not enough that it made them feel uncomfortable.

Names were exchanged. Bill and Fran Maczis were both retired elementary school staff. Bill completing his career as the principal of the school and Fran was one of his teachers. Bill was a tall, slightly balding, dark haired man whose skin looked leathery as if he spent a lot of his time out of doors. Bill had been a Marine during the Korean conflict and was very interested in military history. Juan explained he was a Vietnam veteran, and an immediate bond was created. Fran was a diminutive blonde woman, with a southern accent, quick to smile, and displayed a natural gift of gab. The other couple was Jim and Shirley Powell who lived just a few miles from Bill and Fran on the outskirts of the city. Jim was a retired transportation executive who had traveled all over the nation in the trucking business. Shirley, like Fran, had been one of Bill's teachers. Jim was a short, gray haired curmudgeon sort of a fellow, with a quick grin as if there were a little devilishment in him. Shirley also had gray hair, was just slightly taller than Jim and bore the charisma of a loving and kindly soul. Shirley explained that she dabbled in oil painting, but wasn't really very good, to which the other three present scoffed. They said Shirley was really very good, and her paintings had won numerous prizes at art shows and county fairs. The four of them had cruised with each other to other parts of the world, and they enjoyed getting away on these hotels that floated.

Juan and Mary delved into their backgrounds and Mary was congratulated when she announced the to be arrival of their first child. A couple of bottles of wine were ordered, tasted, approved, and their glasses filled. A toast to new made friends was made, and everyone clinked their glasses together in salute to a new friendship.

The waiter arrived at the table, dressed in the likeness of the host, with a white cloth draped over his arm in the French style. They opened their menus to a delicious set of choices. They could choose from three appetizers, a hot or cold soup, three salads, five entrees, and six desserts. Mary had a hard time deciding which to chose, but soon made up her mind. The waiter took their orders and disappeared into the kitchen. Mary was certain that if she continued to eat all of this wonderful food, she would weigh more than her physician would allow. She had been cautioned not to gain too much, and she vowed to violate the code this one time, but resolved to watch what she ate the rest of the trip.

The group retired to the lounge area to take in the evening's show, a Broadway tribute to Cole Porter. They found some seats, ordered a nightcap, and sat in stunned silence as the curtain rose on a chorus of spectacularly dressed, young entertainers.

The rest of the week zoomed by like a NASCAR tournament race. Bingo in the afternoon, dance lessons, gambling in the casino, a workout in the more than adequate gym, lounging by the pool, walking the top deck, and course, more food. It seemed like the cruise lines had an endless supply of calories for their payers to consume. Not only were three standard meals each day, but there were snacks in the morning and afternoon, an ice cream bar open all day, a cafeteria line on one of the upper decks, and a midnight buffet complete with a different ice sculpture each setting. After the first day, Juan and Mary simply limited themselves to a light breakfast, a small afternoon snack, and banishment of the bewitching hour grub.

They enjoyed the on-shore excursions. When the ship docked at Mazatlan, Puerto Vallarta, and Los Cabos, they hopped aboard the bus, and were shuttled into the cities to shop, watch cultural shows and visit the tourist spots like "Senor Frog". They watched the native Indians tie a long rope to their ankles, climbing up a very high pole, winding the rope as they went, then casting themselves out into space and spinning around the pole as they descended closer and closer to the ground. The crowd sucked in its breath as the ground came up to meet the daredevils, but the rope played out just inches shy of total disaster.

They bought the usual stuff, Mexican silver, tee shirts, serapes, painted gourds, and other local crafts. Juan, having a command of the Spanish language was more adept at haggling with the merchants, and assisted others on the cruise in purchasing their goodies. Juan and Mary didn't go to excess, realizing there was only a finite amount of room in their luggage, and they didn't want to go through the expense of having to ship their purchases back to the states.

In Mazatlan, they watched a bare skinned diver position himself on a rocky shelf above the cascading surf, poised at a height that would scare most people. The diver timed his leap off the shelf to coincide with the upsurge of the wave, allowing the diver to enter the ocean with the maximum level for safety purposes. History had revealed that many of these young male divers mis-timed their dives, and crashed into sunken rocks at a very shallow depth, and were killed. As the diver exited the ocean at the conclusion of his performance and placed himself back at the base of the rock, the tourists tossed Pesos at his feet to pay for the excitement they felt. He collected the shiny silver coins, and bowed in gratitude to the crowd, ascended the rock and repeated the dive. Juan wondered how many times this challenge would take place in a day as he and Mary walked back to the bus for the return trip back to the ship.

After a small dinner, Mary told Juan she just preferred to rest and not take in the show. Big dinners and late evenings were taking their toll on this young mother to be. She just wanted to go to the cabin, read for awhile, and go to bed early. Juan walked her back down the spotless corridor, unlocked the door with their pass chip and let her inside. Juan wasn't ready to turn in a just yet, so he told Mary he wanted to walk around the ship for a spell. Mary kissed him lightly on the lips and said okay.

After Juan closed the door, he decided to take the elevator to the fifth deck and to stroll completely around the ship at that level. The fifth deck was one of the few decks where one could circumnavigate around the ship. Most of the decks did not have walkways, or were comprised of rooms with verandahs. Juan crossed the luxurious reception area, noting people were still making arrangements for land excursions at Cabo and other arrangements when they returned to the United States. On the other side of the reception, crowds of people were milling around getting ready to move on to the show. Everyone was in a festive mood, the adrenaline still flowing from the first day. Juan wondered if some of these individuals ever slept.

He ventured out of one of the large teak doors and into the soft, balmy night. There were a few other strollers, but for the most part, Juan was alone. As he moved about the decking, he would pause on occasion to look at the beautiful Pacific Ocean. As he neared the bow of the ship, he paused to watch the vessel slice through the ocean, forming a vee shaped wake of white water cascading onto the dark blue water on each side, like icing on a frosted cake. The deck chairs used during the day had been neatly stacked against the bulkhead, ready for the next usage.

As Juan finished approximately three quarters of his stroll, he noticed Bill Maczis leaning over the railing looking deeply into the azure blue of the ocean. As Juan neared, Bill was just lighting up a long, black cigar. Even though Bill knew smoking was a filthy and nasty habit he had picked up with the Marines in Korea, during times of relaxation, Bill just couldn't resist the savor of a good cigar. Bill was forced to retreat to the outside of their cabin as Fran would have nothing to do with these stinky creatures anywhere near her. She complained about the stench on his clothes, so after Bill finished, he would walk about enough to clear out most of the smell.

"Good evening Juan", Bill said as he watched his new found friend approach. "What brings you out on an evening like this?"

"Oh, Mary didn't feel like taking in any entertainment and wanted to lie down and rest for a while. I didn't feel like joining her, so I thought I would walk off some of the calories so I can continue to get into my pants. That cigar surely smells good. I don't smoke, but that aroma might make one consider it strongly."

"No, you don't want to take up this habit, it would turn you into an isolated figure in less than a minute once you put the end ablaze and your wife was within smelling range."

"You are probably right," commented Juan.

For the next several minutes, Bill and Juan chatted about the trip, all of the high lights they had seen, people they had met, and nourishment they had over done. Juan had told Bill much about his past, but it was speaking of politics that brought out the sparkle in Juan's eyes.

"Juan, what are your plans for the future? I know you are the District Attorney of Santa Barbara County, but what's next?"

"I guess I will see what I can accomplish in that job and possibly move on to the California State Legislature. Who knows, maybe even Governor of the state. I see so much that needs to be done, and more efficient ways to do it. The state has been rife with corruption and the immigrants are a problem we all have to do something about. The cost of living is increasing so rapidly in that part of the U.S., housing and medical care have spawned a new generation of welfare recipients and our Medical Insurance coverage is beginning to become a huge funding problem. I know the current administration is in the hands of the big corporations, but they are so strongly ingrained in the system, it may take years to uncover just how bad things are, and then get elected to do something about it."

"It sounds as though you have an ambitious task facing you. I applaud your courage to project yourself into the future with such lofty goals. I like your fire and if it weren't for the Constitution of the United States prohibiting a foreign national from becoming President of the United States, I'll bet you would try for that as well."

"You know Bill, that wouldn't be a bad aspiration. I know it would take an amendment to the constitution for me to get a shot at the highest office in the land, but stranger things have happened. One never knows."

"Well Juan, if you ever reach that plateau, get in contact with me. After I retired from being a principal of an elementary school, I got involved with the local Democratic Party and did some part time lobbying for the educational system. In my travels, I have become to know quite a few powerful Senators, Congressmen, and local Democratic people. Maybe, someday, I can give you a helping hand."

Bill Maczis could not have said a more prophetic word. Little did he know that fate would revisit him and turn his life upside down.

The cruise ended much too quickly. On the final morning of the cruise, the six friends sat at the familiar table for their last communal breakfast. Their luggage had been taken ashore, to be reclaimed later when they left the ship. When the last of the greasy eggs and syrup had been wiped from their lips, they returned to their cabins to brush their teeth, gather up their carry on items and disembarked from the ship.

At the bottom of the gangplank, they gave embraces and kisses all around, and vowed to keep in touch as often as possible. Fran and Shirley insisted that Mary get the word to them when the baby arrived so they could send an appropriate gift. Mary said it wasn't necessary, but the other women they wouldn't hear of not doing something for the little tyke. The six of them parted, Juan and Mary heading directly to the parking lot where their limo awaited them for the trip back to Santa Barbara.

CHAPTER FORTY-EIGHT

The frivolity was over. The time had come for Juan and Mary to get back to work. It was hard returning to the grind after such a wonderful outing with newly found friends. The transition between Juan and Sarah went smoothly. Juan officially took office on January 1st, but Sarah indicated she would be available to assist him for the next three months just to tie up any loose ends that he might have questions about.

When Juan arrived at the District Attorney's office, the staff was there to greet him. A banner hung over the door to the reception area and the area was filled with floral arrangements of every description. The staff all sang "For He's A Jolly Good Fellow", Sarah standing right in the middle, chirping away with the best of them. Sarah escorted Juan to his new center of authority for the next four years. Sarah had cleaned out her personal items which would allow Juan to decorate the space to his own liking. The room was Spartan, richly lined with dark wood paneling, and floor to ceiling windows behind an antique teak desk that came with the position. Dark red, velvet drapes hung along the windows, items Juan had not noticed when he had visited Sarah there. There was a dark mahogany leather couch against one wall, and two matching leather chairs in front of the desk. Two floor lamps were neatly tucked into the corners to offer indirect lighting for effect when desired. Sarah had once had a large fish tank along one wall, but that was gone. Juan was going to have to think for a while about filling the room, but that would come later.

Sarah called in Juan's secretary Shirl Margee, so that she, Juan and Shirl could go over the pending cases for which Juan would have to make assignments to the assistant district attorneys. As Shirl briefly gave Juan a synopsis of each case, Sarah inserted a recommendation on which assistant was the best choice to receive the assignment. Juan knew the assistants, but did not have access to the intimate files or knowledge Sarah had. The meeting went well, and in a couple of hours, all of the pending cases were completed. Shirl left Juan and Sarah alone, to attend to other pressing phone calls, messages, and emails. Sarah closed the door, offered Juan a drink from the wet bar hidden in the wall paneling, another perk of the office, a well stocked bar. They joined each other on the leather couch, touched glasses, took a sip and relaxed.

Sarah spent the next hour giving Juan the lay of the land, the powers-that-be in the county government, those who could trusted, and those who couldn't. She spoke to the alliances she and her predecessors had forged, and encouraged Juan to contact them to create the link necessary to continue the ease at which the District Attorney's Office operated. Juan didn't take any notes, he committed everything Sarah said to memory. Juan had learned long ago that information of this nature, once written down, could sometimes come back to bite one. The information Sarah was relaying to Juan was of the highest quality, and would give Juan a formidable edge in the future. They finished their conversation, polished off their drinks, and stood. Sarah reached up, pulled Juan's face to hers, and gave him a soft, motherly kiss on the lips. Juan knew that if anything were to happen, he could certainly count on Sarah as if she were his own mother.

The staff came together like a well oiled machine. Each morning Juan conducted a meeting to go over the cases the assistants were working on, to give direction, and receive input. The meetings were short. Juan had always felt meetings that lingered on and on were not well thought out, and were a waste of people's time. He cautioned the staff always to be prepared when their turn arose, so as not to impede the speed in which the office work was getting done.

Juan reaffirmed the two activities which were the major part of his election. One: to reduce crime in the county, and second, to go after corporate fraud. Juan knew the country sheriff, working in close cooperation with the city chief of police could take care of the first item, but the second would need a little more finesse by himself and his senior staff. Juan decided to tackle the reduction in crime first. He put in a call to the Police Chief, getting the Chief's administrative assistant on the first ring. She told Juan to hold on a few seconds and she could put the call through. Juan was lucky, the Chief was a very busy man, and trying to capture him in his office was usually a monumental task.

The Chief came on the line, expressed his congratulations for Juan's new position, and asked how he could be of service. Juan spent the new few minutes explaining his expressed desires in the area of crime, and suggested that the Chief and his major division leaders join Juan for a Sunday bar-b-que at Juan's house. Juan wanted to let the top dogs in the police department hear what he had to say without the pressures of the office standing in the way. A date was selected, the Chief letting the District Attorney know he would contact his minions and he would have them there.

The agreed upon Sunday arrived. Juan and Mary had the party catered except for the meat. Juan had chosen New York cut steaks, ribs, chicken, and wurst. This way, Juan reasoned he could please everyone. Of course, the wives were also invited. To round out the food fare, there were three types of salads, rolls, corn on the cob, baked beans, beer, soft drinks, and hard liquor. Juan was well accustomed to the idea that the best way to a man's heart, or a woman's for that matter, is through their stomach. Having everything except the meat ready would allow Juan some time to mingle, get to know the Police

Department top dogs, and discuss the problem areas they need to face while the meat was cooking.

The guests began to arrive. Juan estimated approximately twenty or so would be attending. The Chief was the first to arrive. Rod Fuller was a veteran of four other police departments, and had spent over twenty-five years in serving the community. He came from an Army, Military Police background, having served in Vietnam as had Juan. Rod was a large man, holding a bald head directly upon his shoulders. His neck was not visible. He was dressed in casual clothing, similar to what one would expect while on vacation in Hawaii. A brightly flowered shirt, a pair of shorts, and sandals without socks. A huge gold chain hung around his neck, matching a solid gold watch on his left wrist. His wife was a short, lovely woman, several years his junior. Juan surmised that she must be the Chief's second or third wife. Juan greeted them warmly, and asked them to stand with him to greet the others.

One by one, the directors of the divisions arrived with their spouses. The Chief introduced each one to Juan and Mary, kidding each with some personal information about their job, their families, or their shapes. It was all in good humor. Juan directed everyone to the bar for the first round. It didn't take long for the party to get into full swing. Soon the meat was done, and the feasting began.

After the crowd had gorged itself, Juan invited the wives to join Mary along side the pool, and he escorted the policemen off to another corner of the spacious yard. For the better part of the next hour, Juan solicited information from them. He wanted to know where the critical crime areas were in the city and county, what types of crimes the police force was experiencing an increase in, and what solutions they thought might work to meet the goals Juan was seeking. None of this was recorded. Juan had a brain that could absorb tons of information, and have instant recall once he got back to his office. When the informal meeting was over, Juan let the group go back to the party, but retained the Chief for just a few seconds more. Juan thanked him very much for his cooperation and input from his staff. Juan told the Chief that he would draft up a battle plan, and send it to the Chief in a week's time, asking for comments, suggestions, and recommendations. When all of the input was received, Juan promised to get together with the Chief and formalize their operational document.

The chemistry between the two men was extraordinary. Juan now knew he had a wonderful ally, not only in reducing crime, but in furthering his political career.

CHAPTER FORTY-NINE

Over the next twelve months, the plan the Chief of Police and Juan had masterminded, started to pay dividends. Violent crime against people and property was down sixty percent. This included murders, aggravated assault, and home robberies. Vandalism in the county was down almost as much. The people of the area were starting to feel safer, and they expressed their satisfaction by awarding Juan the title of "Santa Barbara County Man of the Year." Another punch in the go-to-the-top card for Juan, one he could salt away in his bank of treasures.

With things going so smoothly on the crime front, Juan turned more of his attention to the task of ferreting out fraud and corruption in the corporate world. His first target was the largest construction company in the county. Juan's investigators had uncovered flagrant abuses of city and county contracts, inasmuch as the contractor had grossly overcharged both municipalities for work involving highways, low cost housing, and governmental buildings. Not only was overcharging uncovered, but a growing list of complaints were coming in about the sub-par caliber of the work being done. Once one complaint was uncovered, the word spread, and complaints came rolling in like the tide.

In one instance, a four story parking garage had collapsed, killing several people and doing untold damage to hundreds of cars. It was later determined the cause was inferior concrete which could not hold the weight placed upon it. The CEO of the corporation called on Juan one afternoon, to stem the bleeding. This big shot tried to bribe Juan into dropping the investigations, by offering him a large sum of money and lavish trips. Juan threw him out of the office. As the CEO was leaving, he turned to Juan and threatened him with dire consequences if Juan didn't call off his dogs.

Mac Murphy, the CEO, was a third generation Irishman whose grandparents had immigrated from Ireland just before the turn of the century. Mac was typical of many Irishmen, coal black hair, blue eyes, and a constant frown. Mac worked his way up through the construction business originally started by his father. He worked as an apprentice, hauling lumber, digging foundations, pounding nails before there were air guns, and working long and arduous hours building the company. Now he wore thousand dollar Armani suits, alligator leather shoes, silk shirts and silk ties, and a Rolex watch. He had his nails done every week, and was still clean shaven by a local barber every morning before going to the office. The calluses were gone now, replaced by soft pink skin. He tried to stare Juan down, but Juan had grown up in a hostile environment as well, and would not back down.

The air was as thick as chocolate pudding after Mac left, Juan placed a call to the staff person he had given the case to. Juan instructed the young assistant lawyer to proceed digging into the corporation's financial records, contracting files, and memorandum drawers. A friendly judge had given the District Attorney's Office a subpoena to confiscate this material as part of building the case. The investigating officer along with the FBI raided the corporate headquarters before Mac had a chance to destroy some or all of the incriminating evidence.

A couple of days after Juan had started the case in earnest, he discovered someone had run a sharp object along the passenger side of his BMW while it was parked in the county administrative parking garage. The garage was supposed to be vandalism free, heaven knows they were paying a security company for just such protection. Juan suspected the on duty guard had been taken care of financially to allow the dirty deed, but Juan had no proof of that.

Over the next two weeks, additional random acts of violence took place. A car had streamed out of the night on to his beautifully land-scaped front yard, digging the car's tires into the wet grass and leaving huge ruts of dirt and grass in its wake. Someone had killed a neighbor-hood cat and had flung the dead animal onto Juan's front porch with a note that Juan and his wife were next. The Chief of Police wanted to put a twenty-four hour a day policeman on duty to guard Juan and Mary, but Juan refused. He reasoned that any action of this nature would signal some weakness, and Juan wanted to avoid timidity at all costs. Juan reasoned Mac may have come from a tough background, but Mac was not the murdering kind.

The investigation proceeded for six months and finally went to trial. Mac threw his entire legal staff into the fray to defeat the lawsuit, but the evidence against the corporation was just too overwhelm-ing. The staff had done an outstanding job in documenting the many complaints, the unofficial rebates to sub-contractors, the laundering of money, and the raping of the employees retirement funds. Mac, the CFO, and six vice-presidents were found guilty. The fines amounted into the millions and the prison sentences ranged from house arrest for a year to two and one-half years in prison. Juan was not satisfied with the decision, but now knew that contracting with the city and the county would return to a more efficient form, and that minority com-panies would be given a golden opportunity to bid for the jobs. When Juan ran for a second term as DA, these same minority companies poured money into his re-election campaign, and he won handily.

Juan continued to uncover corporate greed and fraud, targeting a big sky country big-time tax dodge for California RV buyers wherein the laws in Montana would allow the California buyer to take advan-tage of the loose registration laws, without having to set foot in the state, shaving perhaps as much as $20,000 off the cost of a luxury motor home. This arrangement was costing the State of California an estimated $160 million to this particular type of fraud.

Juan went to the legislature in Sacramento to see if there wasn't something which could be done to stop this abuse, and to recoup the lost revenue. Juan found some sympathetic ears, but the process he encountered was slow and mundane. After doing as much as he could with the help of others, Juan knew in his heart the only way to get things done was for him to get inside the state government as a District Senator, and change things.

Juan's staff continued to uncover weird and bizarre corruption schemes and other scams against the public at large and the system of equality to all involved in their daily lives. The second largest corruption to come across his desk involved a major fundraiser for the California governor. The fundraiser was charged with trying to collect millions of dollars in kickbacks from companies seeking state business. In one case the fundraiser squeezed a company for a $1.5 million contribution "to a certain public official."

Juan told the press, if the charges are true, the fundraiser should be held accountable to the fullest extent of the law. The governor is running for a second term, and his opponent is smacking her lips at this disclosure. She said this fundraiser was the governor's right hand man even though the governor disclaimed the charges. The governor was also hard pressed to answer questions about a $1,500 check to one of his daughters from a man whose wife got a state job.

And so the cases went. The threats diminished, and Juan and Mary got back to some sort of normal life. It was during all of the commotion, that Mary deliver their first child, a baby boy who they named, "Jose", after one of Juan's closest childhood friends from the trash dumps. Jose was a large baby, giving Mary some troubles at the time of birth, but Jose was healthy and all of the body parts were in place and perfect to the new parents. Jose was also a good and happy baby. He started to sleep at night early on, which gave Juan lots of relief with the hectic schedule he was keeping. Over the next few months, Jose continued to grow and be such a joy in Juan and Mary's life.

With each new life, an old life goes away. Juan had flown his mother to Santa Barbara to witness the birth of her grandson, and shortly after his mother had returned to Mexico, she had a stroke and died. Juan's uncle informed him the tragedy and Juan returned home for her funeral. He was glad his mother had gotten the opportunity to see Jose, and Juan felt a piece of himself dying inside. He had truly loved his mother, and often rued the day because she had not moved to the U.S. so she could have had a better life. Juan had asked her to come to California, but her roots were in Mexico, and she didn't want to go through the legal hassles in becoming an American citizen.

Juan didn't stay long. Many of his relatives from the past had also died, and most of his siblings were now married and had to devote their time to their own families. Besides, Juan rationalized, this was the old world, and the new world was in California where the money and the fame resided. One of the younger sisters had moved into his parent's house, the hovel Juan called it, but the sister, her husband, and their five children seemed content to have a roof over their heads. Juan had made overtures to the family about coming to the United States, but did not receive any positive feedback. They all knew Juan had made a success of himself, but they were so mired down with their poverty, they didn't seem to have the energy to think beyond their day-to-day routine. Juan knew while the rich got richer, the poor got kids. He had seen some of the same poverty in the slum areas of Santa Barbara County. He couldn't understand how there could be such poverty in such an affluent county, but clearly understood the trash heap. Juan vowed to carry on the fight against this kind of life style as part of his desire to reach the top of the governmental pile.

As Juan prepared to depart, the older relatives all shook his hand, and the women cried real tears on the front of his shirt. Many of his nieces and nephews, who didn't know him, stood back and eyed him with their deep brown, doe like eyes. He tried to encourage them to come closer so he could get a better look at them, and get to know them, but they seemingly didn't want to cooperate. Maybe someday, when the children were older, they would meet again and be closer.

Juan threw himself back into his work with such a fervor, he rarely got home before the bewitching hour. Jose was growing by leaps and bounds, but Juan never got much of a chance to observe. By the time he got home, the baby was asleep, and Juan was relegated to just stand over the crib and gaze down at the wonderment of infants. Mary never said anything, but Juan would feel the abandonment vibrating from her soul. Mary knew of Juan's complete immersion in the political arena, and she knew it was what made him truly happy. Often she felt she was playing mistress to his first love. Their lovemaking became less and less. Many times when Juan fell into bed after his shower, totally exhausted, Mary would rub his manliness, but received no arousal. Juan was usually asleep as soon as he hit the pillow.

At her wits end, Mary decided to return to nursing. Juan was initially against it, but conceded when Mary explained her reasons. They both agreed to hire a nanny to take care of Jose while Mary worked. They interviewed several recommended candidates, and selected a British student who was attending night school at the University of California at Santa Barbara Law School. Her name was Violet Tonks, explaining that although Violet was a name used back in the 1920s and almost unheard of in the modern times, she had been named for a great grandmother who had immigrated from England around the turn of the century. Violet was a short, dowdy blonde, slightly older than most of her counterparts at the Law School, but she had a cherubic glow about her persona. Violet immediately fell in love with Jose, an attraction Jose shared immediately with her. That sealed the deal, and Violet was hired. Juan and Mary agreed to let Violet occupy the guest bedroom and bath, thereby saving her some money, which she desperately needed for her education, and keeping salary expenses for Juan at a reasonable level.

The next week Violet moved in. She didn't have much by way of clothing, dressing in jeans and sweatshirts to attend class, and a pant suit for going out in the evening, and one white blouse and a skirt when she wanted to feel womanly. Juan took Violet to an office close out sale, and purchased her a useable desk to store her books and where she could study when Jose took his naps, or when the lord and lady of the manor were in residence. The arrangement worked well. Juan also found Violet to be helpful in a secondary way. They would discuss Violet's studies, Juan quizzing her on the different areas of the law. This way, Juan found himself getting a refresher course in some parts he had let slide when he became the DA.

The plan the judicial enforcement and Juan had put together continued to pay dividends. Crime had reached an all time low and corporate fraud and abuse was being attacked with a vengeance. Juan's notoriety continued to grow, reaching outside of his immediate sphere of influence and into the surrounding counties and other parts of the state. Juan now found himself being asked to consult with other county DA's and to speak at a variety of service and civil clubs across the California territory. It has started to become rumor that Juan was indeed timber of enhancing the leverage for the Democratic Party within the state.

Even though Juan was enjoying the new found celebrity status, the threats from the corporate world didn't disappear. He would get hate mail on his computer and telephone calls at odd hours during the night. Even though he changed his private telephone number several times, somehow people were able to access it. His car was also vandalized on numerous occasions, almost to the point that he thought he couldn't afford the deductible. He hired someone to watch the car during the day, not worrying about the evenings when it was safely enclosed in his garage. At this point in time, it was a struggle between greed and righteousness. Juan swore he would weather this storm, and come out victorious in the end.

In spite of the interruptions in his life, Juan continued to flourish in his career. Major drug rings were being investigated, and the hospitals reported a sharp decrease in overdose related deaths and emergency room visits by addicts. Juan not only threw himself into his work, but he became a pillar of his community. He joined the Rotary Club of Santa Barbara and in a year was elected the president. He volunteered to work at the Boys and Girls Club mentoring young people headed for problems, and making them motivated young adults, improving their self esteem and worth. He hardly ever saw Jose or Mary, but Mary didn't mind, as long as Juan was happy doing what he was doing, and was grateful for the quality time they shared together when he was home.

The death threats didn't stop however. One morning early, Juan decided to take a run in the park near his house. He needed to let off some steam, and be by himself to think through some difficult decisions he was being faced with at his office and in his political life. The morning was crisp as he jogged down the dew laden asphalt path winding through the trees turning gold and red with the coming of fall. He passed by other runners out for their exercises, and neighbors taking their canine charges out for a daily run before they had to be off to work. Juan didn't know many of them, but they waved a friendly wave, nodding their heads as if Juan were some sort of idol. Juan vowed to become a larger part of his neighborhood watch and get to know the individuals who comprised his part of town.

As Juan was winding down his run, he circled a large Elm tree, a half way point in the park he always ran to before returning on his final trek back to the house. As he was reversing his direction, he heard a sharp crack, and saw a large chip of the tree break off just over his head. A few inches more, and it would have struck him squarely in the middle of his forehead. He was suddenly aware he was the target of an assassin, who had nearly ended his young life. Juan glanced in the direction he thought the sound had come from and raced to face his attacker, only to see the bushes move and then become silent as if a ghost had been there and suddenly vanished. Juan searched the reaches of that part of the park for a few minutes, but the assailant had vanished as quickly as he or she had appeared. Juan decided not to report the incident, he didn't want to unduly upset Mary or his office staff, but did vow to exercise extreme caution on his next outing. After he had taken his shower and gotten dressed in his blue suit with the light blue stripping, the button down shirt, and the Ivy League striped tie, Juan sat on the edge of the bed, still rattled with his recent experience. In spite of the fact he had completely dried himself off after the shower, he felt soaked through to the skin. He looked at his shirt, but didn't detect any moisture seeping through, so decided it was just his imagination. As he kissed Mary and Jose goodbye for the day, he couldn't shake the feeling of some sort of looming doom hanging over his head. He started his car, but before he put the car in gear to back out of the driveway, he inhaled several long and deep breaths to calm his racing heart. The drive to the office was unnerving, but by the time he arrived downtown, the feeling of foreboding had subsided and was soon forgotten.

Juan contacted the Chief of Police to let him know about the attempt and asked for a small, quiet look into the matter. If any suspect was apprehended, the case against him could not involve Juan. Some other charge would have to be made and the individual convicted of that charge. The Chief sent a Crime Scene Investigative Unit to the area and within three days, had a person of interest in custody. Enough evidence was gathered to bring the assailant to trial and a conviction came about. Unfortunately the criminal could not be tied to Mac.

The week went swiftly, as all of the weeks seemed to these days. Friday rolled around and gravitated from a furious beginning to a more sedate afternoon. Juan was just putting the finishing touches on some paperwork, which required his signature when his secretary Shirl buzzed him on the intercom of an incoming phone call. Juan didn't feel much like taking any calls, he just wanted to be left alone to finish his business and go home. He asked Shirl to tell the interloper he had left the office and to leave a number for Juan to get back to him on Monday.

"I think you had better take this call", she said, "it is your old friend Kyle Smith and from the sound of his voice, he wants to speak to you."

Reluctantly, Jose pick up the phone, pushed the button on the line the incoming call had originate from and said hello.

"Juan, it is so good to hear your voice. I am sorry for disturbing you, but I wanted to let you know that I am hosting a small get together at my house tomorrow evening, and wondered if you and Mary could give me the pleasure of joining me and a small group for cocktails and dinner by the pool. I know it is short notice, but I think it will be well worth your time to come. We are on fall break from congress, and I need to fill you in on what has been going on as it affects California, and to receive your wise counsel. I have been told of all of the wonderful things you have been doing, and the success you have made as District Attorney, and I wanted to show you how much I appreciate your efforts in making this state a better place to live."

Juan knew bullshit when he heard it, but also knew Kyle had agendas well worth listening to.

"I hope you can get away. Put that Nanny to work on overtime, and pay her handsomely to take care of Jose. I am sure she can use the money, and you can certainly afford it."

Juan had to agree. He and Mary had not had the occasion to go out for a long time, and Juan knew Mary liked and admired Kyle and his wife Tara and would love a nice evening out with friends. Mary also knew Kyle spared no expense in the catered meals he procured for such happenings. Juan was getting tired of sandwiches and TV dinners and late night leftovers, and could certainly use an elegant dining experience to cap off a long and arduous week.

"Kyle, Mary and I would be honored to accept your invitation. I can give you my assurance we will be there without even asking Mary.

You know she thinks the world of you and your wife, and wouldn't miss one of your affairs for the world."

Juan had become a master of bullshit as well.

"Good, please drop by the house at 7:00 pm. We will have a few drinks, then have a scrumptious dinner. See you then." With that Kyle rang off, Juan hung up the phone, closed the file folders he had been using and left the office. As he exited the office, Shirl greeted him with a know it all smile. Juan wondered if she knew something he didn't. Shirl had a way of anticipating things, a trait Juan wished that he could have. He told Shirl to get out of the building, and to enjoy her weekend with her family. He knew she would be back in the office for part of the next two days, she always was. Juan couldn't figure out how he had been so lucky as to have inherited her, but knew he had found a gem.

CHAPTER FIFTY

The night of Kyle's party arrived. As directed, Juan wore a comfortable pair of Dockers, white pants with an Hawaiian style colorful shirt over the top. He put on a large gold necklace, which accented his olive colored skin. He also wore a pair of expensive, leather shoes without socks. Juan had become so Anglo, he could fit into California circles as if he had been native born. He had lost all trace of his accent, conversing in either English or Spanish at will.

Mary put on a lightweight linen dress with a red sash around the middle. She wore matching red earrings, and painted her fingernails to blend the outfit together. She, like Juan, wore a pair of sandals without hose. She had recently had her haircut short for the summer, the sides enveloping her face in cherubic fashion. She didn't wear a bra, but little could be seen of her moderate breasts through the fabric. Just enough to be tantalizing, and for the men to wish to see more. Juan admired his wife as she was putting on the finishing touches. He almost asked her to stay home with him, to make love, and forget the party, but Mary reminded Juan of the purpose of the get together, and he begrudgingly agreed.

As they descended the stairs from above, they witnessed Violet and Jose sitting on the living room sofa watching cartoons. Fits of laughter came spewing from Jose's mouth. The pair were thoroughly enjoying themselves. Juan told Violet where they would be, and where to find the phone number in case an emergency came up, then he kissed the baby and out the door Juan and Mary went.

The drive to Kyle's house was not a long one, but it gave Mary and Juan a chance to talk about what might happen at the party. Kyle had been very cryptic about their meeting, so many things hung in suspicion without basis. Mary speculated that perhaps Kyle wanted Juan to come to Washington D.C. to work as part of Kyle's staff, a move Mary would have hated, but would bear if it meant advancing Juan's career. Juan thought Kyle was just being generous for the backing Juan had given him in the past, and wanted to reward Juan for his efforts. Other ideas were bantered around, but nothing could be decided without more information. They finally decided that trying to guess the unknown was fruitless, so they turned to talking about their son, and how happy they were.

As Juan negotiated the driveway, he was waved to the side of the house by a valet, assigned that evening to park the guest's cars, unburdening the guest of that chore. As the valet held Mary's door, a second young man held Juan's. They smiled, hopped into the BMW and drove off. Mary and Juan walked up to the beautiful stained glass and wooden door, and were greeted by the host and hostess. Kyle and his wife were most gracious, treating them like royalty instead of the other way around. As they entered the foyer, Juan was surprised to see his old Law Professor, Professor Tillman, the other U.S. Senator from California, a dowdy woman whose name Juan could not recall, Gus Bell the Democratic district committeeman, the Mayor of Santa Barbara, the Chief of Police, the County Sheriff, and a smattering of other local and regional governmental officials. Some Juan recognized from his Rotary Club, some only by reputation coming out of the press.

Juan was greeted warmly by his old professor, and shook hands with those good friends he knew, and was introduced to those he didn't. Mary was escorted off to meet the other ladies, and to be ogled by all of the men as she circled the room. As if by Pavlovian command, a bell sounded from poolside, announcing the dinner was ready.

Along the far side of the pool, a long banquet style tablet was laden with a Hawaiian style Luau buffet consisting of fresh island greens, spinach, Koi cucumbers, Kula tomatoes and Maui onions, croutons, bacon bits, and papaya seed dressing. There was Lomi Lomi salmon, oriental chicken salad, pipikaula, poi, grilled Mahi Mahi with crushed macadamia nuts, teriyaki chicken, kalbi ribs, roasted suckling pig with giner guava sauce, Hawaiian sweet potatoes, steamed white rice, fresh vegetables, haupia, banana and macadamia nut cream pies, tropical sliced fruit, lahaina chocolate cake, fresh rolls and Hawaiian lavosh.

Next to the food was a bartender mixing any alcoholic drink a person could want. Juan had never seen so much food in his life. This table alone could have feed his village in Mexico for a week. Juan felt a pang of disgust over the opulence of the feast, wondering how America could flaunt it's wealth while other countries' populations were starving. He watched the guests heap their plates with lavish proportions and then head off to find a seat. Juan handed Mary a plate, a napkin, and some silverware, then retrieved the same items for himself. He went through the line, but didn't put much on his plate. Kyle asked if Juan wasn't hungry, but Juan countered with the fact that he was trying to lose weight, and a spread like this would do too much damage to his girlish figure. Kyle seemed to accept this explanation when Juan said he might consider coming back for a second helping later.

The food was delicious, and the disgust Juan had experienced slowly abated. Juan sat at the table with Kyle and his closest friends, delving into the meal with some gusto. While the food was being eaten, the liquor flowed, and the noise of the group continued to increase in volume. A small musical combo had been hired to provide evening music, but was drowned out by the conversation and laughter. Juan wondered why Kyle had gotten the musicians when their rendering couldn't even be heard, but that was not Juan's problem.

The evening wore on, the food and beverage was consumed, and the tables were cleared of the dishes and leftover waste. After dinner brandy was served along with Cuban cigars for those who wanted them. Juan declined both, he had had enough to drink, and didn't smoke. When everyone had comfortably settled in, the music stopped and Kyle rose to address the gathered throng. He recognized the members of the crowd for everyone's benefit, then turned his attention to Juan. Staring directly at him, Kyle said in a loud and authoritative voice, "Tonight, our special guest is Juan Cardova, the District Attorney for Santa Barbara County. I wanted not only to recognize Juan for the outstanding job he has done for the County, but for the involvement he has exercised in the community. Juan is innovative, creative, hard working, and full of potential. It is time for him to leave his current position and move on to bigger and better things. I, and many of those assembled here have decided to start a feasibility committee and to establish a campaign war chest to support Juan in a run as a member of the California legislature. The State of California needs this kind of leader in Sacramento."

Juan started to rise, but Kyle held out his hand and Juan sat down.

"I know this is a surprise to you, and I should have told you of our intent before, but I didn't want to give you the opportunity to consider the move and turn it down. We need you Juan and hope that you will accept our proposal right here and now." The crowd erupted with "We want Juan, we want Juan." How could Juan refuse, his life had reached another critical juncture.

CHAPTER FIFTY-ONE

The next several months centered around finding a feasibility committee to test the depth of interest in Juan running for the state house. Mixed in with his job, his family, and this new twist, it seemed Juan hardly got any sleep at night. It was fortunate he was young, and had learned a discipline of keeping things in perspective when all chaos was swirling around him.

Juan would be running in the California 35th congressional district, which included the city of Santa Barbara, Santa Barbara County, and small pieces of other counties in the Santa Barbara vicinity. The feasibility committee's report was finalized and given to Kyle Smith for review. Kyle called in Juan, Gus Bell, and several key staff members to discuss it. The report was glowing, indicating that Juan, as the democratic candidate, would lead all potential opponents anywhere on the scene. The decision was made, Juan was to run for the state house vacancy from the 35th district in the next election.

Kyle put up the seed money to get things started, and convinced many of his powerful and influential friends to do the same. Funds raisers were scheduled, speeches prepared, and the circus began. Juan spoke at service clubs, in schools, at colleges, to senior groups at retirement centers, at shopping malls, and at any opportunity which presented itself. As the word spread that Juan was running for governmental office, the minority businesses began to implode with cash givings, swelling the coffers available to Juan to more than adequate to meet his budgetary needs. Signs were printed and place on lawns, in vacant lots. Television ads began to appear. Juan didn't want his ads to appear to be negative, so he directed his staff to stay away from smear type tactics. A professional consultant was hired to produce the ads and to polish them, presenting Juan as the man to fill the needs of the populace. Themes of better education for the children, more affordable health care, improved employment opportunities, less crime, and an improved economy became Juan's mantra.

Juan's opposition was a little known businessman the Republican Party put up as a token. No one felt he stood a snowball's chance in hell of creating any stir, but Juan, Kyle, and Gus were surprised when the novice came on strong with backing from sources which were not easy to determine. As the months rolled along, the margin of support between the two candidates narrowed to an almost dead even heat. Juan intensified his efforts, increasing his speaking engagements and spending long hours outside of work and shopping areas shaking hands and kissing babies. Then, the break came that Juan had needed. Someone leaked some information indicating the businessman had, at one time, been associated with the mob in Las Vegas. It was alleged this businessman still had ties to the underworld, and could easily be influenced by them. The fear of increased drug trafficking, gambling, and control of local businesses sent a shiver of fear through the citizens. Even though these allegations were never proven, the damage had been done. By the time Election Day surfaced, Juan was leading the businessman by over forty points, and won easily.

This was November, and in just two short months, Juan would be sworn in as a junior house delegate in the California assembly. Another surprise was coming Juan's way. At breakfast one morning, Mary announced that she was pregnant with their second child, the doctor confirming the baby was a girl. Juan was overjoyed, he knew Mary wanted to have a little girl in the household, especially with an older brother to watch out for her. Juan and Mary hugged and kissed and decided to name the child Maria, the Hispanic equivalent of Mary. It wasn't anything unusual, just a common name to go along with Jose, another common name. This meant they would have to get a bigger house, one with a room for the boy and a new bedroom for the crib. Juan and Mary began to look in the Santa Barbara area for the new residence. They hated to move away from the neighborhood where they were living, and their friends, but there really wasn't any choice for them. Besides, Juan would be spending time in Sacramento at the legislature, where he would have an apartment, commuting back and forth whenever he had a chance. He didn't want Mary to be alone too much with the new infant, but knew that the nanny would be there to help as well as Mary's mother, who had consented to stay for a few months after the birth.

Now that Juan was a member of the state government, he could no longer be the District Attorney for the county. He hated to give up his county legal profession, but the conflict of interest was an issue that simply couldn't be avoided. The county commission selected one of Juan's primary staff to fill the position until an election could be held to find a permanent replacement. They had asked for Juan's recommendation, a female with a strong personality, who Juan knew could handle the responsibility, and who stood a better than average chance of running for the office and being elected in her own right.

On the last day as District Attorney, Juan's staff threw a wonderful "Hail and Farewell" party to wish their boss the very best and great success. They lavished him with gifts and mementos reflecting the close relationship they shared. Juan knew he would miss them terribly, but also knew that he wanted a couple of them to join him at the seat of power in the state to function as his legislative aides.

Again, Juan was a civilian attorney, finding a job with a very prestigious law firm in the city of Santa Barbara. Again fortunate to have Kyle Smith lend a hand to ensure Juan had a steady income, and the flexibility to operate in two different spheres at the same time. Juan went out of town for a few days to find an apartment in the state capital, having little problems locating a space that would meet his needs perfectly. Juan met with the property managers of a Sacramento reality company, signed the lease, made a down payment, and returned to Santa Barbara. Although things seemed to be going smoothly, when Juan arrived home, he found the nanny comforting Mary through episodes of pain that Mary had hidden from Juan. Violet explained to Juan that Mary had developed a prenatal diabetic condition, which left her weak, and caused painful side effects from the prescriptions her OB/Gyn had ordered for her. Juan knew things weren't right. Alarmed, Juan called an ambulance and had Mary taken to the hospital for some tests and observation. Mary's physician went through a thorough examination and battery of tests to determine the best course of action in treating the problems which had arisen. After a couple of days in confinement, the medications were changed, and Mary was ordered home to bed rest.

Juan didn't want to leave Mary in this state, but the freshman legislative orientation was rapidly approaching, and Juan would have to leave. A relative of Mary's arrived and assured Juan all would be just fine, and he should move on to his new challenge. With reluctance, Juan kissed Mary goodbye and drove to Sacramento.

The first few days of the orientation were a flurry of activity. Juan was settled in his new office in the legislative house building, and began attending the orientation sessions where elder legislative personnel conducted classes to explain the process this body was to go through in order to create, discuss, and possibly amend the myriad of bills that may or may not be enacted into law. The new freshmen were given a thorough course in how the house and the senate functioned, and how they were supposedly going to work together. Most of what Juan heard seemed like Greek to him, but the sense of power he had experienced in the past took an entirely new meaning. Here he was about to make decisions and to exert pressures on other legislators to put into law policies that would influence a state of millions of people. Juan almost became heady with the prospects. After each day's classroom presentation, Juan spent most of the evening going over policy and procedures manuals, and the notes he had taken during the day. Of course, he checked several times a day with Mary's status, and felt comforted she was experiencing less pain, and was improving. She didn't cotton to having to spend so much time in bed, but was resigned to the fact the baby was of greater importance. She would survive the inconvenience.

After the orientation was over, the leadership of the house set about making committee assignments, the key roles going to those who were in power, and who had been in the legislature the longest. Everything was keyed to seniority. The freshmen were all assigned to sub-committees, not having enough experience to be participants of a full committee. This was standard procedure until they had gone through the initiation process of their first term in office. Juan noted that some committees exercised more power than others. Not understanding why, Juan was assigned to a subcommittee in the house Ways and Means Committee, the committee which determined which bills would be forwarded to the full house for vote, and those that would die in committee, be tabled until a future time, or discarded entirely. Juan was also selected to participate in a subcommittee for the Health and Human Services Committee. This committee oversaw the legal control of billions of state and Federal dollars dedicated to the purchase of medical care and services for the indigent, the poor, the disabled, children, mothers, and others who fell below the Federal poverty line.

Juan was also selected as a member of the House Democratic caucus, where strategies were formulated to ensure the agenda of the Democratic Party was met. Again, Juan was uncertain as to why he was selected to such a prestigious post, but didn't have time to concern himself about it.

The orientation ended with a power breakfast in the house dining room, hosted by the house majority leader and chairman of the Ways and Means Committee, Marty Hoyt. Juan had heard much about Marty, a consummate charmer who came from the poor, south side of Los Angeles, and one of the first black members of the legislature to reach this high of a pinnacle. Marty was a standout athlete at his high school, only because some teacher talked him into joining the Boys and Girls Club of LA. Through this encouragement, and with quite some reluctance on his part, Marty met a member of the LA Lakers professional basketball team. A player who not only sat most of his career on the bench, but a person who would set an outstanding example and define the career paths for scores of young Afro American young men. This pro didn't take any guff from these young punks, and spoke to them in the language they all knew, street talk. He was a product of the street himself, and had gotten his chance through this same system.

He taught them teamwork and physical discipline. He ran their tails off at practice, making them so tired, all they wanted to do was go home and go to bed, not having the energy to get into any kind of trouble. He also insisted on academic excellence, noting they could not rise above their environment without a high school education. Marty was mesmerized by this individual, while doting on each word the new basketball teacher was saying. Marty did rise above his environment, graduating from high school with honors and receiving full scholarship to play basketball for the Bruins of UCLA. While at UCLA, Marty had majored in communications and sports psychology, two areas that were to bode him well. Marty was a light skinned, handsome man, who exuded confidence at every turn. Marty had worked hard to get elected for his first term, and had worked even harder to maintain his work ethic while returning his campaign promises to the district electing him.

As Juan was leaving the breakfast to return to his new office, the elevator door opened and out walked the infamous Marty. Recognizing

Juan, Marty put his huge hands on Juan's shoulders and said, "You are on my sub-committee and I am truly delighted." Juan was so in awe, he hesitated for a few seconds until he gained control of himself, mumbling something to the effect that he was delighted as well. With the pleasantries over, Marty turned and disappeared down the hallway.

Like most legislatures, the one in California meet for over 100 days every other year to pass key pieces of law and to approve an operating budget for a two year biennial period. The in between years were to clean up or discard what was not passed at the start of the biennial period, and to agree on a supplemental budget if needed. The supplemental budget process was generally only thirty days unless the governor called for a special session to either extend the biennial portion, or if a critical need arose requiring the legislatures to re-convene.

This meant Juan would have a lot of time at home with his new family and his new job. Maria Elena Cardova was a large and healthy baby, blessed with dark hair, flawless skin like her father, brown eyes like her mother, and for some reason dimples. Juan didn't remember dimples as being any part of his family's characteristics, and Mary couldn't either. It became a private joke between Juan and Mary when Juan accused the child of having a different father while Juan was away safeguarding the state from itself. Maria was a good baby, taking to breast feeding whereas Jose had had difficulty with it. Following in her older brother's footsteps, Maria also started to sleep all night almost immediately, a rarity among children for the most part. Mary and Juan were pleased.

Violet, the nanny, was also pleased. Violet had been an only child, and had wished all of her life to have had a sister. Maria didn't exactly fill the bill as a sister, but more as a niece which Violet accepted in lieu of a sister. Although Jose was at that stage of comprehensibility, he wasn't sure who this creature from outer space was, yet when the two children were placed side by side in the crib, they touched each other and recognized each other as brother and sibling.

The California legislature began with a bang. Bills were being created by the dozens, in every sector of the organizational structure. The overriding issues were the homeless, the rising costs of medical care for the poor, the uninsured citizens of the state, the rising increase in illegal immigrants, low cost housing, highway projects, agriculture subsidies, higher education, and a myriad of other social and health issues.

Juan got his first taste of lobbyists when an attorney from the Master Builders Association asked for an appointment to get Juan to sign on as co-sponsor of the bill that would rezone parts of the state from rural agriculture zoning to commercial/residential. The lobbyist, dressed in an expensive Italian suit with a button down white shirt and striped tie, reminded Juan of the con artists and used car salesmen he hated so much. The interloper was slick, making feasible arguments on the surface, but hiding the agenda the builders were really after, gross profits at the expense of the buyer. Juan listened to the speech, thanked the lobbyist, then ushered the unwanted guest out of his office.

Marty had warned Juan about the lobbyists, telling Juan never to commit to anything until the proposal rendered could be thoroughly checked out by Juan's staff, and a decision made. Marty also instructed Juan to limit the amount of time spent in talking to this group of individuals. Marty felt it was better to have the organization or association send their proposals in writing in advance of any meeting, this way a legislator could be prepared to ask more intelligent questions, and shorten the time of discourse. Juan found this to be very good advice. Juan still had so much to learn and so little time to do it. Juan signed on as a co-sponsor for a number of bills, watching some of them pass on to the floor for vote, and some go down in defeat, not passed out of committee, or tabled for next year.

The other biggest part of Juan's time expenditure was sitting in on committee and sub-committee hearings. It would take Juan some time to fully understand the rules of order that were applied to the process.

He felt two things. One, too much time was spent over trivial procedures, and the hatred he had for the arrogant and powerful leadership positions that seemed to go to the heads of some people. He didn't say much, but deep inside was festering a mistrust for such individuals. Juan often thought to himself, it wouldn't be war or the economy that brings down this great nation, but arrogance.

After awhile, Juan just became numb to what was transpiring around him. He learned in a hurry how to approach other members of the house so they could compromise with each other, mutually supporting each other's pet projects. He learned the art of persuasion and cajoling that paid the most dividends. Juan used his extreme good looks to their full advantage, especially with the female members of the assemblage. Although Juan suffered some minor defeats, his victories were numerous and his prestige among his peers soared. He was recognized for his intelligence and for his ability to gain a consensus with the minimum amount of effort. He became a favored consultant to the power brokers, along the way garnering favors that Juan knew would become useful later on.

Juan's ability to work with the lobbyists, the committee chairs, his peers, and the public became legendary in just a short time. Juan kept his quiet demeanor, often displaying his quick wit, and deep intelligence. Soon he was a participant on several of the local talk shows airing during prime time during the week or on Sunday when all of the pundits were watching. Somewhere along the line, a national reporter caught wind of Juan and suggested that his national network to feature up-and-coming state legislators for appearance on the big screen.

The executives at CBS thought this would be a good project to be featured on their premier show "Sixty Minutes". CBS spent the next several months traversing the countryside, interviewing local congressmen and congresswomen from the state capitals. It was decided to bring on six of what seemed to be the most dynamic rising stars from these interviews. Of the six, four were male, and two were female. Juan was chosen as the representative from the west coast. An assistant producer was flown to Sacramento to meet Juan and to prep him on his upcoming debut on worldwide television.

After a couple of days of preparation, Juan was flown, all expenses paid, by the network to New York City. They put the interviewees up in a swanky hotel, and wined and dined them to their hearts content. Juan had never been in New York, and immediately fell in love with the city. In the evenings while he was there, he would walk the crowded streets at night taking in the swells of the Big Apple and to marvel at its diversity. He found the food to be outstanding, discovering gourmet cooking in little hole-in-the-wall places obscured by high rise office buildings.

The taping was scheduled for early morning on Thursday. This would give the network a chance to draft the outline of the interviews earlier in the week, tape on that day, and edit the tape for showing on Sunday. A limo came by the hotel to pick up the six people, and escorted them downtown to the CBS studios. They were taken up to the 22nd floor where they met the producers, the make up artists, the wardrobe outfitters, the staff, and the celebrity interviewers, like Mike Wallace, Morley Shafer and others. When they were properly dressed, they were then taken into the studio proper, arranged in chairs facing the cameras, and had last minute touch ups on their makeup.

Juan was amazed at how small the studio was where the tape was being made. He never realized you didn't need a large setting since the camera was able to focus on the smallest area necessary for the picture to be beamed to a household's television set. The studio was totally surrounded with lights and cameras to eliminate all shadows and to capture people at every possible angle. The interviewees were told not to look into the cameras, but to focus their attention on the person conducting the interview. Juan was also amazed at how hot the lights were. He felt as if he were back in the trash dump in Mexico during the high points of summer. Technicians continuously moved about dabbing the sweat from their foreheads and reapplying makeup.

A hush fell over the studio as the director proceed to count down to the start of the segment of the show Juan was participating in. Background music came on with the familiar ticking of the "Sixty Minutes" clock. An announcer talked the audience through the introduction of the cast of announcers, and then the director pointed to Mike Wallace to begin. The interview went by like a blur. The questions ranged from the backgrounds of the interviewees, to where they stood on local and national issues, as well as what they liked to eat, and what were their aspirations for the future. All of the interviewees came across as smart, well controlled, and as rising stars. Juan showed the brightest profile, eclipsing John F. Kennedy who debated Richard Nixon for the presidency of the United States. Juan felt like he was only on the air for a few seconds, but realized the segment he participated in ran for over twenty minutes. The director called a wrap, thanked everyone for their participation, and walked out of the room. The technicians returned them to the dressing rooms where the make up was removed, the studio clothing exchanged for that which belonged to them, and they were driven back to the hotel for a gala dinner, compliments of CBS. Juan was so wired after the dinner, he couldn't sleep. He realized it was three hours earlier on the west coast, so he called Mary and told her all about the experience.

The group was gathered onto a bus on Friday morning to travel to the airport for their return flights home. Juan arrived back in Santa Barbara just before six P.M., was met by one of his house staff members and driven to his house. That Sunday, Juan and Mary invited some of their closest friends and allies to come to the house to see the show. Mary had the affair catered with the best of finger foods and wines. As the crowd fed on the delicious cuisine, a hush feel over them as the television commercials stopped and the latest episode of "Sixty Minute" took center stage.

Juan's segment was in the middle, so the crowd of onlookers suffered through the introductions and the first segment, something about an exposure of corruption and incompetence in hospitals. The first segment ended, a commercial about some beer ensued, and then the breathless moment happened. There was Mike Wallace and a panoramic view of the six legislators emerging on the color screen. Even Juan was impressed with the job the editors had done with the tape. The friends viewing the show with Juan were enraptured. At the conclusion, everyone gave Juan a round of applause and congratulated him with hugs, kisses, and slaps on the back. Juan had certainly shown like a diamond on display. When the guests had gone, Mary turned to Juan, put her arms around his waist and snuggled her head into his chest. Juan savored the moment, then pushed her gently away.

"Well, what do you think?"

"Oh, Juan, you were wonderful. I think the sky's the limit, there is no stopping you from going to the apex of your desires."

"I love you Mary, and now there are other desires I need to take care of first."

CHAPTER FIFTY-TWO

Juan's career seemed to blossom, like the ugly duckling turning into a beautiful white swan. After he finished his first two years in the state house, he was re-elected to a second, two year term. By the end of his third year, Juan was feeling bored with the house, and wanted to elevate himself to the real seat of power, the State Senate. The terms were longer, and the prestige was much greater. He wanted, no, he needed the rush power gave him. It was like a narcotic he couldn't get enough of. He again met with Gus and the Democratic Party, and it was decided Juan would be the candidate for the Senate seat from the Santa Barbara district. This seat was currently held by a Republican, who was aging, becoming forgetful, and saying things detrimental to the GOP cause. Via the grapevine, it was rumored the Republicans were going to drop him like a hot potato and find someone new, more dramatic. Juan was given some inside information that the new GOP hopeful was a member of his law firm who had served on the city council, as a precinct committee chairperson, and as the director of the United Way Fund for the county.

Bob Hamilton was from the upper crust of the Santa Barbara aristocracy. Bob claimed his family history could be traced back to the Pilgrims landing on American soil in the seventeenth century. Bob had been educated in the east, getting his undergraduate degree in English from Boston University and his law degree from Harvard.

While at Harvard, Bob became editor of The Harvard Review. Bob had practiced his profession in New York City as part of Wall Street, specializing in urban planning and development. He was the brain-child for the wealthiest contractors and developers in the nation. He was revered not only in the USA, but internationally as an individual who could bring thorny development contracts to fruition.

Bob had moved from the east coast because of an asthmatic condition, the doctors advising him to seek a warmer climate. Santa Barbara had meshed with his desires perfectly. He brought with him a lovely Bostonian wife with flaming red hair and two, well mannered, and intelligent children. One boy and one girl. They had moved into a ritzy guarded community, and frequently made the society pages of the local newspaper. The couple belonged to all of the right clubs, did charity work, and basked in local acclaim. When Juan found out this information, he knew he had an uphill struggle to overcome, but was willing to take on the challenge.

When the filing date arrived to announce his candidacy and turn in the required forms to the Secretary of States Election Office, Juan, Gus, and other staffers made a public show of the occasion. Not to be outdone, Bob also had his group there at the same time. Photographs were taken of the two men shaking hands and wishing each other well. The newspaper sensed a real shootout at the OK Corral, and was making plans to exploit this competition to its fullest. Never in the memory of the newspaper editor, could the paper remember such a pairing, and the newspaper owner smacked his lips with the possibility of profits falling on the publication like manna from heaven.

Millions poured in the coffers of the two individuals. War chests of this magnitude were unprecedented. The race took on the demeanor of a national run-off, not a state event. As the campaign progressed, national news coverage elevated the struggle of the Titans to a new level. Juan and Bob were consumed, debating not once, but four times with the consensus being each garnered half of the kudos. Again, as in the race for District Attorney, Juan found himself slightly behind in the polls, but within gunshot of Bob.

The intensity of Juan's campaign increased. More television ads popped up, more signs sprouted on residential lawns, more appearance were made in parades, at mall openings, and at ballgames. In spite of the increase in pressure, Juan's approval rating remained stagnant. He couldn't seem to erase the deficit and gain any ground. Juan pulled his staff together to see if they could come up with a newer and fresher strategy to resolve the dilemma. After the staff had given Juan their recommendations, he dismissed them, remaining to talk to Gus privately.

"What can we do now, Gus? I don't seem to be getting anywhere with this Lily white character who is matching me point for point. I'm feeling like I'm standing in quick sand and slowly sinking. Do you have any suggestions?"

"That I do. Why not bring in your old pal Wilson to help you out."

Suddenly the clouds separated, and the answer was clear. Juan had not approved of the dirty politics used in Kyle Smith's run, but that was water under the bridge. Juan wanted to become a Senator in the State of California, and he was willing to condone any dirty tricks.

"I think you are right Gus, I will give him a call."

"Good, I think you have made a wise choice. I know what Wilson did for you in the Kyle Smith project, and I know now is the opportune time to use that expertise yourself. Good luck Juan, and let me know how things turn out. I appreciate you're keeping me in the loop and up to date on this."

Juan turned off the lights after everyone had gone, and sat there in the silence of the room thinking to himself. Am I doing the right thing? He couldn't feel any pain in his gut, nor could he get any satisfaction stirring in his brain. It seemed everything lending itself to reason was idling in neutral. Juan hadn't been drinking that much, so he knew it wasn't the alcohol, he just couldn't focus. Juan arose from his seat, walked to the outside doors, opened them, and peered out into the night. Mary had gone to bed, and the lights from the bedroom window on the second floor had gone out. Juan could smell the soft, sweet aroma being carried through the yard on a light breeze. For a few moments, he was being transported on Aladdin's Magic Carpet to places mystic and foreign to him. He lost touch with reality, but soon regained his composure. Then it came to him, the feeling he had been waiting for, the feeling that he was making the right decision. Juan didn't want anyone else involved in this liaison, so he could have to think up some excuse for going back to Virginia to see Wilson.

As Juan was shaving the next morning, he looked in the mirror and saw Mary's reflection as she got out of bed to go and check on the children. He knew he would have to tell Mary about his trip, and feared the rebuttal she was about to give him. He wouldn't argue with her, just look her in the eye and tell her it was what he had to do. He knew that Mary would cave under his spell. He knew she wouldn't like it very much, but would agree to support him once again.

He wiped the shaving cream from his chin, splashed on the after-shave lotion Mary liked the best, and entered the bedroom just as she was returning. As Mary approached, Juan put his arms around her and kissed her lightly on the lips. She smelled the lotion.

"My, my, didn't you get enough last night?" she teasingly taunted him while reaching down to feel his manliness starting to become arousal seeing her in a near naked condition. Juan withdrew her hand and looked her squarely in the eye. He explained his trip, intensified the stare and waited for the explosion, which never came. In fact, he was surprised when Mary immediately agreed, letting him know that she wanted him to continue his trek to higher political office and she agreed with what he must do. She then turned, walked away, stripped off her nightgown and stepped into the shower. Juan joined her.

Juan called his office and gave some lame excuse about not coming in for a few days. Although the excuse was barely believable, his boss gave him permission to be absent without any questions. Juan then called the airlines to arrange for a flight to the east that afternoon, and arranged for a rental car to be picked up at the Virginia airport. He slowly packed a small suitcase, Mary helping him select the items he was going to take. They poked the clothing in the small case without conversation. When they were finished, Juan lifted the case, kissed Mary goodbye and went to the garage to drive to the Santa Barbara airport for his journey.

Throughout the flight, Juan went over what he was going to ask of Wilson, sifting through a variety of reasons why he needed the help. He finally decided just to level with Wilson and let him know the true purpose of the assistance he needed. Juan arrived at his destination, filled out the paperwork for the car and drove to Wilson's residence. The drive this time was easier, Juan having been there once before. As he traversed the small town, reaching the outskirts, he came to a stoplight just turning red. Juan didn't notice a large truck pull up behind him. Suddenly, Juan felt a jolt as the truck struck the rear of his car and began pushing his vehicle forward into the path of an oncoming car angling in from Juan's left. No matter how hard Juan applied the brakes, the truck continued to push into the intersection.

In a panic, Juan released the brakes, stomped on the gas pedal, and shoot through the intersection to safety on the other side. Unfortunately the driver of the truck was caught unawares. The oncoming vehicle hit the truck full force on the driver's side, spinning the truck around setting off a fire storm of flames which consumed both vehicles. Juan shook off the adrenaline rush, not completely understanding what had just happened, but also not wanting to stay around to be involved in the consequences.

He drove slowly down the side streets, letting his nerves settle down, finally locating Wilson's street and pulled into the driveway. The house was dark and no one appeared to be home. Juan killed the engine, turned off the lights and walked up to the front door. The place was a dark as a tomb, and smelled of misuse and abandonment. He looked through the front window, and observed that the house had been swept clean of any furnishings. Wilson was gone.

Surely, Juan thought to himself, Wilson would have notified him that a relocation had taken place unless Wilson had gone completely underground and didn't want to be found. Juan shook the confusing cobwebs from his brain, not really certain what to do next. The trip, apparently, had been a wash and Juan must now come up with a different strategy for defeating Hamilton.

As Juan stepped off the front porch of Wilson's house, an ominous wind came up, almost like Wilson's spirit was somewhere in the vicinity. As he turned to go to his car, he almost bumped into an elderly gentleman who was out walking his dog. The dog, one of those small yappy types was certainly giving Juan an ear full. The old man shushed the dog and apologized for not paying attention to what he was doing. Juan assured the man that the fault was all Juan's, and he should have been more observant. Once the niceties had been exchanged, Juan asked the man if he knew who lived in the house. The man replied he didn't know the occupant personally, but had seen him come and go over the past few years.

"Strange", the man said, "the owner always seemed to go to the corner convenience store each morning about the same time to get a cup and coffee, a donut, and some conversation with the attendant. It was about the same time I walked my dog in the mornings. Perhaps the store manager can give you more information."

Juan thanked him for the hint and trudged toward the store and gas station situated a few blocks away on a corner lot. It was a typical twenty-four hour a day operation, filled with items desired to fill the full spectrum of needs from food and drink to automotive supplies to health and beauty and everything in between. As Juan entered the establishment, as a soft bell rang to announce his presence. A dark skinned man, probably of Eastern Indian extraction looked up from the counter to inquire what Juan was looking for.

The man was dressed in a dark jumpsuit accentuating his mahogany toned countenance. He spoke with an extreme accent, one Juan could barely understand. As the man eyed Juan with suspicion, Juan asked if the man knew to owner of the house down the street.

"I am not sure I know which house you mean. Please come to the front door and point it out to me."

Fulfilling his request, Juan went to the front door and thrust his arm and finger squarely at Wilson's home. "That one there, the one with the white shutters."

"Oh, I know that one. Yes the owner comes here every morning and every evening for a cup of coffee, a donut, a newspaper, and to chew the fat as they say in America. I have known him for about two years now, but do not know much about him. He is a very private person. What is your name and what do you want of him?"

Juan didn't want to divulge too much information so he said, "My name is Juan Cardova, I am from California, and the man and I are old friends from the conflict in Vietnam."

"Can I see your driver's license please, just to verify your name?" Juan wasn't sure about doing this, but felt a trustworthiness flowing as an aura surrounding the man. Juan extracted the wallet, opened it to his driver's license and held it out for the man to see.

"Just a minute please." With that the man retreated into the back of the store and quickly returned with a white envelope sealed across the back with a piece of tape and addressed to Juan Cardova.

"The man down the street told me to give this envelope to someone with your name if you should ever show up and he was gone. I am certain you are who you are and now I have done my duty. Now if you will please leave, I am not feeling very comfortable with you here."

Juan placed the letter into the inside pocket of his jacket, thanked the attendant and walked out to his car. It was getting late, and Juan needed to find a place to stay, so he began driving around until he located a motel which seemed to be in relatively good repair and which offered a reasonable rate with color television and a free breakfast. Juan entered the reception desk area and asked if a room was available for the evening. There was and Juan filled out the necessary paperwork, was given his key and directions to his room. He drove around to the backside of the building and used his room key to gain access to the hall leading to his room. He swiped the electronic key through the slot, a green light came on and when the door handle was depressed, the door opened into a well appointed, spacious and clean room with a king size bed, a table and two chairs, a television and a bathroom.

Juan placed his bag on the luggage rack, hung his jacket in the closet, turned on the television and sat down at the table to open the letter. Inside was a single sheet of paper with Wilson's small handwriting taking up only a small portion of the page. It read simply: Juan, I had to leave to protect myself and you. Someone is out to get us, and I think it is coming from the highest levels of the U.S. Government. They may have already attempted to take your life. If you need to reach me, I have a secure telephone system. The number you can call is numbers of your military identification cubed. Good luck, and watch your back. Wilson.

A cold sweat came over Juan. Suddenly the truck pushing him in harm's way leapt into his thinking. How did they know he was in town and who were they? Were there more out there that would be seeking him out. Juan went to the window, peered out and could see nothing. He would try to get a good night sleep and leave early in the morning. He had paid the motel manager in cash so there wouldn't be any paper trail via his credit card, and his leaving early wouldn't be noticed. He decided to skip the free breakfast and find a restaurant down the road at the next town.

Surprisingly, Juan did get a good night's sleep, then backtracked through a neighboring town to the airport for his flight home. As he drove, Juan kept looking into the rearview mirror for signs of someone following him, but saw nothing. When he arrived home, Mary could see the concern on his face, but didn't ask about it. She had been married to Juan long enough to know when to pry and when to let things alone. She was just glad he was safely home. Little did she know how close Juan had come to making her a widow, and leaving their two children without a father.

Back at the office, Juan took a few minutes during his lunch break to compute the telephone number for Wilson based on the cubing of his Army service number and placed the call. As the call was going through, Juan could hear the mechanics of electronic scrambling, a sound he had become so familiar with during his intelligence days in Vietnam. A muted voice came on the line asking Juan some personal information no one else would have known to verify that the caller was in fact Juan. The voice instructed Juan to place the request for action in writing and then fax the request to a specified fax terminal. After the fax had been confirmed, Juan had to shred the paper so no evidence of the transaction would be left behind, to be found. Juan, in very brief sentences, placed the request for information about Bob Hamilton on paper, went to his fax machine next to his desk, punched in the numbers, listened to the dial tone and watched as the paper went through the bowels of the machine. Just seconds after the paper had made its cycle, a confirmation date and number was printed ensuring the fax had reached the right end point. Juan then stepped to his shredder and destroyed both documents.

In about two weeks, the local newspapers began to print stories about the private life of Bob Hamilton. The sources weren't given, and even though Juan was accused of starting these so called rumors, Bob could find no credible evidence that Juan had anything to do with it. Finally the whole story hit the front page like a missile striking a tank directly into the turret, with fallout occurring immediately. It seems Hamilton was a wife abuser and sadist. Medical records, which were supposed to be sealed and private, were now open for review by the public. Hamilton brought a slander lawsuit against the paper, and charged invasion of privacy, but the damage was done, and Hamilton could not produce any retort to discredit the information. Two days after the bombshell struck, Hamilton withdrew from the race. The Republican Party did not have a backup candidate, being so sure Hamilton would win, and conceded the election to Juan. After the November election was held, Juan took his place in the California State Senate that coming January.

It didn't take long for Juan to recognize the difference between the House and the Senate. The power of the Senate was almost palpable. Members of the House bowed to the senators, as if they were older brothers, and wiser in the inner workings of the state government. Juan's office was larger than his House office and his staff larger as well. Instead of going through a short campaign and term every two years, Juan was now secure in his position for a much longer span. This was another facet of a senator's power, the ability to have more time in which to persuade, leverage, and enact into law those things that would not only benefit Juan's constituents, but would bring him more and more recognition as a go getter and leader.

Juan was almost heady with power, but reflected back on his background and the way he had been able to accomplish things, and reverted to the normal way he conducted business. It didn't take Juan long to wrangle himself into some of the most prestigious committees, eventually becoming the Chairman of the Ways and Means Committee and a member of the Appropriations Committee, two of the strongest and most influential positions to be had.

Juan worked hard to lessen the immigration problem, to reduce unemployment, to draw tourism into the state, again to control corruption at the corporate level, reduce crime, fight discrimination of the minorities, reduce the state's budget deficit, improve the educational systems, and even build a budget surplus for the first time in many years. He formed coalitions not only between the political parties, but between labor and industry, the religious sects, and the gang factions blighting the inner city. Wherever he went, he was greeted with adoring crowds, who shouted out his name and wanted to touch him and get his autograph. His name became legendary from one end of the state to the other. His political capital was growing by leaps and bounds. Never in the history of the state had anyone achieved the pinnacle of success Juan seemed to enjoy. He relished the adulation, and gave back more and more of himself to the public he served. At holiday times, Juan could be seen serving the needy at a homeless shelter, or marching in ceremonial parades, or speaking at veteran's remembrances celebrations, or visiting schools and hospitals. He appeared frequently on local and national television programs and threw out the first pitch at the opening day of the major league baseball season. His name became a household word, and he grew and matured.

Juan sailed through his first term as a California State Senator, and was re-elected by an even larger margin the second time. Juan was aging now. Streaks of gray hair were showing through his otherwise black strands. The gray didn't detract from his appearance, it only enhanced it. Now in his mid life, Juan still exuded youthfulness, but had taken on the embodiment of the elderly statesman. He had the State of California squarely in the palm of his hand. Everywhere he went, he was swarmed by well wishers and supporters.

CHAPTER FIFTY-THREE

In spite of the fact Juan was throwing himself into his senatorial duties, the craving for higher office never abated. He would lie awake at night and think about the possibilities. Never in the history of the State of California had the Governor been anything other than a rich, moderate, white man. To think a foreign national could be the leader of the state was unthinkable, but was it? Juan had come this far, what was there to keep him stymied at the senatorial level when he had all of the resources he needed to make the next move.

One morning Juan called Gus Bell and invited him to the office for a businessman's lunch. This was to be a private meeting just between the two of them. Gus agreed and arrived at the office a little before noon the following day. Juan asked him into the office, closed the door and poured each of them a drink. It was a Friday before a holiday, and Juan had given his staff the rest of the afternoon off, so a drink during the day was not out of hand. A small round table had been set up in the corner of the office. As Gus sipped his drink he was joined at the table by Juan. The lunch consisted of Gus's favorite, a Rueben sandwich with a dill pickle and some French fries. Gus knew the cholesterol was bad for his heart, but he didn't care. Going off one's diet once in a while wasn't all that bad. He would just take an extra pill and swear to be stricter with himself. Juan had settled for the club sandwich with coleslaw. The two friends exchanged small talk as they savored their meal. When they were finished, Gus waited for Juan to start the opening dialog.

Juan leaned forward with his elbows on the table, looked Gus straight in the eye, and said, "Gus I want to be the next Governor of the State of California." The statement hung there like the mushroom cloud of an atomic bomb. Gus was speechless. He had no inkling Juan was considering such a bold move for a naturalized Hispanic. After the initial impact, Gus gathered his senses about him, shook his head, and headed for the wet bar for another drink, which he downed in one large gulp. Holding the empty glass in his hand, he turned to Juan and said, "Are you out of your mind? You know the history of this state. No one from a Mexican background has ever even mentioned such a scenario. Hell, in the just recent past, there would be a lynching if such a proposition were put forth. You have been lucky so far Juan, what on earth are you thinking now?"

"I know it sounds crazy Gus, but I want this more than anything else I can think of. Look at what I have accomplished so far. Why can't I grab for this brass ring as well. What have I got to lose?"

Gus knew Juan was right. Juan had entered the governmental arena against all odds, and had somehow managed to defeat all comers. If ever there was a chance for Juan to recognize a status this high, now was the time. Juan had paid his dues.

"Alright, let's bring in some key players in private, talk about this, and formulate a plan. Who knows, today the Governorship, tomorrow the Presidency." How little did Gus know that was the next item on Juan's agenda.

It was decided the meeting would take place at a secret hideaway, far from the prying eyes of the public and the press.

"I know just the place." Gus said. "I have a friend who owns a cabin deep in the backcountry of northern California near Lake Tahoe. I know he will be more than happy to let us use it for a short period of time. Once we put our group together, we can make arrangements to meet there incognito. We should be able to wrap up our deliberations in a couple of days, so I would suggest we meet from a Friday evening until Sunday afternoon. That way, we can be there without having to make excuses for missing work. I am sure the wives would understand a few men getting together for a weekend of poker out of town. Especially since we are all friends. We don't have to tell the better halves who will be attending. That way we can keep the back fence gossip from letting out the membership of our mutuality."

"I agree, who do you recommend be included?"

"Oh, I think we should start with Kyle Smith, then we can add some strong forces within the state. You know some of them by name or you have met them at political functions. I would recommend Wallace "Wally" Jenson, a black committeeman from Central Los Angeles, Jerry Wurtz, a gay Jew from San Francisco who is affiliated with the Better Business Bureau system, Pete Thomas, a venture capitalist from San Jose, Bill Brockman, a powerful figure in The State Farm Association who knows the farming community of Northern California, and of course myself. All of these men have extensive experience in organization, communication, and finance. I don't think you can get a better mixture of talent anywhere. Let me feel them out and see if they are interested in participating with us. I will keep it low keyed and confidential. I know for a fact they can hold their tongues."

"That sounds good, but I'd like to add Carl Evans, an attorney from Los Angeles. I met him and his wife on a cruise and was very impressed. Do you know him?"

"I certainly do, and he would be a great addition to our group."

"Alright then, you do the leg work and get back to me. I really appreciate what you are doing for me Gus, I know things will come to fruition. I can feel it in my bones."

The two comrades embraced each other, Gus leaving to start his negotiations.

That night Juan suggested he and Mary go out to the finest restaurant in town, just to have great food and to be alone for an evening.

Juan knew the teenager next door was in dire need for some money, and being that it was a weekend coming up, she wouldn't mind staying up a little later since she didn't have school the next day.

Mary was a little curious about such an offer all of a sudden, but was mollified with the explanation Juan gave. Juan hated to tell white lies to Mary, but felt deep in his soul he need a place with atmosphere to reveal his plans. He wanted to ply Mary with good booze and French food.

"Let me make the reservations at Jean Pierre's, I am sure they will be able to find a table for us, even at this late hour. Why don't you call the babysitter, and if she is available, I will contact the restaurant."

About thirty minutes before they had to be at the eatery, the fourteen year old baby sitter from next door rang their doorbell. Juan and Mary had given Violet, the nanny, a couple of weeks of vacation to visit family and friends, and were very appreciative a capable young lady lived next door, and could fill in during a pinch. Mary gave the young lass instructions on the care of the children and handed her a note with the telephone number of the restaurant on it. "Don't hesitate to call now, we can be home in just a few minutes. If any situation arises that you can't handle, contact us immediately."

"Oh, I don't think there will be any problem, I have been baby sitting since I was twelve, and can take care of almost anything that might arise."

They agreed on the price per hour for the job and promised her that they would be home within three hours. Mary slipped into her black velvet evening jacket, and Juan put on his Navy blue sports coat covering his Cambridge baby blue, buttoned down shirt with the Ivy League tie. Mary liked the combination Juan was wearing along with gray slacks, black shoes with tassels, and black socks. It made him seem, well, all American, and distanced from the Hispanic background.

They drove the short distance downtown, parked the car and went into the building. The restaurant was mid block on the main street, sandwiched between a department store, and a jewelry store. The owner was the chef who could have been hired by any five star hotel in the heart of Europe, or anywhere else for that matter. However he chose to invest his time and energy in this moderate undertaking. The money wasn't the greatest, but the satisfaction of creating the finest cuisine in the city was priceless. Juan had met the chef at state occasions when the chef had been asked to cater some political functions, and over time they had become good friends.

Juan and Mary stood by the gold plated sign informing the guests to please wait to be seated. It didn't take long for the hostess to escort them to a lovely table near a window looking out on the garden, a location that offered a full vista of the facility and easy access to the small dance floor. The hostess handed them each a menu, took their cocktail orders and departed. Juan ordered a scotch and soda neat and Mary a glass of white wine, knowing she was going to order some sort of fish. They each scanned the menu which was filled with delightful choices. Juan noticed there were no prices next to each menu item. He guessed if you wanted to know the prices, you couldn't afford to eat there.

Mary indeed did order the fillet of Sole and Juan a fillet mignon, medium rare. The repast started with the two of them clinking their glasses, and then tasting the rich liquids they had been served. The first course was a raison, dark wheat bread, cut into very thin slices and served with creamy butter. The bread seemed to melt in their mouths. This was followed by a cheese plate with four assorted cheeses, all French, and all mouth watering. Then came the main course with steamed vegetables. The fish was splendid and didn't taste fishy, which Mary hated. The steak was cooked to perfection. The vegetables retained some of their crispness, but were cooked and not mushy. Once the main course was finished, then came the desert. They each had chosen the crème Brule, a custard with a caramelized coating on top. The meal was completed with a small snifter of aged brandy. Juan couldn't remember when he had had such a meal. As they were enjoying the after dinner drink, the owner came to their table and inquired if they had enjoyed the meal. Juan lavished praise on the chef, letting him know he would tell all of his friends what a wonderful place this was to eat. The chef doffed his tall white hat and retreated back to the kitchen. Juan and Mary languished for awhile, then paid the check with a visa card and drove home. Mary settled up with the babysitter and reflected on the conversation she and Juan had had during the meal.

Juan carefully couched his words on the impending gathering to let Mary know what his intentions were. Mary had surmised what Juan's hankerings were for some time, and offered little in resistance. She knew Juan wanted to be governor more than anything in the world, and she was willing to make any sacrifice necessary to have him achieve that goal. She reinforced her support as they were getting ready for bed by wrapping her arms around his waist and placing her head in his chest. Juan could not believe he had found such a wonderful jewel of a wife, and after turning out the light, drifted off to a dreamless slumber.

CHAPTER FIFTY-FOUR

Gus called Juan to let him know the five men he felt were best qualified to get Juan elected had agreed to the clandestine meeting. They would be meeting in three weeks over a weekend. As Gus had stated before, the site was a getaway cottage high in the mountains looking over Lake Tahoe near North Incline village. Each participant would be traveling separately, but should make arrangements to gather no later than nine o'clock on the Friday night. Juan knew most of them would probably travel by car, but he decided to fly to Reno, rent a car and motor to the lodge. He called the airlines on his own to avoid any possibility of his secretary knowing about his plans. He would leave Santa Barbara and arrive in Reno in the late afternoon. That would give him plenty of time to procure the rental car and drive the distance to the site.

The three weeks went by swiftly. On Friday morning, Juan announced he was giving his staff another Friday afternoon off for their good behavior and as a bonus for all of the wonderful work they had done for him. This didn't seem unusual to them, since Juan was very generous with those who worked for him. After the staff had departed the office, Juan finished up some last minute items, drove to his house, and packed enough clothes to see him through the next two days. The flight was indeed short, which Juan appreciated. He had flown so much lately, as little time on a airplane as possible would be a welcome relief.

After deplaning, Juan picked up his medium sized automobile at the Hertz counter, signed the documents, obtained the keys, and found the car parked in space 6 next to a large Lincoln Town Car. Although the vehicle he had chosen was much smaller by comparison, it was new, clean, and certainly would meet all of his requirements. Now was not the time to choose a car that would make him conspicuous, and possibly compromise his situation.

Juan had always loved this part of Nevada. He had been to Reno several times to gamble, see a Broadway style show with a big name celebrity, or to just get away. He always stayed at Harrah's right in the middle of town on Virginia Street. He found the rooms to be plush, the hotel personnel friendly, and the food excellent. The location also allowed him to walk to most of the other hotels and their casinos without requiring any form of transportation. As Juan drove out of the airport parking lot, he wanted to turn left and do some gambling, but thought better of it.

Juan angled south on Highway 50 from Reno until he came to Highway 431 where he exited and began his ascent up into the mountains. Juan never ceased to marvel at the splendor of that part of the country. As the road wound up through the pine trees, Juan could look into his rearview mirror at the lights of Reno rapidly disappearing from sight. He felt as if he were traveling in time, through a blanket of mist, to an unknown destination. The dark trees began to swallow him up, as if to devour him and prevent him from meeting with these man-creatures from another planet. The landscape almost became surreal as he journeyed forth.

Gus had given Juan directions, spelling out certain landmarks to watch for. The vegetation was so dense and overgrown, it could be extremely easy to miss the signposts indicating the address of the owner. It was starting to get dark, and the unfamiliar road was becoming a hardship for him to concentrate on. He slowed the car as he watched the odometer roll over the number of miles from Highway 50. The measuring device told him the entrance to the cabin was close, so Juan stared more intently to the right side of the road. He almost missed the marker which was partially obscured by overgrown shrubbery, but there it was, just as Gus had said it would be.

The pavement stopped at the cutoff and Juan found himself on an improved dirt road still containing some remnants of gravel spread some time ago. The road curved left and right for about a half mile, then the trees parted and the cabin appeared. It was a wonderful sight, all lit up like a Christmas tree, surrounded by several cars parked along the circular driveway and beside the cabin. Juan recognized Gus's car, but not the others. Like himself, they had chosen small cars which were non-descript to avoid undue attention. He parked as close as he could to the structure, shut off the engine, exited the car, and opened the trunk to extract his small suitcase. As he neared the front door, the door opened and Gus appeared, framed by the light from the living room, to greet Juan.

The cabin must have cost a fortune. It was constructed of logs from native trees found nearby, and configured in such a way as to blend into the surroundings as if it were meant to be there. The roof was made out of a dark brown colored tin and was pitched at a sharp angle to allow the accumulated snow to easily slide off and not damage the place. There were several out buildings designed to house equipment and the well which to supplied the necessary water to the kitchen and the bathrooms. The center of the living room was dominated by a huge stone fireplace, and was filled with expensive overstuffed furniture. There were heads of deer and elks mounted on the upper walls, and Navajo blankets fastened between. The bedrooms and the baths were on the upper level, the living room with large glass windows taking up most of the space below. Behind the fireplace was the kitchen and utility room. The kitchen would have been the envy of most chefs. It was outfitted with modern appliances, counters, and an array of pots and pans suspended from the ceiling. Standing in the kitchen were the other men, each having a drink, some smoking, but all waiting for the hired cook to prepare their evening meal. The aroma of the food made Juan realize just how famished he really was.

Gus made Juan a drink, and then made the introductions. Bill Brockman, the farmer, was an overweight man standing just over six foot six and verging on the obese. He was dressed in a long sleeved flannel plaid shirt with a leather bolo string tie, Levi's with a leather belt and a large silver and gold buckle, and cowboy boots. He complexion was ruddy denoting the fact he spent so much time outdoors. As he shook Juan's hand, Juan could feel the calluses, and knew this was a man who worked for a living. Bill had a friendly face, and was immediately likeable. Gus told Juan that Bill hired a multitude of Mexicans to work on the farms, spoke Spanish fluently, and respected any Hispanic who had made a success of him or herself.

Next Juan met Wallace (Wally) Jenson, a city councilman from south central Los Angeles. Wally was a large Afro-American with a light brown complexion. He could have almost been mistaken for someone from the Middle East. He was about Juan's age, but looked older. Wally was dressed in a pair of Docker pants, an opened collared casual dress shirt, and tennis shoes. He had a slickness about himself that reminded Juan of a scam artist. After Juan shook his hand, he checked to see if he still had on his ring and all of his fingers. Wally didn't say much. Juan got the impression Wally was a man of few words, but when he spoke, there was meaning behind what he said. Pete Thomas reeked of money. He had on light blue slacks, a dark blue silk shirt, and a Navy blazer with some crest on the pocket patterned to look like some house of royalty. His shoes looked as if they would have cost Juan a week's salary. His hair was dark brown and stylishly cut. He wore gold colored framed glasses, his nails were manicured, and on his right hand was the largest diamond Juan had ever seen. Gus told Juan that Pete has bankrolled some of the most profitable companies in America and had connections not only in the State of California, but across the nation and the world.

Pete had grown up on a sheep farm in Southern Idaho, went to high school, then to college at Stanford where he received his doctorate in Electrical Engineering. After his schooling, he then migrated to Japan to build satellites for the large Japanese electronics companies. He married a Japanese girl who came with him to San Jose. Pete had provided the money to open a restaurant for her, which had become highly trendy and very profitable. Pete's salaries and bonuses had already made him a multi millionaire when he had partnered with other rich young men to get into the business of financing start up enterprises. Pete's group had been so insightful, their share of future profits exploded. Pete's wife had recently divorced him, and Pete was now living with his secretary.

Jerry Wurtz was the oddball in the crowd. Jerry was a gay Jew from San Francisco, and was very active in mobilizing gay rights initiatives. He was a consultant for a number of public relation firms, and businesses that catered to the homosexual communities. Juan had always thought gay men would look like women, but not Jerry. Jerry struck Juan as being able to be a convincing leading man and lover in any romantic movie, especially since Juan had been surprised to learn that Rock Hudson was gay after watching him make passionate love with some of the most beautiful ladies in Hollywood. Jerry spoke with a deep baritone voice, was dressed in a conservative fashion, and gave Juan a firm handshake.

Juan spent a few minutes reminiscing with Carl. He inquired about his wife and her health. Carl returned the question about Mary and the two men finished their short chat.

The feeling of urgency in the room was instantaneous, but the heavy deliberations could wait. The men mingled freely, exchanged private information, and all sat down to devour an outstanding steak dinner with all of the trimmings. After dinner they retired to the living room for more drinks and then to bed. They had a full day's schedule ahead of them in the morning.

CHAPTER FIFTY-FIVE

The dawn broke wonderfully and spread its shimmering glow across the cabin, warming the very innards of this magnificent place. Juan was an early riser, so jumped out of bed immediately, showered, shaved, and dressed in an Adidas jogging suit. The suit was expensive, and displayed his sculpted body well. He wanted to make a good impression on his newly found friends figuring even small details can help.

He was surprised when he walked downstairs that all of the others were in the midst of breakfast. Juan knew these individuals were on a mission and they didn't want to waste any of their precious time. The group only had the day Saturday, and half a day Sunday to get everything done. Juan knew the discussions would be intense, and Gus had told him they planned to meet for about six hours the first day, which would allow some time for the men to take a walk in the woods and to relax in this gorgeous setting. The cook asked for Juan's breakfast order and then set about to fixing it for him. Gus poured Juan a cup of black coffee and a glass of fresh squeezed orange juice. The others engaged Juan in small chatter, not bringing up anything about the meeting, just items of interest to them on the state level and within their family arena.

Juan had ordered a Spanish omelet, hash browns, crisp bacon, with a little salsa on the side. Jerry Wurtz, good heartedly ribbed Juan about eating ethnic foods. The others all laughed. Everyone took their time devouring the wonderful meal, then Gus asked all of them to sojourn to the living room to start the meeting. In the room, Gus had arranged six easels with large paper pads on each. The pads would be used to record the proceedings and saved for typing into notes to be distributed later. The chairs and couches were arranged in a horseshoe configuration so everyone could see the pads from any angle.

Gus set the ground rules. Everyone was asked to participate. Everyone had a right to his own opinion and the others had no right to criticize. Everything would be recorded however trivial. They would take a break each hour and would have lunch at exactly noon. The session would terminate at 3:00 P.M. All agreed to these terms and the meeting began. The strategic plan to get Juan elected governor of the State of California took on the ferocity of a hurricane. Gus was having a hard time keeping up with the remarks as he was recording them with felt tipped pens. The group developed a time line for the campaign, highlighting critical dates when each task must be completed. Groups of constituents were identified and members of these groups were recommended to be on the master team. Advertising, a very high budget item took some thought. Before beginning this abstract endeavor, the first break was announced. They all went to the kitchen to refill their coffee cups, got some more juice, and to eat some wonderful cinnamon rolls the cook had just taken out of the oven. When the juice was consumed, the last of the icing was licked from their fingers, and the coffee cups refilled, the conversation again resumed in earnest.

Juan's head was exploding. Never in his life had he participated in a roundtable discussion where so many great ideas were floated in such a short time. So many things were put on the charts. So many aspects and angles were espoused many of which Juan would never have thought of even though he had managed a major senatorial campaign for Kyle Smith himself. He knew he was in the midst of political genius and appreciated the group so much. The day flew by and before Juan knew it, a halt was called to the proceedings. Lunch had been light, but with all of the extra trimmings. Some of the group decided to take a short nap on the chaise lounges on the expansive redwood deck, while other put on their walking shoes and started for the forest.

Juan remained in the living room with Gus and spent approximately an hour going over the comments to ensure Juan was fully grasping the concepts and the various parts of the plan. When they finished, Juan joined some of the men on the deck to marvel at the grandeur surrounding him. That evening, after dinner, the group decided to start a high stakes poker game, which lasted well into the night. Juan was lucky, drawing to an inside straight, and taking his share of the pots. Juan was a good poker player, but knew he was playing with equal competitors whose faces he could not read. When the game was over, the losers anted up to the winners with cash or a check and everyone retired to their rooms to shower and to sleep.

The next morning, the process was the same, the group finishing up just before noon. Another small lunch was prepared and each individual wished Juan a fond adieu and good luck for the coming months. As each of the group drove away, Juan felt a small piece of his soul leaving with them. He sensed he may not cross their paths again to any great degree, but knew in his deepest recesses they would be in the background guiding his fortune. Gus had gathered up the papers, stowed the easels in his station wagon, paid and dismissed the cook, straightened up the cabin, checked to see all of the lights had been turned off, and locked the front door. The two friends shook hands, and set a time to exchange the notes and to begin the journey. Juan's drive back to the airport and the drive to his home gave him time to reflect on the meeting and the course looming before him. If he were prone to ulcers, they would have been spouting gushers of red cells into his inner cavity by now. He pulled over to the side of the road, calmed himself and let the wave of foreboding subside. He knew he would get through this massive undertaking, he just had to take it one step at a time.

Safely inside his residence, he held Mary tight, walked her slowly into the front room to sit her down on the sofa and tell her of the happenings. Mary listened without comment, nodding in the appropriate places, and sighing when Juan could not continue. Mary stood, embraced her husband and gave him the comforting words she knew would sustain him for the many new months to come. Mary knew when Juan was due to arrive, so she had prepared his favorite meal. After handing him a fresh cocktail, she opened her favorite wine, and toasted the new governor of the State of California. Juan was appreciative, but warned her not to count her chickens too soon. There were still mountains of work to be done.

Silently, without fanfare, and as covert an operation as would have done the CIA proud, the facets of the plan to elect Juan governor began to take shape. Volunteers were being recruited in all of the groups identified by the gang of six. They weren't told who was going to be entering the primary elections for the Democratic Party, but were given schedules for reporting to work, and outlines of the chores they were to perform. The arms of wealthy contributors were gently twisted. No money was given at this stage, but pledges were taken for a future time. Change was in the air. California had been suffering an economic status quo for the past two terms of the current Governor, and the people were sick and tired of it. There were still problems in every facet of the state's infra-structure. These problems were reminiscent of the same problems Juan had faced in his other bureaucratic endeavors. It was almost uncanny how the six of them had zeroed in on the same subjects the populace were venting their anger on.

The Governor, for some reason, just couldn't seem to come up with any compromises with the legislature to alleviate the situation and help the state overcome the adversities. When the time was ripe, Gus advised Juan he should announce his candidacy at a press conference just as the state legislature was to commence.

CHAPTER FIFTY-SIX

The state legislature was due to convene in early January to start the spring session. The legislative assemblage met twice a year for a short period, this year being an off year where the body contemplated a supplemental budget and passed or eliminated small bills not enacted into law during the fall session. Next year would be an election year, and a year to set into place a biennial budget to fund the state's government and its support service for a two year period. Juan knew he had less than two years to put his run for the governorship in place, and time was of the essence.

Juan had been given key committee posts by the legislative powers, and as such, was contacted by the press media for his thoughts on the upcoming session. The press conference was live from Sacramento and was broadcast from the steps of the Senate building. The day was sunny, yet cool, but in spite of the chilliness, Juan stood tall in a dark suit without showing any signs of shivering. The press asked the standard questions about what the legislature hope to accomplish, his opinion of what the key issues facing the California economy were, and what he thought could be done about the crime situation. Juan handled the questions flawlessly, shying away from answering directly any question considered well within the realm of the legislative body to consider, and not within his sphere of influence. As the session was winding down and Juan was about to turn and leave, a diminutive female in the back raised her hand. Juan didn't see the hand, but one of his staff aids did, nudged Juan, and suggested he take one final question.

"I have heard it rumored you might be interested in running for Governor, is there any truth to that?"

Juan knew some of his advisors had planted the seed with this reporter, and now was the golden time to let the state know he was running without bringing up the subject himself.

"To answer your question, yes, it is my intent to run for governor. I know the present governor is planning on running for re-election, and I feel I am ready to challenge him and bring stability to the state. I feel I have paid my dues, and can put together an administration based on professionalism and experience. There will be more to come in the next few weeks, but first I must meet the filing deadline. When all of the paperwork is turned in to the elections office, I will be more at liberty to explain my platform and how I hope to accomplish those items that must be accomplished."

Juan turned and exited the forum. He did not respond to the many following questions shouted at him as he moved up the stairs and into the beautiful, white marbled building. Once he had settled into his office, and was going through some briefing papers his staff had prepared, his phone rang. It was Shirl letting him know there was a phone call from a Mr. Carl Evans, and would Juan wish to take it. Juan told Shirl to put him through.

"Juan, I was just watching the television broadcast and heard your announcement. Congratulations. As I told you at the conclave, you will make an excellent leader for our state. I also wanted to let you know I have put my assets to work on your behalf. I have many political favors to call in, and I wanted to direct them your way. I would appreciate knowing of any groups you would like me to assist you in getting their endorsements, and any names of people of influence I should contact to let them know of my intent." Juan rattled off a half dozen groups. Carl and Juan conversed for a few more minutes, and

Carl rang off promising he would get back to Juan in the following months. The first major cornerstone in Juan's quest had now been cemented into place.

The state was abuzz. After Juan was the first to declare, four more democratic candidates threw their hats in the ring. As Juan was perusing the paper, he ran across an article about these newcomers, knowing they would present a formidable challenge for him. Included in the list of want-to-bees, was Wendell Gillette, a very successful lawyer, and a fellow member of the State Senate. The list followed with Perry Weatherspoon from the Green Party, a devoted environmentalist, known for his tree hugging abilities and ocean pollution prowess. There was also Bill Styker, a lobbyist of some renown. Bill had been a governmental representative and lobbyist for a major pharmaceutical company housed in the same section of the state as were the megalithic software giants. Ty Vu, an immigrant from Vietnam, and a wealthy and self made developer in the San Diego area who wanted to see the state become the bastion of the foreigner and the minority segment, offering them the same equal opportunity as that enjoyed by the other, longer established citizens. The list was rounded out with the name of Kristine Duncan, the California State Attorney General.

Juan didn't know much about Ty Vu, or Perry Weatherspoon, but had met Bill Styker on occasion, and was well acquainted with Wendell Gillette who had served on several committees and sub-committees with Juan. He did know Kristine as well, and felt she would be the most dangerous opponent. She was not only good looking, but came from money and power. Many said she had engineered herself into the Attorney's General office with her family's wealth, and had devilishly rich friends scattered throughout the state. Kristine was extremely bright, having graduated from The University of Michigan Law School at the top of her class. She could charm the skin off a snake and the snake would thank her for it. She would deserve Juan's full attention.

The papers required for the filing were completed by Juan's staff, and personally carried by Juan to the elections office, accompanied by Mary and Shirl. As he stood at the counter, transferring the bundle along with his cashier check for the filing fee to the chief clerk of the office. Juan took every opportunity to press flesh with the employees, and to smile radiantly for the cameras. Those honed communicative skills Juan had developed over the years were now starting to pay off their dividends. The filing hadn't taken long, but had given Juan the edge since he was the first one to do so. The others would follow, but would be treated as less efficient and competent. Juan needed all of the edges he could get, and tickets punched to solidify his position.

Now the balancing act and management of his time began. He was supposed to keep many balls in the air at the same time, while not wearing himself out in the fray. He had a law office, a family, a senate job, and a community presence to keep on top of, as well as a campaign to be an intricate part of. He knew his physical stamina and his experience would be tested to the maximum, but he also knew he had the best people in the world on his side. Now it was Just a matter of delegating and coordinating with those people.

The pieces of the mosaic were falling into place. Campaign offices were being established within critical parts of the state, staffs were hired, and volunteers recruited. Endorsements began to mount. Juan received the backing from the Police Officer's Guild, but not the group representing the county sheriff organizations. Most of the unions fell on Juan's side of the ledger, but the two most powerful, the Teamsters and the Longshoremen had not declared as yet. It was any one's guess as to how that hammer would land on the anvil. The teacher's union was leaning to Juan's side, but still was waiting in the wings to see what would develop as time passed. Each day, Juan would receive a consolidated list of endorsements reflecting if they supported Juan, if they were pro Juan, but had not declared, were in other camps, or were staying neutral for the duration. The list looked most favorable for Juan, but he knew the winds of politics could change in the blinking of an eye. Now the "Go for the Gold" was in full stride. The days were flashing by at a speed Juan had never known before. He knew the ins and outs of this business, no longer a cog in the background, but in the forefront of the fighting.

It wasn't time for the signs to go up in the yards, or for the advertisements to air on television and on the radio, but requests for public appearances increased sharply as did the rhetoric in the press. For the first year, the bantering was hospitable, but as everyone predicted soon would turn ugly. The smear components were starting to come out, old skeletons revealed whether true or not, and claims of incompetence made. The spin doctors were working overtime to refute some statements or to turn the statements into positive images. Juan was even starting to believe he had done some of the wonderful things they were saying about him, knowing full well that some of them he had not done, but the public would never be the wiser.

Juan received a tremendous boost when the Hispanic population moved in his direction. The experts were saying if the primary election were to be held at this date, Juan would receive over 60 percent of the vote. The pressure to increase the voter registration among the minorities took on a greater importance. He would bring this up as an agenda item at his next strategy meeting.

CHAPTER FIFTY-SEVEN

Jose and Maria Elena were continuing to grow and develop, and Juan was missing out on the most critical parts of their lives. He knew Mary was resenting his absence and involvement, but she never gave any hint otherwise. He knew he was placing many demands on his loved ones, so at a rare evening dinner, he announced he was taking three days off, and they were going to the beach to lie in the sun, play beach ball, and just hang out together. He need to recharge his batteries and couldn't think of a better method to do it. Everyone at the tabled cheered in unison, and the rest of the evening was spent with hugs, kisses, and intricate planning. It would be a marvelous time, and something from which everyone could benefit. Juan went to bed happier than he had been in many months, swearing to himself that nothing would interfere with these plans so help him God.

Everything went as planned. The staff was told to keep the media at arm's length, and not to disturb the family for any reason. The location of their gathering at the beach was kept quiet, so little if any interruption transpired. The staff kept their word and saved the myriad of chores for Juan's return to the headquarters. The family gamboled in the surf, lay on the beach and thoroughly enjoyed the sun. In the afternoon, the children would take a short nap while Juan and Mary would lounge in a hammock on the deck of their room and sip colorful drinks with little umbrellas in them. Paradise had truly come their way, but reality set in when they realized the short vacation was coming to an end and they must get back to the bump and grind of the real world. Jose and Maria Elena cried when the morning came for their return. Juan promised them they would come back just as soon as possible, which barely placated them. Finally, through urging by their mother, they ceased their grousing.

The return to the fray was almost overwhelming, but Juan, because of the getaway, felt rejuvenated and ready to get down to business. As time moved along, three of the Democratic candidates began to filter to the top of the list of hopefuls. The state's Attorney General Kristine, Wendell Gillette, and of course Juan. The pollsters put the three at almost a dead heat. The lobbyist and the environmentalist were a far distant fourth and fifth, and in Juan's estimation posed no threat. Kristine came out swinging with the first salvo. It wasn't just mud slinging by the handful, but slime throwing using a backhoe. She attacked Juan from every aspect, focusing in on his record as District Attorney in Santa Barbara County. Somehow she was able to get her hands on files from his ancient office for cases that had been botched by his staff, had been bargained away to control the damage, and should have been forgotten. She took parts of each case, and bent them out of context. Juan recognized what she was doing, but was impotent to stop her. He put the best spin on it as he could, but damage was being done. After the first popularity poll, Kristine was leading Juan by twenty percentage points. Even Gillette had taken advantage of this and leaped ahead of Juan in the polls.

The Gods were truly smiling on Juan when Kristine brought forth a case in a press conference, and a reporter who was familiar with the case took her to task on her accuracy. He, in front of all of the media, forced Kristine to admit she had been wrong in her assumptions and assessments. Juan's staff took immediate action and for the most part put Kristine in a position of having the public question all of her previous statements. Juan gained ten points back.

As the rhetoric continued, it was suggested the candidates get together in a neutral place and debate the issues. This was to be patterned after the Kennedy-Nixon debates, which Kennedy won handily. Juan wasn't too crazy about the idea, but felt with his experience, he could hold his own. A site was chosen and a date selected. The candidates were to be placed on stage behind individual daises, with a moderator assigned who would ask questions of the candidates and limit the time of their responses. One morning, as Juan was preparing for the debates, he picked up the morning paper from Los Angeles, and blazoned across the top of the paper was the headline, "CANDIDATE DIES IN FIERY CRASH". According to the report, Wendell Gillette had been involved in an automobile accident on a county road in eastern Los Angeles County. It was alleged someone had run him off the road and into a tree where his car caught on fire and he could not escape. The police and other criminal investigative agencies were looking into the incident as suspicious, but had no leads at the present time. Juan had this funny feeling in his gut that people surrounding him were to blame, but were they? Certainly no one he knew would resort to such tactics would they? No matter how hard he tried, Juan could not shake this feeling, but when he asked around his camp, everyone claimed pure innocence. Gus told Juan not to focus on the horrible accident, he had larger fish to fry.

It was back to the debates. The lobbyist and the environmentalist decided not to join in the debates, but to sit back and take the spoils from the procedure. They knew they had no chance to win, but felt they could siphon off votes from one of the candidates so the person they liked the best would win. Their plan was to meet with their preference and to garner favors for positions in government that would ensure them a wonderful salary and many benefits. Unknown to Juan the preferred person was Kristine.

The debates were to be held in the Los Angeles arena seating over twenty thousand, with millions watching on television. The arena was gaily decorated with patriotic banners and flags giving it an almost Fourth of July atmosphere even though it was springtime. Backstage, Kristine and Juan were in their dressing rooms, attendants going over their wardrobes, hair, and makeup to guarantee the best projection onto the screens in the homes in California and to the audience in attendance. To Kristine, makeup was vital. It was necessary to cover up the many lines that had gouged her face and had given her a haggard look. She had contemplated plastic surgery, but just had not had enough time to have anything done. The makeup the cosmetologist applied was nearly flawless. As Kristine peered into the mirror, she was gratified. No way did she feel she would lose the debate, and felt every confidence she would advance in the polls and finally win the Democratic nod.

The hour had come. A producer knocked on Juan's dressing room door and announced there was five minutes to airtime, and that Juan should be on stage as soon as possible to be placed into position. The makeup artist put the finishing touches on Juan's face and neck. Juan had near perfect olive skin, so very little makeup had to be used. Juan rose, adjusted his tie, looked back into the full-length image, smiled, licked his finger and drew it across his eyebrows. The trip to the stage wasn't far. He knew he would not cross Kristine's path on the way, it had been scheduled for him to enter from the right, Kristine from the left. As they appeared in the lights, a large roar mixed with infrequent boo's resounded throughout the hall.

Juan had never felt butterflies like this before. His advisors told him just to act natural, hesitate after each question so that the question was fully understood, then speak slowly and distinctly. The floor director signaled to each person holding up his fingers and counted down, FIVE, FOUR, THREE, TWO, ONE. As the director lowered his hand, a red light came on the TV camera. Juan had been warned not to look directly into the lens, but to focus on the moderator.

The first question came. It was a simple question, one to loosen up the debaters and to set the mood of the performance. Juan and Kristine handled the question well, and the butterflies suddenly went away. As the questions proceeded, Juan's confidence grew. He had a sense about him clearly discernable by the crowd. Their attention was beginning to shift onto his presence. Kristine could feel this shift in momentum. It was almost palpable. Her otherwise stoic demeanor showed a slight crack as she hesitated a fraction of a second too long in answering.

As the debate worn on, the bright lights began to take its toil on Kristine's makeup. As the covering began to melt away, the witchlike lines began to appear. Her face went from ravishing beauty to one slightly haggard. She didn't dare wipe the makeup away, which would only make matters worse, so she suffered through as best she could, hoping the ordeal would be over. Mercifully it came to a conclusion. There was no doubt in anyone's mind that Juan was the clear victor. His rating in the polls jumped. He was now back neck and neck with Kristine.

Another major break came Juan's way. He received a notification from Bill Kobus, Director of the San Diego State Alumni Association that he had been nominated and selected to be placed in the Aztec Sports Hall of Fame, an honor reserved for only the very best in the university's sports field. He had been chosen to represent the field of soccer at a ceremony to be held in the sports arena at the school. He was one of seven individuals chosen. The athletes would be brought to the university at no expense to them, housed at a local, upscale hotel, transported to the ceremony where they would receive a plaque inscribed with their name. Their picture would then be installed in the Walk of Fame hallway down a major corridor at the arena. It was an especially proud moment for Juan, as this ceremony marked the one-hundredth anniversary of the establishment of the award.

Mary sent Juan to San Diego alone. This was an honor he had achieved by himself, and she didn't want to distract a single iota from its importance. She would stay and work, watch the kids with the nanny, and wait for his return. Juan wanted Mary to go with him, but realized from whence she came and agreed to go solo to his old school.

CHAPTER FIFTY-EIGHT

Juan drove to San Diego, and checked into the hotel the university had selected. As he carried his bags up to the registration desk, he was greeted by a representative of the Alumni Association Office who was none other than Wally "Chipper" Biggs, the Athletic Director who had given Juan his scholarship to play for the school. Chipper, of course had retired, but still looked the same. He had gained a few pounds, but was still lean and mean, and looked like he could run over any line backer known to man. He welcomed Juan warmly, and they conversed about old times, and what Juan was doing in his rich and full life. Other athletes started to arrive, Chipper recognizing some of them, and shaking hands with others who had not come under his domain.

The honorees were told to relax, explore the hotel, chat with friends, and come to a dinner in their honor at 6 o'clock in the hotel main dining room the following day. Juan was given a packet for information about the ceremony which he glanced over once he got up to his room. The evening was to be formal and the menu looked superb. There would be a hosted cocktail hour, followed by introductory speeches, then the meal. Each athlete would then have a video snip projected on a large screen displaying parts of their lives and their accomplishments. Each person would receive the honored plaque, and a gold medallion suspended around his neck with a ribbon emblazoned with the school's colors.

As Juan entered the dining room, he glanced toward the center of the room and saw Shannon, his long time friend and mentor. They stood and gazed at each other for a few seconds, then Juan approached his old friend. Shannon was not known for her affection, but did slide her arms around Juan's neck and planted a kiss on his lips. Juan almost felt like he was committing adultery, but the feeling passed and the old friends waltzed, arm in arm to the bar. After they had gotten the drink of their choice, they circulated around the room, exchanging pleasantries with the members of the crowd, and stopping to reminisce with fellow teammates.

The cocktail hour ended and Juan along with Shannon went to their assigned table. The round tables were distributed around the room, seating eight persons to each table. Juan, the award recipient, joined former members of the soccer team during his heyday, and members of the current team, a group that comprised and emulated the glory teams of the past. Joining Juan was Bubba Hendricks, Mark Goddard, the former soccer head coach, and Tim Ryan, one of the former assistant coaches who now was head coach at College of the Redlands. Introductions were made all around, and the honors banquet began. The attendees were welcomed by the President of the University. His speech was short, and the words well chosen. The President was a brilliant individual, but also a notable politician in his own right. The head of the university was followed by Bill Kobus, and the current athlete director. The speeches ended and the food was served.

Salads were followed by wine, then a thin broth soup, and the main entrée "Surf and Turf". The steak was exceptionally tender, and the seafood poached to perfection. The desert was a smooth chocolate mousse topped with real whipped cream. More wine came, the glasses hardly touched, but still filled to the rim. Juan stopped after two glasses, he knew he must be lucid enough when his turn came to present his acceptance talk. The lights were dimmed, and the video appeared on a three large screens dropped from the ceiling. The first person honored, was a football player who had been a star about the time Juan entered the academic area. Scenes of the player's life, including pictures of him as a child, uniformed as a high school player, his marriage, and action shots of the days when he played for the Aztecs. The clip wasn't long, and the screen went dark. The lights were brightened and the player came to the platform. The President placed the medallion over his neck, shook his hand, and offered words that could not be heard in the crowd. The player then walked to the podium, reached into his coat pocket, unfolded a small piece of white paper, and recited the honor he humbly was experiencing. The speech was brief, sincere, and very touching. The next recipient was announced, and the same procedure followed until it was Juan's turn to be recognized.

The alumni association director appeared at the podium to announce Juan. He gave a few remarks, and with a burst of energy, he said, "and the next governor of the State of California, Juan Cardova." A thunderous cheer erupted from the crowd. Juan was taken by surprise, but knew he could count on almost a thousand votes in the upcoming election. Juan's video began. Whoever had prepared the tape had done a masterful job. The visions put Juan in the best light possible, unbiased and capitalizing on his best traits and accomplishments. Juan didn't remember going to the stage or what he said, and found himself back at his table being slapped on the back and hearing the din of the applause. Juan spent almost an hour after the dinner was over, renewing old friendships, and being every inch the candidate. His fifteen minutes of glory were over. He returned to his hotel still exhilarated from his evening, unable to sleep, but finally did. The next morning he drove back to Santa Barbara.

He had a brass ring to catch.

One debate was followed by another debate, some times alone with Kristine, and sometimes with the other two strivers. More television ads appeared, the tenure of the mud slinging increasing. Claims and counterclaims continued unabated. The public was getting sick and tired of the personality bashing, so Juan's advisors decided to have the ads changed to reflect more of Juan's position on the needs of the state. This change in direction seemed to help. The polls showed a slight increase of a few percentage points going Juan's way. Then unexpectedly, a series of newspaper articles started to break in the Los Angeles Times about Kristine Duncan's character. The reporters would not list the sources, but cited reliable information obtained from individuals who had been associated with the attorney. Kristine was inundated by the torrent of reports alleging everything from her sexual orientation to bribes taken. She denied the facts as they were presented, but no matter how hard she tried, the damage was done. Finally, in an unscheduled press conference, she attempted to defend herself, but was not very convincing. California being a fairly liberal state, seemed to forgive her, but a large majority of the conservative right wing of the Democratic Party mounted a "Get rid of Kristine" push. Things were not going well for Kristine. Her numbers in the polls plummeted and when the primary election was finally over, Juan had won by a landslide.

Juan didn't know who had leaked the lesbian information, and hated to win this way, but since he was not involved with the action, he prepared himself and his staff for an encounter with the Republican selection to determine the sovereign of the most populous state. The chosen Republican was a political protégé from the family of a previous governor. California had almost always been a democratic state, but several years past, a charismatic man with the last name of Brown came along and convinced the populace he could lead the state. He had been successful for two terms and was about to create a dynasty. The incumbent picked to marshal the Republican troops was a well known banker and lawyer named Nelson Brown Neely, the grandson of the former governor on his mother's side. Nelson had been raised a political animal. He had the education and money to make the race a potentially miserable one for Juan. Juan knew those in office had one leg up, but was determined not to let that sway him.

The media had a field day with the two choices, comparing them to the classic heavy weight boxing matches between Ali and Joe Frazier. Long articles on the backgrounds of the two were paraded out in all sorts of printed and aired mediums. If there were any skeletons in their backgrounds, the investigative reporters were not able to uncover anything. Juan began his journey traversing the state from end to end, doing all of the things politicians do, kissing babies, cutting ribbons, holding town hall meetings, and sending out his message via the radio talk show circuit. Juan visited the gang ravaged ghettos of the big cities, and the barrios of the Hispanic. He attended Bar Mitzvahs and Protestant weddings. Nothing was left untouched. He appeared to be everywhere at once. Everyone wondered how he was able to keep up the pace. Mary was concerned for his health, but when she had a rare occasion to see him, it appeared that he was thriving on the attention. He said he was eating and sleeping well, and had never felt better in his life.

Surprisingly, the war between the two Titans was fairly clean. There were some offside remarks made, but they contained very little substance. Both of the men seemed content to promote their platforms and let the people decide. As the general election neared, the intensity increased by volumes. It was a general election year to elect a new President of the United States, so the percentage of voters going to the booths was estimated to exceed the normal average. In spite of the fact that America was founded on the freedom to exercise one's right to vote, over the years the numbers actually exercising that right barely exceeded a third of those eligible. Most of the youth remained apathetic, not trusting anyone over thirty years of age, and more concerned with their lives and not the welfare of their fellow citizens. Juan knew he would have to work hard to get the minority groups registered to vote, to woo the gray panthers, and to capture the imagination of the unions and large associations. His planning partners began to deliver. Juan's war chest continued to swell, and his exposure continued to grow. The endorsements continued to come in, but the polls still reflected a near dead even status between the two men.

Election Day finally arrived. Juan had chosen a swank hotel in Santa Barbara to cloister with his friends, staff, and volunteers. He had rented several suites for the higher ups in his campaign and the ballroom for the victory speech and celebration if he were lucky enough to pull it off. Juan sat in his suite with Mary and his closest allies watching the returns come in from the national scene. The national consultants and network anchors were shifting from state race to state race and the results of those voting for the leader of the land. The trend seemed to favor the Democrats who were going to garner additional seats in congress and for the first time in many years were projected to control both houses. It also was predicted the next President would be a Democrat. Even though the polls in California still had three hours before closing time, the networks were making early decisions on who the winners would be, and Juan knew this would influence the results in his state. He was concerned about this approach taken by the national media. He felt the predications should be held in abeyance until the voting places were buttoned up in the Pacific time zone. He wanted every voter to render his or her decision without undue influence. Maybe, someday, Juan thought to himself, I will be in a position to change this fact of life.

Television sets were strewn all about the suite, one in every room, many tuned to different channels so those in the suite could get a more complete picture of what was transpiring. Juan and Mary sat in the bedroom, Mary trying to relax on the king size bed, and Juan sitting in an awkward position in a lounge chair. Juan was dressed in a tuxedo, but had taken off the bow tie and loosened the collar of the fluted shirt. As Juan watched, he felt as if he were swimming through molasses. The time seemed to drag on at a snail's pace. He wanted a drink of scotch, but knew he better not. Finally he got up from the chair and strolled into the front room to be with other members of his contingent. Even though the channel was set differently, the announcer seemed like a clone of all of the others.

Surprisingly, when almost eighty percent of the district votes were counted, the margin between the two candidates was too close for even the computer generated statistic machinery to predict, it was simply just too close to call. With all of the ballots counted in Los Angeles, Orange, San Diego, and San Francisco counties tallied, Nelson was only leading by less than 7,000 votes. The northern part of the state was slower coming in because of the rural nature of that part. Juan hung his head in silent prayer, begging Fritz to deliver the farming community and logging industries. With just ten percent of the votes to come in, the north began its march on the Capitol. Without fanfare, the votes shifted in favor of Juan. Just a few at a time, but then the count began to resemble a large rock rolling downhill, slowly gaining momentum. Juan was leading by just a few thousand, then ten thousand, then twenty thousand, and finally the drama was over. Juan was in the lead with twenty two thousand votes out of millions. Nelson would not concede the election. According to state law, if the margin of votes did not exceed a certain level, a mandatory recount would have to take place. The victory celebration would have to be put on hold. Juan finished getting dressed and with Mary, went down to the ballroom. He went to the microphone, and told the gathering to enjoy themselves, since the party had already been paid for, and he didn't want all of that good food and drink to go to waste. The well- wishers took his advice and began to gobble up the victuals. The crowd had a festive mood about itself, but at the same time subdued. They didn't want to put a jinx on Juan, but felt he would survive the recount. The night ended and everyone went home or to the rooms that had been reserved in the hotel.

Two days later, the Secretary of State and the state elections officer put their stamp of approval on the final count, and Juan Cardova, an alien from another country was declared the next Governor of the

State of California. Kyle Smith again arose to the occasion, hosting a huge congratulatory bash at his home. He invited everyone who was associated with the win, regardless of how many came. Juan was overwhelmed with the generosity. The party wasn't to the magnitude of the victory ball in the hotel, but close to it. It started in the early afternoon, and didn't end until the next morning. Cars and people continuously streamed to and from Kyle's mansion. Many came to seek Juan's favor including the lobbyists and the press. No matter how hard they tried, Juan gave them very little information about his administration or what his priorities were going to be. Juan had become very artful at dodging those leading questions intended to pin him down while at the same time not offending anyone.

Shortly after the election, Juan was informed that his campaign was being sued by the State Republican Party for advocacy groups using membership money to produce and air "issue" ads. At issue was a bipartisan campaign reform act which restricted corporations, labor unions and special interest groups from using their general funds to run ads that named a candidate for state office within 30 days of a primary or 60 days of a general election. A huge concern surfaced in the Democratic ranks. If this law were upheld, it could possibly nullify the election and a new vote would have to take place. The State Democratic Party immediately filed a counter suit with the state Supreme Court. In a six to three ruling, the Supreme Court of California said organizations have a First Amendment right to speak on political issues in ads that address policy, not the election. Juan was reaffirmed as the Governor.

CHAPTER FIFTY-NINE

On a cloudy, rainy morning in early January, Juan would take the oath of office, and be sworn in by the Chief Justice of the California State Supreme Court. What fitting irony that the head of the body which ruled in Juan's favor over "issue" ads would be the person to make his title official. The inauguration was scheduled to be held outside on the steps of the state capitol building, and in spite of the fowl weather, that is exactly where it was held. A huge throng gathered on the streets in front of the massive gray granite building, a sea of umbrellas dotting the landscape. As Juan stood at the front of the platform, he looked down on his citizens who appeared to be a sea of black silk. He wished he could see their faces, but knew inside that his acceptance speech would be heard by all, and he would achieve solidarity for his efforts. Juan had chosen to use an old Bible his mother had given to him when he left Mexico to seek his fortune. Although the Holy Book was tattered and well worn, it seemed like a red hot griddle as Juan placed his left hand on it and raised his right hand to repeat the oath now being administered by the Chief Justice. He could feel the warmth of his family, his friends, his staff, and the people gathered coming through the very core of the book he held. Slowly, Juan stated, "I Juan Cardova do solemnly swear that I ……….."

When the oath was completed, the Chief Justice shook Juan's hand, Mary gave him a kiss, and he turned to the microphone to give his inaugural discourse. Juan didn't want the speech to be lengthy. He knew the crowd was getting restless because of the cold, so he hit home with goodness and light for everyone. When he was through, the crowd roared its approval and the ceremony came to a close. That evening, by invitation only, the inaugural ball was held. The ball tickets were the hottest item in town, many people paying huge amounts just to get one. Two thirds of the tickets were allotted to the Governor's office to be distributed to those who had helped Juan the most, the remainder going on sale to the general public. The ball was the most opulent gathering in the history of the state. Many local leaders groused about the expense, but were placated by promises of an equal amount being made available to support local services and projects. The festivities were over, and the time had come to put together the administration geared to bring fruition to the goals and aspirations Juan had for the state.

The first week was given to moving into the Governor's Mansion and the Governor's Office. Mary hated to leave their comfortable home, but knew what was expected of her and the two children. Suddenly she felt as if she were a beetle being examined under a microscope. She knew every phase of their lives would now be out in the public eye for all to see. She wasn't sure if she would wilt under the pressure, but Juan assured her she would do a marvelous job as the State's First Lady. Since the Governor's mansion was furnished, there wasn't much to be moved from their other house. Juan and Mary decided to lease their home for the next four years hoping they would find a family who would take care of it. It didn't take long and the right people came forth to rent. In fact, it worked out perfectly, the husband of the new renters had just been hired to head one of the major divisions in the state, and Juan knew him. At least one problem was solved.

Now the daunting task of putting together the new administration loomed over Juan's head. A transition team had been formed to accomplish this purpose. Some of the smartest minds were brought together for a retreat in the Sierra mountains to map out how the building of this state's administration would look. Juan cleverly brought together some of the old guard from the state legislature, new blood from the private sector, consultants for business, farming, health, and education. Juan wanted a mix of gender, age, race, religion, and background in his administration. The transition team in small part mirrored this desire. For a week, the group labored and finally came up with an organizational table which Juan felt would fit the bill.

Juan selected an old Army buddy to head up his Department of Personnel. It would be the responsibility of this director to fill the key positions as Secretaries of the Departments, the Deputy Secretaries, and the staff closest to the flagpole. Juan contacted his old friend Colonel Jim Easton, US Army Retired. Jim had spent over 30 years in the Army having been commissioned through the ROTC program just like Juan, serving in a variety of positions in the personnel management area. Jim had served his initial three years in the Regular Army in an infantry unit, then decided he would much rather ride a desk, than jump out of aircraft into enemy territory, so he requested a transfer to the Adjutant General Corps. Juan met Jim in Vietnam, and over the years they had exchanged correspondence and Christmas cards.

Jim knew the human resources game. He could determine the value of Army officers with a simple interview, and would make assignments appropriately, or instill in them the desire to get out of the service for the good of the nation. After he had retired from the military, he was hired by the nation's top head hunter agency. Jim was responsible for finding many of the Presidents of major corporations and Chairmen of key boards of directors. Jim had the innate ability to put the right person in the right job at the right time. Juan didn't have much money to pay Jim for his time, but that didn't matter. Jim felt an obligation to Juan and money was no object. Over the years, Easton had been fortunate to have received not only his military retirement pay, but had been generously reimbursed by the firm he worked for.

Jim flew to Sacramento and his work began.

In state government, top jobs were classified as exempt positions. This meant the status of the job depended on the wishes of the governor. A person who was hired to fill an exempt position knew his or her job depended on the wave of the political climate. They could either be retained in their current position, be moved to a position of lesser importance, or outright replaced. It was a risk the person had to take when opting to work within the state structure.

Jim was a large redhead, quick with a smile or a laugh. Highly intelligent and extremely well organized. Since he left the Army, he had put on a couple of pounds, and felt his age, but his energy level had never been higher. He relished a new challenge. His demeanor was tricky, many people of low potential who had thought they had pulled a fast one on him, suddenly found themselves looking for other employment.

Juan had asked for a chart showing all of the major positions in the state, the current incumbents, and a brief resume of each. He met with Jim in his office and together they poured over the documents. To the right margin of the list, Jim had placed four columns. One was labeled retain in position, one labeled move to lower status, one promote to higher status, and one "get rid of". In a couple of days, red checkmarks were made in the columns in approximately eighty percent of the names. The remaining twenty percent were labeled as questionable as to disposition. Jim wanted to personally interview that twenty percent. Interviews were schedule over the next week, each person was given an hour for questioning and for their input. At the end of the week, final decisions were made, and the rotation of personnel began.

The first major change was in the Department of Health and Human Services. It was one of the largest departments in the state, providing money and other services to the state's low income population, to elderly individuals, and to disabled children. The budget for this department was staggering, and growing out of control year after year.

It was true the client population was increasing, especially because of the influx of aliens from Mexico, Asia, and Russia, but there were many other factors which accounted for the increase in expenditures. Even though the Federal Government provided an established match for money allocated by the state, there never seemed to be enough to meet the demand. It was estimated over thirty percent of the low income children were without an medical insurance coverage. The prescription drug program had ballooned out of proportion. There weren't enough case workers to keep up with the demand, and fraud and mismanagement ran rampant. The ranks of the mentally ill swelled to a level which overwhelmed the mental hospitals and clinics. The food stamp program was broken and needed to be fixed immediately. The more the staff looked into the problem, the more apparent new leadership was indicated. Someone must be brought in to stem the tide. The best person for the job was found within the confines of The Humana Corporation, a corporation providing health care coverage for a huge majority of the private pay citizens of America and subsidized most of the major hospitals and other health care providers.

The new director agreed to a four year contract, but that was all. He knew he must accomplish a turnaround during that time frame, and if he did, he would probably be burned out due to the effort, if not he would probably be replaced. Juan met with the new director, and they arrived at a meeting of the minds. Juan had set reasonable expectations, and target dates for meeting their objectives. The director was to report to Juan on a monthly basis, outlining the progress being made to correct the problems. The biggest challenge was to stop the fraudulent abuse of the system. Subsistence checks were being sent to individuals who were dead. The families of the deceased cashing checks with no one the wiser. Information provided to the financial intake staff was falsified and ineligible people were put on the rolls. People throughout the state couldn't figure out how people on welfare could go to Kmart driving a new car. Information was not being shared across agency lines. Some individuals had applied for several programs or from different addresses, and were receiving duplicate or triplicate payments. The state was not being reimbursed for elderly folks who were on the Medicare rolls and considered dual eligible. The computer system was antiquated and not doing the job. In short, the situation was a mess, and something had to be done immediately. Because of the mismanagement, the State of California was about to lose its Federal match. Juan had the director contact the Health Care Financing Authority in Rockville, Maryland to obtain a delaying period before this could be allowed. Fortunately, the Federal government saw the situation, and was willing to give California some time to correct things.

The Department underwent a massive reorganization. Monies were allocated to upgrade the computer system, and all agency heads, which consisted of Juan's cabinet, were told point blank to share information. Eligibility lists were compared and duplications eliminated. Medicare eligible populations were identified, and the state started to bill the Federal government for a fair share of the funds available under that entitlement. It was also discovered that some of the people who were feeding at the state trough had private health care insurance. The state became the payer of last resort. Providers of services were identified who were filing fraudulent claims, and their offices were shut down. The leaks in the dike had been fixed, and the money was flowing to those spaces where it was needed, and the totals were declining. Surpluses were being generated which allowed Juan's administration to reallocate to fill un-funded requirements. The number of uninsured children who now were covered jumped. Juan was on the right track thanks to Jim and his astute selection.

Health and Human Services was not the only area needing revamping. The Department of Corrections had been a pork barrel for many years. The jails and prisons under private management contracts, were being reimbursed by the state at an alarming rate. These contractors saw this gold mine and were padding the expense account into the millions. The jails and prisons were being filled with inmates, put there for minor crimes due to the sentencing laws enacted by the state. The records of sex offenders were not complete as required by law. Many re-offended because their whereabouts were unknown, and they moved into unsuspecting neighborhoods without the resident's knowledge. Gang killings were up, and good officers were leaving the force because of poor pay and benefits.

California's economy was tanking. The initial rush of money into the silicone valley when the software giants were at their peak, was waning. Jobs were being outsourced to foreign countries, and labor unions were raising hell. The old administration did little to offer incentives for companies to move into California or expand their operations. Many cities had lost their bond ratings and were scrambling to pay their debts.

The educational system was another disaster. There weren't enough bilingual teachers around to handle the influx of Hispanic children born in the United States, who had reached elementary school age, and therefore were entitled to an education as American citizens. Classrooms were overcrowded, and the need to provide security guards in the high schools was on the rise. Students weren't safe anymore.

As if this weren't enough, Juan was faced with bickering within the state legislature. Since the balance of power had shifted from Republican to Democratic, egos became more important than the welfare of the area. Power struggles were everywhere, and nothing to benefit California was getting passed. Military bases, once a tremendous source of income to the state were being closed as the nation was reducing its forces after the close of the Vietnam Conflict. Juan hated that term. Vietnam was a war, it looked like a war, acted like a war, and therefore was a war, but the Federal Government never recognized it as such. Juan remembered coming home from Vietnam and having to ditch his uniform at the airport so people wouldn't harass him. He remembered the Veteran's of Foreign Wars (VFW) not allowing Vietnam Vets into their organization because it was not declared a war. Many vets had made California their home, and were suffering from wounds received or from post traumatic stress. The Veteran's Administration hospitals were not keeping up with the demand, and the untreated veterans were becoming homeless or seeking help from civilian hospitals. Drug use was increasing, as was HIV/AIDS.

Air pollution was creating a haze over Los Angeles and other metropolitan areas, obliterating the skylines of these beautiful cities. Interstate highways were crowded as more and more cars added to the problem. Morning commutes were becoming a nightmare, cars gridlocked on the major thoroughfares for hours. Juan was fortunate living in the Governor's mansion in Sacramento, but he felt the thrust of the claustrophobic traffic when he traveled within the state assessing what was going on. Something had to be done, and soon. The state could no longer afford the luxury of being what it had been in the past. The state reveled in its Hollywood image as the Sunshine State, but the infrastructure was decaying at an alarming rate.

Juan's first initiative was to bring together the leadership of the state legislature. Many of these individuals were close friends of his, and helped him get elected. He knew he could count on their support if he stroked their inner Baja the right way. A meeting was set for his conference room shortly after the legislature convened. As Juan glanced around the large oaken conference table, he recognized his peers, the power brokers, and egotists. The mix was a homogenous one. There was a smattering of ethnic, religious, gender, and cultural segments. Juan could say one thing, if you wanted diversity, come to California. Everyone was there a little early, but then again there were the usual late comers who wanted to be recognized as someone they weren't, and used the last minute entrance as their cue to immortality. Juan had planned for this. He had his staff set up a side bar with food and non-alcoholic drinks. When the late comers entered the conference, they were greeted with jocular humor spewed from mouths crammed with a delicious menu. They dropped their superior attitudes, clasped hands, slapped each other on the back, and joined in.

When everyone had exchanged pleasantries, they assumed an assigned seat and sat down. Juan had learned in group dynamics classes to put the people he wanted to control on his right and those he wanted to ignore on his left. Place cards were arranged to fit this axiom, and after a few seconds of searching for their names, the assembled group sidled up to the table ready to hear what Juan had to say.

Each participant was handed an agenda and a three inch thick document. They all knew Juan was not a person who wanted to waste time in meetings, so the agenda was rigorous, but manageable for the time allotted for the meeting. Juan hoped to accomplish the agenda within the day, so the group could get back to its primary mission, that of running the state's government. The document was Juan's blueprint of how California could solve its many problems. It was a masterpiece put together not only by his consultant group, but by some of the most brilliant minds Juan knew. As he leafed through the pages earlier, he was amazed at the depth of the analysis, and the simplicity of the solutions recommended. Although Juan didn't agree with all of the approaches, he fell in line with the majority of the recommendations.

As Juan normally did during meetings, he explained the ground rules so everyone was on the same page. Microphones were placed around the table. Juan told the group not to take notes, each would get a copy of the tape for future reference. This would allow the participants to focus on the discussion, and not be distracted with note taking. Most of the group knew each other, but there were some unfamiliar faces. Juan wanted everyone to introduce themselves, tell the group their position in life, and a brief biographical sketch of their lives. Each person was given five minutes. Sitting next to Juan was a small wooden box with three lights mounted on top. One was green, one amber, and one red. Juan had learned to use a box like this when he was a member of Toastmaster's International. The green light indicated the speaker designated was to begin. The amber light meant there was one minute to wrap up, and the red light meant to stop immediately. Juan not only wanted to use this technique for the intros, but when a member of the group was asked for an opinion, or a conclusion. It took some getting used to, but the effect was profound. Little time was wasted on superfluous dialogue.

The pace of the meeting was furious, but remained controlled and calm. Egos were put aside and everyone understood the gravity of the state of the state. Every fifty minutes, a break of five minutes was announced for smokers to adjourn outside for a quick puff or others to refresh their coffee cups or other drink containers. Juan was glad to see there were only a couple of smokers in the crowd. Smoking had been the demise of some of Juan's relatives and he knew well the effects it had on people illustrated by the current health statistics about the effects of cigarettes and second hand smoke. Juan knew the bad outcomes of this addictive behavior, which was reflected in the discussion documents with a recommendation the state sue the tobacco companies and then use the reward money, if the case was in the state's favor, for a Public Health initiative to portray the ill effects of the habit, and to provide funds to support smoking cessation programs.

Methodically, the agenda was exhausted. Tapes in the recorders were changed often, and consensus was reached on each item. It wasn't necessary to agree with every recommendation or approach, Juan just wanted everyone to understand they could go along with the recommendation even though they didn't necessarily agree with it. Juan truly displayed his mastery of consensus building, using every beguiling asset he had. He knew there were tradeoffs, gains and losses for everyone, but as long as each person felt they had gained something for their efforts, and had lost little, they went along.

The revised plan was a wonderful accomplishment. It was recognized it needed some fine tuning as the legislative year moved along, but for the most part, it was workable. Later in the week, copies of the tape were made, and each member of the discussion group received one. In addition, Juan followed up with a personal telephone call to everyone to cement the group's understanding and cooperation and to thank them for their diligence.

CHAPTER SIXTY

The biggest hurdle to overcome initially was the creation of the budget. This task was made much easier with the strategic plan. Money for past projects now viewed as frivolous, were shifted to priority targets. The lawsuit against the tobacco companies proceeded with a stunning victory for the State's Attorney General. Based upon the recommendation of the task force, the State of California had co-joined with twenty other states in presenting their arguments. The tobacco companies had sent legions of lawyers into the battle, and spent millions of dollars, but when the last legal barrier had been breached, the states had won. When the final settlement was announced, California would receive enough money to meet every recommendation the public health department had made.

Favors were called in from the unions. Juan's administration was willing to increase the minimum wage and give a stronger voice to the union in the operation of the state government, if the unions were willing to provide incentives to their members to increase the efficiency of their farming and manufacturing practices, and to root out the individuals who were freeloading on the system. Contract terms and conditions were strengthened, and minority companies were awarded a larger share of those contracts given by the state. Confidence was building with the consumer, and spending increased moving the economy forward.

Juan extended pardons to minor offenders who were taking up

valuable space and increasing the problems with overcrowding. Each person receiving a pardon was counseled, and the consequences of violating the pardon explained to them. If they tried to circumvent the provisions of the pardon, they would receive sentences far worse than they could imagine. They were given training opportunities and job skills to supplant the profits they were making from the drug trade. Marijuana was legalized and put under prescription for those on chemotherapy, or in rehabilitation programs. By making the availability of this controlled substance legal, the profit motive was destroyed.

A clean syringe and needle campaign was initiated. If drug users were using contaminated needles, that practice was no longer needed. Used needles and syringes could simply be traded at various outlets throughout the state for ones that were clean and sterile. The rate of HIV dropped dramatically. More money was pumped into new school construction and the hiring of teachers. Class size was reduced, and additional bilingual teachers and teacher's aides were added. Tax laws were revamped which allowed city and country municipalities to offer incentives for light industry to come into the state, thereby increasing the demand for labor, increasing the tax base, and reducing pollution. Contracts were negotiated with health care providers and pharmaceutical companies to reduce health care costs to the low income. Neighborhood watch and clean up efforts were funded in the pockets of the greatest poverty. Self esteem was returning the to neighborhoods. Citizens were taking a more active room in controlling the gangs roaming the streets undetered by the police. Curfews were put in place and parents became more responsible. Gang related crimes and drive by shootings made a dramatic dip.

Juan began a major television innovation by placing television ads on national media inviting tourists to come to California. He solicited movie stars, Rap artists, and famous personalities to help him appear in these ads. People who were once afraid to come to the crime ridden core of the country's most populace state began, once again, to flock to the wonderful treasures of California, Disneyland, Hollywood, Yosemite, San Diego, Monterey, and San Francisco. Major corporations loosened their purse strings, and began to sponsor major golf tournaments through the state. A new arena was built for the Los Angeles Lakers, the Los Angeles Dodgers, the San Diego Chargers, and the Sacramento Kings. Owners were putting more of their assets into their teams, garnering a better caliber of professional athlete and drawing bigger and bigger crowds to games.

More and more illegal aliens from south of the border were being taught English and were becoming American citizens. The money they made through their labors remained in the state and was not shipped back to Mexico. Border crossings saw a marked reduction, and the services expenditures to those who were not citizens was dropping.

Juan ordered a review of all of the state laws. It was his contention the laws were written in such a manner, the ordinary citizen couldn't understand them. He also ordered that rules implementing the laws be reviewed to eliminate duplication. He directed that statues be passed to open governmental meetings to the public. This would allow pressure to be exerted on law makers from their constituents when the full disclosure of the meetings was made available to the common man on the street, and who in turn could apply the same pressure to those elected within the district. The day of the backroom politics was over, and the stay at home mothers, the small businessman, the advocates, and the seniors now felt they had more of a say in those matters affecting their lives, and the lives of many others. California was shining.

But all was not well in Peyton Place. Some powerful people were having their feathers ruffled, and their illegal treasuries disemboweled. Death threats once again began to appear in the mail received in the Governor's office and in the offices and homes of the leadership of the state. Heightened security became more in evidence. Resources from the Federal government, namely the FBI were solicited. Massive crackdowns were launched against the cartels and the underground.

Open war had been declared. Juan and his administration met the challenge head on. Raids were made at homes of suspected criminals. Bank accounts were investigated when they concerned known gangland officials. Even though the criminal element felt they had placed the muzzle of their pistol against the head of those in power, the wrist had been twisted, and now the gun was pointed squarely at the head of the aggressors.

Indictments were leveled at hundreds of the offenders, and the word soon got around that making threats against California was a losing proposition. The threats began to abate.

Juan's national star was rising. In just a few short years, he had gone from little known Mexican upstart, to a prominent figure in charismatic circles. National leaders were now starting to take notice of his prowess, and inviting him to come to Washington D.C. to consult with them about matters of the nation. In his third year as governor, Juan was elected as President of the National Association of Governors, a role he relished. This gave him a chance for broad recognition and power. He made the most of every exposure on the wider scene, not missing any opportunity to appear with the trendsetters, and the power brokers. Again and again, he used his charisma and organizational abilities to woo those about him. He was the nation's darling. A successful story of an underprivileged, minority person rising to the highest level of competence. Little did they know Juan's ultimate goal was not to terminate with being Governor of the State of California, but with attaining the most powerful position in the most powerful nation in the world. Juan never confided, even with his closest friends, his desire to become President and Commander In Chief of the United States of America.

CHAPTER SIXTY-ONE

Juan's first term as Governor of the State of California went smoothly. The timelines and end points for the accomplishment of the task force's recommendations were being met, and new initiatives formulated to ensure the successes in the past would continue into the future. When election time returned, Juan won a second term. Hordes of well wishers spilled out onto the pavement of the cities to attest to his popularity. He ran virtually unopposed. This time, he didn't have to wait in his hotel suite for his victory celebration. Only minutes after the polls were closed, the national media declared him the victor, and he put on his tuxedo jacket and joined the tumultuous crowd in the largest ballroom in Los Angeles.

Juan's popularity continued to escalate. He was given the privilege of throwing the first pitch at opening day for the Los Angeles Dodgers. He was hired for a cameo part in a major blockbuster movie. He visited elementary schools and children's hospitals. He raised money for a great many charities, and was the honorary chairman for the United Way Campaign for that year. He seemed to be gliding through life on an Aladdin's magic carpet. He could do no wrong. Oh, there were minor set backs, but nothing that would offset the accomplishments mounting up. He was considered for a federal presidential cabinet post, which he turned down desiring to remain as governor rather than occupy what he considered a staff position.

His children were moving along in maturity. They were a handsome pair, having captured the best traits of their parents. Jose was growing like a weed. He was going to be tall like his father. They were in public schools now, Juan didn't want them enrolled in a private setting for fear his electoral base would view that as uppity and out of character. His children did well in school, but never really got used to the celebrity status of their father. Sometimes Jose wished his dad could just be a businessman, or a blue-collar worker like so many of the parents of the other children. One night at supper, Juan asked Jose how school was going.

"I don't think I want to go back there tomorrow" Jose replied.

"Why in the world not?"

"Well, every day when I play on the playground during recess, there is this man standing by the chain link fence watching me. When I leave to go back inside, he turns and walks away. Dad, he is creepy, and I am afraid of him."

"Don't you worry son, I will contact the State Patrol and have them put an undercover policeman in the yard. He will pose as a teacher, but will have his eye on the intruder. I can guarantee you that you will be safe."

Thusly assured, Jose finished his meal, took his bath, and was tucked into bed by his father. It had been an exhausting day, and Jose fell asleep immediately. Juan closed the door, descended the stairs and went into his study, shutting the door behind him. He had to make a very important phone call.

The phone was answered on the second ring. It was the home of the Chief of the State Patrol. Very few people had access to his private number, but the governor was one so endowed. Juan quickly described the situation. The phone remained silent for a few minutes, and then the Chief said he would get right on it. The Chief was a good man, handpicked for the job by Juan, and promoted ahead of some of his peers. The selection had been a good one. In spite of the displeasure of some of the senior members of the patrol, the new Chief brought with him a capability for organization and efficiency that was sorely needed. The former Chief had been discovered to be doing favors for some shady characters and receiving monetary reimbursement for his involvement. The former Chief looked the other way when he was told to. He was in the pockets of the mob and was more than willing to do their bidding for the compensation he was receiving. He probably would never have been caught, but he insisted on a lavish lifestyle unbecoming a man with his limited salary. Juan had long suspected this was happening, and had secretly asked the local FBI agent to see if there was some validity to this appearance of impropriety. The allegations were true. When Juan read the FBI report, he called the Chief into his office, handed his a letter of resignation, and told him to sign it. The Chief hedged, claiming innocence. Juan had been forcing the Chief to stand in front of his desk, an affront which made the Chief unhappy, but which had to be tolerated. With the denial, Juan arose from his red leather chair, walked around the desk, and thrust a large envelope into the chest of the Chief with some force. The Chief was rocked backwards, but regained his composure.

"Open the envelope Chief. I think it contains enough information to make you change your mind."

Slowly the Chief ran his fingernail along the sealed edge and removed the contents. With shivering hands, the Chief read each piece of paper, looked intently at each photograph, and hung his head in shame. The evidence was overwhelming. Juan didn't want a scandal, so it was agreed that the Chief would sign the resignation letter and they would jointly announce his retirement with full pay. The reason would be described as relating to poor health brought on by the rigors of the job. The retirement was to take effect immediately.

Following the dismissal of the Chief, Juan received a confidential letter, unsigned, written on ordinary paper, and typed on a generic typewriter. The letter was delivered to his office via messenger. Shirl opened the letter, glanced at the words and rushed into Juan's office. Handing him the letter as if it were a red hot iron, she said, "I think you had better read this."

A thin line of sweat beaded Juan's brow. The letter threatened Juan's family for the action Juan had taken against the Chief. Juan knew without doubt there was a connection between the letter and the strange man who was stalking the playground. Juan asked Shirl to contact the messenger service, and to have them ask the delivery person who had given him the letter. The person explained the letter had been in outgoing container with several others, and he had no clue as to where it came from. Likewise, none of the other message service employees had any information which would shed any light on the source of the correspondence.

Juan turned the letter over to the state crime lab, but no forensic information was found that would identify the originator. Juan was shaken, but grateful he had been assigned an officer to watch his children. The more Juan thought about the letter, the angrier he became. He again contacted the new Chief of the State Patrol and ordered that the strange man be picked up for questioning. An undercover van was stationed around the block from the playground, and when the suspected individual appeared at the time of the recess, he was apprehended, pushed into the van, and taken downtown for questioning.

He was placed in a holding cell with several others awaiting interrogation, and before he could be moved into an interview room, one of the other suspects plunged a small knife into his chest, killing him instantly. The knife was never discovered, nor would any of the cellmates confess to any wrong doing.

The crisis had been averted, but each day the children were escorted to school and returned home promptly. The trauma of this ordeal was telling on Jose. He would wake up in the middle of the night screaming, and calling for his father. Juan would comfort him until his eyes were closed and he had returned to a better state of dreams. Eventually, Jose was seen and treated by a child psychologist, and the nightmares stopped. This was all done under the tightest of security. Juan didn't want any of this leaked to the press.

It was at this juncture when Juan felt another family vacation was in order. A trade mission was arranged with the Mexican Secretary of Commerce and Industry and the meeting was to take place in Cancun, Mexico. Cancun, one of the most beautiful spots in the world fit the bill nicely. Juan could conduct business during a portion of the day, and could spend time with Mary and the children doing what they liked the best, swimming in the ocean. There weren't any fears of intrusion. The resort where they were staying was sealed off tighter than a spacecraft "O" ring. The hotel was completely booked with the delegations from the two countries, and security personnel were stationed twenty four hours a day both inside and outside the hotel.

The weather couldn't have been more perfect. The temperature during the day was in the low to mid seventies, and at night a balmy high sixties. A gentle breeze wafted through their beachfront apartment, so no air conditioning was necessary. At last Juan was relaxed and his soul rejuvenated. He needed this break. His nerves lately had been worn to a frazzle, and he was critically close to a nervous breakdown. Even though Juan presented a persona of calmness under all situations, internally, he felt as though he were coming apart at the seams.

The apartment was huge by any standards. The children each had their own rooms with baths, and the master bedroom which Juan and Mary shared was accentuated with a king size water bed, a stand alone shower, and a Jacuzzi tub. The floors were of the finest terra cotta, and were always cool to the touch of bare feet. The roof was made of thatched palm branches, and the walls plastered with adobe stucco. There were windows everywhere to let in plenty of light. The master bedroom and the great room just off the kitchenette faced the ocean on the Gulf side. Juan had never seen water so crystal clear and blue. The beaches were festooned with white sand and the land gently sloped into the water at such a gradual pace, a swimmer could walk for many yards before the water came up to his chest. The waves were small, and could hardly be heard as they moved across the beach. In the afternoons, after the meetings, Juan would sit with Mary on the deck chairs watching Jose and Maria Elena romp in the surf.

Juan wished he could have spent more time with his family, but he also knew the trade talks were vitally important. In the past, too much friction had been generated between the Mexican government and the United States President and Congress. America wanted to put tariffs in place to reduce the balance of payments between the two countries and protect the American worker. Congress wanted free trade, but with the advantage going to the US side. Reduction in foreign aid to Mexico was threatened if American demands could not be met. The immigration department was also rattling its sabers with promises to build a wall separating the two neighbors. Juan and his advisors had studied the problem well, and Juan was able to forestall US actions that would not have been beneficial in any form. Juan struck trade agreements between Mexico and California that seemed to be fair to everyone involved. The dialogs were congenial, each side feeling each other out until common ground could be found. The documents were drafted and redrafted until agreement had been reached. After ten days of back and forth bargaining, the pacts were signed by the two trading entities and the mission came to a close. That evening, the Mexican delegation hosted a party to end all parties.

The resort grounds were alit with colorful lanterns. The children were treated to piñatas suspended from poles, each containing candy and other goodies dropping to the ground when the piñata was bashed open. Margaritas were everywhere. Juan had never tasted such wonderful Tequila. The drinks went down just a little too smoothly. Experience had taught Juan to take these mixtures seriously, and to drink them slowly and to limit the number consumed. The men were all dressed in fashionably decorated silk shirts worn outside white denim pants.

Sandals were the footwear of the day without socks. The women all wore flowing dresses, their hair done up in bright ribbons. Mariachi bands flowed around the party playing some of Juan's favorite Mexican melodies. For a while, Juan was transported back to his youth when the village bands would get together on a Saturday night to bring a little music and joy into the otherwise drab lives of his village.

The next day marked the departure of most of the participants. Juan had decided to stay an extra day. The afternoon was getting hot, and as was the custom in these types of climates, it was siesta time, a time for sleeping, and a chance for the body to repair itself for another charge at the nightlife. Juan didn't really feel sleepy, so he sent Mary and the children off to the apartment, and he casually walked down the shell strewn pathway to the poolside bar. He liked this bar. It was set in the middle of a spacious life size swimming pool, with a short breezeway from the mosaic tiled outer rim to chairs which were arranged in a circle around the bar itself. Juan thought this was a unique concept where a person could sit in the coolness of the water without getting wet, and admire all of the young women who were cavorting in string thong bikinis.

The bar was decorated much the same as the apartments, in thatch with exposed beams. The chairs were made of bamboo and were cushioned with a soft suede covering. Juan ordered a Mai Tai. He really preferred harder liquor, but decided to forgo that pleasure this early in the day. Besides, he liked the little decorations that came in the glass. He sipped slowly on the drink, and closed his eyes to reflect on the wondrous things that had happened to him and his family over the past several years. He had been lucky, surrounded by an adoring family, good friends, close political allies, and a public who treated him like some movie star. As these pleasurable thoughts drifted throughout his mental cortex, a hand gently placed itself on Juan's shoulder. Usually, Juan would have jumped at such a maneuver, but there was something about the grasp which radiated a charisma like a healer sending soothing rays of power onto his body. He opened his eyes, turned slightly and was shocked, but pleased to see his lawyer friend Carl Evans, whom they had met on the cruise.

"Carl, what a surprise" Juan said. "Where is your wife Nedra?'

"Oh, she is taking her nap, and I didn't feel like joining her, so I thought I would come down and see who was at the bar, and have a drink with them. How are your wife and the kids?"

"They are wonderful, and enjoying their siesta as well."

"Good, but to be honest with you Juan, I knew you were here, and I wanted to catch you alone. I have something that might interest you. I had my feelers out, and was informed you were taking a short respite from the Governor's job and coming here, so I booked a flight and I followed you."

"Really, what could so important that you would take your valuable time to come here just to look me up?"

"Well, I wanted to start a discourse with you about your future. You can never start too early to reach out for the goals you have established in your life. Soon you will be finishing up your second term as Governor, and what will you do then. Return to a legal practice? I think not. Becoming a consultant, doesn't fit your personality or ego either, so what is left. I suspect the answer is to move on to bigger and better things. I know you aren't fully aware of the role I have been playing in your development, but let me assure you it has been a significant one. I like you Juan, and the country needs people with your ability to lead it in its destiny. You have done just about everything there is to do in the State of California, so the next logical step is to run for an elected office in the Congress of the United States. I would suggest the House of Representatives as a starting point, and who knows where that will lead."

Juan was stunned. He had known all along strings were being pulled by someone, but could never put a finger on the source. He knew his political movements were orchestrated like a father guiding a young son on a new bicycle, which had the training wheels removed. He knew intuitively someone was bringing all of the loose threads together on his behalf, it was just going too smoothly. Juan was afraid to ask Carl any particulars, knowing Carl could easily divert the questions, so he remained silent.

Carl let the offer sink in as he ordered a drink from the bartender.

"Carl, I really hadn't thought much about my future. I have been so embroiled with the task of running the state I have not really given the aspects of the future down the road much of my attention. I know hints have been dropped my way about this subject, but I just haven't picked up on them. How naïve of me. How could I have been so stupid, not to see what was before my very eyes. What you are telling me makes perfect sense, a progressive outline to the next level."

"I thought you would see it my way. Now, let's have fun tonight, and when you get back to Sacramento, I want you to join me and some of my friends for some meetings to cement the concept."

Juan held up his glass and an alliance was formed when the two glasses clinked together with a sound of church bells announcing the anointment of new leader. The vacation was over, but before Juan and his family returned home, they had dinner with Carl and Nedra. Mary was thrilled to see old friends again. The dinner was magical, and Mary noticed a glow about Juan that had not been there before. She had learned over the years not to ask questions about these occurrences, knowing at some juncture, Juan would tell her all about it.

The children were thrilled too. They were allowed to have foods that normally would have been restrictive, including ice cream with chocolate syrup and ground nuts on top. Jose asked for a cherry, and the request was granted. Of course, Maria Elena had to have a cherry too, everyone had to be treated equally. The next morning, the old friends shared a van to the airport since both of their flights were departing at approximately the same time. Deep down inside, Juan knew his fate had taken another twist.

CHAPTER SIXTY-TWO

Now it was back to the business of running the state. As Carl had promised, secret meetings were held from time to time as Juan traveled about the state. The usual places were private clubs where large mergers and developments were schemed by people with wealth and status. They usually went by the names of athletic clubs, and the premise for Juan was that he needed to workout, leaving no one on his staff the wiser. Juan was amazed with all of the new faces. He remembered many of them from the Fortune 500 magazine, and now was meeting them up close and personal. Everything about them exuded money and power, from their clothes to their carefully styled hair to their expensive smelling cologne.

As these meeting progressed, Juan could not shake the feeling he was becoming mired in a situation where the payback would someday be extracted for the effort these individuals were putting into his future. They didn't say as much, but the vibes were clearly there. These business tycoons didn't waste any time giving Juan all of the tools he would need to make a successful run as a new US Congressman. The current member of Congress from Juan's district was retiring. The Republicans weren't even bothering to put up much of a resistance. The district had been Democratic since the founding of the state, and probably before that if you believed some of the tales being told.

As Devine guidance had dictated, Juan completed a second term as Governor leaving the state with a budget surplus, marked improvements in the educational outcomes of the children, a reduction in the rate of unemployment, a likewise reduction in major crimes, and an economy that was booming. Juan's approval ratings were off the charts, and when he announced he was seeking the seat being vacated in the House of Representatives, the deal was closed without further fanfare. Juan ran a skeleton campaign, merely going through the motions to satisfy his constituents. His television ads were slickly produced, and none of the mud slinging was in evidence. He was the Golden State's Golden Boy.

Mary wasn't thrilled about leaving her home for a part of the country she cared little about. She had never enjoyed her tour at Walter Reed. She had always felt that US Congressmen and Senators were sleaze balls, out to feather their nests at the expense of the taxpayer. She didn't like local politics, much less those on a national scale. She hardly ever turned on the tube to watch the Sunday broadcast of "Face The Nation", or "Hardball". It disgusted her to watch these supposedly honest men lie through their teeth while smiling and facing the camera. Mary was not a political animal, and she never would be. But, she knew she had made a commitment to Juan to support him in his profession. Deep inside there was a kernel of hope that Juan would not succumb to the temptations most certainly to be placed before him. She knew politics was like a mistress, highly seductive. She kept reflecting on the old adage, "Power corrupts, but absolute power corrupts absolutely." She knew Juan was a good and idealistic man, but like everyone else, vulnerable. She reaffirmed her support with Juan, telling him in wifely terms she would go with him, but he must be true to his convictions and not be swayed with the aroma of pork for California.

Juan tried to calm her fears as best he could, promising to adhere to her counsel and to the ethical principles he had set and followed for himself throughout his life. The race was run, and Juan was declared victor, and was now one of the new Congressional freshman to take their place in the hallowed halls in Washington, D.C.

Changing jobs and moving was always a hassle, but things seemed to take place without much struggle. People materialized out of nowhere to pack up their belongings, put their home under caretaker status, find them a home near the Capitol, enroll their children in the finest schools, and get them settled in. Juan knew he was seeing the first vestiges of the IOU's he would be returning with payment down the road. The family flew back east, and were met at JFK airport by a long, black limousine complete with a tuxedoed driver, who took care of their luggage and seated them inside the luxurious sedan. Like celebrities, they were whisked away from the terminal, and were soon on the beltway which traversed the airport and the District of Columbia.

Their new home was a three story apartment in the Georgetown area, replete with upscale shops, restaurants, and other amenities most desired by those living in this location. Juan couldn't help but wonder how come he was able to get something like this when his peers couldn't, but he put the questions aside. He was comfortable, and he knew the family would be comfortable. Another IOU.

The house was furnished in an old Victorian style, befitting the area where the house was located. The furniture was a heavy, dark maple, with drapes of burgundy and gold. The kitchen was very modern, with a cooking island in the center complete with hanging pots and pans from the ceiling. All of the floors were a teak hardwood, covered with expensive oriental rugs in matching colors. The bedrooms reflected the ambience of a fine hotel. Mary joked that she hoped the children wouldn't fall out of bed with so much room to roam in. The kids loved the beds, jumping up and down on them to their hearts content. Mary finally had to put a stop to the frivolity, reminding the children that beds were to sleep in not to jump up and down on.

The house also had a wonderful den and library where Juan could conduct business when he was home. There were bathrooms at all three levels which would give the children a chance to have a shower of their own, and one for Juan and Mary to share. The thought struck a chord with Mary, it had been some time since she and Juan had shared a shower together. She was looking forward to the idea.

There were a few days before the freshman orientation at the Capitol, so Juan, Mary and the kids explored their environment. They were thrilled at the sights, the smells, and the bustle of that part of town. It reeked of affluence. They dropped by the school to enroll Jose and Maria Elena into their classes. The teachers and counselors were top notch, as good as anything Juan had seen in the education system in California. Juan and Mary were very pleased with the caliber of the teachers and the capability of the principal and his administrative staff. Mary could only speculate how well the children would do in this environment. All the telling signs were there. Likewise, Juan came away with the sense that the family had truly fallen into a proverbial bucket of shit, and came out smelling like a rose. Another IOU.

Settling in was easy. Most of the work had already been done for them. A welcoming party and house warming was next on the agenda. Neighbors came by with casseroles of food and drink to welcome the new people into the neighborhood. Friends were quickly made. So many names were passing by Juan's conscious effort, he knew he would have to reintroduce himself to the people who had shown up at the party. He had no intention of alienating any of them. He would make every effort to relearn their names and to become close friends with those who surrounded him and his family. The infusion of Juan's family into this living and breathing structure made Juan giddy. Of course the drinks more than amply enhanced the effect. Life was good, and Juan was enjoying every minute of it. Promises were made to have a series of parties over the coming months, and to set up a database for birthdays, so people could be pampered as they grew older, including the children.

Juan felt like Dorothy when she went to the Land of Oz. He looked down at his imaginary dog, and said. "Toto, I don't think we are in Kansas anymore."

With most of the logistical tasks being taken care of by people Juan hardly knew, he could now focus on his new job as freshman representative from the great state of California. Before the congress convened, it was tradition for all freshman representatives to gather on the granite steps of the capitol to have their picture taken. For the first time in over twelve years, the Democratic Party was in control of the congress. The mood was upbeat, and was reflected in the smiles of the new members of Congress, as they posed side by side in front of this magnificent structure of the US Capitol. Men and women alike were dressed in dark suits based on gender. Their faces polished, teeth brightened, and their heads held high. The picture taking was an old tradition tracing its heritage back many centuries to the inception of photography. It was a handsome group. A mixture of young and old, male and female, black, white and Hispanic, with a little ethnic and religious fervor thrown in.

The picture was breathtaking with the Capitol building in the background. The edifice which stood for the greatest power on the face of the earth, was now Juan's home for the next two years, and maybe beyond, who could tell. The group split up, many of them introducing themselves to others, some saying hello of old friends, and some just standing in awe of the baptism by fire that awaited them.

Juan's office was in the old congressional building, the newer offices given to the more tenured representatives. Although the office was old, it was roomy with high vaulted ceilings and ornate work in masonry around the door jambs. The office held three rooms, one for Juan, one a work area with copiers and storage, and one for the small staff who would serve Juan during his time there. He did have a window with a view of the back parking lot, covered with dusty maroon colored drapes badly in need of cleaning. Most of the office furniture was governmental issue, an old wooden desk for Juan and gray metal desks for the others. Juan, as Governor, had much better trappings, but he knew it wasn't the furniture that made the position, it was the position itself that really mattered. He and his staff would manage very nicely.

The first week of the session was primarily devoted to organizing the Congress to conduct the business of the nation. The most important struggle was to form working committees and subcommittees that would determine the priorities relating to the legislative process. This was a drill Juan was extremely familiar and completely comfortable with. It was the prerogative of the Speaker of the House, the Majority Leader, the Majority Whip, the Minority Leader, the Minority Whip, and leaders of the Democratic and Republican caucuses, the senior chairman, and consultants whose names would go without mentioning to see the accomplishment of this organization.

Juan wanted to be on the House Appropriations Committee. He lobbied the Speaker of the House without avail. He enlisted the help of the two California Senators, Kyle Smith, and Barbara Baxter. These two powerful senators with the assistance of the House Majority Leader paid a visit to the Speaker's office. Freshmen were rarely appointed to such an important committee, and Juan faced formidable competition, including a former Vice Presidential candidate. In the end, it was a combination of political maneuvering and a chance meeting with an old friend and former student of Professor Tillman's which procured Juan a seat on the committee. Another IOU.

Juan's career wasn't all a bed of roses. Some of his fellow congressmen and women felt threatened by him and his ability to work his magic. They knew there had to be something behind this straw man, no one can be this perfect. One day as Juan was passing down the hall from his office to the house chambers, a friend of his pulled him aside and whispered in his ear.

"Watch your back, someone is out to get you. I hope you don't have any skeletons in your closet. I am sure you don't, but just be careful." Before Juan could ask the friend what he had meant, he was gone. Juan stood there for a few minutes stunned, then realized he did indeed have enemies he didn't know about. Perhaps he had been too trusting to appreciate the fact that in the circles he was now in, jealousies do exist. Over the next few months, Juan viewed all of his colleagues with suspicion. As he glanced into their faces, he tried to read what was behind the fake smiles, and eager eyes. The foundation Juan had built reaching this plateau was starting to crumble. One evening he confided in Mary the turmoil he was experiencing. She assured him there was nothing in his past that could hurt him, and just disregard the feeling and go about his business. Juan took her advice, putting his doubts on the back burner and continued to do his job. He felt much better when several people told him they were glad to see him back to his old self.

Because of this incident, Juan took his surroundings a little more acutely. He watched what he said carefully, and spent extra time editing what he was writing. He went out of his way to be cooperative, but still exercised his independence in a smooth and convincing manner. Juan was gaining the respect of more and more of his peers, but did notice two congressmen who tended to shy away from him. He also noticed some strange cars were parked on his street. Cars which pulled away when he arrived home. One afternoon, he received a call from Kyle Smith inviting him to the Senate dining room for lunch. At this lunch, Kyle let Juan know that someone had asked the FBI to dig deeper into Juan's past. In previous background checks, Juan had come up clean as a whistle, but these newly requested probes seemed to be much more in depth. Kyle advised Juan just to sit tight and all of this would go away. Kyle just wanted to let Juan know that these kinds of things were part of belonging to the institution, and should be expected. There were always people who wanted to get the upper hand, probably due to a lack of self confidence on their part or a super ego they could not control.

Strangely, the two congressmen Juan had doubts about suddenly resigned from their offices. One cited reasons of health, and the other family matters which needed his attention. The FBI probes stopped.

The inquisitions had abated. Somewhere on Capitol Hill the guardian angel again stood over Juan and protected him. Another IOU.

Juan received one more top committee assignment, as deputy chairperson for banking. This went along with many sub-committee assignments in the fields of interior, agriculture, justice, intelligence, armed services, and energy. Juan was getting an education far beyond his wildest expectations. Everyday brought new challenges and experiences. He was held privy to policies that could lift or sink this country. He was invited to state dinners and given choice seats next to foreign dignitaries and heads of countries. Juan's diamond was being polished to a luster and would be the envy of any jeweler.

The months rolled along quickly. Besides his congressional duties, Juan was involved in trade commissions, a role he had relished in California, and of course returning to his district to report to his constituents. Before Juan could grasp the time, his term was over, and he was running for re-election. He won again with very little effort. It was easier the second term. Once an incumbent, the less a congressman had to worry about being re-elected unless he or she pulled a boner to end all boners. It was hard on a first term congressman to lose. It meant he had to give up his office, a part of his character, and a part of his prestige. Trying to get re-elected would become a mountain some just couldn't seem to climb. Many of these types became lobbyists, or went to work for think tank groups in the Washington D.C. area, or opened consultant offices. Juan ran across some of these individuals from time to time. He was always a gracious person to them, sometimes letting them make appointments to try and persuade him to vote for a certain bill that would benefit entities they worked for.

Juan had his share of exposure in the print, radio, and television medias. He was even invited to star in a cameo role on Saturday Night Live, a new, and very popular new show. Juan was highly photogenic, and his picture appeared on the covers of several publications, as well as within the bowels of the text. His name was becoming more and more familiar across the land. Even political cartoons were kind to him. Then he was dealt a crushing blow. For some weeks, he had been experiencing a sharp pain in his lower abdomen. Quietly, without letting Mary know, he made an appoint to see an internist at Walter Reed Army Medical Center, the primary health care facility in the D.C. region with a mission to provide diagnostic and treatment services to the members of the Federal government. Walter Reed, known more familiarly as "Walter Wonderful", was one of seven regional medical centers scattered across the United States and Hawaii. It was one of two major military medical centers along with the Bethesda Naval Hospital in Maryland. Walter Reed was a teaching hospital, containing a medical school, intern and residency programs, and helped to furnish the uniformed services with physicians and other health care professionals, and was Mary's old home.

One afternoon, under the guise he was due for his annual physical, he arrived at the clinic, reported to the receptionist, and took a seat in the waiting room. It didn't take long for his name to be called by one of the technicians. Juan was weighed and escorted to an examining room where another technician or nurse, Juan couldn't determine which, took a medical history from him, asking about any childhood diseases, injuries, medications he was taking, or other health concerns he had. The nurse also took his pulse, his temperature, and his blood pressure, recording all of the findings in his chart. When the preliminaries were completed, the nurse excused herself and Juan was left alone to look around the room. Charts about smoking, proper eating, and preventive health care were encased in glass frames on the walls. In one corner was a stainless steel cabinet holding disposable latex rubber gloves, various injection products, bandages, and other supplies. A small desk and chair were placed against one wall, obviously for the physician, a smaller chair next to the desk, obviously for the patient. An examining table was in the center of the room, made of metal with a black vinyl skin on top, which was covered by a sheet of disposable paper. Juan wasn't sure where he was to sit, at the desk or on the examining table, so he chose to stand. A soft knock came to the door, and in walked a tall, thin, slightly bald intern about Juan's age. The physician introduced himself as Dr. Bill Nickelson, M.D. They shook hands and Dr. Bill asked Juan to be seated on the examining table. He asked Juan to disrobe down to his tee shirt and boxer shorts. Dr. Bill kind of got a kick from the sight of Juan's shorts. There was a picture of a wolf on one side, apparently chasing a good looking woman on the other side, with a twelve inch ruler down the front. He didn't comment.

Carefully, Dr. Bill placed his stethoscope on Juan's back and asked Juan to take a deep breath. He then repeated the procedure on Juan's chest. He had Juan lie on his back. Dr. Bill probed Juan's stomach and sides. He paused for just a few seconds when he pressed just to the left of Juan's navel. Juan draw a sharp sigh as a thunderbolt of pain shot through his body.

"Congressman, I think we need to get an MRI to see what we have found." With that, Dr. Bill picked up the phone and called the radiology department. He had Juan dress and wait for a corpsman to come with a wheel chair to take Juan to the X-ray unit. Juan asked Dr. Bill what he found, but was told that nothing could be confirmed until the diagnostic tests had been done. Fortunately, the MRI machine was available, so the procedure didn't take long. The corpsman returned Juan and the images from the MRI back to the examining room for Dr. Bill to look at. Dr. Bill withdrew a pen from his white jacket pocket and traced the images one at a time, stopping a various places to ponder what he was witnessing. After a few minutes, Dr. Bill again picked up the phone, spoke into it briefly, and hung up the receiver.

"Congressman, I think we have discovered a tumor on your large intestine. I can't be sure, so I am having the Oncology Chief come down and take a look. He knows better than I what is there."

Dr. Bill and Juan chatted for a while until the oncologist appeared. The doctor in charge of the cancer service was a bird colonel, a tall man with prematurely graying hair, and a Marine Corps cut about him. He wore a butch trim haircut, and his white coat covered a sharply pressed shirt and trousers. The white coat also accentuated his highly polished shoes. The two physicians approached the films, passed comments between themselves in a lingo Juan didn't understand. When they were finished conversing, they told Juan he indeed had a small tumor. They weren't sure if it was malignant, or non-cancerous, only a biopsy could reveal that fact. Juan was taken to the minor surgery suite where he was tranquilized, and a long needle was inserted through his stomach wall. Based on the x-rays, the oncologist knew exactly where to put the needle and how far it had to go to come into contact with the hard lump. The physician withdrew the plunger on the syringe holding the needle, and extracted some fluid with bits of tissue floating in the mixture.

The fluid was then placed in a sterile tube, capped, and labeled with Juan's name and identification number. The sample was then sent to the pathology lab for analysis. The oncologist, a Dr. Glenn Peck, Colonel, Army Medical Corps released Juan to go home telling Juan he would be contacted the next day with the results. Juan left the hospital shaken, but controlled himself in such a way it didn't appear he was in any kind of difficulty. He spent the rest of the day in his office, and then went home.

Mary sensed something was wrong. Juan took her to the kitchen, poured each of them a stiff drink, and told Mary about the examination he had just undergone. Mary sat there in silence. Being a nurse, she was familiar with cancer, and assured Juan the possibility that it was cancerous was less than that it was just some foreign tissue which shouldn't be there. Mary's assurances and a few more drinks didn't help Juan sleep any better.

CHAPTER SIXTY-THREE

Juan went to his office the next morning, but had a hard time concentrating. Thank goodness his schedule was light for the day. Most of the morning was spent going over brief notes on upcoming legislative bills with recommendations on how to vote or to amend. Juan found himself reading and re-reading the briefs almost to a point of distraction. He decided to change his focus. Ever since he had come in contact with Dr. Peck, he was curious about the man. Juan called the military liaison office and asked if he could get some information about the doctor. A young Air Force Captain said he would fax over a biographical sketch within the half hour. Shirl brought in the fax as soon as it arrived.

It seemed Dr. Peck was a graduate of the United States Military Academy at West Point, and after completing his undergraduate studies, had gone through the Army system and obtained his medical degree within that system. He had completed his internship at William Beaumont Army Medical Center in El Paso, Texas, and his residency in Oncology at the Fred Hutchinson Cancer Research Center affiliated with the University of Washington Medical School in Seattle. He had held various assignments in the United States, and was now Chief of Oncology at Walter Reed. He had been promoted on the fast track reserved for outstanding young people who demonstrated the potential for leadership. His father was a Marine Corps officer and a veteran of Korea and the early part of the Vietnam conflict, so his bearing was explainable.

Among his stated objectives, Dr. Peck hoped someday to become the Army Surgeon General, a three star rank, and head of the Army Medical Department overseeing the activities of the Army Nurse Corps, the Army Dental Corps, the Army Medical Corps, the Army Medical Specialist Corps, the Army Veterinary Corps, and the Army Medical Services Corps. In addition, the Army Surgeon General also was responsible for the planning, coordinating, and conducting medical operations, both in peacetime and war, with the other Surgeon Generals of the Navy, Air Force, and Public Health Services. Dr. Peck had been involved in the development of new drugs to fight the scourge of cancer and was a well published author in medical journals. Juan was comforted knowing he was in good hands.

Later that afternoon, Juan played host to a group of young Californian high school students who were in Washington D.C. attending a National Youth Forum sponsored by the State Department. Juan, along with other congressional members from California met with the exuberant youngsters, having his picture taken, and answering the myriad of questions so often asked by this age group. His beeper vibrated against his hip let him know he had a very important phone message awaiting him back at the office. Juan excused himself, anxious to find out what the message was all about.

The phone call was from Dr. Peck asking if it were possible for Juan to drop by the oncology department at Walter Reed. They had the results back from the pathology department, and Dr. Peck wanted to discuss them with Juan in privacy. A sudden rush of adrenaline hit Juan and he almost fainted. He had never experienced such anxiety before, and if it had not been mid afternoon, he would have poured himself three fingers of his favorite Scotch.

He arrived at the reception desk at the Oncology Department, and was immediately escorted past a roomful of patients to Dr. Peck's private office. As Juan entered the office, he was struck by the fact that the room was so uncluttered. He had expected to see piles of medical magazines, and patient's charts scattered about, but there was none of that. Dr. Peck's walls were blanketed with certificates and pictures of Dr. Peck with various governmental celebrities including presidents, vice-presidents, congressmen, department secretaries, and foreign diplomats all arranged in tasteful rows.

Dr. Peck was intently examining some x-rays on a wall mounted screen, not hearing Juan come in. He finished, turning to find Juan standing in front of his desk. Dr. Peck invited Juan to take a chair. "Congressman, we have gotten the results back from the sample we took of the tumor in your stomach. It is indeed malignant." Dr. Peck waited for a few moments, giving Juan a chance to absorb the information, and overcome the initial shock.

"We think we have found the tumor early in its development, and it hasn't spread to any other parts of your body. I have discussed your case with other members of my staff and we had chosen a treatment plan that hopefully will rid you of the problem."

Juan was struck by the candor of Dr. Peck. He seemed too detached, but Juan theorized this detachment was normal for individuals with high intelligence who didn't want to get personally involved.

"Okay, Doctor Peck, let's hear what you have decided."

"To start with, we need to schedule you for an operation to remove the tumor, but before that, we want to give you some chemotherapy and radiation treatments to shrink the tumor and prevent any additional growth. You won't have to be hospitalized for this. We can have a home infusion team come to your house. This way, there will be less exposure to the public, and we have found patients do much better when they are at home. This should take about three weeks. Of course, you will have trouble with nausea and hair loss, but we have drugs to control the vomiting, and the hair will grow back in time. After the chemotherapy, we will complete the radiation and when the tumor is the size we want we will operate and extract the tumor, making sure we have it all. After the surgery, we will schedule you for a couple of follow-up sessions to make sure everything has been done. After three months, we will bring you back in and conduct tests to see how things went, and what the prognosis is. It is my recommendation for you to take a four month leave of absence to get everything done. I have had experiences like this with other congressmen, and that amount of time, even though highly valuable, won't hurt your efficiency on the job. Are there any questions I can answer for you?"

Juan noted a slight change in Dr. Peck's facial features. Juan saw for a fleeting moment, compassion and concern, which quickly disappeared.

"No, I don't think so. I will inform my staff and my superiors in congress of the situation, make a press release, and have my secretary coordinate with your staff on the timing of the chemo and the surgery. Let's hope for the best and see what happens."

The two men shook hands and Juan walked out to meet his destiny.

The next day, Juan made his announcement to take a leave of absence after he had met with and confided in his leadership. He was assisted by the spin doctors who put a face on a deadly disease which even amazed Juan. They minimized the severity of Juan's condition while basically sticking to the truth. Juan had a small, and they emphasized small, tumor which would be surgically removed, then after a period of rehabilitation, Juan would return to the congress as good as new. No matter how hard reporters tried to probe deeper into Juan's condition, the less was said. Finally they gave up and the hubbub died down.

After the press conference, Juan went back to his residence to prepare for the chemotherapy scheduled to begin in the morning. At promptly 8 A.M. a young female arrived and knocked on Juan's door. She was dressed in casual clothes drawing little attention to herself. She carried a small black leather bag over her shoulder similar to a large purse, or a small suitcase, or an gym equipment bag. She was tall for a woman, and thin. Her hands were a soft white with well manicured, unpolished nails. Juan estimated her age at about thirty or maybe a little younger. She had clear green eyes demonstrating compassion and friendliness. Juan bid her welcome and she stepped inside.

The young woman showed her credentials to Juan, confirming she was a registered nurse with experience in home infusion, or the delivery of drugs and other chemicals via an intravenous route into the veins of a person's arm or hand. She spread a clean, white cloth on top of a coffee table in front of Juan's favorite lounging chair, and laid out the equipment she was going to use. There were two IV bags of clear liquid, various lengths of clear plastic tubing, shutoff valves, antiseptic swabs, syringes and needles, and bottle of injectable fluids. She carefully went over each item and explained them to Juan. She told him to relax when he sat in his chair and she would insert a large needle into the vein on the top of his hand through which the chemo would be infused. The IV bags not only contained the liquid mixing fluid, but other drugs to increase the effectiveness of the chemo without raising the level of the cancer fighting chemicals to dangerous heights. A drug to counteract the nausea was also included in the mix. From her bag, the nurse took out a collapsible metal stand to hang the IV bags from, popped it up and placed it next to the chair.

Carefully she examined and shook each bottle. Juan had been instructed not to wear any restrictive clothing or clothing he didn't want to get ruined if he did have to vomit. He wore an old pair of jeans and a short sleeved tee shirt with some design which had long since faded beyond recognition. She placed a cloth type bib around his neck to protect his body, placed his arm on a soft flexible plastic board and secured his arm to the board and the board to the chair with strips of tape. She cleansed the back of his hand with the antiseptic and carefully inserted the needle. She hung one of the IV bags to the stand. She then attached a plastic coupler to the needle and to the IV tubing.

She opened the line from the IV bag and the fluid started to drip into a chamber and from there into the tubing. Juan watched as the liquid came down the tube and into his hand.

The nurse then told him she was going to put the chemo into the IV bag through a portal, and that Juan should start to experience a slight warming sensation in his hand and eventually his body. She explained that this was normal and it should go away in a few minutes. She also explained the treatment for that day would take approximately three hours, and she would be there at all times to make certain everything went smoothly. She told Juan he could read, or watch television, or close his eyes and snooze, whichever seemed to be best for him.

The chemo was withdrawn from the bottle and injected into the IV fluid, and the trip had begun. As she had predicted, Juan did feel a warming go through his hand and into his body. It wasn't uncomfortable, and true to her word, the sensation went away. Juan did feel a little wave of nausea hit him, but it was mild and soon dissipated. He was so nervous, he couldn't sleep, and he couldn't concentrate on any reading material, so he used his remote to turn on the television, switching to a football game in which he had no interest, but it was something to watch.

CHAPTER SIXTY-FOUR

As predicted, Juan's beautiful black hair began to come out in clumps. In less than a week, he was completely bald. Mary kidded him, saying he was very sexy and reminded her of Yul Bruner. She suggested maybe he should give up government, and go into acting or star on Broadway. He wasn't in any mood to take the ribbing, but understood what Mary was trying to do, so he didn't say anything. During the chemotherapy, Juan had to return to Walter Reed to have Dr. Peck monitor the progression of his disease. The MRIs did indeed show that the tumor, after three weeks, was now approximately twenty percent of its original size. Dr. Peck felt Juan only needed one more week of chemotherapy, then the radiation, then the surgery.

The infusion nurse came for the last time, withdrew the needle from Juan's hand, put all of the bandages, tape, and empty vials into a hard shelled container for contaminated waste disposal, and said good bye. She wished Juan the very best, and hoped she would not seen him again. Juan thanked her for her wonderful support and her professionalism. Juan wasn't sure how much the home infusion had cost, but he did know federal employees did have the best insurance available, and the taxpayers would be picking up the tab.

The removal of the remaining tumor came off without a hitch. The operation was simple and straightforward, only taking a couple of hours from start to finish. When Juan came out of the anesthesia, Dr.

Peck told him he would kept in the hospital for a few days, to return in two weeks to start a final brief regimen of radiation to make sure the cancerous cells had all be taken care of. And then it was over. By the end of the four months, Juan's hair had grown back, his energy returned, and he was ready to tackle the task he was elected to do. A final MRI was done, and Juan was given a clean bill of health and clearance to return to his office. A few return visits to Walter Reed were scheduled just to make certain everything was the way it ought to be.

Juan's career continued to flourish. He was re-elected twice more, and by this time had forged himself into the position of majority whip, one of the most powerful position in Congress. He was now chairing committees, and serving on others. Work was like a drug to him, he seemed to thrive on it. He used his ability to foster cooperation between the opposing parties, and became the sponsor of some of the most impacting legislation to be passed. He was now in greater demand as a speaker than ever before. Lobbyists continually sought his favor, tempting him with tickets to sporting events, vacations, gifts, and other favors. Juan knew his bounds, and never succumbed to any of these offers. Juan was one of the most ethical individuals anyone knew. Juan saw how other congressmen fell to the evils placed before them. Some got away with it, but others were brought before the House Ethics Committee, and eventually lost when they ran for re-election.

During the legislative winter break, Juan again had occasion to meet with Gus Bell, Kyle Smith, and others to continue to develop strategies for the upcoming session and for future elections. As always, the group brought in only the finest minds to assist. By now, Kyle and Juan had amassed an enormous fund which would allow them to do this. Another vacation was in the offing and this time Juan and the family decided to go to the National Parks in southern Utah to camp, hike, and enjoy the great outdoors. They flew to Salt Lake City, rented an RV, purchased what equipment they needed, and took off to see some of the most beautiful scenery known to mankind.

Juan had his staff make the arrangements through the National Park Service for places they would be staying. As they traversed the land south of Salt Lake, the desert type landscape suddenly turned into rock formations of every color. Mostly reds, rusts, browns, yellows, but sometimes greens, blues, and whites. Juan was struck with the marvelous beauty of this place. He knew that God must have had a wonderful day when he created the parks now called Zion and Bryce. In the evening, the family would sit outside their RV on folding chairs, and watch the sun set, the formations changing colors as though they were choreographed by a famous dancer. Juan was mesmerized as if he had taken an overdose of LSD and was hallucinating. The feeling was addictive, and when the time came for them to turn in the RV and fly back to California, Juan almost didn't want to, but knew he must. When they returned, the pictures they had taken were developed, and painstakingly placed in special albums for later reflection. As each photo was placed in its proper place, Juan relived the experience and was so pleased they had made this trip.

The political meetings continued, interspersed with visitations around the district to get a feel of the pulse of his political worth, listen to the needs of the people who lived in his district, and gather more information which would better assist him in the drafting of future laws. After much of this activity, Juan was getting anxious to get back to Washington D.C. and get busy. He was somewhat annoyed when Kyle asked him to join him and Gus for an hour or so as they had something they needed to discuss with him, but he relented knowing how important these two individuals had been to his development.

They met at Kyle's house, in Kyle's den, the most comfortable room in the place. Kyle took orders for drinks, completed the orders, and began his conversation with Juan. "Juan, Gus and I have been discussing your future. We didn't include you initially, because we wanted to test the waters before we made any decisions or gave you any expectations which we could not fulfill. As you know, the other Senator from the state is not running for re-election, and we want you to take up the challenge. You could do so much more good as a Senator, and the party needs you in this role. What do you think?"

It didn't take Juan long to respond. "I appreciate what you and Gus are doing, but I have had some time to think about this, and I think I am at a point in my life where I should reach out for the one thing I have been striving for during the majority of my life. I don't want to become a Senator from California, I want to be President of the United States."

You could have heard a pin drop in the room. Kyle and Gus sat there, their mouths agape, not knowing what to say. Then Kyle responded. "Juan, that is an admirable goal, but not a realistic one. As you know, the United States Constitution prohibits a foreigner from becoming President. I don't remember the exact wording, but I think I have a copy of the Constitution around here someplace. Kyle walked to one of his bookshelves, withdrew a dark leathered book, thumbed through the index and opened the book. "Ah here it is, and I quote. Article 2, Section 1: The President. No person except a natural born citizen, or a citizen of the United States, at the time of the adoption of this constitution shall be eligible to the Office of President; neither shall any person be eligible to that office who shall not have attained to the age of thirty-five years, and been fourteen years a resident within the United States. So you see Juan, there is no way you can fit this criteria and become the Commander in Chief."

"I hear what you are saying Kyle, but let me run this by you. The Constitution was envisioned by the founding fathers as a guide to a young nation. They wanted this document to be a living, breathing entity. Not static, but flexible enough to be changed as the needs, and experience of the national grew. As you know, the original piece has been amended several times, including the section following what you read. You know that the succession to the presidency, in the event of the death of the President, while in office, was amended to change

394

the order of precedence amongst the hierarchy of the government. That means, under Article 2 and Section 1, it could be amended just as other sections have been. At the time of the adoption of the Constitution, America was made up mostly of British and other European citizens. It wasn't until many years later our nation expanded to incorporate other ethnic groups like the Irish, Italians, Slavs, Africans, Germans, Spanish, Mexican, South Americans, and so on. Our nation is different now. It is time the people elect the most capable individual regardless of his or her origin. I remember when John Kennedy was running for President, people said a Catholic could never be President. It might mean the Pope in Rome would rule through a puppet government. Well, that didn't hold true, and he was elected. Who knows how great a President he would have become if he had not been assassinated. I can see, down the road, the possibility of an Afro-American or a woman becoming our chief executive, so why not a naturalized citizen. Why should I be discriminated against? I learned to speak English, went to American schools, served my country in the military, governed a very large state, and have been highly effective in keeping this place operating. No Kyle, I will settle for nothing less that the Presidency."

"I applaud your candor Juan, but I think people in Hell would be served ice water before that would ever happen. If your decision is not to run for Senator, then we will see how things shake out. Think about our offer. You don't have to decide this minute, but give us some consideration. Mull this over, and after a good night's sleep you may take a different tack on the subject."

Juan knew he wouldn't, but he told Kyle and Gus he would consider what they said, and let them know. Kyle sighed a sigh of relief, the men finished their drinks, bade each other goodbye, and Juan went home to his family. In spite of what Kyle thought, Juan knew there just had to be a way to make his desires come to fruition. There just had to be. Maybe if he prayed hard enough, he would receive the inspiration to conceive a workable plan. Stranger things have happened, so why not this? Juan was becoming obsessed with the idea. He felt like a bulldog with a bone and he was not willing to give up for any reason. He would not be satisfied until he accomplished this aim or he would die trying, but that was a battle for another day. Now he had to return to the tasks at hand, his job, his responsibilities, and hope some inspiration would come to him.

CHAPTER SIXTY-FIVE

Even though Juan had been raised Catholic, he had never really been a religious man. Oh, he treated everyone in accordance with the principles of the Bible, lived a code befitted to a healthy life style, and gave to the needy, but he wasn't a church going person per se. He believed standing in a church doesn't make you a Christian any more than standing in a garage makes you a car. But this time, he felt he needed to go to a holy place to seek guidance. There was a chapel in the congressional building, open twenty four hours a day for the use of the members. Juan sought the chapel out. There was no one in the chapel, so Juan approached the altar, crossed himself, and knelt down. He bowed his head and started to pray.

It didn't take long for Juan to finish his prayers. He arose, left the chapel and returned to his office. He asked Shirl to get Kyle Smith on the phone if she could locate him. About twenty minutes later, Kyle was on the line.

"Kyle, I have decided to take you up on your offer to run for Senator. I talked it over with the Divine Power, and I know this is the way to go. I recognize the difference between a Congressman and a Senator, and feel this is the next logical step. I still haven't forgotten about the Presidency, but that is something for another day."

Juan knew America wasn't quite ready for a major change to their Constitution, but the six years Juan would spend as a Senator would give him the opportunity to lay the groundwork to get the amendment considered and put in place. He knew he had many IOU's out there, but he also knew there were many who owed him big favors. He, if elected to the Senate, would work on those groups of immigrants that had powerful clout, like the populations in Florida, California, Texas, New York, Washington State, and other places which had experienced such an influx of people coming from other countries to settle in the states.

Kyle Smith's counterpart, the other Senator from California, true to her word, did retire from Congress, leaving the seat open. When the California Democratic convention was held, Juan was selected to replace her by unanimous vote from the floor. His acceptance speech thrilled the crowd. He delivered every punch line with force and conviction. He touched on every issue that had been harboring resentment from the citizens of the state. Many times, he had to stop and wait for the applause to subside. After the speeches were over, Juan worked the crowd like a seasoned veteran. His arm ached from shaking so many hands. It was a good thing there weren't any babies to kiss, or he would have worn his lips out as well.

After the filing papers were in, the campaign for the Senate began. It was getting to be old hat, but Juan relished every minute of it. One would think after all of these years, it would be boring, but Juan found it invigorating, a reason to get up every morning and go to work. Again, he did the usual things. Stumped the state, visited senior centers, debated his opponent, met with community groups, appeared on national television, and cemented his name as a household word all over the nation.

The election was held, and Juan won handily. He was now Senator Juan Cardova. The next time congress convened, Juan was shown into his new office. By comparison to his house office, would be like comparing a VW Beetle to a Lincoln Town Car. His new surroundings had more room, and were beautifully decorated. The number of staff members increased, as did his workload. He wanted to receive assignments to committees and subcommittees concerned with the interior, banking, intelligence, armed services, and foreign affairs.

These were the areas he felt he was lacking the most to round out his credentials. Because of his work in the House of Representatives, and his association with Kyle, now a senior Senator, he received most of what he wanted. Kyle and Juan now made a powerful tandem, exercising muscle very few states could lay claim to. It harkened back to the days of Magnuson and Scoop Jackson from Washington State, with buildings, highways and naval ships being named after them.

One of the primary duties Juan had to perform was to chair Senate hearings, probing into matters that plagued the various Federal Departments. Juan didn't like some of the tactics members of his committee or subcommittees used, but he understood they had every right to handle things in their own way as long as the proceeding fit the proper protocol. It was well known around the beltway that Juan was a compassionate, fair, but firm Senator, and whoever testified at a hearing he was in charge would be treated with respect and candor. Juan didn't use his hearings to further his career or to stroke his ego as some did, but to get to the bottom of problems and to find solutions that would benefit the nation. As a result, he received kudos from most of the political pundits and analysts. Slowly but surely, Juan was weaving a mystic about himself that would someday return great dividends.

Mary and the kids were by now well used to the Washington D.C. scene. Jose and Maria Elena were doing well in school, and had adjusted to the lifestyle. Public appearances no longer terrified them. They were growing up to be handsome and well mannered individuals, a proven asset to Juan. Jose was becoming an accomplished soccer player, taking after his father. Juan tried to make it to as many of his games as possible, and was so pleased to note the progress Jose was making. Juan would give him helpful hints on the game, but never interfered with what the coaches were telling him. Juan didn't want to come off as an intrusive parent, a fact the coaches appreciated. Who knows, someday Jose may receive a scholarship to play for some major university, and follow in his father's footsteps. Maria Elena was becoming a young woman.

CHAPTER SIXTY-SIX

It was during a formal state function, that Juan was seated next to an envoy from a foreign government, which had been subsidized by the United States for many years at a cost of billions of dollars. The envoy, during a lull in the dinner, leaned over to thank Juan for his gracious hospitality and inquired if Juan had ever considered becoming president of such a great nation. Juan acknowledged the compliment, and explained the Constitution of the United States prohibited him from ever becoming the President. The envoy was amazed at the explanation. He told Juan in his country if some change needed to be done to the leadership, either there was a coup or the law was changed. He suggested Juan move forward to change the Constitution and be done with it. Little did the envoy know this was the exact thought Juan had come up with many years ago. Like Yogi Berra once said, "It is Déjà vu all over again."

As Juan became more and more comfortable in the Senate, he took every opportunity he had to point out the weaknesses of the present administration. He did it in a kind way, well armed with facts and figures. People were starting to take notice as Juan deftly was putting together a platform to run on later, without anyone understanding what he was doing. Juan traveled extensively to other countries to encourage open and free trade, and to build secret alliances with them. Juan was a moderate, so he appealed to more sides than did the extreme liberals or conservatives in Congress. Juan was for the working class, and spoke often at union conferences and other trade organizations. Even though he was a Catholic, he was for the woman's right to choose, and was against the repeal of Roe Vs. Wade. He supported The Headstart Program to assist children in getting a good foundation to a lifetime process of learning. This also included better nutrition, especially in the morning. Juan and Mary were patrons of the arts, giving generously to performing centers and to San Diego State University. Juan created a scholarship endowment at San Diego State to help a struggling student meet the ever increasing cost of tuition and books. He laid wreaths at national cemeteries and even gave a sermon at a local, all black, Baptist church, singing and clapping right along with the choir. He participated in Cinco De Mayo celebrations in the Hispanic communities, and marched with the crowd on Martin Luther King Jr. days. He threw out the first pitch at baseball's opening day, and had pasta in Little Italy. He wore green on Saint Patrick's Day and red on Valentine's Day. He attended the Rose Parade on New Year's Day, and the Christmas Macy's Parade during the holidays. He kept a schedule exhausting to most men, but he thrived on it.

When he felt all of the groundwork had been laid, he called together the most loyal of his inner circle, people who worked for him, and had no obligations to anyone else. In complete secrecy, he gathered the young minds, and charged them with complete confidentiality. In the meeting room, which had been swept for any bugging devices, Juan met with four individuals. Two males and two females. Four of the sharpest minds Juan had ever seen. As they were seated around the room, Juan made his grand announcement, he was going to run for President of the United States, but needed to know what it would take to get this done. The group debated various strategies, but didn't come up with anything that seemed to be workable. Then Juan remembered the envoy saying why not change the Constitution. Juan floated this idea to the assemblage. One of the staffers, a whiz at Constitutional

Law, gave an overview of what this strategy would take. First, the amendment would have to be drafted with the support of key leadership figures. Then the Congress, both houses, would have to pass the amendment, followed by two thirds of the states ratifying it before it would become effective. The group mulled this over for several hours, while Juan wrote down the ideas on a large flip chart.

It was finally agreed that Juan needed to call in all of his favors, and strong arm those who might be opposed to this action. This would take more than the gentle nudge of persuasion, it would take an all out war under the guise that it was the best thing for the country. The group also discussed Juan's qualifications. Did he have enough experience to be President and was he old enough? Research told Juan he had all of the qualifications. He, by no means, wasn't the youngest or inexperienced to run for this office. Several candidates like Wendell Wilke and Woodrow Wilson had little if any experience in government. Wilson had been the Governor of New Jersey, but had not been involved at the national level. The meeting was concluded, Juan again warning the four about leaks, and the repercussions that would befall them if any word of this meeting were to get out. When everyone had left the room, Juan tilted himself back in his chair, closed his eyes tightly, massaged his forehead, and made a decision to get a hold of his old friend Wilson. The word strong leverage suddenly translated itself into blackmail. Juan would get Wilson and his cohorts to find skeletons in the Senators and Congressmen's closets, and with a threat to exposure them, get their agreements to support his move. In some ways, this tactic ran against Juan's grain, but the desire at this point in his life was stronger to be President, than to stay truly ethical.

Juan labored over this decision for several days. He spent restless nights trying not to let Mary know such things were bothering him. He wasn't much of a liar. Mary had suspected something for some time, and at breakfast one Sunday morning, set his bacon and eggs in front of him, stared him in the eye like a snake would address its meal, and asked the question.

"Juan, you have been as nervous as a cat lately. What is going on?'

Juan knew he could not lie or hold out on Mary, she was too perceptive. She could see right through him in an instant. He wanted to attack his meal before it got cold, but knew she wanted an immediate answer. Slowly, like a teacher explaining a difficult math problem to a student, he recited his plan. He didn't have to explain his desire to be President, Mary already knew that, but she was appalled that Juan would stoop so low as to betray his friends in the name of self gratification. She could not imagine what had come over him. Juan hemmed and hawed, but the words came out all wrong. When Juan finished, he asked Mary if she was going to stick with him or not.

Without hesitation, Mary told Juan that she was taking the kids to see her relatives for a few days to think things over before Juan could wield his magic over her. She had to digest the impact of his decision, and to determine the impact it would have on their lives. Juan attempted to persuade her, but she shrugged it off and left the kitchen. Juan ate his cold eggs, and didn't enjoy them very much. He knew he would have to retreat back to square one and come up with scheme that Mary could accept and support. He knew this would be a very difficult task.

The next day Mary bundled the kids up, loaded them in the car and drove away. In spite of everything Juan tried to do, he knew Mary had made up her mind to see this scenario through to its bitter end. As he watched her car pull out of sight, he was filled with remorse, and hung his head as tears began to well up in his eyes. Mary had given him a hard time in the past over issues, but had never left him alone to stew before. He was seeing a different woman than the one he had married. He tried to think of the ramifications if Mary decided not to go along with the plan, and the hair on the back of his head stood up in the same way it did when he watched marching troops parade to a Sousa tune. The eggs had not set well on his stomach, and the scotch he poured down upon them didn't set well either. He decided to tie one on just to spite her, and the results were disaster prone. He spent most of the morning making love to the ivory throne, his toilet. He had been sick in college from drinking too much, but his age renewed the experience with a vengeance. He spent most of the day sleeping it off, awakening in the late evening with a headache to end all headaches.

Several times over the next week, Juan tried to reach Mary by phone. Each time the telephone rang, it was answered by someone who said Mary was not available. Juan knew that Mary would not reveal everything, but was concerned about how much Mary would let slip. Juan was told in no uncertain terms to stop calling and harassing her, that Mary would make up her mind what she wanted to do, and would reconnect when the time was right. Juan knew his efforts were futile, and Mary's protectors were right. He would hear from Mary in due time, but that didn't stop the anxiety or the frustration. Trying to control his emotions on the job was not an easy task. Juan had always been able to hide his feelings well from his staff, and he continued to do so. He busied himself in congressional matters, hoping to hear from his spouse soon.

Juan lucked out again. Without requiring any further explanation, Mary agreed to return home with the kids and support her husband. She kind of made a joke about it, stating that she thought she would make a great First Lady, and it was well worth the try. Juan was elated. This night he did get drunk, but took it easy to avoid a duplication of a Sunday, which was forever burned into his mind.

CHAPTER SIXTY-SEVEN

Before Juan could put together an exploratory committee to test the waters, he had to put the major pieces together giving him a much better chance. First was to contact Wilson and start the information gathering about the backgrounds of the influential Senators and Representatives. Second, he needed to increase his support network, instilling in them the concept that times have changed, and a person, regardless of where he or she came from, as long as they were naturalized citizens of the United States could become President. Third, he had to call in his favors. And last, Juan needed to make sure the media was on his side. He knew there were reporters and anchor men out there that might look at his concepts as feasible and help him make an argument to the people.

Juan knew he would have to go slowly, but he also knew if someone was told something often enough, they would tend to believe it. Hitler had used that propaganda method quite effectively. Even though Juan knew he wasn't any Hitler, the paradigm remained the same. With the seeds in place, Juan began sowing them as rapidly as he could. He needed to reach Wilson, but didn't have the least notion where he was. Then he remembered Wilson had told him of a telephone number and a code word to be used in the event he needed to be reached. But remembering that, and remembering where the piece of paper was with the information on it he needed, was another hurdle. Juan racked his brain, and could not come up with the answer. He started with his address book, the black leather coil bound one which held all of the contracts he had made over the years. Names and numbers of old classmates, business contacts, old girlfriends, consultants, and a multitude of others.

It wasn't there. Next he began a drawer by drawer search of his desk. Methodically he removed the desk drawer, placed it on top of the desk and sifted through everything that the drawer held. He laid each item to one side, and when the drawer was empty, he rechecked each item as he placed it back. It took most of the day, mixed with a few drinks, to conduct a thorough search. Juan finally gave up the quest. He simply couldn't concentrate anymore. He stumbled to the couch, dropped onto it in a dead faint and fell asleep. He didn't know how long he had been out, but the sun was no longer present, and the house was completely dark. Juan switched on a lamp, went to the bathroom, downed a couple of Tylenol, and went back to work trying to find the telephone number. Finally, he could longer think, and gave up. He would start again in the morning since it was a Sunday, and he would have more time.

Sunday morning, Juan rifled through his desk and again came up empty. He next attacked the bedroom drawers, removing all of his underwear and socks, but found nil. He knew he hadn't placed it where Mary would find it, so he skipped her areas. He went through the books on the library shelf, thinking he might have placed the item inside one of them. One by one, he gripped the spine of each book and shook it. Nothing dropped out. Juan was getting desperate. Suddenly, a thought hit and he struck himself on the forehead. The safe, he said out loud, it has to be in the safe. Juan had installed a wall safe behind one of the oil painting he and Mary had purchased at an art auction in Silver Springs, Maryland. Juan didn't really like the painting, but had to agree with Mary it did help to blend the colors of the room together. He lifted the painting from its mounting, spun the dial, stopping on each digit after the correct number of spins, twisted the black handle and opened the container. Methodically Juan again went through each item, placing them on a coffee table placed underneath. After looking at each item he returned them to the safe. He found nothing. Juan was beside himself when suddenly it struck him like a thunderbolt.

The piece of paper wasn't a piece of paper at all, it was a photograph taken of himself and Wilson in Vietnam. Juan had written the information on the back of the photo and placed it into one of the many albums they had stored in an upstairs closet. Juan leaped up the staircase, taking the steps two at a time. Now if he could remember which album it was in. Someday, Juan said to himself, I am going to go through these albums, identify what the photos are, and re-arranged them in some kind of logical order, labeling the albums so the contents would be known on the outside. Then again, there were lots of things Juan was going to do if he ever had the time.

All in all, there were approximately twenty albums lined up across the shelf. Juan didn't know whether to start at one end and work to the other end, or start in the middle and work to one side and then the other. Juan knew whatever choice he made, it probably would be wrong. Too many times Juan had sorted through something only to find it was at the very end, and could have been found easily had Juan started in a different direction.

All of this labor had made Juan hungry, and the day was moving on. He had to get back to the office in the morning, but knew he needed something to fill his stomach. He fixed a tuna fish and pickle sandwich, tossed some potato chips next to it, and opened a bottle of his favorite light beer, a microbrew the region was so famous for. As the last morsel was washed down with the beer, Juan placed the dishes in the dishwasher, and tossed the bottle into the recycle barrel.

Back to the albums. Juan decided to start on the left and work to the right. He had gone through six of the albums when the photo he was seeking appeared as he turned a few pages. The photo was one of

Wilson standing with his foot on a fallen tree stump resting his rifle on his boot. Juan was standing behind and slightly to the right of Wilson. Juan found it hard to imagine how young they were. They were both deeply tanned and their short hair was dark. Now Juan needed more sun, and the black hair was tinged with gray. The photo had been taken by one of Juan's friends and was now starting to fade with age. Juan carefully removed the photo, turned it over and breathed a sigh of relief. He had used indelible ink, and the information was still very legible. He copied the information onto another piece of paper, replaced the photo, and made the call.

The telephone was answered on the first ring by a female voice Juan didn't recognize. She answered the phone with a "yes" and waited for Juan to go through the coded process to allow him to get the information he needed. When he finished, the female told him he would be contacted by a young woman posing as a student representative from some high school in the D.C. area. He was to give her his request and she would return to give him further instructions when she had relayed the request to Wilson. Juan said he wanted to speak to Wilson face to face, but the female said that wasn't possible. Wilson was in hiding from an adversary seeking to kill him. Juan knew Wilson lived in a constant threat of death because of the work he did, but he also knew Wilson was smart enough to outlast any problem which would like to dispose of him.

Years ago, Wilson and Juan had worked out a method of coding text so that they could exchange messages without compromising the information if it fell into the wrong hands. They had spent hours in Vietnam devising the code, and had perfected it to their satisfaction. They even gave the code to several military decoders to see if they could break it, and no one could. Juan wasn't certain about the new computers, but felt by the time the code was broken, he would have been in touch with Wilson and things would have been changed.

Juan sat at his desk and composed his request. It was really straightforward. Juan wanted Wilson and his associates to find anything in the past of selected powerful individuals that could be used to blackmail them. Here again was the word blackmail, which Juan hated. He would have preferred to use the word provide leverage against, but blackmail was the truth. To these few lines, Juan encoded the names to be investigated. Juan knew amending the Constitution was in the hands of the Congress, so he carefully chose those who could get the job done. Juan wanted to get to those who had tremendous influence with the governors and legislatures of the states, since it took two-thirds of the states to ratify any constitutional amendment.

Juan knew he had a daunting task ahead of him. The Constitution had been amended twenty seven times. The twenty sixth amendment was done in March of 1971 and ratified that same year. The twenty seventh amendment was written in September of 1989, but was not ratified until May of 1992. Many years had passed since the first ten amendments, The Bill of Rights were long passed, before the other seventeen were put through. But Juan also knew his seeds had started to take root and grow and the process was well on its way to being accomplished.

The next day, as predicted, a group of students from a local high school was touring Congress as part of their civics class. One of the students, an attractive brunette, wanted to see Juan since she had previously lived in California, and was aware of him from past experience. Juan granted a short interview. When the young lady was finished with her questions, she asked Juan for his autograph. She handed Juan her autograph book which he signed with a short message, and then slipped his request to Wilson into the back of the book. She thanked Juan for his time and left his office. Juan sat there for a few minutes, soaked in sweat. His office wasn't hot, but initiating this request brought forth all of the adrenaline needed to elevate his core body temperature. He closed his door and went to his clothes closet where he kept extra clothing and changed his shirt and tie. He wanted to appear fresh when he went to the floor to hear some of the debates.

CHAPTER SIXTY-EIGHT

The background work Juan's staff was conducting was revealing the American people were more concerned about a person's religion, their gender, or their race than they were about whether nor not the candidate was a native born citizen. This news elated Juan. Now he knew he had opened the door just slightly, and with care would continue to wedge his idea through the portal. He continued his propaganda campaign, meeting with cells of influential friends who were easily convinced and then moving on to the media where they casually floated the concept as hypothetical. Letters to the editor were written, but only a small percentage of them were negative. This gave Juan even more hope. In the meantime, Juan was starting to receive incriminating evidence about the backgrounds of key Senators and Representatives. It was amazing to him what checkered pasts these individuals had.

In one case, the person had belonged to a fraternity at a well-known Ivy League school, and after an all night beer fest, got into his car and hit a jogger. The jogger died. The family sued, but because the boy's parents were rich, the family was quieted and bought off. The case never went to court. In another, the representative had taken thousands of dollars worth of trips, kickbacks, and bribes from corporations to garner his favor and to assure bills were passed to included vast fortunes for their companies. Of course, prior drug use showed up in many cases, most of those involved growing up in the era of the Hippies when free love and drugs were the thing of the day. One of the more unusual cases was an individual who had been in prison for murder, had served his sentence, been paroled, and finally set free. He had gone through extraordinary pains to change his name and create a whole new identify for himself. Somehow he had managed to escape detection, and had wrangled himself into a respected government position.

Juan was receiving information on slum lords who hired others to do their dirty work while they reaped the profits. Others were connected to the underworld, but no one could even make the connection, and as long as the suspicions were unfounded, nothing was done. Certainly these devious individuals were in the minority, but surprisingly, they were the ones in the seats of power, and the ones Juan could go after when push came to shove.

All of the information was rock solid. Confidential records that should never have been made public were showing up along with photographs, tape recordings, and other damning documents. There was a sprinkling of homosexuality, spousal abuse, and pornography thrown in just for good measure. Juan, while leafing through the information, felt that even if he didn't get to be president, he had enough stuff to open a daytime television show, like many of the shows now in existence.

Juan put together his exploratory committee, and began his fund raising. The supporting funds started to come in at a snail's pace, but soon started to snowball. In no time, Juan was beginning to amass a war chest bigger than any the nation had ever seen. Like the New York Yankees, he was putting together the best team money could buy. He was millions ahead of his nearest competitor. Now to await the Democratic Convention. The nominating festival was to be held in Los Angeles, and Juan could not be more pleased with the choice of this city, his home base. Before he could get to that point, Juan knew he would have to start with New Hampshire's primary, then to Iowa, and across the states. He selected his campaign manager, a versed lawyer from the D.C. area. A person well known and well liked by most of the insiders and in the media. Offices were opened in all of the fifty states and staffed with some paid, but mostly volunteer types of people. The race was on to see who would be the chosen one from the party.

When Juan arrived in Baltimore, Bill Maczis was there to deliver the support he had promised. Juan thought to himself, I wish I had fifty men like Bill working for me. Bill invited Juan out to his lovely home near Catonsville, but Juan was on such a tight time schedule, he declined gracefully. Bill understood and wished him well.

The next few months were like an exhausting nightmare. Juan began to crisscross the land, not knowing what day it was. Advance men and women laid the groundwork for his visits, making sure his short stints there would pay the maximum dividends. He rolled up his sleeves, speaking at county fairs, from the backs of trucks, and in town meetings. He soothed the furrowed brows of the senior citizens in nursing homes, and kissed babies. He spoke to the Hispanic populations in their native language and danced the polka in Minnesota. His charisma was taking on matinee idol proportions. There was a ground swell of approval never seen before. His ratings were sky high as the best choice of his party. The time had come for Juan to make his calculated move to amend the Constitution.

The time for the Democratic Convention wasn't that far off, and timing was everything. The process for amending the Constitution wouldn't take that long if Congress would get to it, and with everything in place within the state organizations, a two thirds ratification could probably be accomplished in about a year. That would give Juan about six months to get ready for the convention, which should be plenty of time if everything went smoothly. Juan's backup plan, in the event the Constitution couldn't be ratified in accordance with his timetable, would be to find a plausible excuse to back out of the convention this time, and re-address the situation later.

Juan didn't like the thoughts of this, but he had to have an escape valve in place just in case. The opening move of this chess game started with a phone call to Kyle Smith. Juan had some very damaging information on Kyle, and he hated to use Kyle as a pawn, but Juan's thinking had become so warped, friendship no longer mattered. All that mattered was the presidency. Juan had become totally obsessed with this notion to the point of no longer being rational. He would spend every spare minute contacting his agents across the country to make sure everything was as it should be. He had arrived at the point where he could no longer sleep, and had the Congressional physician prescribe some hypnotic tablets for him. Juan knew he must have some sleep or his body would simply burn itself out.

Juan had Shirl take the prescription to a local pharmacy which filled most of the medications for the members of Congress and other governmental offices. She waited, signed for the prescription and returned to the office. The medication was inside a standard white bag with the logo of the pharmacy emblazoned on the outside. Juan opened the bag and extracted the prescription vial, amber in color to stop the sun from damaging the ingredients, with a child proof lock top simply stating, "Push and turn to open."

Juan hated these types of openers. They were just like the over the counter products that the Federal Government has imposed a regulation in an effort to decrease the number of child poisonings when the little ones gained access to the medicine cabinet without parental supervision, and ingested the substances which could make them ill or even kill them. It was often remarked by the older generation that these tops couldn't be opened by adults, but could be opened by children quite easily.

Juan rolled the vial around in his hand, reading the label that was affixed to the outside. On the label was his name, the prescribing physician's name, the date the prescription was filled, the name of the medication with its strength, the number of tablets in the vial, and the directions for taking the medication. "Take one tablet at bedtime for sleep" it read simply. Also accompanying the vial was a printed information sheet which told the patient of any side effects or potential dangers. Juan threw the instructions into the wastebasket without reading them. That night, he took not one, but two of the tablets, immediately fell into a deep slumber and barely heard his alarm the next morning. He chided himself and resolved to only take one tablet next time.

CHAPTER SIXTY-NINE

Shirl had contacted Kyle and set up a meeting in Juan's office. Kyle arrived just a few minutes early. Shirl offered him a cup of coffee. Kyle liked her coffee, pronouncing it the best in the building. Shirl blushed slightly with the compliment. Shirl really didn't like Kyle at all. He was much too smooth with the women and too free with the sly remarks. Shirl felt like he was undressing her with his eyes whenever he looked in her direction. She felt he was the epitome of the classical "Dirty Old Man". Juan was occupied on the phone, but did hear Kyle's loud voice through his closed door. Juan felt Kyle could wait just a few minutes until he had finished his important business. Juan knew Kyle had kept him waiting on many occasions, so turn about was fair play.

Juan finished his conversation, hung up the phone, walked to the door, opened it, and invited Kyle in. Juan asked Shirl to bring him a cup of coffee, and after handing it to Juan she retreated back to her desk. Juan closed the door, and sat behind his desk. Kyle took a seat in the comfortable leather chair at the side of Juan's position.

"Well ole buddy", Kyle started, "what is the reason for this wonderful chance to see you again."

Juan briefly told Kyle his plan and the urgency to get things moving. Kyle listened sympathetically, nodded his head and replied.

"Now Juan, you know how Congress works. You know I support your theory on the need to change the Constitution in order for you to be able to run for the Presidency, but these things take time. You just don't change the course of history overnight. This has to be thought through and through. There are a lot of I's to be dotted and T's to be crossed. Rome wasn't constructed in a day you know."

Kyle continued to ramble on uninterrupted. Juan just closed his eyes, blocking out the sound of Kyle's voice. Juan had seen Kyle in action on the floor of the Senate, droning on for hours thoroughly involved with himself and his own importance. Even though Kyle had been a long time friend, Kyle was now becoming an old bore. His time had passed, his apex had been reached, and his effectiveness was at a point of critical mass. Juan knew he had to force Kyle to do what Juan needed this very instant. It couldn't wait as Kyle would disintegrate over time. Juan suspected Kyle was starting to exhibit the early stages of senility, and would be tolerated by other members of the Senate until he was no longer able to function, just as they had for other Senators who had reached an age approaching one hundred years, but the folks back home just couldn't seem to let them go.

Juan had finally had enough. He opened his eyes, held up his hand and spoke. "Kyle I understand what you are saying, but before you continue any further, we just don't have that much time."

Juan spent the next few minutes outlining the mechanisms that had been put into place, the strategies that had been adopted, the infrastructure that was now ingrained into the fabric of the nation, the thousands of people who were primed to rally to Juan's banner, and needs of America. During the past two terms of the current administration, the very essence of forward movement had stopped. The rate of unemployment was going up, the foreign policies weren't working causing our former allies to shun us, inflation was running rampant, the deficit was ballooning out sight, and Juan went on.

Then Juan outlined the plan to amend the Constitution and to get the amendment ratified. Kyle sat there stunned, his mouth open, a small film of saliva drooling from the corner of his mouth. Juan gave him a short respite to consider what had been said, then asked Kyle to agree to begin.

"I can't do what you ask Juan, it would be impossible. I am overwhelmed you would think otherwise. There is no way I would even consider adhering to your timetable. I need to think this over."

"The time for thinking is finished Kyle. You will do what I say, and you will do it in accordance with my timetable, and I'll tell you why." With that Juan dropped the bombshell on Kyle's head. It seems Kyle had impregnated his Mexican housemaid who had given birth to a baby boy outside of the country. Kyle knew he was the father, and had supported the mother and child since the delivery. In addition, Kyle had been grossly unfaithful to his wife, keeping a bevy of young women at his beck and call. Juan handed Kyle the brown envelope containing the revealing and damning information. Kyle carefully went through it, his face taking on an ashen pallor. Juan thought at one time Kyle was going to have a stroke or a heart attack, and the medics would have to be called. Juan steeled himself for just such an eventuality.

Kyle finally took a long, deep breath, composed himself and said. "I didn't think you would ever do anything like this to me Juan. I thought we had been friends for far too many years. It galls me to even contemplate assisting you in this manner, but my ego and my marriage couldn't stand the scandal, so I will do your biding. Let me have copies of the backgrounds of the other key Senators and I will do your dirty work for you. Just leave the thirty pieces of silver in my office someday, and we shall never speak of this again."

Kyle was very unsteady when he arose, but regained his strength and exited the office. Juan was elated, the first salvo had been launched, and the war was on. Juan didn't feel any remorse at all, in fact, he felt vindicated.

CHAPTER SEVENTY

Very quietly, but steadily, the wheels started to turn to put the amendment in place. Juan could feel the change as he passed his colleagues in the halls of the Senate chambers. Some gave him a knowing grin, others a slight nod of the head, and others a look of distain and disbelief. No one was saying anything, but Juan would feel the energy emanate through the fabric of the building. Casual articles were starting to show up in local newspapers, and talk radio hosts began to bring the subject to the surface. Juan was starting to get feedback from his sources, which pleased him greatly. At one Hispanic rally, the participants vocally shouted their desire to have Juan run as their President, and to give him the right to do so. The time had come for change. True, in the olden days, the Presidency was reserved for the white, colonial landlord who held riches and people in their hands, but now the landscape had changed. Just as black children had been banned from attending white schools, the thought was, why ban a naturalized citizen for becoming the leader of the nation.

The debates started to rage, but the change seemed to gain the upper hand. The issue wasn't about who was the person born in the United States, but who was the best person to run the government as long as that person was a citizen of America. Other examples began to emerge. Women were denied the right to vote until the women's suffrage occurred. A poll tax kept certain segments of our population from being able to vote and that was repealed. Individuals had the right to free speech, so why didn't they have a right to hold certain offices in our government. And so the issue was dissected and mulled over by everyone. Newspaper editorials started to be published, the majority in favor of changing the way the government did business. The money Juan had spent to buy off the mob, the unions, and the minority groups was also starting to pay off. Kyle rarely spoke to Juan, but he was doing what Juan had asked him to do. Kyle, the Democratic majority leader held his secret enclaves and urged his fellow senators to go along. Kyle didn't reveal too many items of information, but he instilled in his peers the necessity to conform. The fear of having their sordid past revealed brought the targeted Senators and Representatives in line. The power, the privileges, and the personal egos were at stake. This amendment wouldn't hurt their reputations, so why not go along with the idea.

In history, many outsiders had improved the well being of this young nation. French and Austrian military men help America through the Revolutionary War. Immigrants from Europe had established the garment industry of New York, the coalmines of West Virginia, the cheese factories of Wisconsin, and the railroads of the west. America had become the melting pot of the world, so why shouldn't the top job reflect that change.

The twenty eighth amendment to the Constitution was introduced into the House of Representatives by a Mexican American from Arizona. The amendment went through its usual process, and was passed by a narrow margin, and sent on the to Senate Committee charged with overseeing these sorts of issues. Likewise, the Senate didn't spend much time discussing the matter, and passed the amendment just as the house had done. The deed was accomplished, now on to the states for ratification. From this point on, the amendment would be known as the "J" Amendment which stood of Juan's accomplishment.

Again, the preplanning paid its dividends. The states took their sweet time to address the issue, but in the end, two thirds or more of them ratified the amendment. Juan was now free to join with the Democratic convention in the run of his life.

The date for the Democratic convention had been known for some time, so no more extensive planning had to be done on Juan's part. He and his crew were ready. The Los Angeles Convention Center was a large facility, which would house the main floor where delegates to the convention would sit in folding chairs. The rows were marked with the name of the state for easy identification. At one end was the platform from which the speeches were given, and off to one side were the press boxes where the national television commentators would send their pictures into millions of homes. Of course, there would be roving reporters who would pigeon hole different celebrities and ask them inane questions. The entire area was covered with red, white and blue bunting which was always traditional, and a large net full of the same color balloons was suspended from the rafters in the ceiling. Inside the structure were also meeting rooms, dressing rooms, and hospitality rooms designed to meet all of the needs of the delegates.

The National Democratic chairperson called the meeting to order. The last of the delegates had marched into the room and were now seated. Banners for each candidate were well displayed. The race for the Democratic nomination had started out with nine individuals, but it had since narrowed down to three. Of course, anyone could be nominated from the floor, but rarely had this type of nomination ever seen reality.

The speeches began with the keynote address, rendered by a young Afro-American member of the House of Representatives. He delivered the address in a booming voice, carefully outlining each plank of the party platform, pausing after each item to a thunderous applause. The tone for the convention was set high in expectations. The keynote speaker had stirred the crowd in a frenzy. Following the keynote address, each candidate was nominated by someone chosen for that task. The profiles of each candidate were extolled, and reasons given for why they should be chosen over all of the others. This took several days, with the proceedings interspersed with entertainment from the Hollywood scene.

Finally, the time had come for the delegates to cast their votes for the candidate of their choice. The state didn't have to cast all of its votes for a single candidate, but most did. The national chairman rained down his gavel and called out the first state's name. "Would the State of Alabama please cast it's vote." A tall gentleman with long white flowing locks, a white mustache and beard stood up. He would have reminded one of Colonel Sanders of Kentucky Fried Chicken fame. He was wearing a white suit with a red bow tie, and perched on the top of his head was a white Stetson hat.

His deep voice rang out, "Mr. Chairman, the great State of Alabama casts its 13 votes for the next President of the United State, Juan Cardova." The mood had been set. The chairman proceed down the list of states until all of the votes had been stated. Juan Cardova had been nominated on the first ballot. Juan, Mary, Jose, and Maria Elena appeared at the center of the main stage, holding each other's hands high in the air to acknowledge the acclaim from the crowd. Juan's ego was pushed to new heights when he heard his name shouted over and over. The crowd came to order, Juan went to the microphone and delivered his acceptance speech, one he had written years ago, and now had the chance to speak the words.

After the speech, Juan grasped hands with his new Vice President, a Senator from the Midwest. Together they basked in the glory of the moment. The new Vice President was young and vibrant and helped Juan by portraying a man who was capable of assuming the duties of President if anything were to befall Juan.

While all of this madness was going on inside, outside a small group of protesters held up signs degrading Juan and the people who had changed the Constitution. Slogans like, "Go home and rule your own country" were held up. The group was orderly, but was moved, by the police, to a location where they could hardly be noticed. When they tried to surge toward the main entrance, their efforts were stifled. No matter how much they hollered, little notice was taken of them. Finally, they dispersed and went home. The deed had been done, and there was nothing any of them could do about it. Quietly, the din subsided about the change to the Constitution. It wasn't mentioned in the media anymore, nor was it a topic of discussion on the talk show circuit. America had finally accepted the fact an outsider, a person who met all of the qualifications, could become the Commander In Chief.

Standing on the platform with Juan at the end of the convention were some of the powerful in the party. Kyle Smith was there begrudgingly, but some notables were very conspicuous by their absence. With all of the commotion, no one seemed to pay any attention. As the new candidate and his party were leaving the center stage, Kyle leaned forward and whispered in Juan's ear.

"I won't forget what you did to me you traitor. I will support you becoming President, but don't make any mistakes, don't slant your mouth the wrong way, and don't forget who got you here, or I will make you the sorriest son of bitch in the world. I will abide by my loyalty for now, but if you step out of line one inch, I will give it my all to see you disgraced even if it costs me dearly. Remember that."

With that remark, Kyle separated himself from Juan, joined his wife, waving gladly to the mass and left the convention hall.

For the first time, Juan seemed rattled and threatened. He must make sure all of his defenses were in place, and that Kyle could never do anything to interrupt his efforts. Juan was certain he would be able to weather the storm and see this thing through to its conclusion.

The victory party went on for the rest of the night. Juan had never shaken so many hands or had so many slaps on the back in his lifetime. He tried to watch how much he drank, he didn't want to make love to the ivory throne again, and there was so much to do in the ensuing days to come. They sent the kids back to the hotel with an escort and then Juan and Mary danced together for the first time in a long time. They were floating on cloud nine, hardly aware of the historical impact they were making on the nation. The evening of gaiety was over. Juan and Mary retreated to the hotel, released the escort who had been watching over the children, undressed, showered, and fell in bed to an immediate slumber.

The next morning, coffee and breakfast was served in their hotel room by a Secret Service agent. Now that Juan was a candidate for President, he and his family qualified for Federal protection. It took some getting used to, having people around you all of the time, but Juan figured it was a necessary evil to be tolerated. From here on out, he would be traveling in an unmarked car, his schedule would be unannounced, and he would be surrounded by bodyguards.

The campaign, which should have been old hat, took on a new atmosphere, grander in scale. Juan was in a high stakes poker game now, the winner coming away with the grand prize. The Republicans had chosen a worthy opponent, and Juan knew the climb to the top of the heap would not be an easy one. The Republican candidate chosen at the convention in Chicago was another Senator and former governor of the State of Michigan. They held several things in common. They were both young, good looking, well spoken, and full of charisma. The basic way they differed was in the party's platforms and their religions. Juan was Catholic and the candidate from Michigan, Michael Riley, was from a Utah background. Religion has not become an issue, so Juan knew he had to focus on the issues and convince the voting public his approaches were the best choice. The race was on.

CHAPTER SEVENTY-ONE

Juan was consumed with the desire to win. He would stop at nothing, as long as he could defend it legally. He knew all of the wooing techniques, and the efforts needed to traverse the country attending meetings, rallies and functions. He knew about the debates and television coverage. He knew about the newspapers and the endless dissection of him and his family, so those parts didn't worry him much. It was the clandestine part that he was unfamiliar with. He had gotten a taste of it in the past, but this time it wasn't a nibble, it was a seven course meal. He knew there were people who would be bussed to the polling places, and maybe even given a few dollars to put in their pockets, but he didn't know who would carry that out or how it would be done. He knew there would be arm twisting within the ranks of the blue collar workers, forcing members to vote a certain way. He knew there would have to be political favors handed out down the road, and he would need some help to determine who would get which piece of the pie. He knew he would have to start now with a search group to pick potentials for the various cabinet positions and major department heads, who would ultimately pick their own underlings. It was a daunting task, but one Juan was so looking forward to.

Juan basically was distanced from his duties within the congress. He ran the office from phone booths and hotel rooms, casting votes by proxy, or on rare occasions when he was in town. Juan really didn't want to be baby sat by a bunch of high testosterone muscle men of the Secret Service, but he knew it was the law for presidential candidates to have the same protection afford for them and their families as did the sitting President. He thought having these bodies around was a waste of the taxpayers money, who would want to destroy him? He was going to the savior of the greatest land on earth. Then he remembered the tragic end to Bobby Kennedy in the kitchen of a Los Angeles hotel as he was leaving from giving a speech. He also harkened back to Martin Luther King Jr. who was shot on a balcony. He made peace with the protection, but never agreed with it.

Little did he know that history was about to repeat itself. It was in New York City. Juan was addressing a convention of the Veteran's of Foreign Wars when he looked up at some commotion in the back of the hall. There was scuffle going on with loud shouting, and then suddenly the sound of gun shots. One agent grasped his shoulder and turned to one side in obvious pain. Another agent seemed to be in a death dance with some crazed wild animal. A third agent was trying to wrestle a gun away from a very large man dressed in workman's attire. The workman had gained access to the hall under the ruse that some repairs had to be made to the sound system and lighting. There had been complaints both system were having problems, so no one gave it another thought until the workman extracted a pistol from his tool chest and started to shoot toward Juan. The gun was an automatic weapon small enough to fit into the toolbox. The accuracy of the shooter wasn't good, which is the reason two of the bullets went wide of their intended target. At last, four agents finally subdued the man, forced him to the floor and placed plastic restraints around his wrists as his arms were twisted behind his back.

As soon as the crowd realized what was transpiring, part of them burst towards the man to see if they could be of assistance, others hit the floor remembering what Vietnam and Korea and even World War II had been like. Some started to panic and head for the exits. It was as if someone had yelled "Fire" in a crowded theater. Members of the audience were shoved down and trampled on. Immediately, a call was made to 911 to summon emergency vehicles and medical staff to take care of the carnage. Soon sirens could be heard heading in the direction of the center where the convention was being held. Juan was hustled off through a back door and into a waiting limousine to remove him from harm's way. Juan was stunned and light headed. He needed a stiff drink and he needed it badly. The limo streaked down a side street and into the alley in the back of Juan's hotel where he entered the service elevator and was taken to his suite.

He did indeed have his stiff drink and immediately turned on the television to see what was still going on. It never ceased to amaze Juan how quickly the media could get to a crime scene with little or no notice. A beautiful young woman who looked like she had just stepped out of a beauty salon was bathed in a bright light. She held a portable microphone to her lips and was attempting to describe what she had been told about the attempted killing. She said there were little details about the shooter, but there would be more to come when he had been questioned by the police. The assailant was reported to be of Latin American extraction, but nothing further was known. Juan was also amazed that something that took only seconds could be analyzed for an hour or more. All he was hearing was speculation and nothing more. Juan didn't sleep well that night, and for the next few months constantly looked over his shoulder and into the faces of the crowds for any telltale signs of someone who wanted to do him harm.

The next morning, it was revealed the gunman was hired by a drug cartel from Central America to accomplish the deed. It was a well known fact that part of Juan's and the Democrats platform was to infused more money into the war on drugs. Especially those coming from Central and South America. Billions were at stake, so what was a few thousand to acquire a deranged individual to snuff out the life of someone who would have put a dent into the huge profits being recognized by the drug lords. The gunman would be charged with the crime, tried in a Federal Court and probably would receive a life sentence in a Federal facility without the possibility of parole. A disaster had been averted, but what else was lurking just around the bend in the highway.

The campaign progressed just as Juan and his party had planned, keeping the rhetoric clean, pushing all of the right buttons, and holding the ratings in the polls as close a possible. They didn't want Juan to appear to be an underdog, nor did they want him to get a large lead too early in the match. There were just too many independent and undecided voters out there. Even though less than a third of the people who were eligible to vote did exercise their right to vote, the American voter was becoming more sophisticated. They wanted to be wooed and to have all of the facts laid before them so they could make an informed decision. No longer did women vote for the best looking man, but for the man who would represent their lives, their families, and their dreams.

The second attempt on Juan's life came from an unexpected source. Juan was visiting the beautiful city of Seattle in support of the congressional delegation in that state as well as his own group. Seattle, the Emerald City, was built on seven hills and offered quite a challenge for drivers who were going from one side of the city to the other. Juan had just visited Harborview Medical Center, one of the nations best trauma centers, and then was headed downtown to the Pike Place Market for a rally. As his limo started on the Denny Hill retrograde, the brakes suddenly failed, and the car began to accelerate at an alarming rate. The driver started to push on his horn to warn other drivers that he could not stop his vehicle. Fortunately, the limo was equipped with red lights, which were switched on hoping the other cars would see them and pull to the side as they would for any emergency. The car had barreled through a couple of stop lights that had turned red, when the driver executed a skillful "U" turn reversing the car's direction and pointed it back up the hill. The car could not maintain its momentum and finally came to rest at the side of the street. The driver applied the manual brake which held the limo in place. A replacement car was summoned and Juan was whisked out of town.

It was discovered that one of the mechanics who provided maintenance for the cars was a subversive, totally opposed to Juan and the Democratic Party. Although he had undergone a background check on his loyalty by the FBI, there was no way any agency was going to get inside his head. He had neatly sliced through the brake fluid line just enough for the line to rupture after a few miles. The fluid had leaked out just before the downhill run, and had it not been for the dexterity of the driver, a fatality might have occurred. The car was later inspected and the severed brake fluid line was detected. The mechanic was arrested and charged with attempted murder.

CHAPTER SEVENTY-TWO

The campaign was moving along to its conclusion, and Juan wondered if it would ever come to an end. Even though he was fully immersed, he was beginning to tire. One city or town seemed just like the last. He had repeated his speech so many times, he could now do it from memory without a script. He had to struggle to make the same speech sounding new and wholesome. He didn't want to make a mistake and misquote his intent. Reporters were waiting in the bushes for something like this to happen and then to play the miscue to the hilt in the media. The campaign, like the others Juan had been involved in started to turn ugly. Claims about Juan's character and counterclaims to blunt the rhetoric, began to come forward. The spin doctors were working overtime to distort the truth or to make the lies seem plausible. The two candidates were like Knights of the Roundtable who were the tops of their breed in jousting with each other. Then November rolled around, the campaigning ceased and the people went to the polls.

Again, Juan had secured a hotel in California to either celebrate his victory or to thank his staff in defeat. This time, no results were announced in the election until all of the polls had been closed. Congress, in its wisdom, had passed a law which stabilized this, making sure each candidate had an equal chance. Juan was losing in the popular vote, but was capturing the electoral votes from the larger states like New York, Illinois, Michigan, and Florida. It looked like history was again repeating itself when Juan lost the total vote, but was elected by the Electoral College when all of the electoral votes from California were given to him. It was reminiscent of the Harry S. Truman vs. Thomas Dewey race when Truman held up a copy of the New York Times newspaper which displayed the headline "Dewey Wins", a premature declaration after the electoral votes were counted, and Truman was the new President.

All of Juan's hopes had come to fruition. This Mexican kid from the trash dumps of Mexico City had been elevated to the highest level imaginable. Like pro athletes who had risen from the ghettos of the inner city to become members of the various halls of fame, Juan had beaten the odds. He kept saying to himself, "Only in America."

Juan's next daunting task was to put together an administration, knowing it would take Senate confirmation of each cabinet member. The consultants Juan had hired for his transition team were well worth their money. The Vice President elected along with Juan had a strong background in government, education, an national security. He was esteemed in the Congress, and favored by the nation as a person who could assume the Presidency in the event Juan was removed from office for some reason.

In addition to the cabinet appointees, Juan was given the challenge to nominate two members to the United State Supreme Court. This was going to be a greater challenge than the cabinet. Juan wanted diversity in his cabinet. He wanted a mix of cultural, ethnic, gender, and racial factions that would solidify his promise to represent all of the citizens. Eventually the mix was achieved and forwarded on to the Senate for confirmation. Juan chose two women to head the Departments of Education and Energy. A Latino became Labor Secretary, and two Afro-Americans headed up Commerce and Transportation. A Jew from Wall Street was named for Treasury, and a retired four star general for Defense. And so the list went on until all bases were covered. Confirmation came easily for most of those nominated. Juan and his staff had done their homework well, but a couple of the chosen were not confirmed, and suitable replacements were found. The replacements in the Supreme Court would take more thought, but would wait until after Juan had been sworn into office.

CHAPTER SEVENTY-THREE

It was a cold and blustery day in Washington D.C. when Juan was to be inaugurated. Massive bleachers had been erected in front of the Congress to seat the spectators, and a platform with American flags was positioned on the steps leading up to the building. The sun came out, but the wind chill factor dropped the temperature to near freezing. Juan didn't care, he would have stood there naked. When announced, Juan rose with Mary and the children and faced the Chief Justice of the Supreme Court. Juan raised his right hand and placed his left on a copy of the Bible, the same one used when he was elected Governor. The Bible was written in Spanish, but no one could tell from the distance. The Chief Justice said, "Repeat after me, I (state your name) as President of the United States do hereby......."

Juan barely remembered taking the oath of the office or the inauguration speech he rendered. His lips were so cold, he could hardly speak. When his warm breath escaped from his mouth, he felt as if his brittle teeth were going to fracture, but he was up to the task. He started slowly, but soon rose to a crescendo as he made promise after promise. His speech was so stirring, the crowd barely noticed the cold. When the speech was over, the parade down Pennsylvania Avenue began. Juan and Mary rode in an open topped car with protective, bulletproof glass on all sides. Near the end of the street as the White House was coming into view, Juan and Mary had the car stopped, and hand in hand, they walked the rest of the way waving at the crowd. They were a handsome couple, just what was needed in these times of economic downturn and distrust of the Federal Government. It was a rebirth of JFK and his lovely wife back in the 1960's. The afternoon was spent preparing for the inaugural balls to be held through the D.C. area. It was planned for the new President to attend each one, so a short nap was in order.

Juan and Mary were escorted by the secret service from hotel to hotel, each decorated in the grandest style. The food was prepared by Washington D.C.'s best chefs and the champagne flowed like water. All of the men were decked out in the latest tuxedo cuts, and the women in the trendiest designer gowns. Orchestras played dance music, and couples whirled about the floor as if in a world class dance contest. The music would stop and the crowd would applaud when Juan and Mary entered each ball. The couple was surrounded as though they were royalty. At one point, Juan almost felt like the walls were caving in on him, but by the fourth or fifth gala, he had gotten used to the crush of the crowd.

At last, the evening was over. Juan had never felt so exhausted in his life, but he knew he must stay in excellent shape to put up with the state dinners and other functions the president was expected to attend. He didn't remember going to sleep, but it seemed like only minutes when the alarm went off. He arose without waking Mary and met his secret service agents who took him to the White House for his early morning briefing by his Chief of National Security. This was a ritual that every president had to endure, the rattling of the intelligence world at six o'clock in the morning. Juan wondered to himself, doesn't the CIA and the NSA have anything else to do but stay awake all night and try and predict what all of the other nations in the world were up to. After reading several of these briefing reports, Juan closed his eyes and envisioned a bearded man in a white robe strolling the streets with a sign which stated simply, "The end of the world is near." This vision brought a smile to his face, and he went on with the job.

Juan's first cabinet meeting was similar to the ones he had as Governor of California. He set the ground rules early and wanted each Secretary to be forthright and honest in their evaluations and to be brief, so that the time of the others was not wasted. His cabinet liked this approach, and Juan held true to his word. Juan's days were filled with activity, from greeting foreign dignitaries, to posing for pictures with championship teams. Juan reveled in his glory. He was just entering his first one hundred days, another honeymoon, when he could set the tenure of his administration and get away with it. His popularity rose in the polls and he received a near perfect rating from the people. His policies began to address the problems of the nation, and Congress was willing to go along with most of the legislation he had proposed. His first hurdle came when he was asked to nominate a new member of the Supreme Court.

Supreme Court nominees normally came from the ranks of the appellate courts across the country. These judges generally, were the best versed in the law from all of its aspects, but Juan broke from tradition and nominated a friend from his law firm in California. It smelled of political favor, and congress wanted nothing to do with it. During the hearings preceding the confirmation, the opposing party was brutal in its questioning. Certain aspects of the qualification of the nominee came to the fore which did not reflect well on the choice Juan had made. It became abundantly apparent the candidate was not aware of many aspects of the law, and his leanings were not in sync with the majority of congress. The Supreme Court of the United States had been a liberal court, but was moving more toward the center. This nominee was to the far right, and such a radical change could not be tolerated. The individual was not recommended for the position, and Juan withdrew the nomination.

Juan's second try was to nominate a woman from the ninth circuit appellate court in San Francisco. He wanted to stay in the State of California, and chose this female whom he should have chosen in the first place. She was a graduate of a good Law School. She had gone through the ranks as a defense attorney, a prosecuting attorney, a superior court judge, and an appeals jurist. She looked like Sister Theresa, wearing a subdued black pants suit with a white blouse, her hair done up in a bun in the back and wearing horn rimmed glasses. She was the epitome of what a Supreme Court Justice should look like. She was dignified, yet motherly at the same time. She went through the confirmation process with ease, and joined her fellow justice as the second woman on the court. Juan was learning.

Juan's successes with Congress outweighed his failures, but his second hurdle came when he proposed a fair trade agreement with Mexico. Congress almost blew the lid off itself. Here was a Mexican native who was favoring his former country. This would mean more unemployment to American workers, higher taxes, and cheap labor. In addition the balance of trade payments would shift to the Mexican side, and the trade deficient would increase. The possibilities of a horrible recession loomed ahead if such a policy was implemented. Congressional leaders on both sides of the aisle sent messages to Juan counseling him not to go forward with this idea. Juan decided he was going to bull up his neck and not listen to Congress. Anyway, who were they to tell him what to do. He knew better than they did what was good for the country. Juan immediately put his staff to work to determine, legally, what Juan could do without the consent of Congress. Juan knew there were mechanisms available to the President to allow him a certain amount of latitude.

His staff found a way. There were provisions where the President could consummate certain treaties using his own power and authority. He blindsided Congress when his declaration was announced. Juan was immediately challenged in court by the unions. It looked as though it were going to be a brutal and bloody fight, but Juan knew he had unlimited resources. Although the unions had money, they could not match him. Rallies were held at the union halls, ads were taken out in the nation's newspapers and on television, and hate mail started to arrive at the White House in bundles. Juan was losing the support of the organizations that got him elected, but he was not going to bend or break. His mind was made up.

More fuel was added to the fire when Juan appointed his wife Mary to head up a commission to reform the nation's health care system. Juan decided every American should have equal access to hospitals and physicians. He surmised there were too many individuals who couldn't pay for their primary care, and were using the hospital emergency rooms instead of going to the doctor's offices. In part, Juan was proposing a socialistic system similar to that practiced in Canada. One of the many think tanks in Washington D.C. did an analysis of the proposal, and determined major health care agencies and hospital corporations would reap huge profits, as would the insurance industries.

Mary put together this blue ribbon panel whose report took over a year to finalize and publish. Eighty percent of the recommendations were immediately discounted by Congress as being unworkable. Lobbyists were having a field day on both sides of the issue. Confusion reigned. In the meantime, physicians, clinics, and allied health organizations were no longer taking poverty clients, citing the low reimbursement rates being imposed, and the increase in administrative costs just to prepare the paperwork to get paid. The business of medicine was becoming a nightmare. Physicians, in order to make a living had to see more patients and the quality of care was suffering. Expensive emergency room visits continued to escalate.

Knowing there were no price controls on drugs, the pharmaceutical companies began raising their prices to distributors at a rate three times the rate of inflation. Even though the new concept of generic drugs had come about, the overall costs went up, pricing those seniors on fixed incomes out of obtaining the medicine they needed. This resulted in more illness in the senior sector, and an increase in the workload at the hospitals. The plan was a disaster, but again Juan was again, not bending. He knew it would work, just give it a little time and the nation would see. People began to stream across the Canadian and Mexican borders where pharmaceuticals were cheaper. These two countries did not have agreements with the pharmaceutical companies, and had placed caps on what the companies could charge. Money was leaking out of America like a sieve.

Behind the scenes, Mary was making the staff at the White House crazy. She had adopted some of Juan's regal characteristics and was ordering the help around like serfs. Nothing they did pleased her. She fired the kitchen chef who had created meals for four presidents, and was spending huge amounts of money to decorate several of the rooms in the residence. She had become very adept at putting on a false front for the guests at state dinners, but when the guests had gone, she spent time criticizing the preparations. She was becoming impossible to live with. The heads of the service departments taking care of the daily operation of the White House complained to the Chief of Staff, but the words fell on deaf ears. He merely told them to listen and then do as they were told. It was his policy if they continued to complain, then they should look of employment elsewhere. Many of the staff quit, but many had seniority and were still just a few years shy of retirement, so they gritted their teeth and bore it.

Juan's presidency was only two years old, and already his popularity had gone from near perfect to a sixty percent approval rating. Juan justified this as being higher than many other presidents, and laughed it off. Juan continued to put forth his directives as if they were edicts to the peasants. The political cartoonists were having a field day caricaturizing him as a king. Juan scoffed at the notion, but deep inside he felt what American really needed was a king. Was Juan becoming bi-polar? His closest friends started to see the change in his personality, and when they were invited to lunch mentioned it to him. Rarely were they invited back. Juan was becoming one of the most hated individuals inside the beltway. He didn't care, he was untouchable.

Juan continued to make matters worse. He moved to eliminate the Headstart Program which had functioned well for a couple of decades. Juan wanted the money being spent to be channeled into educating the Hispanic population in English as a Second Language or ESL. He rationalized that if this segment of America was growing by leaps and bounds, then they should be given the opportunity to learn the official language so they could adjust to living north of the border. Juan was not aware that the predominate feeling of the immigrant was that they came to this country expecting an entitlement, and the United States was obligated to provide them with everything they needed from the time they crossed the border. They didn't feel they needed to assimilate into the environment like immigrants had in the past. Unfortunately Juan agreed with them. Rumblings were starting to be felt in the Asian groups, along with the Russians. They were demanding the same approach. The states were starting to expend precious dollars in providing interpreters, printing informational booklets in dozens of foreign languages, and hiring teachers who were fluent in more than one language. These immigrants didn't seem to want to do anything for themselves. Instead, they expected to have everything handed to them. Why should they be responsible for themselves when the richest country in the world should be obligated to them.

Juan wanted to eliminate the Department of Education as being unnecessary. He felt it was the responsibility of the states to fully fund education. He felt national standards no longer applied, since each region was unique unto itself. The National Education Association (NEA) rose up in arms, denouncing this statement as catastrophic. At the national NEA meeting in Atlanta, Georgia, the NEA passed a resolution condemning the President for narrow mindedness. They wanted him removed from office.

CHAPTER SEVENTY-FOUR

As Juan was nearing the end of his first term, his advisors gathered to advise him on what steps needed to be taken in order for him to be re-elected. Juan started to make a one hundred and eighty degree turn in his administration. Suddenly, he was himself again. He reversed some of his directives, was more open to suggestion, and began to work closely with the Congress on matters he had been in opposition with before. The economy started to turn around, his popularity started to rebound, and America drew a sigh of relief. Maybe Juan was just going through a phase for some reason. This phenomenon was bantered around the talk show circuit. No one could explain it, but the rallying cry was "let us give Juan the benefit of the doubt". He had created more good than bad. Mary eased up and the White House staff was most grateful. The old adage, "Time heals everything" was certainly true in this case. When it became time to run for re-election, most of the animosity toward Juan had been put aside. Fortunately, the opposition for the presidency was weak at best, so Juan had little pressure from either party. Juan waged a good campaign, but far less intensive than the first one. Juan won a second term.

Behind Juan's back, the powerful senators were meeting to consider checks and balances of a second term. What if Juan were to revert back to his former self, and the nation once again was going to be put in peril? The Senators smiled to Juan's face, but Juan didn't see the daggers hidden in the togas of the Senate, like the ones used in the demise of Caesar. Several bills were introduced to limit the powers of the President. When these bills were passed in both houses by an overwhelming majority, Juan promptly vetoed them, knowing the Congress didn't have the requisite two thirds majority to override his veto. With the congressional defeat, Juan began to reassert himself, and his confidence and ego once again started to increase. Juan was smart enough to know what his mistake had been in the past, so this round, he courted the powers to get what he wanted. He even went so far as to contact his friends in the underworld to bring pressure on the pols.

Strange things started to happen. News items were leaked to the press about some of the skeletons in the closets of members of congress. More embarrassment. Threats were being made behind the scenes forcing congressional members to support unpopular bills and an unpopular President. Kyle Smith called Juan one day to accuse him of being the inspiration for this blackmail just as he had in causing the Constitutional Amendment that allowed Juan to become President. Juan claimed absolute innocence. He swore he knew zilch about any schemes, while smiling throughout the entire conversation. Oh course Juan knew about them, he had directed the effort, but he wasn't going to tell Kyle that. Juan was wily, many people comparing him to a huckster, but Juan didn't care, he still ruled the roost, and so things went. Juan was continuing to think ahead. He knew a constitutional amendment had been passed to limit the presidential term of office to two terms. This was done after the administration of Franklin Delano Roosevelt. Roosevelt was probably the closest to being king as any President had ever come. Roosevelt was in his third term when he died and probably would have been elected to a fourth term if he had of lived. Some very astute Senators viewed this with alarm, trying to imagine how many terms FDR would have filled. People were starting to refer to FDR in terms befitting a monarchy, and the Senate would have nothing to do with this possibility. Juan thought to himself, if I can get the Constitution amended to allow me to become President, then I should be able to amend the Constitution to repeal the restrictive amendment and I shall rule as long as I want. No one knew it yet, but Juan was developing a megalomaniac's personality. Juan wasn't even aware of it himself, but signs were starting to show up in his behavior. Those around him either didn't see the warning signs, or chose to ignore them.

Juan decided he needed to get out of town for a spell, so he scheduled a tour of the European countries, trying to foster good will among our allies. He started in France, which was not a good place to start. The Communist Party had won a majority of the French parliament, and Juan was quoted as saying he never did like the color red. The Prime Minister of France gave him a cold reception, affording him the courtesy he deserved as President of the United States, but barely tolerating it. Juan also criticized the French Government for not providing its fair share of troops to support the NATO mission in case the Warsaw Pact Nations came across the Fulda Gap and attacked central Europe. Juan, in no uncertain terms, accused France of not being a fair trade partner, and even threatened higher tariffs for French wines and perfumes. The French rioted during Juan's visit and the Prime Minister couldn't get him out of the country fast enough. The scenario played the same in Germany, Spain, Austria, Switzerland, and Portugal. Juan was bent on ruffling as many feathers as he could. Congress back home couldn't understand why Juan was doing this, and they attempted to soothe the confrontation with diplomatic messages sent thru back channels to the ambassadors to all of these countries. The bleeding was starting to show, and Congress wanted to stem the loss of blood the best that it could.

The spiral continued when Juan visited the Central American countries. He threatened to send in troops if these countries didn't stop the production, manufacturing and distribution of illegal drugs from their region. The cartels laughed at the possibility. Let the gringo come on down they said, and we will give them a fight bigger than Vietnam, one they will lose just like they did then.

Secretly behind Juan's back, the Speaker of the House, the House Majority Leader, the Senate Majority leader and both minority leaders had joined forces with the White House Chief of Staff and the White House counsel, to see what could be done before this President could destroy the country. They decided to hold a meeting in the Oval Office when Juan returned to confront him with the facts and see if they could indeed change the direction in which he was spinning out of control. When Juan was back in Washington D.C., Juan's Chief of Staff set up the meeting to nip this problem in the bud.

The meeting was held shortly after the intelligence briefing, and the President had done some housecleaning chores and signed or vetoed some bills. As each participant entered the Oval Office, the President welcomed them as old friends, shaking their hands with vigor and speaking words of affection for the jobs they were doing. A sideboard had been set up on one side of the office, containing coffee, tea, soft drinks, bagels, and other pastries. The President encouraged everyone to enjoy themselves by partaking in the goodies that were being offered. They took advantage of the refreshments, but in moderation. They weren't there to gorge themselves on food and drink, but to bring to a head an infection that was seething just below the surface. The group had to confront Juan with the facts and see how he reacted.

When the initial eating and greeting was over, the assembled sat in the various chairs and on the couches surrounding the President's desk. When everyone was seated, the Present opened the proceeding with this.

"Well, my friends, what brings this august body before me in such a somber mood."

The members of the group wasted no time in raising the issues, and asking the President to explain his policies and behavior over the past few months. Juan sat at his desk absorbing the rhetoric thrown toward him, trying to keep his cool, but reviling every speaker as they reiterated their concerns. Juan listened for about fifteen minutes, then held up his hand to stop the conversation, and said, "Who do you people think you are to tell me what I am doing is wrong. How ungrateful of you to attack me now when I was the one who helped most of you get elected or appointed to the jobs you now hold. You are a most ungrateful bunch of bastards." Juan continued to ramble on almost incoherently, not letting the audience get a word in edgewise. Finally Juan stopped and glared at the individuals before him. His eyes had grown large, accentuating the brown deepness of them, and he appeared to have vacated the known world. Spittle started to seep from the corner of his mouth. Some of those present felt he was suffering a stroke or a heart attack. Juan could not gather his thoughts or speak intelligently. The White House Physician was summoned, and when he arrived, the scene in the Oval Office was utter chaos. The physician opened his little black bag, withdrew a syringe and a vial of mild tranquilizer and injected the serum into Juan's arm.

Immediately Juan stopped his ranting and slumped in his chair. The doctor made an initial assessment that Juan had just suffered a mental relapse. The meeting was closed, each person exiting with the mandate to hold what went on here inviolate. Those assembled were in a state of shock themselves. Never had they witnessed such an ordeal involving the deterioration of a human being. When the room was cleared, The Chief of Staff remained with the doctor until it was determined that Juan was stabilized and could be moved safely to the Presidential quarters. Two secret service agents were summoned to escort the President upstairs to his bedroom. Juan could not stand, so each agent placed his arms over their shoulders and lifted him off the ground like an injured professional football player who had wrenched a knee, and couldn't exit the field on his own power.

The agents undressed the President, put on his pajamas and placed him in bed. It was still early in the afternoon, so someone drew the drapes to darken the room and Juan was left alone to sleep until the medication wore off and he could be re-evaluated by a psychiatrist. Those witnessing the occurrence kept their mouths shut. The last thing they wanted was to leak any of this to the press. American didn't need another black eye to decrease its influence in the world. They went back to their offices to await the outcome of the physical and mental evaluation that was coming up shortly.

The Chief of Psychiatry from Walter Reed Army Medical Center came to the President's quarters to examine Juan. The examination took over two hours, after which, the psychiatrist gave Juan an injection, a mild tranquilizer to relax his tense muscles and put him back to sleep. The doctor gathered Mary, The Chief of Staff, the Vice President and the Speaker of the House in the living room and informed them that the President had just suffered a bout of mental exhaustion, probably due to the tremendous pressure he had been under lately. His diagnosis was borne out by the symptoms and the prognosis was good looking at Juan's age and his stamina. He recommended quiet solitude and daily sessions with a psycho-therapist for the next six weeks. The psychiatrist suggested that Juan be moved to Camp David, the Presidential Retreat in the mountains. This would get him away from the pressures of his position, and into an atmosphere of solitude more conducive to the healing process.

Plans were made immediately to move the President and to create a story that the President was going to Camp David to meet with his upper echelon staff to formulate the administration's legislative agenda for the coming session, and to allow the President some time to rest up after the arduous schedule that he had been keeping. All of the people who knew of the ailment were sworn to secrecy, the Vice President promising that if any of this leaked out, he would personally see that the individual responsible for it would be drawn and quartered.

Under the cloak of darkness, the President was placed in an unmarked car and driven the miles to the retreat. Over the next six weeks, Juan was given a well orchestrated regimen of diet, exercise, sleep, and psychotherapy. The turnaround of his condition was remarkable. The old Juan was reemerging, sharp as a tack, and anxious to get back to the duties he was missing. Juan was not an easy patient to deal with, but Juan did recognize the peril he had been in, and he submitted to the treatment. Camp David was a beautiful place set among thousands of trees with winding paths through the forest. The weather was balmy, and the sun shone every day. Juan was lucky, his absence was kept low key, and no suspicion arose. Mary spent very little time at Camp David, but returned to the White House to conduct her tours and to give the appearance that everything was just fine with the President. Juan had dodged another bullet.

CHAPTER SEVENTY-FIVE

Juan returned to Washington D.C. in fine fettle. He had been cautioned not to work so hard, get more sleep, and delegate more authority to his cabinet. These things were not in Juan's nature, and he found them very difficult to do, but with the urging of the Vice President and a therapist who had been brought into the Oval Office undercover, Juan went along with the suggestions. Things were moving along smoothly, but little did Juan know what damage had been done by the exhaustion. The chemistry in his brain had been rearranged, and the potential for another episode with even more serious outcomes was awaiting in the wings of his gray matter. This worried the therapist who kept close watch for any outward signs which might indicate a relapse of any kind. Subtle changes are very difficult to detect, so the therapist expended tremendous energy standing on guard. He asked Mary and the others to also be on the alert, and to let him know if anything should show up out of the ordinary.

Juan suppressed his ego, trying to lock it away in the depths of his cortex. He still had too many things to accomplish; but just months down the road, his mania returned with a vengeance. He became aloof with Congress, refusing to see the minority leaders and the Speaker of the House. He directed anything coming to him must go through the Oval Office staff. Juan curtailed his public appearances and became a recluse in his own world. He cancelled trips to foreign countries, sending instead lower ranking cabinet members, an insult to the leaders of the snubbed nations.

Juan began to produce Presidential directives that flew in the face of orderly operations of the country. He knew he only had a few years as President which was not enough time for him to reach his goals. Internally, he rationalized the need to become a monarch. He knew what was best for the country, and the country could only obtain the pinnacles of dominance in the world if he, Juan Cardova had that power. He again harkened back to the effort he had put forth to get the Constitution amended to allow him to become President. He must now use the same mechanisms to get the Constitution changed to allow him unlimited terms in office.

The thought also crossed his mind on how to use the armed forces to insure this internal coup. Castro became his guru. If Castro could wrest control of a country through this medium, why couldn't he. Juan was becoming more and more obsessed with the idea. He tried harder and harder to keep the frustration under control, but his mind was just too powerful an influence. Juan started to meet individually with members of Congress. He was seeking their support in his efforts. He had carefully sculpted his arguments, to try and convince these members to embrace these concepts. When the congressmen hesitated, Juan gave them veiled threats, insinuating if they let it be known what the discussion had been about, he would search into their private lives and would ruin each and every one of them. During one such session, Juan became so incensed and angry, he leaped from behind his desk, grabbed a Senator by the front of his coat, and screamed into his ears. Juan called for security and told the agent to have this man arrested. The Senator and the agent stood there in utter disbelief. The Senator freed himself from Juan's grasp, and the agent restrained Juan, wrestling him to a couch where the agent sat on him while calling for additional help. It took three secret service agents to subdue Juan and to summon the President's private physician. Again Juan was sedated.

The decision this time was to move Juan to the psychiatric ward at the medical center. Juan was put into a private room away from the general population. For the first few days, Juan was heavily sedated, but the doctors began to wean him off the medication, and slowly brought him back to consciousness. Juan was in a state of not knowing where he was. He attempted to raise his arms, but found them restricted to the metal bed he was in. Juan was very uncomfortable. They had inserted a catheter into his bladder to drain off the urine, and were feeding him through an IV tube. He suddenly realized he wasn't right, and summoned all of his efforts to regain his former state.

His first few words were slurred, but as he became more and more awake, the words started to make sense. The attending nurse quieted him and called for the psychiatric resident. This fresh faced young doctor, looking as if he were barely out of high school leaned over Juan, checked his heartbeat, and listened to his chest. He asked Juan to be calm, and as soon as he was through examining Juan, they would have a little chat. Juan spoke slowly, but made sense. It appeared he was over the hump, and almost sane. The doctor explained the situation, and asked Juan if he understood the circumstances, to which Juan replied in the affirmative. The doctor asked the nurse to remove the restraints, but to watch Juan carefully, and if he demonstrated any signs of remission, the restraints were to be put back on immediately. The nurse brought forth a basin of warm water, and a soft towel. She wiped Juan's forehead and face, then rolled up the sleeves on his hospital gown and washed down his arms. The warm water bath was the most pleasant experience Juan had had for quite a long time. He closed his eyes, dreamed of a soft breeze across a tropical island and fell asleep. When he awoke for the second time, it was again with a start, but this time realized where he was and what was going on. Restorative treatment was begun, and Juan responded well to it. The IV tubes were withdrawn and Juan was allowed to have whole food. The catheters were also taken out much to Juan's relief. From time to time, Juan would feel pangs of anxiety, but this would be subdued with an injection of lorazepam, an anti-anxiety drug. In discussing the case, the panel of physicians in the mental ward estimated Juan would have to remain in the hospital for a minimum of three months to be evaluated further. In the meantime, the Vice President was running the country, and doing a reputable job.

Rumors were flying around the countryside like hornets attacking an invader. The newspapers and television stations only reported what they were told, which wasn't much. Lacking a great deal of information, speculation took over. At first the President was dead, and the people were being kept in the dark. Then came rumors of the President's breakdown and mental condition. He was described as having everything from a mild case of depression to a complete loss of mental function. The tabloids did an even worse job of stirring up the nation. The Ship of State was listing to one side without a Captain at the helm. The man and woman in the street, as well as the Governors of the States were demanding something be done about the course the nation was taking. The stock market was falling, and crime and costs were rising. The majority party in Congress was having a hard time getting legislation through, seemingly out of rhythm with the administration. Kyle Smith decided enough was enough. He called together the Vice President, the Chief of Staff, selected Cabinet members, and the leaders to Congress to discuss the matter at hand.

The meeting took place in the situation room, deep in the bowels of the White House, where a President would gather his staff when a crisis had arisen. As each invitee took a seat around the large oval table, the air in the room suddenly seemed to be devoid of oxygen. The men loosened their ties and took of their jackets. The women likewise, made themselves more comfortable. The air conditioning was turned up a notch, and the climate inside the room became tolerable.

The Vice President called the group to order. "Ladies and gentlemen we have been thrust into a terrible situation which can no longer be tolerated. To the best of my knowledge, the President is no long capable of conducting the business of state. I have been informed his prognosis is guarded, and the medical staff aren't sure just how long President Cardova will have to be in confinement. I asked you all to come here today to help me go through all of the options available to us. I also asked an expert on Constitutional Law from Georgetown University School of Law to be with us and to give us guidance on interpreting the meaning the Founding Fathers put into this document. As I see it, we have three courses of action. We can ask the President to resign, which I am sure he will not do. Or, we can put up with him until his term has expired, knowing he cannot be reelected, or we can recall him and hold another general election to select a new President."

Before the Vice President could go on, a shout came from the end of the table. "Or we could hire someone to shoot him, it's been done before."

"I'll disregard that comment, even though the thought had crossed my mind as well. I don't think any of us want to be an accessory to murder. Let's all take just a few minutes to refill our coffee cups and think about these options, or perhaps come up with a fourth of fifth."

Some members of the group left the table to indeed refresh their coffee, or to get something else to drink, or to go to the bathroom before the session got too intense. When all of the housekeeping chores were over with, and everyone was re-seated, the Veep continued. "As I said before, option one is not viable. Juan Cardova has spent too much of his life getting to the realization his greatest desires. In fact, many of you know he is trying to again amend the Constitution to allow him unlimited terms in office, virtually making himself a monarch. No, we cannot tolerate such a move. The second option is likewise very unreliable. This is the second episode of a mental breakdown. Even if he comes through this in fine shape, who knows how many more there will be. Who knows what policies and directives he will dream up to further his goals. Then again, he might just get back to normal, to the same person he was when we elected him to office the first time, but are we willing to take that risk? I say we are not. Which leaves the third option, to recall him as President. Now let's hear from our legal consultant who can advise us on what a recall would entail."

The distinguished personage from the School of Law stood. He was a Dean Emeritus, well known in the world of Constitutional Law, and revered as a scholar among his peers and colleagues. The professor and Dean of Law stood, straightened his bowtie, and began his dialogue. The professor was dressed in a brown tweed jacket, matching brown slacks, and a button down white shirt contrasting with his tie. His hair was silver like a shaman from an Indian tribe, and he carried a presence about his ruddy complexion. He had a deep bass voice, strong and full of conviction. He very carefully and meticulously went over that section of the Constitution containing the essence of the discussion being held. He outlined in great detail all of the reasons for which a President could be recalled, and the process such an action would take. From time to time, a hand would be lifted to have a point clarified, or to ask a related question. The time was slipping away. Already it was late afternoon and getting on toward evening. The Vice President asked the group of they wanted to recess or continue on. The majority opted to keep going until the issue was settled.

The Vice President directed the situation room staff to make preparations to have meals provided for the group, hoping everything would be nailed down before breakfast. When the professor was finished, time was allowed for the members to mull over what had been said. They were also asked to be thinking about a fourth or fifth option. After some time of deliberation, a Congresswoman asked for the floor.

She was an old timer, having served in the House of Representative for over twenty- five years. She too was a highly respected individual among her peer and the group listened, giving her all the dignity she deserved. She took a deep breath, let it out slowly, sighed, and began.

"I think there is a fourth option. As you all know, Juan Cardova came to the United States from Mexico and gained his citizenship through the naturalization mechanism. As it has been stated before, citizenship is an earned privilege, not a given right. I suggest we consider revoking his citizenship and exporting him back to his native country, bidding him good riddance forever."

A murmur started around the room like a wave going throughout a football stadium. Several people nodded their heads and others turned to the person next to them to share agreement or disagreement. Again, the law professor was called upon to comment on the feasibility of such a move.

"In my considered opinion, the option is viable. There are plenty of court cases setting precedents in this area. However, in this case, since we are talking about a sitting President, the lawsuit may take longer than we wish, and the President will remain in office to do his damage. I would not recommend this course of action, but I also think it should remain on the table."

There were no other options put forth from the group, so the Vice President suggested the group have dinner, go back to their offices, and reconvene in a week to talk about plans to settle this matter once and for all. The week slipped by quickly and the group came together again. It was decided the best way to dispose of the blight placed on the country was to recall the President, and hold a new open election. With the law professor's guidance, the wheels of justice were put into motion. Extra effort was expended to write up the recall brief, outlining the reasons for such a drastic action. Cited were Juan's mental instability, his recent outbursts, his mania, his blackmailing of Senators and Congressmen, and his inability to unite the country. The Vice President knew he was taking a chance by bringing up the blackmail scenario, but also felt the implications of such a disclosure could be spun in a positive way for the people accused, and used as a weapon against Juan.

A clandestine operation was devised to locate and destroy any evidence Juan had accumulated when he put the leverage on to have the Constitution changed. This meant Juan's office, his home, his safety deposit box, and any other conceivable place must be searched, the data confiscated, and forever removed from the face of the earth.

Kyle had a friend at the CIA who he knew owed him a favor, and would be just the man to come up with a workable solution. Kyle placed a call to his friend and agreed to meet him in Langley, Virginia, a much more secure place to meet. On a sunny and bright morning, Kyle entered his limo for the short ride to the CIA headquarters. His car was stopped at the security gate. Kyle showed the guard his credentials, and was permitted entry. The CIA was a nondescript series of buildings nestled in the woods of rural Virginia, surrounded by the tightest security protection known to man. Anyone attempting to penetrate this compound would more than meet their match. The car moved into the visitor's parking space, letting the Senator out and waiting for his return. Kyle left the car, walked a short distance along a well landscaped path of concrete blocks to the heavy glass doors which marked the entrance.

Just inside the door was a huge crest logo of the CIA and a reception counter. Kyle informed the guard at the counter he had an appointment with a certain official and again showed his credentials. The guard ran his finger down a preprinted sheet, picked up an intercom phone and placed a call. After returning the phone to its cradle, the guard invited Kyle to have a seat, an escort would be with him shortly. It wasn't long before a young, lithe woman exited the elevator and approached him. She was stunningly attractive, dressed in a form fitting designer suit, dark navy blue in color with a soft white blouse accented with a single strand of pearls. Her shoes were made of soft black leather and appeared to be made in a functional manner. She introduced herself, and led Kyle to the elevator from which she came. The door closed and the indicator went from the ground floor to floor seven, the crypt were most of the powerful intelligence officers were housed. The doors opened to a mass of activity. Throughout the room were many cubicles from which sounds of voices and machinery were springing. The young woman led Kyle around the cubicles to a corner office where Kyle found the person he wanted to speak to.

The office was well appointed with a magnificent view of the woods on the hillside behind the building. The scenery was serene, giving off a comforting effect, which helped to dispel the tension that must be felt in a structure used for this purpose. Kyle's old friend greeted him warmly, offered him a cup of coffee, filled a mug with the CIA logo on it with a rich smelling brew and sat down with Kyle at a small table in the center of the room. Kyle knew his friend would keep the conversation confidential, so he got right to the point. Kyle explained the situation, not leaving out any detail, the friend seeming to understand as the dialogue went along. At the end of the short speech, the friend told Kyle everything would be taken care of. This was an operation the CIA conducted on a daily basis around the world, so it would be a piece of cake. Kyle thanked his friend knowing the deal had been sealed, and there would be no reason to request a report of completion. The job would be done properly. On the way back to his office, Kyle felt a sense of relief that one possible backlash item had been avoided.

CHAPTER SEVENTY-SIX

The CIA had little trouble getting Shirl out of the oval office for a few hours. They had arranged for Shirl to attend a luncheon honoring her for her service to the President. The function was held under the auspices of the League of Woman Voters who annually recognized those women who gave above and beyond the call of duty. Shirl was thrilled when she was informed of her award, and gratefully accepted. While she was attending the reception, her office and the oval office were sterilized of any incriminating information. Likewise, the residence was searched, and nothing found.

Juan had a safety deposit box at a downtown Washington bank, but gaining admittance to it poised no problem. Some pictures and narrative were found, extracted, and destroyed. Unless Juan was smart enough to have made copies and put them in a safe place, there no longer seemed to be a problem of discovery. Things were moving along nicely for the recall group.

Juan was released from the mental ward of the hospital sooner than expected. Kyle went over the group's plan just to make sure everything was done and in place. It was exactly like Kyle wanted it to be, nothing had been left to chance unless something came up which had not been anticipated, but Kyle doubted they had overlooked anything. He called a couple of members of the group just to feel satisfied the list was complete.

As soon as Kyle heard Juan was back in the White House, he set up an appointment to see him. Juan didn't feel much like seeing anyone, but Kyle was an old friend, and he needed the comfort of an old friend at this particular time. Juan had confided everything in Mary, but needed to be reassured by someone outside of his family. Shirl announced Kyle's arrival and Kyle entered the Oval Office. As Juan approached his old friend, Kyle held up his hands staving Juan off and told Juan to have a seat, he was about to hear some news that would not make his day. Juan sat in his tall backed, red leather chair, confused at what Kyle was saying.

"Juan, I have come here today not as a good friend, but as a concerned citizen. Over the past few months, you have been able to have and survive two mental breakdowns, and to run this country into the ground. I, among many others, feel that you are no longer capable of handling the office and something has to be done immediately. I offer you two options, either resign and go into seclusion staying away from the Federal or State Governments, or The Congress of the United States will recall you. If you are recalled, and wish to challenge it, we will see that your citizenship is revoked and you are deported back to Mexico for the rest of your life, never having the ability to re-enter the United States again. Believe me Juan, we have more than enough evidence to meet the legal test a recall and subsequent actions would need. I will give you one minute to think about what I have just said, and then I want your answer."

"Kyle, you bastard, what did I ever do to you that makes you hate me so badly. Oh, I know I put a little heat on you when I needed the Constitution changed, but I never leaked any of that information on you or the others, so there was no harm, no foul. I will not accept either option. I will stay in The Office of President until my term and my ambitions have come to fruition. Neither you nor anyone else can stop me from making this country into an empire that will rival all other empires that have ever existed. And not only that, you have now forced me to divulge all of the background information I have so laboriously hoarded for these many years. You and your co-conspirators will rue the day you challenged me. I will ruin you and your families to the point that you will be glad to leave and go into exile yourself. Now get the hell out of my office, I have work to do."

"I am not leaving so quickly Juan. I want you to look for the damning information, and if you can find it, I will be more than happy to face the consequences. You see Juan, while you were in the hospital, we purged all of that data, so it can't be used against us in any form, and you will not have time to reconstitute any of it. You've been screwed Juan, and you just don't know it. So stop acting like a dictator and take your medicine, the country will be better off for it. This afternoon, a Congressional panel will be constituted to start the recall. All of the paperwork has been prepared and it is legally sound. I hope to have a Senate vote by the end of the week, and to personally have you escorted back to the trash dump where you belong. I thought we had a great relationship Juan, and I thought we would do great things together, but you have managed to defile everything that I hold sacred, and I want to see you burned at the stake."

With that, Kyle left the office. Juan screamed for Shirl. "I need the background information I entrusted you with on the Senators and Congressmen about their shady lives, and I need it now, so start bringing it in to me." Shirl left only to return in a few minutes.

"Juan, all of the information is gone. I don't know how they did it, but it's gone."

Juan screamed and pounded his fists on the top of his desk. "Not so fast Shirl, I thought maybe someone might try something like this, but I have an insurance policy. I made a duplicate set of everything and stashed it in a safety deposit box at the First Federal Bank. Get me a car, I need to retrieve the information immediately." The car was brought around to the side entrance, and quietly Juan was transported downtown. He had called ahead to the bank to alert them he was coming. He wanted to enter the bank undetected, and returned to his office in the same manner. He called in his security agent and they devised a plan to disguise the President and take him through a back door of the building. A standard, non-descript automobile with darkly tinted windows pulled up to the side of the White House and the trek to the bank began.

The movement went undetected. Juan was met at the rear entrance by the bank president and taken through a secret corridor to the safety deposit room. Only the president of the bank went with Juan into the chamber. The safety box was located, and both keys inserted into the keyholes. The box was withdrawn and placed on a nearby table situated for that purpose. Juan jerked the lid open, and stood there stunned. The box was empty, and the contents were all gone. Juan threw the box against the wall, jumping on it when it fell back to the floor. He stomped until his feet could take it no longer, then he went back to his office.

CHAPTER SEVENTY-SEVEN

His first ploy had failed, but Juan still had other options. Juan knew Wilson must have held a copy of everything that turned up, so Juan went through the same drill he had before to reach Wilson. This time, the contact was a repairman who had come to the Oval Office to fix Juan's phone. Juan gave him instructions on what was needed. Two days later, a letter arrived marked "For the President's Eyes Only". Inside was a single piece of white paper typed on any standard typewriter in the code Juan and Wilson had thought up in Vietnam. Juan hurriedly decoded the message, and his jaw sank when he read, "So sorry, didn't keep any copies." That was all there was on the sheet. Juan's head began to hurt. He felt like there was a little man inside with a hammer trying to beat his way out. His face reddened and he felt flushed and faint. He sat down, sensing his blood pressure was rising to a dangerous point. He didn't need a stroke or a heart attack right now, so he gathered himself and realized what he needed was a good stiff drink. He went to the sidebar hidden behind some paneling, and extracted a bottle of Scotch. He didn't use a glass or any ice, he just took a healthy swig straight from the bottle. It burned all the way down, but the desired effect took place. Juan was starting to calm down, trying to focus on what steps he was going to take next. Suddenly, Juan felt the mania starting to come back. He was losing his grip again, another disaster in the making. Juan summoned all of the courage he could muster to stave off the feeling. As part of his therapy, Juan had been taught how to put himself into a self meditating state, until the feelings had passed. The feelings did pass, and Juan again shuffled through his brain the options still left open to him. A light bulb came on, and Juan again signaled to Shirl he wanted her to contact General Duncan, the Chairman of the Joint Chiefs of Staff, and have him come to the Oval Office from the Pentagon.

As ordered, General Duncan arrived in about an hour, excusing himself with the explanation that some last minute details had to be attended to before he could show up. General Duncan was a tall man, his black hair streaked with the first strands of gray. He was in his Class A green uniform with four silver stars glistening across each shoulder, and so many rows of awards and decorations on his left chest, Juan could hardly count them all. General Duncan was a graduate of The Military Academy at West Point, and had seen service in the waning years of Vietnam. He had spent over thirty years in the Army, rising through the officer ranks, and getting his tickets punched along the way. He was a John Wayne sort of a guy, who walked with a swagger, holding his head up high, and taking no guff from anyone.

Juan looked the General straight in the eye and explained the plans to take over the country with a military coup. "I am your Commander and Chief, General Duncan, and I order you to carry out this plan."

"Sir, I have been a soldier who has never refused an order from any of my superiors. I have served my country faithfully, and have expected those subordinates to do the same, but in this case, I cannot obey you. What you are asking is not a lawful order, but a treasonous act of cowardice. I was warned by the Congress you were contemplating something like this, and I refuse to be a party to it. The country was molded by men who wanted a republic, and to be free of the bonds of a King who was unjust. I am not going to assist you in this lunacy, and turn the clock back to 1776. If I were doing my job right, I would have you arrested and thrown into a military prison until your case could be disposed of. You need to look elsewhere Sir, for help. I nor any of my staff will render you any aid."

General Duncan drew himself up to his fullest height, and gave Juan the snappiest salute he could muster. He turned on his heel and strode out of the office. The alcohol had rendered Juan incapable of saying a single word. Juan just stood there like Humpty Dumpty who had fallen off his wall. No one was going to put him back together again.

Juan sat at his desk, his head cradled in his sweaty hands. The notion of suicide flooded over him like a Tsunami. He was drowning, and couldn't seem to get enough air to breathe. He wondered if this was what a heart attack was really like. Juan had a pistol upstairs in a safe, but decided not to retrieve it just yet. He had many phone calls to make. It was now time to draw in all of the favors he had dished out over the past six years, but phone call after phone call was met with rude rebuttal. He was running out of time and options. His friends all seemed to have deserted him in his hour of need. He even thought about taking the pills from his prescription bottle to end it all, but knew that someone would discover his dilemma, rush him to the hospital and have his stomach pumped. This would give Kyle more ammunition for the recall, so Juan couldn't chance it. Juan resigned himself to his fate. He would not resign, but would wait for the drama to play itself into the final acts. He would fight Congress every inch of the way, but for this, he needed legal advice from his personal counsel.

Juan's choice for his private attorney was a middle aged man, slightly bald and rumpled. He would have reminded someone of Burl Ives, but the blue eyes hid the depth of his cunning and ability. His name was Phil Egbert. He had been a corporate lawyer for many years in Boston, but over the past decade, had moved to Washington D.C. to join a law firm representing large corporations doing business with the Federal Government. He was also a part time lobbyist to make a little extra money. He cultivated friendships in Congress and in the Executive Branch. He spent most of his spare time broadening his knowledge of Constitutional Law and immigration. He was a bachelor, so he had the time to devote to his passion, the legal field.

Juan had met him at a Governor's conference in Boston, and was immediately impressed with him. They kept in touch for years, and when Juan was elected President Phil was brought to the Oval Office immediately. Phil had served Juan well, keeping him out of trouble and up to date on what his executive powers were and how he should use them. Phil was wearing his usual mismatched jacket and pants, both a similar brown, but both with patterns. His shoes were black, but no one noticed. Juan asked Phil to join him on the white leather couch. After they were seated, Juan explained his situation and wanted Phil to advise him on what actions he could take to remain in power and to move his agenda ahead.

Phil wouldn't look directly at the President. He turned slightly sideways and stared out of the large bay windows that framed the rose garden and the beautifully landscaped grounds. "I'm sorry Mr. President, I can't help you. As badly as I would like to, it is just impossible for me. The leaders of Congress have the power to ruin me forever, and I just can't take that chance. I love the law and would be hard pressed to survive without it. In addition, I have researched the matter, and there is nothing you can do. Congress has all of the aces, and you can't bluff them. They are in the highest stakes poker game of their lives, and they hold all of the cards. My advice is to resign. There are many reasons for you to slip into the darkness and never be seen again. It would the most painless thing to do. If you resist, they will recall you, revoke your citizenship, and deport you to Mexico. I am not sure you could tolerate such a defaming of your character. I also wanted to let you know that I have decided to resign as your counsel." With that, Phil took a business type envelope from his inside jacket pocket and handed it to the President.

There was nothing Juan could say, another salvo had been fired, and the walls of Juan's castle were tumbling down steadily into the moat surrounding the estate.

CHAPTER SEVENTY-EIGHT

Kyle's intense preparations paid off. The Justice Department sent Marshals to the White house on the premise the President was a danger to himself and others, so he should be held under house restriction until his fate could be decided. The Senate subpoenaed the medical records from Walter Reed to substantiate the basis for the recall effort. The Senate was hastily called to session to vote on the recall. The Senate is comprised of one hundred Senators, and as Kyle polled each of them, he found an equal number were in favor of letting Juan continue his presidency until tight controls as there were Senators who favored his recall. Kyle knew if the vote were tied, the Vice President would be called in to cast the tie breaking vote, and probably would vote to retain the President. However, as fate would hat it, one of the pro-president senators had a heart attack in his office and died before the recall could come to a vote. There wasn't time for the Governor of the State of this Senator to name a successor, so that meant that a simple majority, fifty to forty-nine would determine the outcome. Being that Kyle was the Senate Majority Leader, he held the right to vote last.

The Senate was called to order. The members assembled, were read the recall petition, and the roll call vote started. The count vacillated between yea and nay. When the last Senator called had voted, the count was indeed tied, forty nine to forty nine. Kyle was now in a position to cast the most important vote of his life. He knew Juan no longer posed a threat to him, and the country needed to rid itself of this vermin, so Kyle slowly arose from his seat when his name was called and in a resounding vote voted yea. The deed was done. The President of the United States had been removed from office. Now to move on to the next step, to revoke Juan's citizenship, and export him back to Mexico. This proved to be a much harder task, but when everything was settled, Juan was no longer an American citizen. The Secret Service made arrangements to pack up Juan and his family and prepare them for a plane trip to Mexico City. The Mexican government had already been alerted to what was transpiring, and arrangements had been made for Juan and his family to have appropriate housing, and supportive services equal to his status.

Juan was livid, but there was little he could do now. He asked for permission to meet with his staff and bid them farewell. The request was granted. All of the staff of the White House met in the Grand Ballroom at a pre-arranged time. A small stage had been erected at one end, and as the crowd of former employees gathered, they found Juan, Mary, and the children seated on the stage. Juan rose, and a hush fell over the staff.

Juan came to the microphone, his eyes slightly moist. He had a large lump in his throat, and took a few seconds to clear it away. He looked out at the people who had been so loyal to him, and thanked them for their service. He told them he would be leaving the United States in the next few days, but offered nothing by way of explanation. Most of them already knew what had been said in the press, or had guessed as to what had happened. Although he was going to become merely a memory, they pressed forward, and when Juan concluded his remarks, they gave him a loud cheer. In some ways, Juan felt he had overcome the situation. He told them if any of them wanted to come to Mexico, he would love to have them work for him in his exile. This elicited a chuckle from the staff. Most of them had bigger fish to fry, and wanted to remain where they were. When Juan finished, he left the platform and joined the crowd. He received hugs, handshakes, and kind words. Some left without saying goodbye, they didn't want to be painted with the same brush. The staff dispersed, and Juan, Mary and the children returned to the upper floors of the White House.

The moving crew came to the residence and packed up the belongings of the Cardovas. For Juan, it was a sad time. He spent a few hours wondering around, gazing out the windows at the spectacular views afforded from this historical place. He reflected on his path to glory, and tried to remember what went wrong. All he wanted to do was to be the leader of these wonderful people. To carry forward the history of independence and courage they had demonstrated since the founding of Jamestown in 1607. He felt he embodied all of the wonderful characteristics the pioneers of the 1800's had shown. He was a true explorer, a Lewis and Clark expedition unto himself. He was an example of what an alien could achieve in this land of opportunity, so how could the people he loved so much turn against him and throw him out? He felt no remorse in what he had done, but he did resent those who had called him friend, and had stabbed him in the back. Et Tu Kyle.

Juan again closed his eyes, and tried to imagine if there was anything he could do now to stop the bleeding of his soul. He tried to stimulate every neuron in his brain to come up with an answer. He did not want to leave America. It was the land of promise and the only chance he had to reach the pinnacle of his goals. But then the reality of the situation came crashing down on his head, and his resolve crumbled. There was nothing he could do but to accept his demise and bow to the wishes of the Congress.

That night, Juan stayed awake most of the night, he knew in the morning the federal agents would escort him and his family to Andrews Air Force Base near Washington D.C., and fly them to Mexico. The next morning, Juan arose early, took his customary shower, dressed in a suit, shirt and tie, woke the rest of the family, and sat in the living room until everyone was ready. A knock come on the door, and Juan's faithful valet told him the escorts were here to take the family to the base. Juan thanked him, and said the family was ready to go.

Quietly and regally as possible, Juan shepherded his flock to the waiting limos. As the cars exited the East Gate, there were signs held high asking him not to go. Across the street however, there were signs displaying just the opposite. What trivial times these were. In his native country, opposing factions would not be pointing signs at each other, but rather guns. How stupid these Yankees were. They didn't seem to have the balls to stand up for what they thought was right. They wanted to stand behind a sign, and pretend they could influence history. Juan harkened back to the Vietnam War. He remembered all of the signs, and being spit upon by the protesters. Where were they now? Most of them were pillars of their communities, or had become the establishment, or movie stars without remorse. Signs didn't prove anything, only weapons did.

As the cars journeyed further and further from the seat of power, the crowds grew thinner and thinner. Finally, the caravan arrived at the security gate of the Andrew's Air Force Base, where a police cadre picked them up and took them to the tarmac adjacent to the base operations building. On the tarmac was a Boeing 747 with The United States Air Force Two painted on the side. They had used the Vice President's plane to fly them back to the south. What insolence, Juan thought. At least they could have afforded him the dignity of using Air Force One. The limo parked along side the massive aircraft, and the Cardovas disembarked. A staircase had been wheeled up to an open door on the fuselage of the plane, which the family mounted and were swallowed up by the enormity of the craft. Even though there was a small crowd at the fence of the base, Juan did not turn and wave to them.

Inside, the family situated themselves in the comfortable seats, the exterior door was closed, and the plane taxied to the runway. In minutes, the 747 was airborne and on its way to another chapter in the lives of these four individuals.

The attending crew tried to make the long flight as comfortable as possible, asking the family if there was anything that could be gotten for them. They all declined, none of them were hungry or thirsty right then. Juan and Mary didn't feel like talking, so Juan closed his eyes hoping to get in a short nap to help pass the time away. Mary picked through the many magazines on the coffee table, finally selecting one aimed at the female population. She leafed through the slick pages, not really noticing anything and skipping over most of the articles. She did stop at a gardening section, an area Mary had always been interested in. She wondered if their new home would have a garden, and if there would be time for her to raise some vegetables and flowers. Mary had come from a farming background, and had always had the smell of wet soil in her nostrils. As a child, she remembered running her hand through the newly tilled black loam and letting it sift through her fingers. It always amazed her to see the green sprouts of the hay, corn, potatoes, and grain start to poke their noses through the brown soil and into the bright sun. She yearned for the farm, but remembered some famous novelists who said you can't go home again.

Jose and Maria Elena sat by the window and just stared out. Maria found it hard to keep from crying. She had to leave all of her school classmates and friends behind, and was fearful of what it would take to make new ones. Although she and Jose were bilingual, she was concerned as to whether they were fluent enough to meet the challenge of being in a place where Spanish was the everyday tongue. She tried to start a conversation with Jose, but he had retreated into his own little world and was oblivious to her overtures. Finally the time since intake of the last food they had eaten had lengthened sufficiently. They felt small pangs of hunger, and asked the attendants if they could get something to eat and drink. The onboard flight crew brought them menus from which they could select any item they wanted. Each made their choice, the attendant writing each request down on a small notepad.

When the food was about ready to be brought from the plane's kitchen, they were asked to go to the dining room where a table, with a white linen tablecloth and white linen napkins had been placed on the table. The napkins bore the Seal of the Vice President of the United States as did each corner of the cloth. The silverware was the same as the silverware they had used in the White House, and the plates, cups, saucers, and salad bowls as well. It was like eating in their last home, only this time they were at 35,000 feet into the atmosphere.

It was a six course meal, each segment orchestrated with the preceding segment. It was delicious, and for the moment, the despair the family had been feeling earlier seemed to dissipate. They hadn't realize how hungry they really were. Since they had been flying in a westerly direction until they reached the State of Arizona, then turning south for the Capitol of Mexico, they had been gaining extra hours translating in a landing in Mexico City in the late afternoon. No arrangements had been made for them to sleep in the available beds, but each of them found a convenient couch or chair and dozed off, only to be awakened by the steward who informed them they were about to land.

The huge plane landed softly on the runway, then taxied to a section of the field reserved for private planes and visiting dignitaries. Awaiting the plane were three, long, sleek, black cars very similar to the ones used in Washington D.C. The aircraft came to a complete stop, a mobile staircase was rolled up the door on the fuselage, and the craft's door opened. Juan, Mary, Jose, and Maria Elena took their time as they descended the stairs, glancing around seeing no crowds, only a few security guards standing at the perimeter of the ten foot high cyclone fences. A driver got out of each car, invited Juan and Mary into one, and the children into the other. The third car was a decoy just in case there was any attempt on the lives of the occupants. The door of the aircraft was closed, the staircase wheeled away, the plane taxied to a long runway, and in moments was airborne back to the east. The Cardovas were now entering a new chapter in their existence.

CHAPTER SEVENTY-NINE

The house the Mexican government had provided for them was much more than they had expected. It was a single story structure surrounded by an ornate metal fence with an electronically operated twin gate at the entrance. It was finished stucco, so typical of that region's architecture. The roof was made of a rich, red tile and decorated with bird facades on the corners of the eaves. The driveway leading from the street up to the house was covered with small, white pebbles. The grounds were superbly manicured, aflame with all the colors in the rainbow. The windows were tinted to prevent the sun's rays from destroying the interior, and to provide some aspect of privacy.

The door leading into the foyer was of solid, dark wood, and carved with pictures of animals set apart by panels. Inside the house, the foyer was inlaid with tiles, each one individually decorated. The house had four bedrooms, five baths, a large great room, a kitchen to die for, an office, a formal dining room, a breakfast nook, and utility room. The walls were painted white as they ascended to a peak of the cathedral ceiling. Flowers were everywhere. The family was escorted throughout the house by a housekeeper, culminating in a tour of the backyard through a set of stained glass French doors. The backyard, like the front was spectacular. In one corner was a large stone waterfall and in the middle, a swimming pool with sparkling aqua blue water. The house also came with a cook and a maintenance man. Juan knew he was protected by a guardian angel, but couldn't believe his good fortune. At one point, he thought he was going to be thrown into prison, and the next moment, he is living in the lap of luxury. The housekeeper suggested the family unpack their bags while she helped them put their clothes away, and then they could take a short nap to rest up after the long flight before dinner. It didn't take much persuasion for them to lie on the soft mattresses and to fall immediately asleep.

A couple of hours later, the aroma of freshly made bread and cooking meat aroused them. Even though they had eaten on the plane they seemed to be famished, and hurriedly showered, dressed, and ventured to the kitchen to see what the cook was preparing. The plump matron of the calories didn't speak any English, so the conversation stumbled along, Juan trying to recall his Spanish which he had rarely spoken over the past decades. It didn't take long for it to come back, the cook speaking in the dialect of Juan's village. Everyone sat down at the dining room table which was covered with a stark white linen tablecloth and matching cloth napkins. Candelabras were set at both ends of the table and the candles were lit casting an eerie glow about the room. They furnished the only source of light, and provided a solemn atmosphere. The meal served was absolutely delicious, everyone ate too much, but were grateful they didn't have to prepare it. Because they had a nap, no one was tired, so they all gathered on the patio to sit and admire the stars overhead. Juan had fixed a drink for himself and Mary, and the children had chosen a soft drink to quench their thirst. The family exchanged small talk, Jose and Maria wondering what was going to happen to them, Juan not having any answers as yet. He told them he sensed something soon was going to transpire and they would be fine.

The next couple of weeks were spent sleeping in, eating well, swimming, and walking around the yard. Juan had erected a volleyball net and they matched up male versus female in a sport which soon became a laughter, the four of them spending most of their time on the ground chasing the volleyball. Juan was becoming bored with the daily routine. There was nothing there to challenge him, or to keep his mind occupied. He tried to read, but the words didn't remain long in his memory and the plots didn't make much sense either. Mary seemed to be content, mastering the ability to withstand long periods with nothing to do. She had taken up art, and was becoming a fairly decent painter in oils. The office was converted into a space for her labor, some of her paintings hanging on the walls as decorations. The children were being sent off to Mexican schools, hopefully, someday, to the University of Mexico for a degree in something. They weren't sure what they wanted to be yet. Jose was leaning towards law like his father, and Maria thought she might like to dabble in journalism and travel.

With the kids in school and Mary engrossed with her art, Juan backed the car out of the three car garage and drove to a small shopping area nearby. Juan enjoyed walking through the market, taking in the sights, sounds and smells it afforded. Most of the vendors were ragged looking farmers from the outer villages, trying to make enough pesos to keep their families fed and clothed. Most of the shoppers were servants of the more affluent in the houses surrounding the market, or workers who labored in the factories or gardens. As Juan watched this kaleidoscope of humanity he harkened back to his own childhood. So many years had passed, and the Mexican people seemed not to have changed at all. They were still tied to the burden of large families and poverty. Juan, as President of the United States had been to the seat of power and the homes of the Mexican bureaucrats, and had witnessed the mountain of money being spent by such a small percentage of the population. No wonder so many of his people were attempting to cross the border illegally, following a dream for a better life. Juan felt deep in his soul the need for this to change. The Mexican government must do something to keep the people at home, to improve their health and lives, and to improve the economy, so Mexico would not be dependent on the U.S. for its existence. Juan purchased a banana and ate it on his way back to the house. He was resolved to contact the government and see what he could do to meet those objectives he was contemplating.

The next morning, Juan had just finished his breakfast and was working on his second cup of flavorful coffee, when the front doorbell rang. The housemaid went to answer it, then came into the kitchen to inform Juan a policeman was there to see him. All sorts of horrible, scary thoughts went immediately through Juan's head. What could a policeman be doing at his house now, what did he want? Juan arose from the breakfast nook table, tucked his shirt into his trousers and went to see who the policeman was.

Standing in the foyer was a large Mexican fully outfitted in a form fitting uniform just a little too small for his frame. He had a wide leather belt around his spacious middle which held his pistol, his walkie talkie, spare ammunition, and a club dangling from the side. He held his hat in his hand and faced Juan. Juan stared for a moment, thinking he recognized him, but couldn't put a name to the face. The policeman came forward, put his massive arms around Juan and gave Juan a hug. He released his bear like grip and spoke.

"Juan, don't you remember me, its Benji Alverez your old buddy and playmate from the dumps." Suddenly the years melted away and the old friendship began to show through. Benji had been a short, skinny kid, nothing like the man who now stood before Juan, but there was no mistaking the eyes and the silly grin on his old friend's face. Juan almost came to tears as he shook Benji's hand and invited him to have a cup of coffee in the kitchen. Benji gratefully accepted and the two men sat down to renew an old companionship and bring each other up to date. Benji told Juan their other two friends, Jose and Alfredo, as well as himself, had been lucky and had extricated themselves from the dump and had made a life for their families. Benji was now the Chief of Police of Mexico City, Jose had become the minister of Commerce for the government, and Alfredo was now a federal judge. Benji described each of their families and what had transpired over the many years. Juan was amazed to hear this story, realizing that an escape from the trash dump was successful maybe one or two times out of a hundred. He never thought any of his friends would accomplish it.

The two of them must have talked for a couple of hours until they had covered just about every possible bit of information. Then Benji said, "But the real reason I came when I heard you were back in Mexico, Juan, was to tell you the story of your father. Your father did not abandon you and your family as so many of your relatives thought. Your father had saved some money and had paid a coyote, a transporter of illegal aliens to America, to take him across the border. It was your father's intent to work in America until he could earn enough to bring all of you there. He didn't tell your mother because he felt she might not let him go. So one night, when all of you were asleep, he took his money and joined the other Mexicans in a truck. Juan, the truck stalled on the way, and the driver just left the truck there in the hot sun. He didn't even have enough sense to unlock the back doors and let in some fresh air. All of the men inside the semi died, and were buried out there in the desert. It wasn't until just recently that the bodies were discovered and identified. There is no question, one of the bodies was that of your father."

Juan felt another chapter in the book of his life close as if by a ghostly hand. All these years he had hated his father for leaving the family to take care of itself, and now he was filled with shame for having such thoughts. He asked Benji if his brothers and sisters knew of this fact and Benji replied they did not. He wanted to wait to tell Juan first and then let Juan take care of notifying the others by himself.

As the conversation was winding down, Juan complimented Benji for his great success and his high position. Juan was impressed also with the achievements of the other two friends. Juan was curious, and asked Benji how the three of them got out of the poverty and the trash. Benji said Juan's mother had begged him to keep silent, but now she was dead, Benji could reveal the secret.

"Juan, when you were in America making all of that money, and sending some of it to your mother, she was giving a portion of it to us so we could someday make something of ourselves. Through her generosity, we were able to go to college or other places to learn the skills we needed. Without her, I would have never gone this far, and I can say the others feel the same way. Your mother was a saint."

It dawned on Juan that his mother didn't live in the lap of luxury which she could have with the money he sent her, but chose instead to live moderately. Juan never questioned what she did with the money, but now he knew the real truth. Juan thanked Benji profusely and escorted him out the door. Juan's next task would be to go back to the village, find his relatives and explain the circumstances surrounding the disappearance of his father. Juan would leave in the morning. He wanted to gather his thoughts now, so he could be better prepared to face them. He wanted a chance to rehearse what he was going to say, just as he had prepared all of his speeches before.

CHAPTER EIGHTY

When the large red ball arose in the east, Juan was on the patio with a cup of coffee to greet it. He was in his house robe, and the sun's rays seemed to penetrate the cloth and warm his entire body. Juan liked the mornings. They sparked a new day, and gave hope for things yet to come. It had been years since Juan had seen his relatives. He wondered how much they had changed, and if they would recognize him when he arrived. Soon, those questions would be answered. Juan had breakfast with Mary and the kids, dressed in comfortable clothes and went to the garage. He waved to Mary as he backed the car out of the space. He had invited Mary to go along with him, but she had declined. She felt this was something that Juan needed to do alone. Maybe sometime in the future she would go with him to visit.

With the horrible traffic of this large city, it took about an hour to drive to the village. When he arrived, the scene had not changed from the time when he was a boy. The trash dump was still there, only higher than before. The smell overwhelmed him at first, but then his nostrils cleared bringing back memories of those days when he sifted through the garbage. Heavy smog, accentuated with smoke, obscured the sun for the most part. It seemed like late evening when it was early morning. Juan found the street where his old home had been and parked in front. Little had be done to improve the place, but it had not fallen into disrepair as many of the structures around it had. He opened the rusty gate and walked to the front door. He rapped on the door sill and heard shuffling in the living room. The room opened a crack, and a small woman's head peered out. "Who are you, and what do you want?"

"My name is Juan Cardova, I used to live here with my mother and my brothers and sisters. I only stopped by to see the old place. If I am bothering you, I will leave."

"Wait, I know who you are. Many years ago, my aunt, your mother, used to tell all of us about you and what you had done with your life. She encouraged all of us to do the same. She gave us money. Some of the family and your friends made something of themselves, and other just spent it on whiskey and cars. I am your cousin Lolita. My father was your mother's brother. Please come in Juan. I didn't mean to be disrespectful, I just don't trust anyone I don't know anymore."

She opened the door wider to allow Juan entrance and accompanied him into the room. She asked him to take a seat on the sofa and she would fetch him something to drink. The house was as Juan had remembered. The paint on the walls had been changed as had the window dressings, but the basic structure still remained. Juan didn't sit down immediately, he moved about reliving his experiences there. All of the good times, and some of the bad came back as if they were just yesterday. Yes he reflected, his mother was a saint.

Juan could hear the hiss of an expresso machine, and soon smelled the rich aroma of the coffee beans. Lolita returned with two small, steaming cups of the dark liquid, handed one to Juan and took a seat on the couch. Juan joined her. For the next several hours, they talked about the years that had gone by, the family, the times, the government, the poverty, the despair, and the hopelessness. With every word, the urge for Juan to do something about all of these surged in his bosom. He knew he had been called to a mission, a mission to change things in Mexico. A mission to make Mexico a superpower just like America. When he finished his coffee, and put the cup in the kitchen sink, he asked Lolita if she would take him around the village and introduce him to the other relatives and people who lived there. She likewise disposed of her cup, put on a colorful shawl, closed the door behind her and locked it. She held Juan's arm and they started toward the center of the village.

It was nearing lunch time, and as usual, the salvagers were leaving the dump and either heading home for some food, or moving toward the cantina for a beer and some burritos. Juan and Lolita followed two men into the cantina spotted a corner table next to a filthy window much in need of a good scrubbing. As they sat down, all of the eyes in the room were riveted on them. Lolita stood, introduced Juan and told the men and women he had returned. Slowly each of them arose, came to Juan, offered their hands and told Juan who they were. It was like a high school reunion, only better. These weren't just classmates from the school of hard knocks, but family and friends. The owner instructed his waitress to bring beer for everyone. Juan was trying to participate in a dozen conversations at once, and finally collapsed with laughter. The food was brought to the tables and everyone joined in. It was like a political rally of sorts, a venue with which Juan was very familiar.

When the food and beer were gone, most of the inhabitants returned to their labors, but a couple of the older men stayed to chat with Juan. Lolita excused herself and went home. One of the men was an uncle of Juan's whom he vaguely remembered. They asked if Juan had come home to help them make their lives better, or to take advantage of them like so many of the gentry of the country did. Juan hinted of his intentions to become a force in the government to improve their status, and at that moment, a cell was formed which would assist Juan in achieving his goals. It was so easy Juan thought. These people are like sheep, and they can be easily lead by the right person. This is a small beginning, but I have nothing but time to travel throughout the land and repeat this process. The door to immortality had just been cracked open, and the light of opportunity shown through. Juan thanked the two men, and promised them he would see what he could possibly do to meet their expectations. He asked them where his brothers and sisters had gone and why they weren't living in the house. Juan knew he had lost track of them when their mother died. He had just gotten too busy to be much of a brother, vowing from time to time to visit them, but it never happened.

They told Juan the siblings had taken the money their mother had squirreled away and had moved into the city. They had never come back to the village, and over the years, they seemed to vanish from sight. No one knew where they were, but perhaps Juan could find out from other sources.

Juan decided not to make the effort. He was sure, because of his indifference, his brothers and sisters could not care less. It was better to let sleeping dogs lie and not interfere with the lives of others. Juan should have felt remorse, but he didn't. He rationalized he was far above them anyway, so why should he waste his time. He had bigger fish to fry. Then he decided he needed their forgiveness, so he would try and locate them the next day.

Today a village, tomorrow a city, and then a nation.

Juan returned to the old home and asked Lolita if he could stay the night. It was getting late and he didn't want to drive into Mexico City in the dark. She consented. There was plenty of room in the house. It wasn't what Juan had gotten accustomed to, but it was clean. Lolita had no children. She said it was a curse for her wickedness of the past. She had married late to an older man who had died of heart failure and now she was living alone. It would seem nice to have a man in the house again she thought to herself.

She told Juan to sit in the living room, to relax and she would make up one of the beds in the back room for him to sleep in. It didn't take long for her to complete this task. Then she began preparations for cooking their dinner. As Juan sat on the soft cushions, he glanced around the room conjuring up memories of the days when he was a young boy here. He closed his eyes and allowed himself to be absorbed into a dreamlike state. He hadn't dreamed long when the smell of the dinner penetrated his nostrils and he became fully awake. Lolita spoke from the kitchen, saying the dinner was ready. Juan sat at the kitchen table with Lolita and thoroughly enjoyed the meal. Lolita had proven to be an excellent cook and Juan showed his gratitude by finishing everything on his plate.

Juan arose the next morning early and bid Lolita goodbye. He thanked her for her graciousness and drove off.

Juan thought he remembered the route to the big city, but it had been so many years and the landscape had changed so much, he got lost several times until he finally found the center of the city. He was looking for the Hall of Records where he would find some documentation of the whereabouts of his brothers and sisters. The records revealed Jesus Jr. was living in the city, in a neighborhood generally inhabited by the middle class. Rather than to look for additional information on the others, he wrote Jesus' telephone number on a piece of paper, thanked the clerk for her assistance and exited outside to use a payphone.

The telephone only rang a couple of times and was then answered by a slight, female voice which identified the speaker as the wife of Jesus Jr. Juan spent a few minutes introducing himself. The conversation ended with the wife giving Juan directions to their home, explaining Jesus would be home by the time Juan got there. The directions proved to be easy to follow and shortly Juan approached a modest two-story villa nestled among many similar looking residences. There was a parking place on the street. He locked his car and went to the door to ring the doorbell. The door was answered by a large, salt and pepper colored haired man Juan hardly recognized. It didn't take long for the two brothers to recognize each other and embrace with great emotion.

The brothers spent the better part of the day and evening talking about family and old times. Jesus explained that Carmen had died in childbirth and he wasn't aware of where the husband and children had gone. Miranda had married into a wealthy family and was now living in the Baja peninsula near the Copper Canyon. They had lost track of each other, so Jesus didn't know her address. Pedro has been killed in an automobile accident several years ago and Pepe, the baby, was somewhere in the old neighborhood, still slaving on the trash pile. Juan vowed he would find Pepe somehow.

Food, drinks, more conversation, and sleep came next. Juan stayed with his brother until the next morning, and then returned to his own family.

CHAPTER EIGHTY-ONE

Now that Juan was safely tucked away, or at least Kyle Smith thought so, the next order of business was to undo the damage the "J" amendment had done to the Constitution. Kyle felt in his heart the repeal of the amendment allowing a naturalized citizen to become The U.S. President, would be a slam dunk. He asked his legal staff to look into the procedure for such an action so that Congress could move ahead. In the meantime, the Vice President had taken over completely the duties of President awaiting the elections just a few months hence. Kyle wanted this repeal to be taken care of immediately so there would be no repeat of the disaster which had befallen America. What Kyle had not taken into account was the opposition to the repeal. Apparently, the issue was not a slam dunk, but an uphill battle all of the way.

When news of the repeal first hit the press, minority groups rose to the challenge. They contended that for the first time in the history of the country, anyone, born in the United States or naturalized had a chance to become President. For too long, the only persons who made it to the top were white, Caucasian, native born individuals. This was fine for the most part, but the dynamics of America was changing. The immigrant groups were smelling blood. They had made an inroad, and were not as willing to give it up as most people thought. They argued, if a female, or a black person, of a Jew could run for President, why couldn't a Vietnamese, a Russian, a Filipino, or any other immigrant do the same. There was a ground swell against Congress, the minorities lobbying hard to stop the repeal. At the same time, other groups were tugging Congress in the opposite direction. The Klu Klux Klan weighed in with their racist rhetoric. Immigration had become a rallying point for the KKK, and now they had a new platform on which to spread their vile. The Aryian nation, headquartered in Northern Idaho also started to exert its bias. America was settled by white, Christian people and that should stand the test of time. There was no reason for America to allow any change.

Kyle suddenly found himself and others in a quagmire. What he thought would be a simple solution to the problem became a dilemma. Demonstrations were being held across the landscape, and Congress was being inundated with letters, telegrams, telephone calls. The business of government was almost grinding to a halt. Never had an issue taken on such high priority. The talk shows were abuzz with the issue, arguing both sides of the coin. Face The Nation grilled top officials, who seemed not to have the answers, but were very slick in evading the question. Newspapers were selling like hotcakes. Many Congressmen and Congresswomen, who were concerned with their re-election prospects, were wavering. Those who Kyle thought were in the fold, were now doubtful. The vote to repeal the amendment was scheduled for a Friday morning when most of the members of Congress were in town. The vote came first in the House of Representatives. When the final tally was taken, the vote in favor of the repeal won by two votes. It now moved to the Senate for action.

The Senate had decided to debate the issue for a couple of days, then after the weekend have the final vote. Kyle needed as much time as he could muster to garner as many votes as he could. Since the House had passed the repeal, the onus rested in the hands of the Senate. The weekend ended with a flurry of persuasion. Again, the Secretary of the Senate began the roll call. All one hundred members of the Senate were in attendance for the vote. When the final name was called, the tally was dead even. Now it was up to the Vice President to cast the deciding vote. The Vice President went to the dais and gathered all of his courage. Never in the history of the country had the Vice President played such a role. Kyle thought to himself, how could the vice president go against the principles espoused by the man he had loved and worked for all of these years. Kyle could only cross his fingers and hope for the best. The Vice President made a short speech. Unknown to the assembled group, the Vice President had been a victim of Juan's blackmail. Upon the conclusion of his speech, the Vice President voted in favor of repeal.

The vote echoed across the land. For years, law professors would attempt to analyze this outcome. In one sector, there was jubilation, in the other pure dismay. Law suits were immediately filed to declare the vote null and void. This would be a long fight, but in the meantime, the amendment had been done away with. When all of this was finished, and Kyle was due to come up for re-election, he decided to not run for an additional term, citing health reasons for his decision. He had won two battles, and he was exhausted with the effort. He just wanted to kick back and relax for a couple of years, play golf, and then return to the fray as a consultant. He had paid his dues, and he was tired. He needed a rest and a chance to regroup. Many other Senators and Congressmen felt the same way. Fresh blood had been interjected into the system.

Juan had been following this controversy in the papers, and was appalled at the vote and the results. He felt that American had somehow removed itself from the modern world and had taken on an isolationist mode. He disagreed with the vote, but he was not in a position to affect what had happened. He was no longer entangled in American politics. He had much larger fish to fry in his native land.

Juan started to build a local support base. He traveled to the small towns and sat down with the elders, consulting with them on how they could improve their areas. He promised them a way to sell their crops, and to receive a larger share of the money that was filtering into the central government. He met with the local priests asking their assistance in controlling the population even though it went against the Catholic teachings. He encouraged the young girls to attend school and become literate. He moved on to the business communities teaching the owners fundamental economics, encouraging the workers to become partners with the owners to share in the profits if they worked hard. He gathered together some of the rich merchants to form a venture capitalist system to help jump start private industry. He contacted some of his friends in the states to show them the advantage of outsourcing their labor needs to Mexico, thereby reducing their labor costs, and increasing their bottom line.

Juan's popularity was growing as he moved about. His ideas were starting to germinate and grow. Not weeds, but healthy plants to nourish those who got involved. He encouraged the Mexican senate to change the tax laws, giving tax breaks to the filthy rich if they, in turn, would divest some of their fortunes into the nation's economy. Mexico was rich with natural resources, gas, crude oil, minerals, and cheap labor. Juan knew other nations like America, Japan, and those in Europe were screaming for these resources to sustain their life styles. Juan helped to start the first labor unions convincing the business owners this was a good thing. It would guarantee the workers better working conditions, health benefits, and some assurances for retirement while at the same time, it would guarantee the owners a reliable source of laborers.

He encouraged families to send their most gifted children to foreign universities to get educations in the sciences, economics, urban planning, and engineering. In just a few short years, these young people would return and pay tremendous dividends. What Juan was doing was not easy, but he moved ahead steadily. Some of his Hispanic friends in the US saw what he was doing, and joined forces with him. They too saw the value of enriching their own people.

Juan was present at the ribbon cutting ceremony of two automobile assembly plants being opened. One was to assemble American brands of cars, the other Japanese. Suddenly new homes, health care clinics, grocery stores, and other enterprises started to spring up. Juan worked with the Department of Tourism to bring northerners and people from across the world to the sun and fun spots of the Mexican Rivera. Major hotel chains started to build high-rise facilities to attract these tourists, bringing in millions of dollars to the economy. Soon, the sandy beaches of the Baja peninsula were filled with white bodies seeking the tan which had eluded them before. Inflation was down to nearly zero and the gross national product had increased four fold. The balance of trade had remained in Mexico's favor, creating even more jobs. Mary didn't care if Juan was gone so much, she was living in the lap of luxury. Jose and Maria Elena were going to college and thriving. Juan knew now was the time to make his move and run for the Presidency of Mexico.

The current President was a fool. Someone who took bribe money for political favors. He was a womanizer and an alcoholic. Suddenly leaks appeared in the newspapers about his failings. Failings he said were untrue, but everyone knew better. The presidential elections were coming up soon, and Juan launched the largest campaign of his life. He used every tool he had mastered in other campaigns to run. He held massive rallies in any venue he could think of. Music played, food was served, and people danced. They listened intently as Juan outlined the Golden Road that lay before them. He was so convincing, even the doubters in the crowd started to believe in him. They were swept up in the dialogue and shouted and clapped after every statement. Men shook his hands and women hugged and kissed him. He was going to be their savior.

Juan knew the toughest hurdle he would have to face was the voter registration and corruption at the voting booths. He sent organizers out to the far reaches to make sure every eligible individual was registered and knew when and how to vote. He contacted Benji and asked for police assistance to ensure the voting places were free of influence and fraud. Benji obliged him by marshalling the other police chiefs and the Mexican Department of Justice. The election went off without a hitch. Of course there was some corruption during the voting, but it was hardly influential to the outcome. Juan Cardova had pulled off another bloodless coup. He was hailed as the next President of Mexico in another landslide. Those who had television sets in their homes or businesses, watched as a triumphant Juan waved to the crowds from his victory platform. Two months later, Juan stood before the capitol of Mexico and became their leader. As he was reveling in the ardor, his brain was seething with revenge against those who had kicked him out of America, disgraced him, and turned their backs on him. He was now in a position to return the favor many fold.

The election of the President of Mexico was not a somber event like it was in America. When the oath of office was taken, the crowd began to dance in the streets. Mariachi bands began playing, bottles of liquor were withdrawn from back pockets, firecrackers erupted, and the party was on. Juan grabbed Mary and danced her around the platform to the beat of the Latino rhythms. Long after Juan and Mary had gone home, the partying continued. By morning, the streets were cleared, the hospital emergency rooms were filled with minor casualties, and a new day had begun.

CHAPTER EIGHTY-TWO

Juan had his plan for revenge in his head, and knew it would take some time to implement, but he had the time and the power to get it done. The first family moved out of the home that they had been furnished, and into the Presidential Palace near the center of the city. This would put Juan much closer to his offices, and would allow him the opportunity to keep a watchful eye on things. The Presidential Palace was a grandiose edifice. Four stories tall, constructed in sheer white marble. It shone in the sunlight like a flawless diamond. The palace was completely enclosed with a high brick wall upon which were mounted security cameras at vantage points to give the security guards complete surveillance of the grounds and buildings.

The grounds were filled with natural plants and flowers, carefully choreographed with matching colors, interspersed with dark green foliage. Groundskeepers were seen everywhere, clipping the shrubs, pruning the dead branches off the trees, mowing the spacious lawns, and watering the vegetation that needed it. The top floor of the palace was the residence of the President and his family. The other floors held meeting rooms, offices of staff members, and other service facilities including a stainless steel kitchen and recreational facility. Juan knew that everything he needed was contained in the building, and perhaps he would never have to leave. But, he knew he had to visit the far reaches of the vast country not only to keep his popularity, but to assess the potential that was out there in abundance.

The first person Juan met with was his new Chief of Staff, Carlos Diaz. Carlos had been educated in American and had gone to law school there as part of a student exchange program with the United States. Carlos had never become a citizen of the U.S., but when he had finished his education, had returned to labor in the Mexican government. He had held several minor jobs, but had risen through the ranks to take on more and more responsibilities. He had been the director of several departments, including finance and commerce, and had closely advised the Mexican parliament in areas of international law. Carlos, like Juan was a handsome man. The two men were about the same age, and could almost be called brothers, they looked so much alike. Juan had known Carlos when he was in the states, and had fostered a close relationship, thinking someday Carlos would be of some assistance to him.

The two men sat at a small conference table made of fine, dark wood, the highly polished surface showing the reflection of the entire room on it. Juan previously had the room swept by his security forces, just to ascertain no listening devices had been placed in the interior which would allow someone to eavesdrop. Juan didn't trust anyone. Not only had he suffered a mental breakdown, and developed other mental aberrations, he was now becoming paranoid as well. Juan was about to reveal his plan to Carlos. He did so in such a way that Carlos knew if any parts of the plan were ever revealed, or he did not fully support Juan, his life would be of little value. Juan didn't want to threaten Carlos because he was his friend, but there had to be some insurance policy with which Juan could collaborate inside the office. They spent the better part of the day laying the groundwork for the next several years. Carlos briefed Juan on those in his administration he could trust fully, and those who needed to be watched carefully. He assured Juan he would have the Mexican Secret Police start a file on those with questionable loyalties. It was not unusual in Mexico for a person who stepped out of line to wind up shot as they were leaving a café, or disappeared into the desert never to be found.

The first step in their strategy was to drawn in foreign companies to improve the harvesting of the natural resources. The abundance had just barely been touched. Juan knew the Mexicans didn't have the money or the expertise to handle this tremendous task, but knew outsiders did.

They decided the first resource they would tackle would be oil. Many nations like American, Japan, Holland, and Australia were highly dependent on fossil fuels to feed their gas guzzling machinery and cars. Juan called in his ministers of commerce, finance, and transportation to discuss the details. It was decided to invite the emissaries of these and many other countries to Mexico City for a four day conclave to discuss the feasibility of expanding Mexico's resource availability.

The representatives were put up in the finest hotel in the city, and were wined and dined in a manner unseen before in this country. Large profits were promised, and incentives given to garner the favors Mexico needed. There would be a large labor pool available along with relaxed environmental restrictions. The conclave was a huge success. Soon companies like Shell, British Petroleum, Exxon, Sinclair, Standard, and others began drawing up contracts to extract the crude oil from the ground, and to build refineries to process the black gold.

Over the next several months, men and materials began to arrive by truck, train, and sea. Overnight, pre-fabricated buildings were going up in the oil fields to house the workers who would be constructing and operating the oil wells. Geologists scoured the countryside identifying the most probable place where oil would be found. It was estimated that the oil reserves in Mexico would be equal to or greater than those in Iran. The countryside was a beehive of activity.

The same process was followed with other industries. Major hotel corporations began to build luxurious high-rises in the major tourist spots. Gambling laws were changed to allow casinos to be built and run by those connected with Las Vegas and Atlantic City. Franchise food sources were invited in or expanded. MacDonald's, Kentucky Fried Chicken, Subway, just to name a few. Regional airports were constructed to accommodate the influx of people. As success and profits grew, more and more entities were sucked into the mix. Foreign money was coming into Mexico at a rate unprecedented before. Mexico was the land of opportunity, so why not get on the band wagon. The Mexican stock market began to rival those in the major financial centers of the planet.

Juan, Carlos, and other trusted ministers watched with glee as these sheep crawled all over each other to get a foothold. Mexican banks were bulging at the seams with capital. Schools were being built and the literacy rate rose immeasurably. Mexicans were learning to read, write, and do math. They were also learning to speak other languages in order to communicate with the outsiders. Public health was improving, the infant mortality rate declining steadily. Teams of nurses and physicians were going out to the remote areas to immunize the children and treat sickness where they found it.

Foreign professors were being drawn into the Mexican Universities to teach the future doctors, engineers, economists, and business leaders from within. Juan didn't want his country to be dependent on others once his plan came into full bloom.

Not everything was going well for Juan. Visitors cruising to the Sea of Cortes were also taking a side train trip to the Copper Canyon to see the breathtaking colors and sculpted rock formations. They were reporting back on the huge hole that was being formed from the mining of the copper ore. Strip mining was ruining the natural beauty of the region, but Juan didn't care, he merely had his Minister of Transportation reroute the train tracks, taking the tourists away from the mine. Soon the furor quieted.

Whenever Juan encountered opposition, he had the police take care of it. Protestors were being arrested, taken to jail, and prosecuted. Being in a Mexican prison was not a desirable thing to have happen, and soon the oppositionists got the message, and fell in step with the government. Mexico was evolving into a superpower. Its status was nearing that of the other industrialized nations. It could no longer be called that poor relative to the south of the U.S. The balance of trade with Germany, Japan, Australia, and America was falling into Mexico's favor.

Then Juan received an unexpected request. His administrative assistant told him a delegation from the U.S. Senate had asked permission to visit Juan to see how things were going with American interests and to pay their respects for the achievements Juan had fathered. He was even more surprised when he learned the head of the delegation was none other than his former old friend Kyle Smith. Juan instructed the assistant to grant the delegation's request, issue the appropriate visa, and set up an itinerary for their visit. Juan wanted to control the playing field since they would be arriving on his turf. It didn't take long for the schedule to be drafted, reviewed, changed and approved by Juan. The visa process, which normally took months was expedited and in a couple of weeks the delegation was leaving from Andrews Air Force Base winging its way to Mexico City.

There were four members of the group visiting Juan. Two Democrats and two Republicans, one old timer, and three new members. Kyle wanted to show them how things got done when the right man was in the right position. Kyle never doubted Juan's ability to govern or administer a nation, he only took the actions he did because of Juan's and the blackmail he had carried out. Juan and Mary were dear to Kyle and he felt great pain in bringing them down. He really didn't care about Mexico. Mexico had emperors and kings before, so Juan would fit right in.

CHAPTER EIGHTY-THREE

The four senators arrived at the Mexico City International Airport and were met on a private tarmac by three black limos with a motorcycle police escort. Security was very heavy around the plane and the fences and entrances to that part of the airport. As they descended the gangplank, they were met by the Mexican protocol officer, the Chief of Tourism, and the Minister of Commerce. A red carpet had been laid from the cars vicinity to the edge of the gangplank. As the senators moved along the carpet, they received a military salute from a Mexican Army Honor Guard. Kyle was impressed with the young men who constituted the Honor Guard. They were dressed in functional uniforms, with highly polished boots, white belts, and shiny chrome helmets. They carried ceremonial rifles from ages past, and snapped to attention to present arms to the visiting dignitaries. The drivers opened the doors of the limos, closed the doors behind the Americans, and whisked them away to the Presidential Palace where they would stay for the duration of their visit.

It was Kyle's desires to see Juan as soon as possible, but after he had been situated in his guest quarters and had contacted Juan's office, he was told the President was unavailable for the rest of the day, and would meet with the delegation at 10 o'clock in the morning. This didn't please Kyle very much, but he understood he should not make any waves. He had alienated Juan enough when he led Juan's recall, and now only wanted to mend a few fences. He would rather have Juan as a friend and ally, instead of an enemy.

The room Kyle had been placed in was very spacious. It was liken unto a suite one would find at a major hotel in New York, Boston, or Washington D.C. The living room was furnished in a modern Spanish style, with bright tapestries hanging from the walls amid oil paintings of the Mexican countryside. The furniture was soft suede, a roan color with matching dark brown suede pillows. A well stocked wet bar stood against one wall. There was a stereo system with music from the 60's and a 21 inch television, which Kyle turned on to catch the news. Unfortunately, all of the broadcasts were in Spanish, a language Kyle had never attempted to learn.

In the bedroom was a king size bed with an oversized mattress and coverlet. A closet with folding doors contained plenty of hangars for Kyle's clothes, and a soft terry cloth robe for casual wear in the evening. The bathroom had a walk in shower accented with Spanish tile and a garden tub with streamer jets. The wash basin area was fully stocked with shampoo, body lotion, shaving cream, razors, tooth brushes, tooth paste, and soaps. Kyle was told that dinner would be served in the second floor dining room at 7 o'clock sharp. Kyle glanced at his watch and noted that he had just over two hours to rest up before dinner. He loosened his tie from his shirt, hung his jacket in the closet, took off his shoes, mixed himself a drink, and went out on the balcony to view the beautiful grounds. He found a comfortable chaise lounge, sat his drink on the glass side table and plopped himself on the cushions. Without intending to, Kyle drifted off into a short nap.

The sound of a lawnmower awakened him. Again he looked at his watch, and sensed he only had time enough to take a shower, get dressed and make it to dinner on time. He knew it was fashionable to be a little late, a power thing, but he didn't want to offend the host. Kyle dressed in a white suit, with a pink silk shirt and a white tie and shoes. He looked every bit the aristocracy of the Old South. All he needed was a cigar, flowing white hair, and his finger draped in his watch fob, and he could have been a replica of Mark Twain.

The other three Senators were dressed casually and had already been seated when Kyle arrived. They acknowledged his presence allowing him a few minute tardiness because of his stature in the group. Pleasantries were passed around, before dinner drinks served, and then a marvelous meal ensued. Juan had gone all out to have his chef prepare a feast for royalty. Kyle kept expecting Juan to join them, but he never appeared. The guests finished up, washed their faces and hands with a steaming towel provided by one of the waiters, and adjourned to the den to have an after dinner cigar and brandy for those who wanted it. In the den, they marveled at the antiquities and trappings with which Juan had furnished the room. It had the look of an expensive museum. The Senators chatted for awhile, then all retired for the evening, it was going to be a busy day tomorrow.

The next morning, breakfast was served in the same dining room, this time a buffet had been set up with everything anyone could possibly want. Kyle was very pleased when he saw Juan enter the room to join them. He was greeted warmly by Juan with a handshake and a non-committal hug. The meal was punctuated with small talk and full mouths. When the meal was over, Carlos, the Chief of Staff give the group a rundown of the next few days activities. The group would be split up, traveling in different directions to see a variety of sites, meeting back at the palace each evening to share what had been seen and heard. Juan asked Kyle to stay after the other had gone, and then Kyle could venture on his rounds.

The Senators were going to see the oil fields, the new medical facilities, the farms, the auto assembly plants, the new communications facilities, and other show pieces Juan had spoken of so proudly. Outside the palace, cars and helicopters were waiting to take the visitors to their destinations. Juan stood with Kyle on the balcony and watched as the cars drove and the helicopters flew away. Juan walked Kyle down to the first floor and into his spacious office, which ironically resembled the Oval Office where Juan had conducted the affairs of state. The only difference being the rug in the center of the floor showing the Seal of Mexico, the Mexican National Flag, and portraits of past Mexican rulers and presidents. The size, shape and furnishings were basically the same.

Kyle sensed an emanation of unreality. He felt like he were in a dream place, a place that was almost unreal. He felt he had entered Never Neverland or the Emerald City in the Land of Oz, and Juan was the Grand Wizard. He saw Juan's lips move, but he couldn't hear the words. The room seemed to swirl around him, almost making him dizzy. He closed his eyes, shook his head, and when he opened his eyes, Juan was staring at him.

"Is everything alright Kyle. You look a little pale. Can I get you anything?'

"No thanks Juan, it must have been the travel and all of the rich food. I don't normally eat this much, and my blood sugar level must have gone off the scale. It will do that sometimes when I eat things that are so rich, but I am fine now, please go on."

Juan was asking Kyle if he had any questions or opening remarks he would like to make. Kyle started with a mild apology. "Juan, I would like to thank you for the kindness you have shown us so far. I would also like to commend you on the successes you have made in this country. It was unfortunate what happened in the United States concerning you, but please be assured there was no malice intended. I have always considered you to be one of my best friends, and I hope we can heal our wounds and move forward as allies and brothers."

"What is done, Kyle, is done. Maybe it was a good thing what you and the others did. It has given me an opportunity to come back home and to really do something for my people. When I left many years ago, I thought I would never want to return, but now I am so grateful that I have. I can never appreciate America enough for the chance they gave me to get a good education, to serve them in war, to participate in the law making process, and to entrust in me the highest office obtainable. All I want now is to work with my friends to further our objectives, maybe someday achieving world peace."

Kyle was drooling on every word, little did he know Juan had tossed him a small piece of the bait, and was slowly reeling him in. Juan had no intention of walking hand in hand with the likes of Kyle Smith. Sometime in the future, Juan would extract his pound of flesh from those who stabbed him in the back, but Kyle didn't know this. He was completely mesmerized by Juan.

Juan continued, "It is my hope that someday we won't need borders between our countries. Our people will be able to move freely from one country to another, sharing labor and wealth. And, if Canada can see its way fit, can join us in the same journey, making the Northern Hemisphere the greatest power in the world. Not even China with its billions of people could dare threaten us. I would like to see every child in the hemisphere with the ability to read, and to speak several languages. I would like to see poverty abolished, unemployment at the lowest possible level. I would like to see a cleaner environment so our people don't have to breath all of the pollutants that abound in the atmosphere. I would like to see all wars end, and the killing stopped. Maybe I am too much of an idealist, but that is much of where I am coming from."

"Juan, in looking at the reports I have been given, and listening to you talk, I am convinced that between American, Canada, and Mexico, we can achieve those goals. It is spectacular what you have accomplished here in so few a years. You have harnessed the will of the people to make a major shift. You have knitted together a tapestry that portrays the soul of your people in what is being done."

Juan listened, thinking Kyle was indeed the master of bullshit, even greater than Juan was. Juan had learned from the master, but he could never equal him. Kyle rambled on for ten minutes more, then drew a breath and stopped. Kyle was most interested in understanding how Juan had done things. Kyle knew that the Mexican government had been corrupt for years, taking the cream off the top of the tax revenues, and putting the money in the hands of the few. Bribes were abundant throughout the military or police ranks. Much of the aid America had allocated to Mexico to improve the lives of the poverty stricken had never reached the intended target. Kyle wondered how all of this had changed.

Juan gave a very simple explanation. Juan had been brought up to be an honest man. He was taught the Golden Rule and to care for the less fortunate. He was honest to the nth degree and didn't tolerate anyone who wasn't. He reviled anyone who feathered their own nest at the expense of those who could not defend themselves. With the help of his friend Benji, the Mexico City Chief of Police, and other trusted friends who became leaders in the Secret Police, Department of Justice, and the Military, individuals who were taking bribes or kickbacks, or who were siphoning money off the top of foreign aid, were identified and withdrawn from office and placed under arrest either at home or in prison. Honest men were brought in to take their places. Councils were established at the village, city, and state levels to administer the money that was now being generated by the booming economy, to ensure everyone who contributed received their fair share. Honesty was becoming a cult.

Union leaders were seeing the value of employee participation and profit sharing. Workers no longer sloughed off on the job, but put in a honest day's work for an honest day's pay. True altruism was sweeping the country. Everyone was watching out for the welfare of each other. Juan's social experiment was working.

The two men chatted for a few more hours, took a short break for lunch, then Juan sent Kyle off to see, in actuality, some of the progress that was being made just outside. Juan was beside himself with glee. He knew the four Senators would be so impressed with what they saw, that they would encourage American investors to pour more money into Mexico, to build more businesses, and to become more indebted to Mexico. He was building this smoke screen as an artist would cover a canvas with brilliant colors, hiding the underpinnings of the work. He knew when the Senators left, they would report their findings not only to Congress and the President, but to the other nations who might have an interest in either entering the venture or increasing their investment.

CHAPTER EIGHTY FOUR

While the visiting party was out in the field observing, Juan was working behind the scenes. The delegation finally finished their business and met with Juan for one last time before returning to Washington D.C. They were very impressed with what they saw and gave Juan their assurance everything would be done to keep things moving in the direction they had observed.

The next morning Juan bid them all goodbye. Juan continued putting together his next step, building an Army, Navy, and Air force equal to the U.S. Juan knew America had a complex system of satellites in the sky taking pictures of activities on the ground around the globe. Juan also knew word would leak out of the build up if they were not very careful to disguise it. The increase in forces must be done in the most covert ways possible. Juan called together his Minister of Interior, the person who had jurisdiction over the military and the top generals of the three branches. For the most part, the military was being disguised as part of the police force, knowing that at a moments notice, they would be federalized to fight a war.

A contingent of twelve men met with Juan in his conference room. He instructed the generals not to be in uniform, and he would explain the meeting was nothing more than a briefing by the directors of the various chambers within the Department of the Interior. The generals had all sworn a blood oath to Juan, as had the Minister. They knew how high the stakes were if they were to be caught in their scheme. They knew America would show no mercy if they were found out before they were ready to accomplish their mission.

As the group sat at the conference table, Juan opened the discussion. He told the persons assembled he wanted a list of objectives to be met, timelines, end products, and costs to bring the military to the standard which was needed. Again, no idea was unimportant. Juan wanted thoughts to flow like spurts of water, as frequently as possible. Every issue had to be addressed from the manufacturing of uniforms and arms, to secret location of training camps. Soldiers would also have to render the oath of silence for fear they would lose their tongues or their lives. Fear and intimidation have a funny way of shutting peoples' mouths for the purposes intended.

The first idea suggested was to manufacture uniforms exactly like the policemen wore, but to have in place Velcro stripes placed in strategic locations, so they would blend in with the normal uniform, but other insignias, rank designation, unit identifier patches, and decorations could easily be attached when the mobilization took place. Special helmets and everyday wear caps were created, and stored in the lockers of the police and in other locations to allow the police and others to eliminate the policeman's cap and put on the military equivalent.

Remote areas were identified for use as training centers. Elaborate camouflage would mask the areas from the satellites and allow the military skills to be developed without observation. Ammunition plants were built to seem to be auto assembly plants. Trucks coming and going from the areas would also be camouflaged and would move only at night, equipped with lights that would be reflective and not detected by night vision apparatus. Lies were told to the families of those recruited into the forces. The families were told the young men and women were being trained to perform civil duties to help build the infrastructure of the nation, and to render assistance to the poorest of the states within the country. The movement had begun. Within months, the armed forces swelled to over a million members. It was becoming a formidable force. Mercenaries were being hired, at great expense, to come in and train the raw recruits. A sense of pride and identity was being to emerge with these forces. They suddenly felt a companionship with each other and the President. There was no shortage of supply for the resources needed to staff the military. The pay was good, the discipline appropriate, and the training facilities were state of the art.

Weapon technology was secured from China and Russia, along with other smaller countries who had been in the arms business for centuries. Aircraft were a little more difficult to hide, but hangers lined with lead were constructed to house the aircraft. Pilots were trained via simulators and practiced in planes painted like corporate jets along with other commercial aircraft.

The Navy was a problem. It was hard to store a large aircraft carrier or cruiser in a location that would remain undetected. The ruse Juan used to justify the Navy was the nation's defense against outside aggression, primarily that coming from Asia. America accepted this premise, because their defense plans also called for a Navy to accomplish this type of mission. It was also suggested that Mexico and American conduct naval exercises to solidify mutual defense positions and mutual support. America was eager to jump at the chance. The top brass at CINCPAC, the Commander in Chief of the Pacific directed his staff to develop operations orders to carry out these joint maneuvers. The current American President was pleased to see the cooperation between the two nations and he felt secure that his country, if attacked by a foreign power, could rely on the Mexican government to come to his aid. Little did he know the reverse was true. The goal of the Mexican navy was to find out the flaws in the American doctrine of Naval Operations, and exploit those flaws in the doctrine when the time came.

The Mexican navy used a portion of its ships for maneuvers with the U.S., but a larger part of the fleet was disguised as commercial vessels, concealed under a façade. The exercises went well, the Mexican navy learning a great deal about their neighbor's capabilities and tactics. All of this information was fed back to the capitol and stored in the war room.

Relationships between the two countries continued to mesh, both growing rich from the progress Mexico was making. The investments in the oil industry were paying off handsomely. There was an abundance of oil, and it was spouting out of the ground just like it did in Oklahoma and Texas decades ago. The price per barrel of crude oil was set by the Ministry of Energy at a level below that of the OPEC nations, but higher than it should have been to those who had invested so much into the development of the product. Some of the companies began to protest, but Juan and his government staved them off by saying the excess profits were necessary to continue exploration and refinement. This seemed to placate the other companies, who were also recognizing abnormally high returns, and the grumbling went away. Oil starved nations clamored for Mexican oil.

The coffers in Mexico City were bulging at the seams. Never in the history of economics had a nation seen such a magnificent turn around. Economic professors from many universities were beginning to write books about the phenomenon. It was a case study to out parallel any other study. Juan could not have been more overjoyed. His plan was working better than he could have ever imagined.

A brief setback occurred, when an Army officer inadvertently gave away some classified information when interviewed by the foreign press. Although the information didn't make the front pages, it did raise questions as to what was really going on within the borders of Mexico. The Mexican government jumped to put a lid on the information. The officer was labeled as an insane malcontent with a grudge against the government, and the statements he was making were to embarrass those who had given him such a position. The information was characterized as the fantasy of a deranged individual. The officer could not be located for comment, and the story died away.

Juan's megalomania was beginning to resurface. After he had been elected to a second term of office as President of Mexico, he urged the parliament to amend the Mexican constitution to allow for unprecedented terms of office, something Juan had been unable to do in America. Getting this done had proven to be relatively easy. The parliament was so in love with Juan, they consented without hesitation. His status had been elevated to nearly that of a king. With the history of the country firmly embedded in his brain, Juan knew this would not be a problem. Kings and emperors had been there before with the people's blessings, so why not now? In due time, the constitution was amended, and Juan could become President for life if he wanted to. Juan began to wear a military uniform. The coat and pants were white and covered with gold braid. He had patterned his uniform after the emperor Maximilian. He was seen regularly at state functions dressed in these trappings. Red flags should have been raising around the world, but no one seemed to notice the warning signs. Many nation's presidents wore military uniforms, so what was the big deal. Juan was flaunting his arrogance in the faces of others, and they were lapping it up. He was on their side, and allowing him his little indulgences was a small price to pay for his friendship.

Another situation cropped up that set off bells ringing at the Presidential Palace. A disgruntled employee, working at a manufacturing plant, threatened to go to a local radio station to let it be known what the government was doing. Apparently he had been promised a promotion to a higher paying position, but when it came time for the advancement, a junior member of the staff was promoted ahead of him. He had stormed into his superior's office and demanded an explanation. When one was given, the employee blew a gasket, turning red in the face, and threatened the company and the government with exposure. The supervisor tried to calm him down, but he was having nothing to do with it. A promise was a promise, and he would rot in hell before he let them trample all over him.

He stormed out of the office, bent on a path to the radio waves. The supervisor ran after him, stopping him in the hall, and asked him to return to his workspace. The supervisor said if the employee would just cool down, go back to work, and remain calm, he would get on the phone immediately and see if something could be done. Back in his office, the supervisor did not intend to do any such thing. Instead, he made a call to the Minister of Communications Office, alerting them of the potential powder keg. Shortly after he made the call, the employee returned to the supervisor's office asking if there had been an answer. The supervisor tried to placate him with a flimsy explanation, but the employee would have nothing to do with it. He stormed out and made a beeline for the radio station. When he arrived, he was met by the secret police, forced into a car, and driven away. The station manager, who knew his livelihood depended on the government, disregarded the allegations, and nothing went out of the building. The government had a virtual stronghold on all forms of media, censoring everything written or broadcast. Juan's destiny was not to be denied.

The next bold move Juan made, with little warning, was to nationalize all of the foreign businesses. Suddenly all of the oil fields, refineries, department stores, franchises, hospitals, colleges, banks, investment companies, transportation systems, communications, docks, airports, and construction came under Mexican control. The upper echelons of these entities were told to pack their bags and to leave voluntarily, or they would be forced out of the country. The foreign workers were told they could stay if they signed a loyalty oath to the Mexican Government. Mexican personnel filled the void. No longer did Juan have to share any of the profits with outsiders. He could keep it all for himself and his nation. The transition went smoothly, just as Juan had hoped. For years, Mexican counterparts had worked side by side with the top brass, so they knew the job as well as they did. Taking over was a piece of cake, and no time was lost or disruption in evidence.

The CIA was now alerted to what was happening in Mexico. Data was being collected on the takeover, and the movement of troops to the border areas. Suddenly, those harmless looking buildings became fortresses. The border stations were suddenly closed and barricaded. All traffic cease to flow from north to south, and visa versa. The President of the United States called together his national security staff in the situation room to discuss the matter.

As each member of the staff contributed their portion, the puzzle was beginning to take on an apocalyptic look. The most alarming scenario was given by the Energy Department. Apparently, the Mexican government had secretly been buying components for a nuclear reactor. Hostile countries to the United States had been supplying the enriched radioactive materials necessary to make nuclear weapons. Juan had told the United States he wanted to develop nuclear energy to provide electricity and heat to his country, but that was a lie as the true nature of this ploy was being uncovered. It was revealed Mexico was also in possession of missiles capable of reaching targets anywhere in the continental U.S. or Canada.

In addition to all that was going on, Juan had for months been dealing with the drug cartel out of Columbia. Juan knew the tremendous profits in the drug trade, and wanted to share in the wealth. Mexico not only was becoming a background for growing illegal plants, but delivery systems were being set up for the drugs to flow from Central America through Mexico into the U.S. and Asia. U.S. satellites were taking pictures of the marijuana growing in the central region, but Juan was doing nothing about eradicating the plants. The DEA was also noticing the increase in availability of cocaine, heroin, and meth-amphetamine. America was spending a literal fortune trying to stop this activity in Central America, and now the business was blossoming in a country hundreds of times the size.

The American President knew the possibility of a war in the northern hemisphere was only inches away from happening. He was hesitant to launch a first strike without absolute confirmation, knowing such an action was also echo disastrous consequences to his own nation. He felt a political solution was preferable to that of war. He was always taught that there are no winners in war, only survivors. He directed his Secretary of Defense to immediately mobilize whatever force it would take to counteract this threat, and to do so in the most covert way possible. He then instructed his Secretary of State to contact the Mexican government to see if there was a way to defuse the threat. Juan was beside himself with glee. At last, he had America on its knees, begging for his cooperation. He rebuffed attempt after attempt to have him reverse his course. He instructed his military to continue to push forward with preparations for attack as well as defense. He finally told the State Department there would be no consideration given to their demands, and that all communications would be halted forever.

The President of the United States again reconvened his security staff to hear the bad news. When everyone had said their piece, the President stood up from his chair, straightened his jacket, leaned forward on the conference table with his two hands and made the following declaration.

"Ladies and gentlemen, we have a problem with Mexico."

THE END